W9-BYT-771

8-19 (10)

Oliver Loving

Oliver Loving

········

Stefan Merrill Block

FLATIRON
BOOKS
NEW YORK

For Liese: beneath every word,
the subatomic vibration

OLIVER LOVING. Copyright © 2017 by Stefan Merrill Block. All rights reserved. Printed in the United States of America. For information, address Flatiron Books, 175 Fifth Avenue, New York, N.Y. 10010.

www.flatironbooks.com

The Library of Congress Cataloging-in-Publication Data is available upon request.

ISBN 978-1-250-16973-0 (hardcover)
ISBN 978-1-250-12286-5 (ebook)

Our books may be purchased in bulk for promotional, educational, or business use. Please contact your local bookseller or the Macmillan Corporate and Premium Sales Department at 1-800-221-7945, extension 5442, or by email at MacmillanSpecialMarkets@macmillan.com.

First Edition: January 2018

10 9 8 7 6 5 4 3 2 1

Oliver

· · · · · · · · · · · · · · · · · · ·

CHAPTER ONE

Your name is Oliver Loving. Or not Oliver Loving at all, some will say. Just a fantasy, a tall tale. But perhaps those labels are fitting; maybe you were born to become nothing more than a myth. Why else would your granny have insisted your parents name you after your state's legendary cattleman, to whom your family had only an imaginary genealogical linkage? Like yours, your namesake's story was a rough and epic one. The original Oliver Loving, and his vast cattle empire, came to an end when the man was just fifty-four, shot by the Comanche people somewhere in the jagged terrain of New Mexico. "Bury me in Texas," your namesake begged his trail partner, Charles Goodnight, whose name your granny later bestowed upon your brother. And so you might be forgiven for thinking that your future was foretold in the beginning. Just as the violence of your namesake's time turned the first Oliver Loving into a folk hero, so did the violence of your own time turn you from a boy into a different sort of legend.

A boy and also a legend: you were seventeen years old when a .22 caliber bullet split you in two. In one world, the one over your hospital bed, you became the Martyr of Bliss, Texas. Locked in that bed, you lost your true dimensions, rose like vapor, a disembodied idea in the hazy blue sky over the Big Bend Country. You became the hopeful or desperate or consoling ghost who hovered over the vanishing populace of your gutted hometown, a story that people told to serve their own ends. Your name has appeared on the homemade signs pumped by angry picketers on the redbrick steps of your old schoolhouse, in many heated opinion pieces in the local newspapers, on a memorial billboard off Route 10. By your twentieth birthday, you had become a dimming hive of neurological data, a mute oracle, an obsession, a regret, a prayer, a vegetative patient in Bed Four at Crockett State Assisted Care Facility, the last hope your mother lived inside.

And yet, in another universe, the one beneath your skin, you remained the other Oliver, the one few people cared to know *before*, just a spindly kid, clumsy footed and abashed. A straight-A student, nervous with girls, speckled with acne, gifted with the nice bone structure you inherited: your father's pronounced jaw, your mother's high cheekbones. You were a boy who often employed the well-used adolescent escape pods from solitude, through the starships and time machines of science fiction. You were also a reverential son, eager to please, and you tried to be a good brother, even if you sometimes let yourself luxuriate in the fact that your mother clearly preferred you. In truth, you needed whatever victories you could win. You were just seventeen; after that night, only your family could remember that boy clearly. But yours was a family that remembered so often and well that it could seem—if only for a minute, here and there—as if the immense, time-bending gravity of their remembering could punch a hole in the ether that spread between you, as if your memories might become their own.

"According to science," your father spoke to the stars on that night when your story began, "our universe is only one of many. Infinite universes. Somewhere there is a universe that takes place in a single frozen second. A universe where time moves backward. A universe that is nothing but the inside of your own head."

At seventeen, you took this bit of soft astrophysics in the way you took all your father's lectures: less than seriously. Your father, an after-hours painter and teacher of art classes at Bliss Township School, had founded the school's Young Astronomers Club and more or less forced your brother and you to serve as its president and vice president. But the truth was that you shared with Pa just an artist's dreamy interest in astronomy. The constellations were mostly twinkling metaphors to you both. But that night, in his Merlot-warmed way, your father was prophetic. Your own journey into another universe, the universe where your family lost you, began very subtly. It began, appropriately enough, with the minute movements of your left hand.

Your hand. That night it was like an autonomous being whose behavior you couldn't predict. For a half hour or more, it had just lain there, but now you watched in silent astonishment as your fingers marshaled their courage, began a slow march across the woolen material of the Navajo blanket on which you were lying on a reedy hilltop on your family's ancient ranch, a two-hundred-acre patch of Chihuahuan Desert that an optimistic forbear of yours named Zion's Pastures. Your eyes hardly registered the blazing contrails and sparkles of celestial brilliance in the sky, the Perseid meteor shower falling over West Texas. Your whole awareness was focused upon your fingers, which were more interested in a different, localized phenomenon: Rebekkah Sterling on a blanket just inches from your own. You breathed deeply, her vanilla smell cutting through the land's headshop aroma of sun-cooked creosote.

"Huh," Rebekkah Sterling said. "That is fascinating."

"You think *that's* fascinating." Your father then proceeded to hold forth on one of his favorite astronomical lectures, about how the basic atomic building blocks for life, everything that makes us us, was produced in the fiery engine of distant stars. But you did not need your father's lecture on the epochs of evolution. Your hand offered a better, in vivo demonstration of life's perseverance despite the bad odds. Your hand, like an amphibious creature clambering out of the primordial ocean, now began its journey over the five inches of hard earth and dead grama grass that separated Rebekkah Sterling's blanket from yours.

Rebekkah Sterling! For the year since her family had moved to town, you had been tracking her closely. Well, you tracked many girls closely in the slumped silence of your school days, but what was it about Rebekkah that set her apart? She was a very slight girl; the outline of her bones pressed against her tight skin. It was true what you would later write about her in a poem, her hair really *did* look like a *piled fortune of amber ringlets*. But she carried that hair like some burdensome heirloom her mother obliged her to wear, something that faintly embarrassed her. She'd tuck that *fortune* into barrettes and scrunchies, pull and chew at its ends. She seemed to spend the durations of your literature class together practicing how to make the least sound possible. When she had to sneeze, she'd first bury her head in her sweater. It was the peculiar sadness of her silence that you found so beautiful. But if not for your father's astonishing pronouncement at dinner one Monday night, your Rebekkah Sterling story would likely have ended the way all your girl stories ended, in your own, far less beautiful brand of silence.

Over the last years, the cumulative effects of disappointment, time, and the considerable quantities of the cheap whiskey Pa consumed had eroded most of your family's old traditions, but you still maintained a Monday night ritual, Good Things Monday, when each Loving, before supper, had to name one good thing to look forward to in the week to come. That night, as the burnt molasses of Ma's meat loaf had wafted from the gray slab set before you, you mustered something perfunctory about a novel, *Ender's Game*, which you were liking; Ma spoke of a slight alleviation of her back pain; Charlie's Good Thing was many good things, three separate parties to which he had been invited that weekend. But the only truly Good

Thing you heard that night, the first certifiable Good Thing you had heard in a very long while, was your father's news.

"Looks like we'll have a visitor," Pa said.

The permanent roster of the Young Astronomers counted no member who did not share the last name Loving, but over the years, Pa had occasionally been able to cajole one of his pupils to attend a meeting. And when your father that night informed his family that he had convinced a former student of his named Rebekkah Sterling to come to Zion's Pastures to watch the meteors, you grasped your seat.

"Rebekkah Sterling?"

"That's what I said." Pa grinned. "Why? That name mean something special to you?"

"No. Or I guess *something*. We have English together."

Before that day you had never exchanged more than a word or two in Mrs. Schumacher's Honors Literature class. You were certain she wouldn't actually follow through on your father's invitation.

Days passed, and you tried to forget that unlikeliest possibility, tried to resign yourself to the glumness of your town in that late summer. That August represented something of a crisis point in Presidio County, but it was a crisis that had been roiling for years—generations, in fact. The border between the English-speaking north and the Spanish-speaking south might have been settled a century and a half before, but it was never an entirely peaceful distinction out in your slice of the borderland. On the white side of that divide, you'd grown up under your late grandmother's alternative Texas history, "the true story of this country they'd never teach in those schoolbooks of yours," a place where for 150 years immigrants had been building the towns and doing the menial tasks, the enduring threat of deportation used to enforce a sort of soft slavery. Granny Nunu had told you how, as recently as her own childhood, your school had conducted a mock burial for "Mr. Spanish," a ceremony in which the Latino students were made to write Spanish words on slips of paper, drop them into a hole in the earth, and bury them. "Shameful,

shameful business, behind us now, thank the Lord, but you can't ever forget it," Granny Nunu told you.

But in your own childhood, these old divides hadn't seemed quite so dire. Spanish was now a required course for all students; in your grade-school days, white and Latino children were often invited to the same birthday parties. And yet, in recent years, as the cartels seized vast powers in Mexico, the white population had been fretting, with growing panic, over the stories of narcotic warfare coming from only a few miles away. Down the river, at the border town of Browns-ville, police had recently found body parts of a number of Honduran immigrants scattered across the highway. Up in Presidio, local ranch-ers were reporting bands of cartel soldiers crossing their properties by night. Immigration had leapt to numbers unknown for generations. And as all these addled refugees came over the river, they arrived to a county blighted by lack of commerce. Ranching and mineral mining had long ago gone bust in your hometown. The only real industries left in the county were sluggish tourism, out in the state and national parks; border control enforcement; and the few local businesses that the employees of these federally funded enterprises could support. The last thing that hardscrabble Blissians wanted was a multitude of new workers, willing to toil for less-than-legal wages.

Something had to be done, was the white opinion, and so it had been a summer of a great many deportations, whole families carted from Bliss to the other side of the Rio Grande. For the TV cameras, the West Texas Minutemen—one of those jingoistic militias that patrolled the desert for surreptitious immigrants—were doing frequent demon-strations at the river, shooting their rifles into the Mexican sky.

Though this fraught border between nations lay thirty miles to the south of Bliss, another border ran down the center of your schoolhouse. Just as the towns all over your county were split in two, neighborhoods segregated by language and skin tone, you'd come to see that Bliss Township School was truthfully two schools; the honors classes were almost entirely white, the "regular" classes mostly Latino. All of the school's officially sanctioned activities—

dances, football games, academic clubs—were white, and the Latino activities were mostly ones that the school officials tried to disperse: the Tejanos' daily gatherings out front, right on the schoolhouse steps, where they blasted music from their cars, causing a minor, perpetual commotion.

It was out there, just beyond the school gates, that something of a brawl had broken out the first week of school, when Scotty Coltrane and his pale cronies began barking abuse at the grounds crew. *"Andale, andale!"* Scotty was yelling at a lawn-mowing man when a Mexican kid crept up from behind and bloodied Scotty's nose. Under ordinary circumstances, it might have ended there, the boys called before Principal Dixon, a suspension issued, but in that tense August the fight turned into a brawl, a dozen boys piling on.

But even in this divided school, you felt yourself to be in a further subdivision all your own, a boy who wanted only to pass his days unnoticed. It was shaping up to be another lonesome year, the worst yet, until that actual miracle happened.

You had been in your father's art classroom, after school that Thursday, marking up your biology homework as Pa worked paint thinner into the student tables. Your brother was sketching something at an easel—a ballerina in a tutu, screaming as two lions devoured her legs—when he turned his head to an arrival at the door. Rebekkah Sterling stepped timidly into the room.

"Rebekkah," you said, feeling ashamed to speak her name to her face.

"So!" Rebekkah said. "Today I get to see where Oliver Loving lives."

Through a blooming blush, you watched her closely, something in her wry grin suggesting her attendance at the meteor shower must have been some kind of a joke. Or, more likely, she had only accepted your father's invitation to be kind.

But then a wondrous thing happened when Pa drove you home. "Shotgun!" Charlie yelled in the parking lot, and climbed into the front seat. And as one of the backseats was piled with Pa's collection of paper coffee cups and fast food refuse, Rebekkah and you had to sit right next to each other, your denim-clad thighs touching snugly, your leg registering each jostle with ecstatic friction.

"A couple hours till nightfall yet," Pa said when you arrived at Zion's Pastures. "Why don't you take Rebekkah for a little show-around, and we'll get the picnic ready?" He winked at you, not very subtly.

Most of the land of Zion's Pastures was just parched country, like photographs you'd seen of the islands of Greece, if someone had vacuumed away the Aegean. But you wanted to show Rebekkah your land's rare swatch of lushness, guiding her down to the fertile earth along Loving Creek. As you led Rebekkah through the machete-cut trails, your anxiety turned you into some kind of historian. "My great-great-grandfather and his family came from Wales, that's near England, and they had this crazy idea that Texas wouldn't be so different from Wales but with enough land for everyone—" You begged your mouth to silence, but it refused to quit its lectures. "This is called a century plant. Its stem supposedly shoots just once in a hundred years." You awkwardly added, "To reproduce." Rebekkah silently trailed your elbow. You elected for the most arduous paths, where many times you had to lift a branch for her to duck the tunnel of your arm. At last you came to your destination, the little creekside cave where you spent many evenings and weekends, doing your homework and writing your rhymy poems at the old poker table you had taken from the storage shed.

"Here it is," you said. "My secret lair."

"Secret lair? What are you, Superman?"

"That's the Fortress of Solitude."

"So no solitude for you, huh?" she asked. "You bring a lot of people here? It's very cool."

"You're the first. The first non-Loving, I mean."

"I'm honored."

"You should be. It's very exclusive."

Rebekkah emitted a faint "ha" and looked up to observe the fleshy knobs of the mini-stalactites that hung from the ceiling.

There had been a time when your boyish imagination could make this pocket of rock seem deep with mystery, a potential burial place for the sort of lost Mexican treasure that your late granny liked to tell stories about. Now it looked to you only like a dim hollow, shallow and gray.

"Oh my God!" Rebekkah shouted, doing a frantic little skip. "A snake!"

You laughed, more loudly than you intended. "That's just snakeskin. Some rattler must have molted here." You both knelt to examine the diaphanous material, the translucent scales making miniature rainbows in the early evening light.

"Wow. It's sort of beautiful," Rebekkah said.

You poked at the iridescent rattler sheath, and the frail substance crumbled under your fingertip. Rebekkah put a hand to her face. "You ruined it," she said.

"Sorry."

"Why did you do that?"

"It's no big deal. Snakeskin is everywhere around here. Really. We can find some more, if you want."

Rebekkah stood away, made a frustrated little snort. You couldn't quite understand what you'd done wrong, but you did understand that you were already failing your first conversation with her.

"Listen," you said. "You really don't have to stay all the way to tonight if you don't want. My pa could drive you home."

"Your *pa*. So Texan."

You shrugged. "Ma and Pa. That's just what we've always called them. I guess it was my grandmother's doing. Always made us do things the old-fashioned way."

"Anyway," Rebekkah said, "thanks for the advice. But when I want to go, you'll be the first to know."

"It's just that I know it's kind of weird that you're here. And now you're looking like you are feeling weird."

"Weird is how I'm looking?"

"I didn't mean—maybe not."

"If anything," she said, "all this is just making me a little jealous. This place. Your family. You get to live like this every day."

But you were the jealous one just then, jealous of other boys better suited for a girl like Rebekkah, with her sad, thousand-yard stare. "My dad drinks alone in his shed most nights," you told her, trying to match your tone to hers, that whispery subdued register. "My mother looks at me like I'm three years old."

Rebekkah glanced up at you, smiled sadly. "Well, I guess we have a few things in common, then." And then Rebekkah reached for you and mussed your hair like a child's. Like a child's, maybe, but on the hike back to the house, your legs throwing long shadows, you could still feel the warmth of her hand on your head, a kind of imaginary crown.

"And have you heard about how scientists have been measuring the universe?" Pa asked, two hours later, on that hilltop. The remnants of the picnic your mother had packed were strewn about. In honor of the guest, Pa had limited himself to wine, the emptied bottle of Merlot now tipped on its side. "They've found this way to take the whole thing's weight. They can weigh the universe now! Incredible!"

"Incredible," you said, but you had much more interesting measurements in mind. Your fingertips had at last forged the great divide, and they fell with exhaustion on the polyester shore of Rebekkah's blanket. You must have been less than six inches from her now; you felt the warmth that her skin radiated. Your fingers took the land's measure, stood, and began the final march. A sudden streak of brightness cut the deep purple above. "Oh! Look look look!" Charlie shouted.

"So, Rebekkah, tell us about you," your mother said, her voice at the edge of that tone she used with strangers, the one she called *skeptical* and your brother called *mean*. "You're new here, right?"

"We've been here for a little more than a year now. My father works for an oil company. Fracking. Never in one place long."

"Poor girl," Ma said. "I know how that goes. We moved around so much when I was a kid, I'd gone to eight schools before I was fifteen."

"It's hard," Rebekkah said.

"I have to admit," Pa said, "I saw a little thing about your father in the paper, something about the surveys his company's been doing around Alpine. Fingers crossed they strike it rich, Lord knows we could use the business."

Rebekkah shrugged. "He never tells me much about it," she said. "Just lets me know when it's time to move again."

"Our family has lived here for about a million years!" Charlie piped. "We never go anywhere! It's not always such a picnic, let me tell you."

"Charlie."

"Sorry." Charlie giggled.

Even setting aside the miraculous identity of your guest, it was very strange to witness your family perform itself for an outsider. You couldn't remember the last time a visitor had come to Zion's Pastures. A couple of years before, your mother had cured the grandfather clock of its mildew infestation by setting it for two days in the front yard. "Just needs a little sunlight to heal," she had explained. A seventeen-year-old boy, unkissed, could be forgiven for already beginning to conceive of Rebekkah like that healing sun upon his whole lonesome, mildewed life at Zion's Pastures.

"So how you liking it?" Pa said. "School going okay so far this year?"

"It's good. I sure miss your art class." You noticed that as she spoke she gestured with her left hand, but kept the other lying there, unbudging in the darkness.

"You know," Rebekkah said. "All this star talk is reminding me of that song. *They call me on and on across the universe—*"

All four of you tuneless Lovings lay there, stunned, as Rebekkah sang a line of that Beatles tune.

"Crikey," Charlie said.

"Beautiful." Pa whistled. "Got some serious pipes on you, good Lord."

"I don't know about that," Rebekkah said. "I just like to sing sometimes."

After a time, Pa resumed his astronomy lesson. "Of course you know that *falling stars* is not really accurate. What you are looking at are just minor asteroids burning up in the atmosphere, but it is remarkable . . ." You were no longer listening. Because your hand understood that it didn't have forever. And so, in one brave and reckless act, your hand called upon the support of wrist and forearm. It crouched low, and then it sprang. And there would perhaps never be a joy as acute as the joy of Rebekkah's downy, warm-soft fingers when they did not stray from the point of contact. Your hands remained there, for whole seconds, their backsides pressed together, turning red hot, generating the atomic material of the future. But your hand was no fool. It understood that the snakeskin had been a kind of sign; if you lingered too long, the delicate thing would crumble.

A half-hour later, you were all sauntering back up the dirt road, the weak flicker of your cheap flashlights casting skittish halos over dust and cacti. "Goodness. It's already nine thirty," Ma told Rebekkah. "Probably close to your curfew, no?"

"Huh," she said. "I guess."

"Well, then, we'd best get you home."

"We'd best," Rebekkah said, and Ma nodded, walking ahead to set a swifter pace. For just a second, you turned to look at Rebekkah. The moon was rising now, and you watched as the thinness of her lips bent into a smile. You smiled in reply. But you were a boy who had developed a nearly anaphylactic aversion to prolonged eye contact, and you looked away, gaped up awkwardly at the sky: a poor decision. Before you could understand what had happened, the intense penny smell of blood had already filled your nose. Your boot toe had caught a rock, sent you sprawling on the path.

"Woot!" your brother hollered. "There he goes again!"

"Oliver!" Ma yelped. "Your nose!"

"It's fine," you said.

"It's not. It's *bleeding*."

"It's nothing."

"Nothing? Why are you *smiling*?"

"I don't know."

As you sat up, you watched your brother hopping from foot to foot, doing what he did with your frequent teenage-klutzy tumbles, turning it into some slapstick act for his entertainment. "I can't believe it! Your best spill yet! Gold medal! Classic!"

"Oh my God," Rebekkah murmured.

"Keep it pinched," your mother said. "Here, use one of the napkins. You need to lie down! Stay here and we'll come pick you up with the car. Or, wait, Jed, what about the couch in your studio?"

"My studio?" Pa said, and paused. "Right. I guess come on then."

The shame of this scene was not inconsiderable, but it was little next to the astonishment you now had to stifle. You were going to Pa's studio? Your father's so-called art studio was a tumbledown cabin, a half mile up the dirt road from the big house, and it was strictly off-limits to his family. And in the past few months, Pa himself often seemed off-limits, too. He occasionally dragged his body to the dinner table, but always his mind remained out there, latched behind a cabin door, in a hazy cloud of Pall Mall smoke and whiskey vapors. This latest absence was longer than his previous ones, but throughout your childhood Pa had disappeared to his painting shed most weekends. Like a controlled experiment to refute the old Texan belief in the direct relationship between perseverance and reward, Pa's countless painting hours had never summed to anything very successful. He spurned the locally ubiquitous landscape art—those shattered canyons and Comanche dragoons in hot pursuit of their bison—that might have fetched him real money in favor of his "true work," which amounted to artful knockoffs of a number of dead masters who piled the bright paint thickly. Van Gogh, Kandinsky, Munch, Chagall.

In his whole stymied, self-poisoning career, you had seen your father sell just a single painting. This was at the start of your freshman year, when Bliss Township threw its fund-raising jamboree on the school's front lawn. Amid booths jammed with foil-wrapped brownies, tin-plated pies, and clunky granny needlepoints, Pa set up a stand to sell his students' work. Of course, nearly all those bleeding watercolors and fingerprint-smudged charcoals sold at asking price—to the artists' own parents. But, late into that Saturday afternoon, a single piece remained unsold. The same oil painting Pa had unveiled at your last Good Things Monday, his wind-whirled rendition of Bliss Township School, the mass of children out front just a bright yellow suggestion, the schoolhouse's cupolas and cornices warping into the shapes of the jolly clouds above. For his own asking price, Pa had affixed a blue sticker that said, *$250.*

As the pies vanished from the booths, as the Bliss Township Marching Band began to fold away their gear, Pa's painting still languished there, unpurchased. Your brother tugged at Ma and you to huddle with him behind the art booth. "We have to buy his painting," Charlie said. "We have to!" Ma touched his cheek. "You are the sweetest boy in the world," she told him. Not to be bested, you felt your pockets for your saved allowance, showing Ma twenty-four dollars. Charlie could contribute only six, and your mother had just eighty-five dollars in her pocketbook. She clutched the gathered money in her fist, worked a finger into one of her curls. "Wait here," she said, and when she came back, five minutes later, she was smiling so widely you could see her back fillings.

"Just watch." She pointed in the direction of your father, whom your school principal, Doyle Dixon, was approaching with an outstretched palm. Principal Dixon showed Pa a stack of crumpled money, and you watched your father fight back a lunging impulse to hug the man. Instead, he pocketed the cash, nodded, and presented the painting to his boss.

"Now listen," Ma said. "Doyle put in the rest himself, and I made him promise he'd never mention our own little contribution. Do you promise you won't say a thing?"

"You—" Charlie was saying, but by that point Pa had practically skipped his way through the crowd.

"Doyle bought the damn thing," Pa said. "Told me he's going to hang it at school. Guess it wasn't the wreck I was fretting, huh?"

"What have I been telling you?" Ma said, working her grin into submission. "It's a beauty."

The sale of this painting, however, had done little for his confidence. "Going through labor," Pa liked to call his long studio sessions, but as for the results of all those painful gestations? He tossed most of his canvases onto the frequent bonfires he'd make in the fire pit. "Have you heard of installation art?" Pa liked to quip. "Well, I make *incineration* art." It had been a very long time since you had seen his work.

But now you were going to Pa's studio—with Rebekkah Sterling! In huaraches, your father walked on ahead into the desert night, leading the way for a grim, dirgelike march, the hard grind of stones under your feet, bats calling invisibly through the air. You let your family lead you, like a blind man, the blood in your nose beginning to congeal.

At the cabin, you settled yourself on the stain-spangled divan in the darkness, and Pa lit two camphor lanterns. Though you felt the blood pooling back into your nostrils you couldn't bear to keep your head tilted away from this rare view. Arranged among the stub-choked ashtrays and empty bottles of George Dickel whiskey, his latest paintings, you were sorry to see, were an immediate disappointment. To your eyes, they just looked like a continuation of his artistic thievery.

Rebekkah, however, walked right up to these canvases and paused, as if she had some silent greeting to make to each one. Pa pushed the blunt end of a paintbrush against his lip as he nervously observed her. "They are a little crude," he at last said. "I know it. I'm having some trouble with my brushes, and I think—"

"No." Rebekkah spoke to the thickly slathered cerulean sky a few inches from her face. "They are beautiful."

"Think so?" Pa watched the back of Rebekkah's head nod slowly.

"Is that *us*?" Charlie asked. Your brother had noticed something you had not. Near the edge of each frame—beneath the swirling paisleys of a van Goghian starscape, at the periphery of a throbbing field of expressionist colors, amid the animalistic swipes and slashes of abstract brushwork—were four unmistakable figures: your parents, your brother, and you.

"It's a series," he said. "Or that's how I think of them. Actually, it's based on what I was telling you earlier, about the multiverse. If that's true about the other universes, then somewhere there must be a whole universe that takes place inside of Vincent van Gogh paintings, right? Another inside of Munch. Kandinsky. And then I thought, what would it be like to live in those other places?"

At the time, you took this cosmological explanation for more of his knockoff canvases as fanciful, sentimental, a little drunken. The whole concept reminded you of the stories that your brother and you, as younger boys, had liked to tell each other about secret passageways, portals to hidden worlds buried in the land, fantasies that you had both outgrown. These paintings embarrassed you a little, on your father's behalf. In this so-called series of paintings, you saw that Pa had married his life's two great failures: the confines of his thwarted artistic imagination and his increasingly silent relationship with his family here on this planet. It seemed a little pathetic, Pa's painting these other universes for his family members when the simpler solution would be just to have actual conversations with you.

"But if there are all these other universes, where are they?" Your brother was always the more credulous, cheery son, untroubled by dark implications. "How do you get there?"

"Don't know," Pa slurred in a grave register, as if this were a question that had been troubling him. "Maybe a black hole."

"A black hole?" Charlie asked. "I thought it was all just dark in black holes."

"No one knows for sure. Could be blackness or could be that it's a wormhole. To another universe. The thing about black holes, I read this, is that the science of them is unknowable. To get close enough for a good look, the gravity in there would tear you apart."

Less than three months later a black hole would open in West Texas, and you would come to see that there was something to your father's naive cosmology after all. His theory held true of the black hole that would dissolve the floor beneath your feet on the night of November fifteenth: you would only begin to understand the truth—about Rebekkah, your own part in that night's horrors—just as you lost the ability to describe it. A terrible brightness would break through you. What would make it so terrifying is that it wouldn't hurt at all.

A beam of light trembled over the thick oils of Pa's impressionist multiverse, a flashlight shaking in his alcoholic hands. "Anyway," you told Pa, "Rebekkah is right. They are very pretty."

And as he grinned, you were grinning, too. Maybe, you were thinking, you didn't need to perform your unhappiness for Rebekkah, maybe she didn't want your own sad stories. Maybe it was the possibility of witnessing a better family that had brought her to you? Tomorrow, you had just decided, you would at last spill the secret of Pa's schoolhouse painting. Despite whatever disappointment you knew looking at his latest output, you were very glad for the promise of this story to tell her, how the three of you had huddled there behind a carnival booth, pooling what little you had to write that day a happier ending for your father.

Oh, of course it would be easy to pity that kid you were then, just a boy feeling the miracle of a freshly touched hand, practicing how to tell his best example of what made his family a family. A boy doomed to a future he could never have guessed. And yet maybe somehow, that night, you were already beginning to rehearse your part in this story? Soon the black hole would open, you would fall to one side, and your family would remain on the other. And after reading all those childhood epics—all those sci-fi, fantasy, survivalist, and tall tales that you so loved, and after all Pa's talk of parallel universes, too—how not to believe that somehow your own otherworldly bed-bound epic really was foretold? How else to explain that unlikeliest sorrow you and your family were made to endure, the mythological transformations you were made to undergo? How not to believe, even still, that you were *chosen*?

No, you wouldn't be able to pity yourself for long. You might have fallen through a black hole, but your family's fate was equally desperate. They had to stay behind, on Planet Earth.

Eve

·····················

CHAPTER TWO

It was that lost, oblivious minute that haunted Eve Loving most. What had she been doing at precisely 9:13 on the night of November fifteenth? Eve wouldn't ever be able to remember, not exactly, of course. Just laundry, most likely. Reaching into the creaking, complaining machine, hefting the clumped, sodden wreckage of a week of dirtied clothes, pitching it into the open mouth of the dryer. She would later retain a faint memory of seeing a pair of her husband's fraying BVDs dropped to the dusty crevice between the machines, of stooping to chuck it into the dryer. *Rotating* was her family's name for this chore.

Eve would remember doing a lot of rotating that night, the last night her universe was still intact. As the old dryer made its monstrous noises, Eve rotated from living room to kitchen, kitchen to porch, porch to bedroom, needing to busy herself. Her father-in-law had died decades before Eve met Jed; her mother-in-law, Nelly "Nunu" Loving, had passed away years ago, but this was still Nunu's house, a granny house, porcelain figurines in the china cabinets, sunny desertscapes in gilt frames, a leering grandfather clock grunting off the seconds. She was alone in the house at Zion's Pastures. Charlie was off at the Alpine Cinemas (*Death Machine Robot 7,* or some ridiculous thing), Jed chaperoning the Bliss Township Homecoming

Dance, Oliver a poor, dateless attendee, who had inexplicably decided, at the last possible minute, to don one of his father's seldom-worn suits and set off to the dance on his own. A fact to haunt Eve for the rest of her life: she had driven Oliver to the school herself.

The night before, Jed had done a highly uncommon thing (was this significant? she would later wonder); when he had come back from his work in the shed, he had slid up next to Eve in the sheets. Over the years, Eve had learned the variety of moods Jed's drinking brought forth. There was the Mope, the Discontent, the Manic, but last night he had scooted up to Eve as that rarest of his species, the Affectionate.

"It's too hot to sleep like that," Eve had told him, shimmying away.

"Who said anything about sleep?"

"Are you serious?"

"Why not? Don't you think it's time the prisoner deserves a conjugal visit?"

"Prisoner? And so in this metaphor I'm the jailer?"

"Eve."

"What?"

"Nothing."

For whole minutes, they had both just lain there, in the humid silence of the bedroom.

"The dance is tomorrow," Jed said at last.

"Oh yeah?"

"Yeah. And I don't think our poor son has managed to wrangle a date."

"I know. But I don't think it's such a tragedy. I never went to any dances myself, when I was his age."

"I think you should come with me to chaperone," Jed said. "Maybe we could convince Oliver to come, Charlie, too. I think we'd all have a good time."

"You are asking me to homecoming."

"Would you do me the honor?"

"Jed," she said, "I'm sorry, but those school parties give me the creeps. Bad memories, I guess."

In her peripatetic youth, Eve had spent her childhood as the New Girl, the perpetual out-of-towner, the vaguely ethnic-looking intruder in classes filled with plain, pale faces. The story of Eve's childhood had been the tragedy of chronic self-reinvention. Each time she had taken her new seat in the front row of a classroom, she faced new eyes tracking her, waiting for her to reveal herself. And even after twenty years in West Texas, Eve still felt the outcast among its white, Christian-cheery people, the wives and husbands of Jed's fellow Bliss Township faculty making her feel like some foreign interloper, some suspect Jewess, some Other slotted in the nebulous racial space between white and Latina. It wasn't a persona she had at last developed so much as a defense strategy. She had learned to behave like a wallflower until approached, at which point she behaved like a Venus flytrap.

"I'm sorry to hear that," Jed said, his body going rigid.

(Might her whole future have pivoted on that late-night rejection? If she had only let his whiskey-loosened body overtake her, for the first time in nearly a year, might she actually have let him persuade her to go to the dance? Might her presence there have somehow changed everything?)

"Jed, listen," she said after a time, but he had already fallen asleep.

The next night, 9:15 passed to 9:16. Did she feel her own Big Bang gathering its hot charge, time and space beginning to warp? Hideously, no. Eve was only puttering about the reliquary of a family that seemed, in her solitary night, already vanished. Oliver's adventure and sci-fi books on the bedroom shelf, her boys' shirts hanging neatly in the tight little closet, the shellacked longhorn bones shining on the walls. Oliver would be off to college in less than two years, Charlie in four, and she was already indulging the empty nester's trick, clicking on the television for the sake of noise.

9:30, 9:45, 10:00. Charlie's curfew, why hadn't he come home from the movies yet? She would remember pushing through the screen door, throwing her weight into a rusted aluminum chair on the wonky fieldstone porch. A November night, summery crickets still chirping. A sound of heavy paws crunching through the scrubby mesquite and bunch grass that lined the creek downhill. Eve was just forty. Maybe, before her boys even left home, she could go back to school, become some sort of a scholar? Maybe she could leave West Texas altogether, leave her sad-sack whiskey-swilling husband, and get a Ph.D. at a school not so far from the one—maybe even the same school?—that Oliver would attend. The truth was, Eve couldn't imagine any future whose every day was not involved with Oliver—well, with both her boys, but (no denying it) with Oliver in particular. She knew it would be a kind of death for her, Oliver's graduation.

Something in her atmosphere fell silent. The dryer, she remembered.

One last cruelty. Eve, glad for activity, took extra care sorting the family laundry that night. It could have been ten minutes she spent there, absently folding and refolding. She arranged the clothes neatly in the wicker basket. She grasped its straw handles and carried it in the direction of the bedroom. She was already well past the television when she paused. Like the time, as a ten-year-old, she had broken her arm in her one failed experiment with skateboarding, at the moment of impact she felt only a perplexing numbness. A picture on the television screen. A riot of squad car lights, the image shaken and smeary. She turned back to the television, but could make no sense of what the woman, Tricia Flip of Action News Six, was explaining into the camera. *Impossible:* that was the first word Eve thought then, the word that already bound Eve to hundreds of mothers like her, mothers whom she had until that night abstractly pitied as she had watched the news of sudden, eruptive violence in far-off places, thinking: *Impossible, no,* why add such a calamity to her long litany of anxieties, a thing like that could never happen in a place like theirs. And yet, in the kitchen, the telephone was screaming. She dropped the basket, its contents spilling on the floor. She stumbled over the laundry, lurched for the phone. She put it to her ear, and try as she might, there would never be a way to forget the instant that followed.

Nearly ten years later: the boundless beige of desert, a flesh drawn tight, freckled with thorned vegetation, rusting industrial equipment, the occasional longhorn kept for nostalgia's sake, subsisting mysteriously on dead grass and stubbornness. A vein of asphalt, running north from the Big Bend of the Rio Grande, cut the desert in two. The chugging gray Hyundai, taking the road at ninety miles per hour, seemed, even to its driver, hardly there at all. An insect on the skin, Eve could have been flicked away.

She gritted particles of sand between her molars, sniffed at the car's stale gassiness, as the road began to widen to link up with the elaborate circulatory system of Interstate 10. And there, at the happenstance flat where road met road, the great cement boxes and oversized corporate signage for the newish shopping center came into view. A shopping center a hundred miles from where her paralytic son shuddered in his sheets, and still she could feel Oliver there with her. Eve knew Oliver had woken to another unmarked morning in Bed Four at Crockett State Assisted Care Facility, but Oliver was also in her feet, her hands, the dampness under her collar, as she turned into the parking lot for the chain bookstore, Tall Tales Books & More, the state's largest bookseller west of the Pecos River. Breathing the heavy fug that her lousy car's AC only pushed around, Eve parked just twenty feet from the wide automatic front doors. It was nine in the morning, the sun already high enough to rouse whirling mirages from the concrete. Glimpsing her reflection in the shop's tinted windows, she thought that it still wasn't too late to turn around. She plucked sharply at her right eyelid, the skin slurping away from the bloodshot globe beneath, and she examined the bulbous white head of the little lash she'd pulled free. The tart throb of pain steadied her for exactly five seconds.

It was July twenty-second, the day of Oliver's first real exam in many years. A hundred miles south of the bookstore, a functional magnetic resonance imaging machine was warming up for him now. Of course Oliver had undergone similar tests before, but that was no comfort to Eve this morning. Eve had long ago learned to believe the unlikeliest promises that her own hope, like some charlatan televangelist, outrageously issued, but she wasn't enough of a believer to fail to understand what today's test would mean. It had been nine years since Oliver's last round of neuroimaging; today likely marked Eve's last hope that the doctors might locate any trace awareness left in her son's jailed mind. To think of this day, over the past weeks, was to invite a dread that was tidal and annihilating, the white wall of a tsunami thundering toward her across the desert floor. Eve hoisted herself out of the car, through the furnace of West Texan July, into the better boxed oxygen inside the bookshop.

Other than a couple of bleary-eyed employees sipping brownish slushies behind the counter, the store was empty. In an attempt to go unnoticed, Eve made swift progress to the Science Fiction/Fantasy section. Since the moment she woke to the terrible fact of today's date, the object had gleamed brightly in the glass display case of her mind, like some kind of lucky charm to ward off bad outcomes. The object: a boxed collector's set that held the five-volume saga of Douglas Adams's *Hitchhiker's Guide to the Galaxy*. Oliver had begged her for it once, when he was fifteen, but she hadn't been able to afford it then, and she could afford it even less today.

But there it was, on the bottom row of one of the faux-oak bookcases. Like a little piece of her son, on a shelf. Her lower back shrieking, Eve stooped and her tailbone landed hard on the navy carpet. As Beethoven's Fifth rattled the PA system, she dislodged the box and palmed the weight, back and forth, like a football. Stage two of her procedure was to assess the store for skeptical eyes and security cameras, but today, with the weight of those books in her hands, Eve's surveillance was lackadaisical, hardly more than a quick eye roll.

Eve knew she was not, as Charlie often liked to claim, *delusional.* She was aware, even as she peeled a magnetic tag from the box's bottom, that even if the impossible thing happened, and Oliver rose from the bed in which he had spent the last nine and a half years, he likely would not have much immediate use for the works of Douglas Adams. But the urge worked like any superstition, something in which she did not really believe, something she could even laugh at inwardly, and yet some atavistic, totem-worshiping part of her was afraid to resist. She couldn't do anything about the test scheduled for today, but here was a self-made test she could pass: Did she believe in a future for her son or didn't she? She unclasped her wide red leather purse, and she dropped the box's pleasing heft inside. She pressed the jagged edges of her chewed fingernails against the bookshelf's lip and rose, made swift progress past the security monitors that flanked the automatic doors. They triggered no alarm. Sweating immensely beneath her blazer, she made it as far as the blinding white pavement outside before a set of thick fingers found her wrist.

"Whoo boy," the man said.

The security guy's name, according to the brass plate on his desk in a tiny, egg-scented back office, was Ron Towers. Eve had met Ron once before, in his previous position at the local Old Navy franchise across the expressway. She remembered his crusty maritime face, as if Old Navy hired its muscle through some casting process. Ron Towers was silently considering her now, like some riddle he was trying to solve. Recognition lit his raw features. "Loving," he said. "Eve Loving."

She nodded, and Ron Towers nodded, too, looking pleased with himself. "It's those crazy eyes of yours. How could I forget those eyes?"

"How could I forget a Ron Towers?"

Ron sneered and typed her name into the computer on his desk. He hit enter and grinned. "Looks like we've got a serious uh-oh here."

"Uh-oh," she echoed as Ron consulted a gray metal filing cabinet. He thumbed through the contents of a drawer, retrieved a document, and displayed it like a certificate of accomplishment.

"Any return will be considered trespassing. Any further shop-lifting will be referred to police action." Ron nudged the document toward her. She didn't need to read it. She was familiar with its content.

The list of stores from which Eve Loving was blacklisted had grown. Over the last nine years, in the sallow back rooms of major Big Bend retailers, she had signed a number of similar contracts. The paunchy or gangly guards always put on the kind of tough-guy bra-vado that Ron showed her now. "We don't need your kind of busi-ness here," they'd unoriginally tell her as they searched her face. But the truly shameful part was that these guys' close attention, their consideration of what she might contain behind her nervous smile, always seemed like a potential antidote to her solitude. As those self-serious men led her by the elbow with a firm hand, she could feel the relieving possibility of confession, the sense that everything in her past months and years was at last coming to a climax. When those men lectured Eve, threatened her, wielded their dinky power behind their cheap nameplates, she felt her whole story rise up in her. And yet, in the end, they were always satisfied by her apologies and a contract. The madness or sorrow that might compel a fiftyish woman to steal a book meant for a teenager: a question that a man like Ron Towers was satisfied to consign to another signed document in a desk drawer.

"So what do we do now?" Ron didn't say anything more, only looked at Eve as if she'd done something other than shoplift a boxed set, as if he really might be trying to suss out a deeper kind of guilt. She eyed the telephone on his desk. She thought of making a break for the door. Ron Towers was grinning, a little lasciviously.

In a decade of many cruel paradoxes, one of the greatest tricks that her tragic forties had played on Eve was the way that grief seemed to have sharpened whatever latent beauty she had possessed. As her

face had thinned, the overlarge eyes had become cartoon-princess-like in their enormity. All the days she had spent outside to escape the musty stuffiness of her house had toasted her Semitic features with a pleasant brownish glaze. Her back troubles made her stick out her pert rear end like a bustle, made her carry her breasts like a waiter offering a tray of hors d'oeuvres. What might it mean, Eve tried not to wonder, that she wore her suffering so attractively?

"Please," Eve said.

"The one thing I'll never get," Ron mused, "is why a nice lady like you would do it. Some poor kid, sure. Some toothless meth head, that's natural. But a lady like you, is it just the thrill?"

She couldn't tell if this was only part of his chest-thumping display or if Ron Towers might actually be troubled. This rosacea-faced man was a poor judge for her life's crimes, but she was relieved to tell him, "I'm Oliver Loving's mother."

He squinted. Did he possibly recognize the name? There was no doubt that he would have heard about her family on the news, back when it happened. In the news stream spectacle that had followed that worst night, the Lovings had perhaps become the most pitiable of all those families to be so piously and publically pitied. But all that was nearly ten years ago. Ron Towers, living a hundred miles away, had likely forgotten all about Hector Espina and Bliss Township School.

"My son is in pieces. He's scattered all over the world," Eve told Ron now. "And I have to pick them up." Eve had learned the trick of the homeless and the imprisoned; bad behavior has an inflection point. Act a little strangely and people will correct you, act oddly enough and people will clear you a wide berth.

"Excuse me?" Ron asked.

She reached across Ron's desk then, for one of his massive, furry hands. Ron did not pull away as she held it like another creature, something injured they had just found together, which they could both worry over. She felt Ron's clunky class ring, its cheap gemstone, and she twisted it loose, as if it were choking his finger. This hand, she knew, was connected to Ron Towers's haughty, reddened face, but it really did feel separate from him now, like some other object Eve wanted to slip into her purse. She lifted its mass, and she kissed it. But then she made the mistake of looking up. Her gaze on him severed whatever strange spell had momentarily altered the space between them. He pulled his hand away, wiped it against the papers on his desk.

"You need help," Ron Towers said.

The clock on Eve's dashboard showed 9:53, the digits dimly throbbing with the engine. The Hyundai, which Oliver had long ago named Goliath, clanked and sputtered as she pulled out of her parking spot. Now that Ron Towers had let her free, she had no excuse not to retrace the route of the morning errand, ninety-four miles deep into the desert.

The roads between the shopping center and Crockett State Assisted Care Facility traversed an emptiness so vast it was claustrophobic. The same five chaparral plants—the goofy heads of grama grass, the Gothic tangling fingers of ocotillo, the low paddled clusters of prickly pear, the surreal candelabras of century plants, the spiny, landlocked sea urchins called lechuguilla—repeated themselves all the way to the deadness of the mountains to the south and the horizon to the north. Thirty years she had been living in the state's westernmost notch, and Eve still had not gotten over the strangeness of all that Texan earth, the extraterrestrial aspect of the empty space that lay in the triple-digit mileage between the Big Bend's few towns. Now shakily powering through the Chihuahuan Desert at a hundred miles an hour, Goliath was like some sci-fi vessel, one of those battered spaceships plundering the galaxy on the covers of Oliver's old paperbacks.

Eve was not a daughter of Texas. She was a daughter of nowhere in particular, the only child of a single-father car salesman, Mortimer Frankl, who had schlepped her around the American West in his maroon 1976 Cutlass Supreme. After her father's death put an end to an unhappy childhood spent mostly in crestfallen hotel rooms and musty sublets where there was never enough space, when Eve met Jed Loving, she had thrilled to the freedom promised by his home's two hundred acres. She could not have suspected how little those acres would hold for her. The Apache, Jed's mother once told her, thought this desert was what remained after the world's creation. The spare raw materials, the leftovers of better places.

"People go to New York to become something," Charlie theorized once. "But they go to the Big Bend to become nothing."

Nearly a decade had passed and even still she couldn't graft this ruined life onto the simple linearity of time *before.* In a single instant, a twenty-one-year-old boy named Hector Espina had shattered time. More than nine and a half years ago Eve had been a full-time mother, already in the twilight years of that profession, staring down the lonesome ambiguities of the forty or so unclaimed, childless years unfurling from the front door of Zion's Pastures. A decade later, she was a de facto (if not yet de jure) divorcée, the mother of one son lost to violence, the other to his own selfishness. She lived alone in the erstwhile "show home" of an abortive neighborhood complex called Desert Splendor, a failed subdivision of unoccupied homes and half-built house skeletons on a high desert flat. Her new house was plagued. It longed to become a ruin. That April, when she tried to start her air conditioner, it spoke its fitful last words and died. "Maintenance," the management company said over the phone, "per our agreement, is your responsibility."

Eve shifted with a grunt in the threadbare driver's seat, unsettled by the grinding pain in her lower back. Having two children with a West Texan had given Eve a vocabulary moralistically devoid of expletives, but now she let loose a hot torrent of them. "Fuck!" Eve shouted. "Fuck, fuck, fuck you!"

She pulled Goliath to a stop fifteen miles shy of Crockett State Assisted Care Facility, into a square of tarmac that framed Señor Buddy's Filling Station. Outside, on a high metal column, stood the old billboard tribute to Reginald Avalon, a faded photo of Bliss Township School's slain theater teacher, back in his youth as a locally famous Tejano musician, in his mariachi getup, singing to the scrubbed blue heavens, a biblical scroll unfurling beneath him: REG AVALON, REST IN PEACE, BELOVED TEACHER. And Eve knew that a couple of lines of Oliver's poem were there, too, just to the right of Mr. Avalon's portrait, and she was glad they were there, but it was just too much to look up at them today.

Oliver's poem, "Children of the Borderlands," had become a kind of anthem for the grieving town of Bliss. It was something that Oliver had written for his English class in the last weeks *before,* and its lines had been reproduced dozens of times now, in local papers and commemorative materials; "Children of the Borderlands" had even appeared once in the pages of a statewide magazine. Though it was true that her son had evinced a startling way with words, Eve understood that the reason for this poem's celebration was mostly just the sentimentalizing sorrow of her town. But, apparently, the highly localized literary renown that tragedy had lent to Oliver had inspired something in his younger brother. Today, somewhere in a benighted apartment in New York City, Charlie was following in Oliver's footsteps, giving his early twenties to some book he was supposedly writing, telling the tragic tale of his brother, the doomed bard of Bliss.

Still trembling a bit from the adrenaline rush of the scene in Ron Towers's office, Eve pushed through the door of Señor Buddy's. When she saw the face of the cashier, Eve felt betrayed. Why did the universe wait until today to place Abbie Wolcott behind the counter? But if it were any other day, Eve would already have arrived at Crockett State for visiting hours. How long had Abbie, her husband's old colleague, her son's old calculus teacher, been working the Señor Buddy's daytime shift? Desert Splendor sat fifty miles from what was left of the town of Bliss, and for the sake of eluding the dreadful heart plunge that was happening now beneath her ribs, Eve tried, as best she could, to avoid the places she knew the old Blissians still frequented.

"Eve! My God!"

"Abbie. You work here now."

Abbie Wolcott's once handsome, blockish frame had expanded to linebacker proportions. Her face, beneath her feathery, bleached bangs, had the blank innocence of a collie. Eve nearly pitied her for a moment, sympathy that a bright burst of Abbie's cheer instantly atomized.

"I do! It ain't glamorous, but it gets me out of the house."

"That's great."

"Plus I get to chat with people all day long. You know me, a regular chatterbox."

"Sounds perfect for you then."

Abbie made a big cartoonish shrug, something from a *Cathy* comic strip.

"How *are* you?" Abbie asked. "It's been forever."

"Yeah, forever." Both women fell silent, considering the last time they'd met, years ago, when Eve turned Abbie away at the door to Oliver's room, declining the casserole that Abbie clearly hoped she might exchange for insider gossip. But Abbie had been only one of a great many visitors to Bed Four. For the first year or so *after,* a few blackly dressed classmates, many teachers, the parents of the dead, the stooped principal Doyle Dixon, and the occasional religious leader would still show up, uninvited, at visiting hours, to put their hands on the one boy for whom the tragedy was still not yet at an end.

"How is he?" Abbie asked now. Eve could see the great effort it took Abbie Wolcott to dim her sprightliness to match Eve's face.

"Advil," Eve pointed to the rows of packaging behind the counter. "He? You mean Oliver? He's fine, Abbie. Just fine. I'm sorry, but I'm in a hurry. Six dollars?"

"Five ninety-five." Abbie Wolcott's voice was glum and empathetic.

"Right."

"You know," Abbie said, "I still keep Oliver in my prayers every night."

Feeling in her purse for the money, Eve pressed the edges of a coin until her fingertips began to ache. "All right."

"And all of you, too. Charlie. Jed. Poor Jed."

"Poor Jed," Eve said.

"Hey, do you want to buy one of these? It's for that memorial they're trying to build. For the tenth anniversary."

Abbie gestured to a corrugated box of bumper stickers beneath a sign that said $5. On the sticker, amid clip art of praying hands, crucifixes, and angels, was the slogan that had become the official death rattle of the town of Bliss, Texas. WE REMEMBER THE FIFTEENTH OF NOVEMBER. Eve hated that phrase, its bombastic, Orwellian undertone. And the memorial dreamt up by the Fifteenth of November set was plainly contemptible. One of those mothers once mailed her an artist's rendering of their vision: four iron crosses, vaguely in the style of the famous cruciform I-beam that was left of the World Trade Center after the attacks. Four crosses, representing the four murdered. But what about Eve's son? A half cross, maybe? Just the horizontal beam? Well, Oliver *was* half Jewish.

"Anniversary, huh?" Eve said. "Like a special occasion."

"It's a nice thing. A good thing they are doing. A way to remember."

"Honestly, Abbie, that whole town is a memorial. Why would we need another?"

Abbie could hardly manage a shrug now. "Eve." Abbie rubbed at her ear. "You aren't alone in this."

Abbie said this with her bland, Christian-comfort voice, but of course Eve knew it was also a kind of reprimand. Abbie meant that small army of grieving families, friends, teachers, and classmates, officially called Families of the Fifteenth of November, who were behind the big memorial plans. It was largely parents who comprised the group; the children had mostly vanished from the area, hoping (Eve supposed, and who could blame them?) to put that night at a great distance behind them, both geographically and psychologically.

Back in the driver's seat, when Eve reached into the brown paper sack for her pills, she found that Abbie Wolcott had slipped in a complimentary bumper sticker. WE REMEMBER THE FIFTEENTH OF NOVEMBER. As if anyone out there could ever forget. As if she and Oliver both were not still sealed inside that date. As if all the questions of that night, all Eve knew and couldn't know about what had happened to her son, could ever fade into the past. WE REMEMBER THE FIFTEENTH OF NOVEMBER. There was so much Eve tried not to remember, her whole past lying stained and shattered on the floor of that schoolhouse classroom. *Why?* She had worked so hard not to think about it, had tried to narrow her concerns to the ten-by-ten room that held Bed Four, but almost ten years later, that question was still in the room with her, every day.

······················

CHAPTER THREE

Eve had no answers that mattered. She only knew the same facts as everyone else. On that November fifteenth, at 9:09 on the night of the Bliss Township Homecoming Dance, a twenty-one-year-old graduate of that school, a scrawny, multiply tattooed, shaven-haired, and sunken-eyed young man named Hector Espina Jr., had parked his pickup outside a rear door of the schoolhouse and entered the building with an AR-15-style assault rifle, which he had purchased at a gun show in Midland. He had walked not to the dance in the gymnasium, where he could have inflicted maximum carnage, but just to a certain classroom near the back door, where the Theater Club was preparing to go onstage to offer its traditional, biannual performance of a few Spanish-language hits. According to that room's surviving students, Hector said nothing before he lifted his weapon. The horror was amplified by its swiftness: the whole thing lasted less than a minute. Within sixty seconds, three children and Reginald Avalon were gone. As Hector left the classroom, he found one more student near the doorway, far from the activities of the Homecoming Dance. *What was Oliver doing there?* A question that Eve knew better than to ask, even if the unreasonable questioner who resided near her heart could never stop asking it. Eve tried to accept it as blunt fact: Hector did find Oliver there, aimed his weapon, and murdered her family's future.

Perhaps Hector had in mind further bloodshed, down in the gymnasium; perhaps he had already completed his heinous mission. No one would ever know, because as Hector walked from the theater classroom toward the school's front doors a janitor named Ernesto Ruiz, working extra hours at the dance that night, secreted himself behind one of the Ionic columns that stood in the atrium. Just as Hector passed, Ernesto lunged from his hidden spot, and in the ensuing scuffle, Ernesto managed to wrangle the rifle from the boy's hands. Hector scampered away, but not—as it turned out—unarmed. In the waistband of his jeans, Hector carried a second weapon that night, a blunt-nosed .45 he had lifted from beneath his father's bed.

Texas, setting to so many of the West's great hangings and blindfolded executions, was a state that still made proud and frequent use of the death penalty, but out there, on the schoolhouse steps, Hector took care of that penalty himself, applying the barrel of his father's handgun to the center of his own forehead, pulling the trigger, leaving the town to tear itself in two with its questions.

In the first weeks *after*, the governor appointed a task force, a bunch of cheap-suited city guys, to investigate alongside the FBI. Most of what this task force turned up the town already knew: Hector Espina Jr. had been a minor dealer of drugs around town and also the son of Hector Espina Sr., a sanitation worker, undocumented and of Mexican extraction. On television news, Hector Sr.'s friends and neighbors tried to distance themselves from Hector Jr.— "psychopath," "strange in the head," "dirt poor," and "loner" were the diagnoses they offered. "Sad" and "angry" and "motherless" were the only explanations offered by Hector Sr. himself. But it had been a year of growing violence along the border, a summer of a great many deportations, an autumn of heightening tensions and occasional skirmishes outside Bliss Township School, and so a certain element of the county's white population rushed to their reflexive conclusions.

"Enough of these madmen sneaking over the border with their guns and their drugs," Donna Grass told Eve, in one of her teary visits to Oliver's bed, just a few weeks *after.* "Something has to be done. We owe our children that much. We owe them that."

"I really don't see what any of this has to do with drugs," Eve said. Her son was still intubated then, unbudging and sallow in an induced coma, and Eve's early grief was still such a combustible, ungainly force that it seemed an accomplishment whenever she could restrain her sorrow long enough to allow any visitor to leave the room unscathed. But Eve reminded herself that Donna had lost her daughter, and so Eve did her best to make a seam of her mouth.

"Have you seen what it's like down there on the other side of the river?" Donna said. "It's practically a war. A never-ending war. You have no idea. It makes them all think that violence is a perfectly acceptable response."

Eve blinked repeatedly, as if allergic to the unwashed, scalpy odor that came off that mourning woman. "And this is what you believe?"

"These are facts, Eve. *Facts.* Did you hear what the governor said? Terrorism, he called it."

"Oh, Donna."

Weeks had passed, and still no one had come up with any persuasive motive that would have brought Hector and his rifle to that particular room, any reason why a graduated student would slaughter a beloved theater teacher and his students, any reason why Eve's son had been there, too. Mr. Avalon—the school principal, Doyle Dixon, told Eve in one of his own Crockett State visits—had never even been Hector's teacher. The only person who might have been able to offer any kind of answer, Hector's father, had vanished from the area.

But Eve's refusal to join in Donna's protests would have made little difference. In a televised news conference, a beefy, red-state character actor named Craig Armison, U.S. Representative for Presidio County, called for further "crackdowns" on "illegals." Facing the ill will of their neighbors and the imminent likelihood of a border patrol officer knocking at their own doors, the majority of the Latino population of

Bliss scattered, draining whole streets of their tenants. Even that night's only certifiable hero, Ernesto Ruiz, fled for the less contentious states to the north. The old school never reopened after that day. At the start of the next semester, the Bliss Township students were incorporated into the drably modern elementary and high schools out in Marathon. Bliss, Texas, had been the sort of town common in the state's western half: with all its former industry dead or dying, the activity of the schoolhouse had been the only reason people still came to town, the only source of customers to Bliss's few weathered businesses. When the school closed, Bliss swiftly slipped its way toward becoming just another ghost town, unmoored in the desert's ancient, evaporated sea.

"There is no *why*," Eve very often told Charlie, told herself. "With some things you have no choice but to accept that fact." Eve couldn't allow herself the luxury of questions: the early grim opinions of the doctors, her worries for Charlie's marred future, the fate of her collapsing marriage, the antipathy that ran down her town like a zipper, baring teeth on either side. Her survival, and so her sons' survival, too, demanded action.

One day, a week after the neurosurgeons had completed the fourth of their procedures, Dr. Frank Rumble released Oliver from his insulin-induced coma and disconnected the respiration tube to reveal the horrible thing he had become, a boy connected to life by electronic umbilicals, his eyes searching in that terrible lost way, his arms snarled like those of a tyrannosaurus. And in that instant, Eve underwent a transformation of her own. It would later seem to Eve that she had actually *seen* her former self leave her body then, like a harp-plucking soul cleaving away from a slain character in a cartoon. Eve ran for the hallway, where she found a trash can. *Impossible.* The first uncomprehending word she had thought that night rose again with the sickness in her throat. Impossible, but it was only now that she understood the reality in which she had been living those last months: the impossible thing, the unfathomable horror actually had become her real life. *There is no why*, Eve had said, and yet she couldn't help screaming the question now, to no one in particular, to the walls.

"Why?" Then she wiped her mouth, walked back into the room, set her gaze on Dr. Rumble. "What do we do now?"

"Now?" Dr. Rumble said, his voice in battle with itself, to accommodate her need and also to tell the truth. "Now that he's off the insulin, we can assess the extent of the damage. But from what we've seen so far—I guess we just wait and hope for a miracle."

"A miracle?" she asked, and Dr. Rumble shrugged.

Oliver, please, Oliver, Oliver, please, please, Oliver: Eve's life, for weeks, contracted to those two words, as she waited for her son's gaze to come back to her face, for his mouth to open, for a word of his own to come.

Eve herself had rarely used the word *miracle* without irony, but this one was different. The world had gone monstrous and wrong, there was a blight on the land. What had happened to her son was something from a gothic horror, a curse from above. And if Eve suddenly lived in a world where such a mythic affliction could suddenly befall her family, then why couldn't a miraculous reversal also be possible? A *miracle*: as time passed she employed that word as antidote to the probabilities of which Dr. Rumble and his colleagues increasingly spoke. Those aging country men intoned falling percentages in the dour tones of priests as they strapped electrodes to the patient's head, tested his reflexes with rubber hammers. The round had entered near the base of Oliver's brain stem; in addition to the structural damage, a blood clot had starved his brain of oxygen for five long minutes during his second surgery. Oliver had arrived at Crockett State with his chance of regaining some consciousness at fifty-fifty. That percentage shrank to thirty, to ten, to five, to far less than one.

And as their hope shrank away, Jed seemed to be vanishing in kind. He appeared to lose track of day and night. When he came back from his shed at wholly unpredictable hours, he smelled like restaurant waste, stale booze, and something sour-creamy. "Tell me what you are thinking," Eve pleaded with him once. "We need to talk about it." There had been a time—a very, very long time before—when their young romance had felt like a marvelously efficient device, a glistening machine that could pack away her old sorrows in words and stories. But now Jed dragged so deeply on his Pall Mall, he might have inhaled the filter. "What is there to say?" he asked. "There are just no words anymore." Eve pitied him, she hated him, it didn't matter. What mattered was that she knew she couldn't have him around.

"I can't have all of this," she told Jed a few nights later, gesturing at the smoke-rimed contents of his shed. And this, she knew, was the story of her marriage: Jed was a seconder of opinions, a placater, a head-nodder. At his excommunication, he only nodded again.

And as for the only other Loving left with her at Zion's Pastures? Eve still panicked at the thought of letting Charlie stray beyond the gates of her family's home, and she dreaded the idea of letting him go to that prison-looking new school in Marathon, where he would sit in those overbright rooms with classmates who would never look upon Charlie as anything but an object of horrible pity. Eve felt that anything important that she'd ever learned she had taught to herself, and she chose to complete Charlie's education on her own, at home.

Despite what he would say about it later, she and Charlie (somehow, implausibly) had many peaceable, quiet days together at Zion's Pastures, in the company of Charlie's snorty new dog, Edwina. Charlie and Eve had to cling tightly together then. That worst night, when a chaplain had brought Charlie to the hospital, he had moved through the hallways as if they were filled with water, his quick little movements now liquid slow, his face panicked and drowning. "When do we go home?" His words had burbled out of him, from some dark and frigid depth. "Soon," she told him, and eventually they did go back to Zion's Pastures, but of course they never really went home again. Shocking to consider now: in that first year of homeschooling, they had used "love you" like punctuation.

One March afternoon, Dr. Rumble summoned what remained of Eve's family into the turquoise and beige tones of his southwestern-motif office, "to make a decision."

"It is very important," Dr. Rumble explained, his ringed fingers pinching the quill of a potted cactus, "that you have no illusions here. Sometimes, you see, death doesn't look like what you'd expect. It is awful to say it, but I feel I must be very clear. From everything we've seen in our tests and observations over the last months, we just can't see any reason to believe that Oliver is still with us. And—this is the hardest part, I know it—the question that you must begin to ask yourselves now is whether you want to keep his body alive."

Eve looked at Jed and Charlie then, but for a long while no one said anything more. Eve rocked forward in her seat, braced herself on her knees. "Ma?" Charlie said, and all at once Eve straightened in her chair. *Liar!*: The word spat out of Eve's mouth unbidden, like something sickly and viscous her lungs had coughed up. "That's a lie," Eve shouted at the doctor in his armchair. But Dr. Rumble only puckered his lips, curiously tipping his head, as if Eve weren't quite speaking English.

In manic bouts of googling, Eve found online several stories of patients like Oliver, patients given those same dire labels of Persistent Vegetative State and Unresponsive Wakefulness Syndrome, who nevertheless emerged from their long paralysis. The chance of a similar miracle befalling her son—less than one-hundredth of one percent—was the little datum she clung to, a fraying rope that kept her from falling into the darkness that had already swallowed her husband. Sometimes, even still, she thought that she could feel in Oliver's clammy left hand something other than the infinite, mindless tremble. Dr. Rumble promised her it was involuntary, just a variation on a perpetually misfiring nervous system. And when Dr. Rumble again enquired about the subject he had raised that terrible day in his office? "We're still thinking," Eve told the doctor many times in the weeks and months that passed, unaware, as the grieving can be, that her indecision was becoming the decision.

Over the years that followed, only one outside visitor continued to arrive regularly at Bed Four. Every three months or so, a man named Manuel Paz would make his way into the room with his slow, wide saunter. Manuel was a kind of police officer, a captain from the Presidio County office of the Texas Rangers, who was also a third-generation Blissian. In Eve's first months in the Big Bend, she had met Manuel Paz a couple of times on Main Street. Even back then, he had seemed like some biological antique, a fleshy, quiet-stoic Texan of yore, almost comforting in his anachronism, a character from a movie about an older Texas, one in which white and Mexican settlers slugged whiskey in the same saloon. But now he had become something else to Eve. Not an official detective—that whole task force had arrived to Bliss, appointed by the governor—but of all those apathetic half-wits Manuel always seemed the only officer who actually cared. "Just thought I'd check in on you folks, see how y'all are faring," Manuel would always say in his sun-dried avuncular way.

All those other officials had gone quickly back to Austin, stuffing loose ends into their bureaucratic attaché cases. It wasn't their town; it was Manuel's town. A town that was hardly even a town at all anymore, disintegrated now into those questions that perhaps only the boy in Bed Four could ever have helped answer. And yet, whatever his doomed motives, Eve was grateful to have at least this one other partner in her hope. "What's new?" Manuel would ask, his gaze quickly falling to Oliver as if, at last, some answer might be in the offing.

"Same as ever," Eve told him, again and again.

And here, Eve would have liked to tell her younger son, was what real fortitude looked like. Even now, even after every good thing had fallen away from her, the future occurrence of that so-called miracle still felt as solid to her as any object she slipped into her purse. She had lost Charlie to college, then to New York City. She had lost her family money, and Jed had long ago quit teaching, hardly turning minimum wage now in his new reception job at a poorly touristed new tourist resort, out in Lajitas. She had lost her home, selling off her husband's ranch to a family called the Quades. She had nearly lost her sanity. She had lost any discernible future. And at last, in recent months, she had lost what little remained of the money from the sale of Zion's Pastures, hardly scraping by now on the tiny monthly sum she received from the fund the governor established for victims of that night and her occasional copyediting work for The Holy Light, a local, televangelically funded publisher of fundamentalist books of Bible stories for children, whose commas, semicolons, and run-on homilies she corrected.

Two months ago, as Eve felt her life approaching a new crisis point, Dr. Rumble had called her back into his mini–cactus garden of an office, where a second presence, a bearded, ferrety man, stood to greet her. This was Professor Alexander Nickell, all the way from Princeton University, who presented Eve with "a very exciting opportunity."

This very exciting opportunity was Professor Nickell's newfangled functional magnetic resonance imaging machine, which he was planning to take on a long road trip of the nation's vegetative cases, and this visit to Crockett State was apparently part of his scouting mission. "What we want to study," Nickell said, as neutrally as if he were speaking to colleagues in a lecture hall, "is how brain death warps and shrinks the size of the organ. We've been looking for people like Oliver, but they aren't exactly a dime a dozen."

"No, they aren't," Eve said.

"What I mean to say"—Professor Nickell pinched at the tight crop of his mustache, as if feeling for its vanished handlebar—"is that they are very special."

"Warps and shrinks?" she asked.

"Yes, there are fascinating structural changes to the brain . . ."

Eve lost the thread of the professor's lecture, but she didn't need to listen. A diligent researcher like herself could not have failed to read about this new sort of fMRI, showing neural activity at microscopic levels, and she of course knew all about how brains of vegetative-state patients were known to shrivel from inactivity. In the first months *after,* among the many EEGs and reflex tests, Oliver had undergone a few rounds on an earlier form of such a machine, all of which, according to Oliver's weathered chief physician, showed Oliver's brain's activity reduced to its core, its cerebellum, its so-called *reptilian brain,* a dim bulb of dendritic light just above his spinal cord that kept his heart beating, his lungs breathing. When Dr. Rumble shined flashlights into Oliver's eyes, they did not dilate properly; when Dr. Rumble rubbed his sternum, Oliver did not lift a hand to bat him away. "Anything? Anything different?" Eve had begged Dr. Rumble many times.

"To tell you the truth, I have to admit I'm just doing these tests for your sake. This charade probably isn't good for anyone."

"Charade? Are you serious?"

"Of course," Dr. Rumble had told her, "you are entitled to another opinion if you'd like. There's a brain center out in El Paso I could refer you to, but I should tell you the place ain't cheap."

But why, really, had Eve not insisted? It was true she couldn't afford it, but of course that was not the reason. The true, unspeakable reason: as Oliver spent months and then years untested, Eve developed a kind of private faith around the lack of quality medical assessment, a faith that spread from that inextinguishable word *miracle*. As if, as long as she could believe that the structure were still intact, it somehow, miraculously, might be capable of life. A new fMRI, Eve understood, might at last force her to see what the doctors saw when they looked at Oliver. Not a trapped and pleading intelligence, not Oliver's eyes searching, in that fast, flitting way they moved, for an escape from his neurofibral thickets. Only a decimated nervous system, misfiring.

Still, Eve had told herself countless times that soon she would insist Oliver undergo testing on the new sorts of brain scans she had read about, the ones that could offer a far more detailed image of neural activity than the clunky, outdated model that their humble little county hospital had employed. *Next month,* she'd tell herself, sometimes going so far as to write the date into her calendar when she would make the phone call. And yet, the next month came and went, and always there were so many reasons to put it off just another month longer: Oliver had come down with a case of pneumonia, she worried about transferring him in the outrageous summer heat, she had too much of her own copyediting work to get done, her finances were at a particularly dire moment. She put it off and put it off, until her putting it off became its own kind of superstition, a ritual in her life. The longer she delayed that second opinion, the more dire its potential outcomes, the more she could not bear to schedule it.

But at last, almost ten years *after,* sitting there with Dr. Rumble and his visitor from Princeton, the faith around which she had arranged her years had come to its end. *Ten years:* that number repeated itself now like a second pulse in her temples. "Eve," Dr. Rumble said after Professor Nickell, glowing with his own informativeness, completed his lecture. "I think this is an opportunity we'd be foolish to refuse. There might not be much we can do for Oliver now, but if the professor here could help at least understand others like him—well, why would we say no?"

Because that last hope is all that's left, Eve did not say. "I suppose you're right," she said instead, and Dr. Rumble looked relieved, dabbing his goatee with the back of his hand.

"The thing is," Professor Nickell added, "we'll need your husband to agree, too." Eve wrote down Jed's phone number on the back of Nickell's business card.

"I'll leave that part up to you," she said.

CHAPTER FOUR

Crockett State Assisted Care Facility was a two-floor stucco cube beyond the dust and gore of insect death polluting Eve's windshield. The repository of her thoughts, labors, hopes, godless prayers looked almost comically diminished from that distance. An outpost on Mars. And her son lived in an outpost of the outpost, the only head trauma patient currently in residence, the balance of the unit's patients afflicted with garden-variety cognitive impairments, Alzheimer's and Parkinson's and muscular dystrophy, aneurysms and strokes. Oliver was the facility's youngest resident by forty years at least. A few times a week, an ambulance came to cart one of the geriatrics to emergency care in Alpine or Marathon.

But today, parked just beyond the side door, was another kind of vehicle, one that loomed much larger than its humble RV dimensions: Professor Nickell's truck, tricked out like one of those mobile blood donation centers, which displayed, in a flourish of corporate logo design, the words PRINCETON MIND-BRAIN CENTER. When Eve reached to unbuckle the seat belt, her back distress blew its buckshot, strafing her from pelvis to shoulder blade.

And now, just before undertaking the arduous work of climbing out of Goliath, Eve paused to let a certain presence pass by, not ten feet in front of her windshield. Margot Strout, in her new bouffant and floral-themed blazer, a golden cross swinging from her neck, pretended not to notice Eve sitting there in her car, as Margot worked her thighs in an awkward scamper.

Margot Strout—the speech pathologist who visited Crockett State three times a week, to help the stroke and dementia cases produce a few words for visiting family and caregivers—was considered something of a saint in that fluorescent-grim institution. She was a blast of excoriating sunshine, a Jesus-loving lady who wore her makeup in operatic proportions, her piney perfume like some chemical weapon attack, her hair teased up to the heavens. According to the story Eve had heard the woman relate many times, Margot had once been the single mother of a baby girl, Cora, who was born with severe birth defects. Cora's mental impairment had kept her from speaking before she died at the age of four, and to the facility's workers, visitors, and Eve herself, Margot had gone on and on about her "calling," about "giving a voice back to the voiceless."

But what about the most voiceless of all the Crockett State residents? At last, seven or so years ago now, Margot had agreed to give a little of her time to Oliver. "From what Dr. Rumble says," Margot told Eve, "you truly cannot expect a speech pathologist will do him any good at this point. But believe me, Eve, I know what it can mean to have someone at least try. You should have seen me, the way I used to badger the doctors about my Cora."

The next week, Margot had come down to work at Bed Four. Margot spent nine hours with Oliver, nine agonizing hours during which Eve had to wait in the lobby, a dangerous hope like a pestle grinding against the stone of her skepticism, her stomach pinched in between. Because of Oliver's draconian insurance policy, Margot worked pro bono that day, and so Eve didn't want to pester the woman, but when Eve looked through the little window into Oliver's room, she was a little appalled at what it apparently meant for Margot to "try": Margot seemed only to be speaking softly to Oliver, putting her hands gently against his body, scanning Oliver's twitchings with her fingers. And at the end of just a single day palpating the patient, Margot seconded the doctors' diagnosis. "Just involuntary tremors, I'm afraid," Margot said, in a voice that was unbearable in its pity. "Nothing he can control. I'm so sorry."

"One day and you just give up."

"No, Eve," Margot told her. "I'm not *giving up*. It's just the truth. And, speaking from some personal experience, the truth is the hardest part."

The automatic doors into the squat stucco box of Crockett State now shushed open at Eve's arrival, and she was stunned by the face she found there, waiting for her to arrive.

"Jed."

It had been nearly a year since Eve had seen her husband and she had to swallow a gasp at what that time had done. Jed's coveralls were spattered with paint and grime, his face was as still and sun pleated as a taxidermy desert animal in a display case. She was looking at the rind of a man, his lips puckered, his eyes red and troubled, his cheeks twin bushels of gin blossoms, his fingers yellowed and quaking.

"Eve."

Jed stood and came for her, extending his arms to strike an image almost perfectly identical to the Crockett State logo emblazoned on the Band-Aid-colored façade outside. Jed's smell was sharp and sour; she felt the bristle of his thinning hair against her cheek. To her chagrin, her eyes watered. "I never thought you'd be here."

"Of course I came. I've been counting the days. I can't believe it has finally come," Jed said in a close voice.

"I can't, either." So this was what July twenty-second looked like. It looked like any other blazing summer day, terrible for its normalcy. Nothing and no one here, other than her husband and the RV, to mark what was about to happen. She felt it was hideous that Jed should show up today, acting like he'd been some partner in all this. He was a trespasser.

But the worst part was that, on a number of occasions, Eve had tried tentatively to crack open the long-sealed gates of their marriage.

From time to time, in the first years after Charlie left for college, Eve would call Jed and invite him to visit Crockett State, as if the man needed an invitation, as if they had decided their son belonged only to her. At Oliver's bed, Jed was always a tremulous, stammering, teary wreck, sitting at a distance, as if his son's paralysis might be contagious. "I'm sorry, I'm so sorry," he'd say, as if the thing had just happened. And yet, after visiting hours, she'd always ask Jed back to her house at Desert Splendor for dinner. Dinner—*ha!* They rarely ate.

Why? Was she trying somehow to undo the thing she had done on that last night *before*, now shimmying her backside against him? No, it was only for the release. Only for those few tumbling, sweating minutes when, for once, she was not thinking of much at all, her mind an empty place, just a bell in which a clapper struck. And yet, after it was over, they came back into their aging skins, the shopworn roles they had long played in the theater of the family Loving. Jed silent, Eve incredulous. After each of their dozen or so "dinners," her husband just acted like one of those bovine-eyed security guys, never saying much or asking much of her, never making her tell the truth about the way she was living, how things had become between Charlie and her, the lengthy conversations she conducted with their silent son in his hospital bed. A life so dire that often, turning the wedding ring on her finger, she could surprise herself to remember she was still a wife.

Waiting for Professor Nickell to appear, Eve and Jed shared a silence in their stiff upholstered chairs. Deep in Eve's gut, the giddiness of her shoplifting and the panic of this appointment did battle, a hot column of something advancing up her chest. Her dread was expansive, taking in everything around her now: the splashy comic-book hues of the vintage western movie posters decorating the walls, the gaudy receptionist, Peggy, clacking at her keyboard, the crackle and wheeze of the facility's air-conditioning, the antique horseshoe bolted over the entranceway for good luck. She couldn't bear the silence a second longer, and she pointed to the neon purple spatter on Jed's jeans.

"Where do you even find paint that color?" she asked.

"Oh. It's not paint."

"No?"

"Nah. It's hipster blood. Turns out, when you flog one of those half-beards to death, he bleeds out in the color scheme of the 1980s."

"Har har." Jed's joking about his hipster cohort in Marfa was one of his few conversational go-tos, as if to prove to Eve he was different from all the vaguely artistic layabouts with whom he shared that town.

"Hey, where do you go to drown a hipster?" Jed asked. "The mainstream."

"Okay, that's enough."

Jed's smile widened a tick too far, became a baring of clenched teeth through which he said, "Sorry."

The reception's swinging door seemed to move, but then it failed to open.

"No, you know what?" Jed said. "Screw you. You don't get to tell me how to deal with this."

Jed was doing that tight smile thing he did when he got mad. Eve nodded earnestly, gladdened and more than a little surprised by Jed's anger, the acknowledgment of what was at stake today. "No, screw *you,*" Eve said, too loudly. She glanced over to find the plump, heavily powdered receptionist grinning behind her desk, her amused eyes informing Eve that later she would be sure to tell her fellow employees of this latest encounter.

Oh, Eve knew what they thought of her, all those nurses and assistants. But Eve had spent four hours a day, six days a week beside Bed Four, and she had learned the routines the doctors prescribed, down to the minute. And so what was Eve supposed to do when the nurses were thirty minutes late in connecting the lunchtime sack of Jevity to Oliver's gastrostomy tube, not mention it? Was she supposed to remain silent when Oliver's colostomy bags overfilled, spilling foulness over his belly? And was she, too, supposed to not raise hell when the nurses failed to rotate his body as often as they should and his pressure sores grew so severe that his fever broke out in a drenching sweat, his hospital gown going translucent against his grayish skin? Should she not mention the unclipped nails with which Oliver's spasming arms could badly scratch himself? The circulation problem that could make his toes and fingers go icy, nearly gangrenous? "Tell me," she often asked the chief nurse, Helen, "am I supposed to just stay silent?"

"All I'm saying," Nurse Helen often recited, in their endless argument over the years, "is that no one else seems to make such a fuss."

But they hardly even came, those children and grandchildren of the dementia and stroke cases babbling down the halls in their wheelchairs and their robes. Eve had come to suspect, by the general failure to visit other than holidays and the occasional hour on the weekend, the true purpose of this institution.

Crockett State Assisted Care Facility, Eve had learned, was a place where people in a particular predicament could displace the burden of their guilt. When stroke or head trauma or Parkinson's or Alzheimer's collapsed a mind and the body beneath did not follow, what was a family to do? Places like Crockett State existed to allow families to commit the coward's form of patricide, matricide, fratricide, filicide: to cede care of your loved one to this place, to tell yourself that you had done everything you could, and then, in the quiet indifference of that institution, to let some infection accomplish the act you didn't have the courage to commit.

Eve would not allow herself that cowardice. She perfected her warning face and would never reward the nurses and doctors with gratitude when they merely followed the prescribed treatments. Eve could feel that her own fixed and pleading eyes were a kind of second and more dependable electricity that powered all those devices, that it was her unblinking gaze that kept the machines clicking and sighing, that fixed Oliver to life. If she let herself look away from the panic of his eyes, the swatting of his reedy arms, the jaundiced pallor of his face, the G-tube might fail, the infection of his bedsores might reach his heart, and Oliver would slip away from her.

To the doctors and nurses, Oliver was just the patient in Bed Four who needed his linens changed. Only Eve was left now to fight for the actual Oliver, the one none of them could know. The boy who loved Bob Dylan, poetry, science fiction, and tall tales. The boy who always insisted everyone stop to look at the sunset, no matter how plain.

Once, watching an old episode of *Oprah,* Eve heard the widow of a 9/11 victim explain that the hardest part was that in her mind, she continued the conversation with her husband, "just as if he were still there, until I remember he isn't." Eve did the same, with the difference that she really had this conversation out loud. She followed Oliver's favorite filmmakers and writers, and she read to him the reviews of their movies and books. She tried to keep Oliver abreast of the news, both international and domestic. She recalled her occasional phone calls with Charlie in vehement detail.

The extent of her motherly faith: Eve really did imagine, and then believe, in Oliver's answers, just on the other side of his trembling skull. When once, during an uncommonly tranquil phone conversation with Charlie, she had mentioned this thought, Charlie told her he wasn't surprised. "Really?" she asked. "Do you sometimes think the same? Then why don't you come for a visit? Why—"

"What I mean, Ma, is that I'm not surprised that you can go on talking without worrying about a reply. Let's just say I have some, uh, firsthand experience with that particular phenomenon."

"I don't know what you could possibly mean."

"It's your way," Charlie told her. "When you don't want to accept something, you just talk and talk, like your talking can make a different kind of world come to be."

"Oh, this again."

"Believe me, Ma, I'm as tired of it as you are. But maybe if you would just try *listening* for once? Maybe, for once, you could ask me a question about *my* life? Maybe you might be interested in hearing what *I* have to say?"

That conversation had ended as nearly all her conversations with Charlie ended, the receiver conducting a thrumming silence until Eve invented some excuse to hang up. Things were different and awful now, but they still ran along the old lines. A mother didn't deliberately pick favorites, but she couldn't help it if one child was more her than the other, just as she couldn't help if one inherited her coltish ankles, the elfin aspect of her ears, her curls. There were people like Eve and Oliver, who understood that survival demanded endless contemplation and skepticism of others' easy ideas, and then there were people like Charlie and Jed, who moved through life like a car at night, never able to see farther than their own dim headlights, blindly trusting the world's dark roads. If there was one modest silver lining to this worst day, it was the phone call she'd get to make to Charlie when it was all over. Whatever the result, she could hope it might summon him home, make him finally see what he had left her to.

The door at last swung open. Professor Nickell looked deeply into his clipboard, a lost man scrutinizing a map. "Mr. and Mrs. Loving?"

"Now?" She scratchily whispered the word, a sound like an unscreamable scream from a nightmare.

"Well." Nickell was already edging back to the door. "No need to rush. We're still getting him ready."

"Eve," Jed said as she hoisted herself out of the chair, shoved her way to the ladies' room. She almost did not make it to the toilet in time. She had not been able to eat that morning, and in the spotless, thrumming stall, only a few drops of ocher acid trickled from her mouth. The truth was that, in nearly every one of those "miracle" stories she had read, the patient did not exactly "wake up." In nearly all of them, a new doctor or scientist simply discovered that the patient had been awake and aware all along, that the patient had only been wrongly diagnosed by antiquated technology or incompetent doctors. And what sort of doctors worked at Crockett State? What sort of a man was Dr. Rumble?

On the slate-blue tile of the ladies' room floor, Eve snapped open her purse and felt for the reassuring shape, half of her somehow hoping she had not actually lifted it from the desk of Ron Towers. But there it was, in her palm. A glistening new phone, which was really just a screen, whose lit face showed Ron Towers delivering a half-nelson to a chubby ten-year-old with Ron's shiny, rosacea-ruddy features. She wondered if Ron had yet noticed its absence. She thought of some surreptitious way to return the thing. And yet, more alluring was the inexorable thought of her son's hands, returned to him, manipulating the glass face of this device. *Geez, how long was I out?*

Eve slipped the phone back into her purse. She rose from the tile floor and ran her palms over the gray polyester blend of her business suit. She freshened her face in the mirror, cupped handfuls of water into her mouth, but could not quell the dryness in her throat.

Back in reception, Eve nodded at Professor Nickell and Dr. Rumble, and the men led her and Jed out into the parking lot, where that trailer that held the fMRI waited, where her son had already been transferred. Eve made the most of the short walk across the apron of asphalt, looking out at the apathetic enormity of the slaggy country, the mountains purple with the false coolness of distance. She trailed Jed into a gray-walled room inside the trailer, a little booth behind a Plexiglas partition, the fMRI just on the other side.

Over the last decade, Eve had watched as machines took over Oliver's body; they had colonized his gastrointestinal regions, his systems both muscular and urinary. And now, as she watched his body shudder into the humming plastic aperture of the fMRI, she had the crazy apprehension that the transformation was about to be complete. As if once the key of her son's awareness docked into the machine, it might suddenly throw forth a holographic image, a Wizard of Oz face, which at last would speak back to her.

And yet, Oliver was in the machine now, electromagnetic energies penetrating the dome of his skull, and to the doctors he was still only a twitching, thoughtless body, a specimen. As the massive computers began to hum, Professor Nickell explained to Eve and Jed what would come next. He pointed their attention to a screen, which showed a human skull in profile. Oliver's skull: a mother could recognize it immediately, even electronically bisected.

Eve looked at the technicians' screens. She was a forty-nine-year-old mother of a massive-head-trauma victim observing the results of an fMRI and she was a forty-year-old woman carrying laundry through the rooms of Zion's Pastures on the night of November fifteenth, when the shaken, emergency-lit image of Bliss Township School on the television caught her eye. Today, the ruin that was left of the man she had married felt for her hand, but Jed also spoke to her, on the telephone, from all those years ago. "Eve—" her name the start of his wail that was not quite human, something animal and dying.

"What? What is it? Tell me. What happened?"

Eve had tried to turn away from the ticking clocks of this world, but time was a vexing, irrefutable math, a tally of prison wall scratches that her counting fingers couldn't resist feeling for in the dark. On that morning, Oliver had been lost in his body for 3,537 days. Leaning into the Plexiglas divide, Eve felt herself grabbing Jed's arm, ropier than before, but the rolling pin shape of it still achingly familiar. She held it against her belly.

And it was odd that it was now, of all times, that a certain memory came worming back into Eve's awareness, from the heavy soil she had long ago heaped upon it. It was something she'd seen on the television coverage in the worst days *after,* playing in the hospital waiting room. Amid the softly droning montage of police officers and weeping students, Eve had seen a single long shot of that girl she had met only once, that night at Zion's Pastures. Only two of the theater kids had made it out of that room wholly unscathed: Ella Brew, who had concealed herself behind the teacher's desk, and also the person Eve now saw on the TV monitor. Rebekkah Sterling, a pale, auburn-haired whisper of a girl, not answering the reporters as she sauntered off into the darkness beyond the school. Rebekkah Sterling ambling away from the violence that had ended the lives of her classmates, set free to disappear into the parking lot shadows.

Eve had never seen her again. Whatever questions Eve had at that moment, Rebekkah carried off with her into that darkness and the years that followed. And yet, what happened that day, what was happening right now inside the fMRI machine in the Crockett State parking lot—the two days, in some unknowable science, were the same blind second, the same question, still unanswered. *Why?* Despite all her vehement claims to the contrary, despite the rational part of her knowing better, Eve couldn't help but feel that at last she was standing at the precipice of some vast and otherworldly presence, that she was finally at the edge of an answer to why this unimaginable fate had chosen her family. That November fifteenth and this July twenty-second, almost ten years later, were connected by the immeasurable heaviness of one of those black holes that once fascinated Jed, pulverizing time, dematerializing her body, atom by atom. Was there light on the other side? Was there anything at all on the other side? Even now, looking at her son's brain coming into the screens, Eve couldn't know: Should she let herself hope, for her own sake, that it would show something, or would it be much better, for her son's sake, if it showed nothing at all?

The professor presented Eve with a big radio announcer's microphone, its output piped through the speakers hung on Oliver's side of the partition. She clenched a fist, struggled to gather enough air to shape a word. And when Eve did speak, it came out very loudly. "Oliver!"

Oliver

· · · · · · · · · · · · · · · · · · · ·

CHAPTER FIVE

Oliver! A shot across the void.

Oliver, when you were twelve years old you brought home a library book you'd found about Philippe Petit's high-wire walk between the Twin Towers. Remember it? It was the technical aspect that impressed you most. The distance between the buildings was vast, and Petit couldn't just toss the 450-pound heft of his tightrope across the chasm. To establish that bridge, first he used a piece of fishing line, which he attached to an arrow that he shot from one roof to the next. Once the line was in place, Petit and his team used it to pull across a thicker string, then a cord, then a rope, and at last they could tug across the steel cable that would let Petit walk into the sky.

Oliver: a single spoken name, and already your family could feel a string drawing taut, the abyss bridged, the line to you thickening with detail. The oily swirl of your hair, like a follicular bonfire. The dreamy, abstracted way you'd sit through a dinner. A teenage-sweet diffidence that could make your every footstep seem tentative, an apology for itself. A seventeen-year-old boy, unnoticed in his school days, becoming visible again.

And it wasn't only your family who came to your bed to try to restore you with a name. "Oliver," the people of your town would say, as their weary faces bent over your bed: a tearful, waddled Mrs. Schumacher, a mustache-fondling Doyle Dixon, a Christianly singing Mrs. Wolcott, a couple of that night's limping survivors, a number of pimple-scraping classmates. Once, even Hector Espina Sr. snuck in to see you, looking down at your body like a darkness to which his eyes could never adjust. Of course, you had been practically a stranger to the great majority of those people and so it was not just grief that brought them to your bed. It was that one same question: *Why?* And though you could not answer, they too could feel the connection to you taking on the heft of the specifics they remembered. Mrs. Schumacher talked to you about the poem you had written: "I never told you how beautiful—" Doyle Dixon blubbered about your first day of kindergarten, when you had brought him an ancient horseshoe you'd found. Your classmates hardly spoke at all; they just looked on, remembering the nervous way you'd skirt the school's masses, wondering if your quiet had been some kind of an omen of what was to come. "Oliver," they would say, again and again, and though you could never make a reply, every one of your visitors could sense it: an explanation that was still somewhere out there, in that impassable, far tower of your memory.

It took Petit's team about an hour to draw across a series of cords until they fastened the cable that let him cross from one building to the next; it would take your family and the people of your town much longer. It would take ten years. But at last, Oliver, in this story split in two, there you are: taking your early tentative steps into that chasm. There you are, walking into your own next chapter, on one September night.

It was September fifteenth, just over two months *before*. A brightness was in your eyes, the dazzle of stadium lights. Banks of them, high over the Bliss Stadium, lighting the first football game in what would prove to be the final season of the Bliss Township Mountain Lions. Though, of course, no one could have known it then. The Mountain

Lions would win that night. No one had any reason to suspect that the good times would not go on and on.

It had been more than three weeks since that night Rebekkah came to your family's ranch, and there you were, in the artificial daylight of 8 P.M., September ninth, just an ungainly high school junior, ascending and descending the concrete stadium steps, a paper envelope of a hat on your head, a tray of peanuts and Coke cups strapped over your shoulders. A truly miserable job for a boy like you, who wanted only to pass unseen. Each school club took a turn at stadium concessions, a way to raise a little funding, and that week the task fell to you as dutiful president of your father's Young Astronomers.

According to an article Pa clipped from an old issue of *Scientific American* and stapled to the bulletin board of his art classroom, which also hosted the bimonthly meetings of the Young Astronomers Club, America's very best stargazing was in your mountainous region, unpolluted by the light of civilization. ("I'm not sure if that is a claim to fame or shame," Ma told him.) It was true what the song said, the stars at night really *were* big and bright, deep in the heart of Texas. But the Friday night lights, the megawattage that lit your matches against the Odessa Bronchos, the El Paso Tigers, the Alpine Bucks, were much brighter.

"Hey, Pizza Face! Are you yelling penis? Ha ha! I don't want your fucking penis, Pizza Face. Stop trying to sell me your penis!"

"Pea-nuts!" you lamely corrected Scotty Coltrane, but your words were drowned in the tide of screams. The Mountain Lions had just put up their third unanswered touchdown. "Pea-nuts!"

Continuing on with your impecunious nut hawking, you thought, for the thousandth time, of quitting the Young Astronomers. But you also knew that, as one of two permanent members, if you quit, the club would cease to exist, and Pa had already suffered too many heartbreaks, ruined dreams, lousy canvases for you to bear to resign. Your club presidency, like your long-ago jamboree purchase of your father's painting, had become your sturdiest notion of familial love: the effort required of you to maintain a loved one's necessary illusion. Still, among the revelry of Bliss Township's hysterical fandom, you were in a particularly rotten mood, and when you passed your brother, high up in the rafters, you showed him an aggrieved frown.

"This is the worst," you told Charlie. "And I've made about six dollars. Subtracting the cost of supplies, I'm at negative thirty-two."

"What are you talking about? This is fun. You just got to work it." Charlie did a slithery thing with his hips, batted at an imaginary hairdo. You were appalled to find his own tray nearly empty, a suggestive nut-metric for the difference between you. How was it that in the west of Texas, your little brother, gay as a box of birds, was so vexingly popular?

Until very recently, you had known a big-brotherly obligation to protect Charlie from the glum truths of your family life—you described the work Pa did in his many liquored nights in his studio as "potential masterpieces"; you called your mother's obsessive worry "just normal Ma behavior"; you many times tried to attribute her obvious favoritism for you as "only a kind of trick she does, to encourage you to get your grades up"; you performed for Charlie many of the ordinary parental tasks yourself, driving him to the movies, taking him for long hikes through the desert. There was a time, not so very long ago, when the two of you could sometimes feel like a sort of better second family, nested inside the larger one. But in recent months, it was Charlie who often tried to lift your mood, suggesting impromptu dance parties and movie soundtrack sing-alongs, flicking at your downturned face until you cracked a grin or at least comically swatted him away. But you saw less and less of him those days. Back at Zion's Pastures you continued, as ever, in your creekside reading, your wistful cacti strolls, but Charlie was always off with one friend or another or another.

"C'mon. Here. I'll take care of your nuts." Charlie emptied half of your tray and really did skip his way back down the stairs.

It was halftime now. Out on the field your school's principal and band director, Doyle Dixon, pumped a baton in front of the Bliss

Township Marching Band, leading a spiraling medley performance of the Eagles' greatest hits.

You spent a while there, leaning against the chain link behind the last row, looking into the sea of school-spirit-reddened faces. A football game, in Bliss Township's tacit racial distinctions, was a decidedly white event, but out beyond the stadium, you observed the loud, boisterous activity of a group of Hispanic kids you recognized from school—an old recess-hour tormentor of yours, David Garza, among them—gathered around someone's pickup, whose subwoofers reverberated in your own chest. Was this a kind of halfhearted protest, the way they congregated near the stadium but did not enter, or were they only drawn to that bright activity on an otherwise silent town night?

You turned back to the rafters, straightened your nut offerings, and that was when you saw Rebekkah Sterling. Not only saw her: through the flittering of paper Mountain Lion paw-mark paddles and jumbo foam fingers, your gaze latched onto hers and held. You had read, again in one of Pa's *Scientific American*s, that if two people maintain eye contact for six unblinking seconds it means they want sex or a fight. This wonderful hypothesis was on your mind when you started counting, all the way up to seven, which—combined with the first two awestruck seconds—must have totaled at least nine. The school's theater teacher, Mr. Avalon, was sitting next to Rebekkah, and he apparently mistook your gaze as directed toward him. He put a hand to his light beard, lifted it and waved faintly. You replied with an awkward Boy Scout's salute. You nearly stumbled in your hurry to get to the bathroom, where you could be alone to marvel at those nine seconds.

Rebekkah might not have joined the Young Astronomers for good, you might not have touched again since that brief grazing of hands, but her one-night attendance at the meteor shower over Zion's Pastures somehow set in motion a wondrous sidereal phenomenon. Rebekkah and you, without ever actually mentioning your standing date, now met each morning in Mrs. Schumacher's literature classroom, empty before school began. For the rest of the day, under the mocking glare of your classmates, you knew that Rebekkah would not have dared to keep your slouched, socially poisonous company. But in those solitary, quiet minutes before Mrs. Schumacher's literature class? In those minutes, your words couldn't come quickly enough.

In that empty classroom, you had already told Rebekkah many things, things you had never tried before to put into language. Your parents' silence with each other, how your mother's love worked like an elaborate and efficient contraption, how your father's love was more like a puddle. You told her about the books you had read and reread, the adventures Charlie and you had invented, the Old Texas tales Granny Nunu told you when you were a kid, the ones that became nearly scriptural to you after she passed. Rebekkah hardly said anything in reply. In truth she usually spoke only when you asked her outright for an answer. "What do you want to do when you graduate?" you asked once. Her face went pensive, as if she'd never before considered the question. "Maybe a musician," she said. "I want to be a musician and live in New York. But is that even a job anyone can really have?"

And it seemed to you that she held whole albums, all those songs she'd one day write, in what she didn't say. Her silence was your greatest inspiration. In the twenty-three and a half hours of your own muteness that constituted the balance of your days, you tried to continue the conversations via the moody, baroque poems you wrote in your journals. You had never known you had so many words in you, that sudden urgency you felt, that need to empty yourself of your entire past, to lay it out and arrange it for her. You talked as rapidly as you could, but your mouth felt too narrow to convey the rush. When you told your stories to Rebekkah, she nodded and listened, and it could seem you had discovered a purpose for your solitary years. An unlikely theory, perhaps, and you were prone to believe other unlikely theories as well. You knew you might never have Rebekkah Sterling, at least not how you envisioned in this universe, but in those parallel universes Pa described? You borrowed from your father's ideas, the very ones you had initially silently disparaged. Every one of the poems you wrote offered a tour of a different place in the mul-tiverse, a physics equal to what your heart required of it. You wrote: *There is another universe / where we do not need a single word / no need to try to converse / when our every thought is heard.*

But even in *this* universe, after many days subjected to the ero-sive sunlight of your many diatribes, Rebekkah's silence began to fissure. You couldn't see what lay beneath, but she did offer you dark glimpses.

"You know, the thing about West Texas is that it was the state's last Indian territory, did you know that?" you were telling her one morning, playing the historian again. "The Apache might still be out here if the Mexicans hadn't had the idea that there might be silver up in those mountains. Of course there wasn't, but that didn't stop them from slaughtering the tribe."

"That's men for you," Rebekkah said. "Not unlike my father, really."

"Your father?"

"With his fracking. Apparently it's not going well. Business as usual, for him."

"But you know what? My granny, she said that there really might be some silver the Mexicans stashed away up there. Supposedly they buried some huge treasure in a drought crack in the earth, but then rain came, the crack closed, and no one could remember where."

"There's a metaphor if I ever heard one," Rebekkah said. "Pre-cious things buried and lost. I should write a song."

You looked at her for a long while. "What things?" you ventured.

"Maybe someday I'll show you, if I can find the map, ha ha."

Rebekkah would never show you that map, but after a couple of weeks in that classroom, you had made a different kind of map, an astonishing mental chart of all the cities in which she had lived, which included impossibly exotic places: Singapore, Rio de Janiero, Dubai. ("Exotic?" she asked. "Not really. For me it's basically just the same McMansion everywhere I go. The same oil people. Only the weather changes.") You knew, also, that she was a great fan of the music of Joni Mitchell, the novels of the Brontë sisters. From her morning snack selection, you saw she was a lover of cinnamon toast. She said little in response to your long lectures, but you learned that she had a habit of chewing at the curling tips of her hair when she was interested in a topic, and also that she had a habit of drumming her chin with her fingers when she was not. Like ripe stone fruit, she was easily bruised, her skin faintly mottled from various light bumpings. And, of course, you knew what everyone knew, that she had a great singing voice, that Mr. Avalon had cast her as the lead vocalist in his Theater Club's annual Homecoming Dance performance, *The Bliss Township Tejano Espectacular,* a selection of Spanish-language standards. And yet, to be honest, you knew little more than that. All Rebekkah had offered to you was her daily early arrival to Mrs. Schumacher's classroom. But you couldn't stop yourself from getting carried away. You couldn't keep yourself from imagining a future with her so unlike your last years. A future that mattered, because she would be there to witness it.

At night, when you considered yourself under the unsparing bulbs of your bathroom mirror, for once you let yourself imagine what your face *could* be. Someday. You looked at the angular dimensions of your jaw and the pleasingly gray eyes you inherited from your father. You let yourself fill in the blanks of your future with all sorts of imagined promises.

You couldn't help it: all this emboldening possibility had made you, for the first time, a little surly with your mother. Just last week, as Ma spoke of a new skin-care remedy she was hatching for you, something involving massive dosages of vitamin A, you had scowled. "Doesn't sound likely," you told her.

Your acne was a particular concern for Ma, as if a much greater affliction than just an adolescent dermatological stage. The sight of those zits seemed to break her heart, proof that you were growing older, leaving further behind the best moment of her life, when you had needed her entirely. But when, that night, she reached across the sofa to probe your particularly hellacious forehead zit with her finger, you slapped her away.

"You can't lose faith, Oliver," she said. "We just have to keep *trying*, don't we? Keep trying and trying until we come up with the solution."

"You don't know that my body is separate from yours," you told her.

Your mother then reached once more for the pulsating mass on your forehead. "That's the sweetest thing you've ever told me," she said.

But your body *was* your own, and at last you had refused to submit it to further humiliations up in the stadium rafters. You were hiding out in the sweet-foul stench of a bathroom stall, gazing emptily at the scratchitti of various sexual positions someone had etched into the aluminum, as you tried to hold fast to the sweet image of Rebekkah's eyes on yours. And yet, as ever, the murkiness of your doubt seeped in, clouding that happy picture. You thought: *she just likes attention.* You wondered if perhaps your daily conversations with Rebekkah were, after all, part of some elaborate prank. Preparing yourself for likely heartbreak, you tried to feed yourself some glib hokum, telling yourself that someday you would be a great poet and make beauty out of whatever might come to pass. But then you remembered a few lines of the last poem you'd tried to write, and you cringed.

You refastened your nut holder, emerged from the bathroom, and walked so quickly for the stands that the tray nearly beamed her in the chest.

"Whoa," Rebekkah said, "hey there."

"Hey," you managed to make your mouth say out loud.

"I was looking for you."

"You were?"

"I thought maybe you'd come say hi, but then poof, you vanish." This was a sentence whose meaning and implications you could have spent a whole weekend deconstructing, reworking into rhyming verse.

"Heavily lays the crown."

"Excuse me?"

"All part of my duties as Astronomy Club president." You gave the nut tray a too-vigorous shake, the Coke shooting up through the straw holes in the plastic lids.

"You are? How did I not know you were *president*?"

"Oh, yeah," you said. "Commander in chief of all the stars in the sky."

"Can't see many tonight. The lights are too bright, I guess?"

"Do you want to?" you asked. "See some stars, I mean."

Rebekkah turned back to the thunderous noise of the rafters, as if considering an obligation there. "What about your job?"

"No one wants my nuts anyway," you unfortunately replied.

You led her past the commotion of the Hispanic kids, presently cheering the bass-thumping pickup as it did donuts in the drive, and made your way to the silent parking lot, where your family's dented Hyundai, Goliath, sat in the back row. Your parents had let you borrow the car for the game, and you felt manly indeed as you brandished your father's key chain, with its little pewter longhorn charm. The hatchback popped, you exchanged the nut tray for the one piece of new technological equipment belonging to the family Loving, Pa's thousand-dollar Celestron telescope in its black Pelican case.

"Geez. You people really are serious about this stuff, aren't you?"

"Very serious." You tried to strike a workmanlike air as you set out into the black flat of desert, the stars above winking back into view. Five minutes later, after making fine adjustments to the Celestron's setting circles, the oblong shape of Saturn, like a ball squeezed from either side, was in the viewfinder. "Look."

"Is that Saturn? Holy shit. You can see the rings. Well, sort of. It looks squished."

"The light you are looking at is already an hour and a half old." Trying to imitate a man, it was Pa's teacherly voice that came to you. "It took an hour and a half to get here. The light from those stars behind? Thousands of years old. Millions. You are literally looking into the past."

"You know," Rebekkah said, "I've been meaning to come back to your astronomy club. I lost track of the schedule, I guess. But I'm sure glad I got to see those meteors. Never seen anything like that before."

"You should," you said. "You should come back."

"Your dad was so kind to invite me and all. He's nice."

You shrugged. "Sometimes I wonder if there is some alien out there," you said, paraphrasing the substance of a sonnet you entitled "The Light from Distant Stars." "Some alien with a very, very good telescope. So good that he can see the whole surface of Earth perfectly. He is maybe watching our medieval period now, knights and wars and castles in Europe, the Mogollon people and bison out here. It's kind of comforting, isn't it? Like our own history is still happening somewhere else. Like it's not really over. Like everything that is happening right now, tonight, won't reach him for a thousand years. Ten million maybe. But he'll be up there, trying to figure us out."

The stadium was a halo of brightness in the distance. The sound of warfare: the Mountain Lions must have breached the end zone again.

" 'Look,' the alien will say. 'Another touchdown for Bliss Township.' "

And that was how it happened, all the students and faculty of a school that would not exist in a year—the victims and the survivors— all howling when the miraculous moment arrived. And though you couldn't have known what was in your future, it did feel like a culmination of something even then, as if your hand's bravery beneath the Perseid shower and all the labors of your before-school sessions with Rebekkah really had been adding to this. As if this night, your fruit- less nut-selling, Pa's amateur astronomy and painting, the poor state of your skin, your loneliness—as if all those glum variables somehow equaled the greatest gift, the rapture (a too poetic word? there wasn't any other) that only a solitary boy like yourself could have known, as his gaze met with his beloved's for too many unblinking seconds to count. There couldn't have been any doubt about what was about to happen. Who moved first? There was a collision of teeth, like an awkward unlatching of a jammed door, and then you were in some other place together.

The incredible wetness; the oddly familiar interior of another mouth; the animal taste, like your own taste doubled; your first good sniff of the truer, deeper Rebekkah smell, as if someone had extinguished matches beneath her skin. Why had she suddenly decided to kiss you? You knew, for once, better than to ask questions. The kiss complete, both of you oddly turned back to the stadium, walked silently through the gates, your hands still clutching.

"Well," Rebekkah said.

"Well."

"I—"

"You what?" you asked, but Rebekkah never answered. Because now the game had come to an end, and the stadium's crowd began to spill out the exits. At this growing tide, Rebekkah tossed away your hand. "I have to—" Rebekkah said, but did not say what she had to do, only walked off in the direction of the bathrooms. Why did you not ask why? Why did you not follow her? You were only seventeen, freshly first kissed; you were a meek, shy, indoor kid, a book lover, and you failed the moment. You watched her march away.

However. Just before Rebekkah vanished into the thickness of the crowd, she paused. Not just paused. She turned, to look back over her shoulder. And before the masses swallowed her, Rebekkah found an instant to give you one last gift. Just a faint smile, and it was all over in a second. But it would linger. A little knowing grin that suggested—what? You didn't know what, exactly, but a grin that seemed at least to promise something more.

You would spend the following weekend writing poems. In your creekside cave, you would press play on your Casio boom box, cuing up your other muse, as recorded on *Blood on the Tracks*. Oh, sing to me, Bob Dylan! *I came in from the wilderness, a creature void of form / Come in she said I'll give ya / shelter from the storm.* But on Monday, you would wait in your seat in Mrs. Schumacher's classroom for a full hour. Just five minutes before the school bell rang, you would at last admit that Rebekkah wasn't coming to see you.

But there was still that backward grin. Of all the many horrors, bad decisions, missed chances that would follow, that would become the moment that perhaps would torment you most. The undelivered joy of that second at the football stadium, the question you would come to live inside—it would take a near decade, and the boy presently turning out a small nut fortune in the rafters, to find an explanation that could bridge the abyss. But at last, there he was: nearly ten years later, your brother taking his own first wobbly tightrope-walker steps over that crevasse, to come find you.

Charlie

．．．．．．．．．．．．．．．．．．

CHAPTER SIX

"If you want to know the story of Charles Loving," Charlie often liked to tell the guys he saw in Brooklyn, "here is a good introduction for you. One of my first memories is of a city I did not actually see."

It was true. One of Charlie's first lucid memories—a memory with clear lines rising out of the blurry brown phantasmagoria of his desert childhood—was of New York City, an impossible island of towers hovering over the plains.

Reason would later tell Charlie that it must have been downtown Houston that he actually saw that night, when he blinked his eyes open in the backseat of his family's old VW. But in a picture book Pa had recently given him for his fifth birthday, Charlie had studied images of Manhattan's towers, and when he saw that gleaming bank of lights, he knew the name for it. "New York City!"

"Ha ha!" Pa laughed. "There it is my boy, New York City! And ain't she a beaut?"

New York City, a miracle! And a miracle was what Charlie needed that night. Actually, all the Lovings were in need of a miracle, if only an invented one, to redeem the week they had just endured.

It had been a miserable little road trip, that July. It was Granny Nunu's seventieth birthday, and for her present she had insisted that "the whole damned clan" accompany her on a trip to the beaches of Galveston. She wouldn't hear her son's apprehension. "After seventy blasted years of dust," Granny said, "don't you think it's time I deserve a little water?"

But the sea they had found at the island of Galveston was just like Texan desert: flat, lifeless, overheated, rich with petroleum. An oil tanker had recently spilled its black guts in the Gulf of Mexico, and their footsteps exposed the tacky slick of oil beneath the khaki sand. The apathetic waves tossed a confetti of tar balls. And Galveston itself seemed on its way to becoming the set of a horror film. The attractions on the old boardwalks were in disrepair—decapitated carousel ponies, a shuttered oceanfront bar whose collapsed tiki huts resembled the abandoned nesting place of some prehistoric bird-monster. Their rooms, at the Texan Paradise Hotel, were damply carpeted, tangy with a vaguely septic smell.

Charlie and his brother spent the week building perfunctory cities from the reeking sand, their hands growing tarred and unwashable. Beneath a plastic umbrella, their parents disappeared into their paperbacks. And as for Granny Nunu? Poor Granny: when a swift, brutal case of pneumonia ended her life just six months later, this trip would come to seem a grim farewell tour, as if the true cause of death had not been a pulmonary infection but rather her outrage at a transformed Texas she could never cotton to. She spent those Galveston days inside the planetary circumference of her straw hat, *tsk-tsk*ing and shaking her head at the disappointment. "You shoulda seen this place before the hurricane hit. It was the greatest Texas city of them all! A true tragedy."

"Ma." Pa looked up from his edition of *Contact*. "That hurricane hit in, what, 1900? You weren't even alive. Your *parents* weren't even alive."

Granny Nunu shook her head once more. "You shoulda seen it then."

On their fifth night at Galveston, as they all suffered the torture of a silent crab dinner at a restaurant called Fish 'n' Chips Ahoy!, Granny smacked a female carapace with a mallet, like a judge ready to offer a verdict. "If you are all so miserable, then let's just go home now." The only real spirit of vacation Charlie had known, on his first and arguably only family road trip, was to pile into the station wagon that night. Back in the VW, Charlie had fallen immediately asleep, relieved to think he would wake up back among their home's many acres.

But then, blinking out of his dreams, New York City! A billion twinkling mirrors, the geometric shapes of buildings outlined in neon, upturned floodlights ablaze. Charlie unbuckled his seat belt, pressed his face to the glass.

"And look!" Ma was driving that night, and even she was getting in on the act now, pointing to what must have been the Enron tower. "That huge skyscraper there, that's called the Empire State Building."

"Charlie!" Oliver said. "Did you see it? I just saw the Statue of Liberty!"

"Where? Where?"

Ma was rocking with laughter. From joy, Charlie assumed.

The New York City Charlie knew about came from Pa's picture book but also from the panels of *The Amazing Spider-Man* he couldn't yet read, the brightly saturated hues of the "Broadway Melody" montage in *Singin' in the Rain*, the stylized black-and-whites of the film noirs that Ma sometimes let him watch with her. "Can we stop? Are we going to stop? I want to see it."

"Um," Ma said. "Maybe it's time to stop torturing the boy."

Pa, sitting next to Ma in the front seat, turned to face Charlie. He reached to put a hand on Charlie's arm.

"That city," he said, "is no place for kids. But someday, when you are all grown up, you should run off for it the first chance you get. No place for kids, but believe your pa when he tells you that our little town is no place for grown-ups."

From the driver's seat, Ma said, "Well then, Jed, have at it."

The station wagon sped into the darkness to the west. The city retreated from view, unthreading into ranch houses, streetlights, and at last the black plains. But upon the generative membrane of Charlie's kid-dreamy brain, as the actual city vanished it only grew larger still, its doors opening to Charlie, leading onto elaborate eateries, gilded elevators that rose among penthouse pleasure domes, rooftop lairs, zeppelins gliding whalelike in the altitudes.

Of course, Charlie soon knew that it hadn't really been New York he'd seen that night. But he wasn't too disappointed. If anything, he was a little awed to understand how it had only taken a few words to remake a lesser city into his own magical Oz. And it was around that time that Charlie and his brother began to test how far that trick could go. Almost every night, in the months that followed, they made up new stories about other impossible places and how they might find their way to them.

"So," Oliver would say, "I was thinking about what Granny Nunu said, about how the Kiowa believed that all people originally came from a hole to the underworld, and then I was thinking, what if we found that hole today?"

"But how would we know where to look?"

"That's just the thing," Oliver said. "What if the ancients hid signs all over the planet, and we had to put together this great big map?"

"Like a scavenger hunt!"

"Precisely."

Those stories Charlie invented with his brother in their bunks: all it took was the nightly twist of a lamp switch to absent them from the purple of the desert night, the angry droning of cicadas, their mother's insomniac footsteps squeaking on the floorboards, the awareness of Pa a half mile away, blowing his Pall Mall smoke at another failed canvas.

Charlie knew that the tales they dreamt up in those bunk bed sessions might not have been anything so extraordinary, just the usual boyish dreamstuff—imagined battles with mythic beasts, discoveries of hieroglyphic maps, spelunkings of underworld chambers. But in their youthful ambition, these stories gradually evolved into an idea of a whole series of fantasy novels they would write, like the pulpy ones Oliver so loved.

They never actually wrote a word, of course, but over the years Charlie and Oliver would sometimes resurrect the tradition and pledge to begin again. And that, Charlie would later believe, was the best escape story they ever told, the story of their someday writing of those books. Unwritten, those novels were like the spirit world they sought, a complete and better world into which they would one day escape together.

And then, one night, Oliver really did find a passage into some other land, but they did not travel there together, as they had imagined. Oliver left Charlie on that ordinary planet to write those books on his own, and many years later, Charlie's exhausted laptop showed the record of a one-man journey through a borderland without end, no magical map to show Charlie's way to the place where he might find Oliver now. And as for New York City? On that July, of his twenty-third year, Charlie had come to understand that it was much better as he'd seen it from the back of the station wagon, better seen from a distance, mistaken for another, better, and imagined place.

On the night of July twenty-second, Charles Goodnight Loving— brother of the famous victim, survivor of the ruined town, failing writer—was a slender body leaning into a fast walk under the anemic Brooklyn streetlights.

At the corner of Seventeenth Street, Charlie steeled his nerve to take a quick glance over his shoulder, perceiving some illusory threat behind him. Charlie was that July an excitable kid, his own archetype of the young man come to New York from the provinces to pursue his visions, but after more than a year in Brooklyn, he was haunted by chronic worry that liked to manifest in mirages of doom. A month before, he had felt the nodule of an ingrown hair in his groin and convinced himself it was cancer until, probing the thing, he'd popped it. When Charlie turned now, he saw no one there behind him on Fourth Avenue, but that did not put an end to his catastrophizing. At each intersection, he searched the shadows for the potato shape of a man named Jimmy Giordano.

And as Charlie looked for the bright cherry of one of Jimmy's cigarettes in the darkness beneath the sycamores, he was patting the cell phone in his pocket, another kind of tumor, the many unplayed voice mails his mother had left that day spreading their deadly metastases into his blood. Why wouldn't she stop calling? Charlie clutched his fists and made swift progress along the dim, gum-spangled sidewalk. Down in the subway station, a train roared to a stop, made its electronic bing. Charlie sealed his eyes, offered a kind of faithless prayer to himself, and stepped aboard.

A couple of weeks before, when Jimmy Giordano—Charlie's gregarious, outer-borough-accented landlord—had knocked on Charlie's door to remind him that he was already three months behind on rent, Charlie had begged Jimmy for a little more flexibility. Jimmy, the sort of guy who usually filled every silence with low laughter, had not laughed. "At four months," he had said, "we can begin the eviction proceedings."

"Eviction?"

"But that's the least of your worries."

"The *least*?"

"Even if we kick you out, there's still the matter of all that back rent. We're talking about, what, five thousand now. Five thousand, it ain't chump change."

Charlie had been the one to laugh then, the way these words, thickened with Jimmy's Brooklyn brogue, sounded sampled from some gangster movie. Such an insinuating threat seemed like a joke in Charlie's neighborhood, a place where Jimmy's beige, vinyl-sided, four-floor tenement was a little blight on the street of terraced gardens and brownstones, where the young professionals ate at locavore cafés and spoke with round-eyed optimism of their careers in media and NGOs. Jimmy Giordano, however, now looked quite humorless.

"I'm sure I can come up with something," Charlie said, and his landlord told him that he had until the first.

"Five thousand you will give me," Jimmy said, in that oddly Yoda-like construction. "On the first of the month."

"Right," Charlie said. And when Jimmy had then mused in his jocularly menacing way about "any further delays or difficulties," he mentioned his "collections guy, who helps me out with tough cases like yours."

Five thousand: that appalling figure, with its three zeroes, rolled like dropped coins through Charlie's mind as Jimmy waddled away. Several months before, Charlie had run out of the money he'd saved working as a bar back during his college years, and he had also spent the decent amount his granny Nunu had set aside for him in her will. But Charlie was still a little too delighted by his life in New York not to find some charm in the scene. *Things had gotten so desperate,* he really did write in his Moleskine that afternoon, *that at the start of my second summer in New York my landlord threatened my life.*

And yet, the next morning, when Charlie had transcribed this sentence into his computer, it did not engender the magic it had seemed to promise. Charlie had not worked a real job since his arrival in New York. Miraculously, he had gotten a little contract with an actual, if very modest, book publisher called Icarus. He received half the meager advance on signing, the other half to be deposited in his account when he delivered a manuscript. How his mother had replied when he had called her, months ago, with the news of his book deal: "Oh, Charlie, what have you done now?"

No fallbacks! Charlie had written, like a rebuttal to Ma, on a Post-it that he fixed just above the kitchen table where he supposedly worked. *Your JOB is to WRITE!* And yet, once more, Charlie was decidedly *not* writing; no following sentence came the next morning or the next. Charlie employed his father's old strategy for dealing with difficulties; paralyzed by dread, he tried to forget his troubles in a self-prescribed course of chemical amnesia. Charlie spent much of the following weeks in a pot-perfumed torpor with a so-called digital artist named Terrance, with whom he lit soggy joints and burned through lazy days on the batik quilt in the guy's East Village bedroom, Charlie's pug Edwina producing watery snores between them.

Back on Eighteenth Street, as the new month approached, Charlie had often seen his landlord out there, skulking around his building, sorting the garbage, smoking his blue packs of Parliaments, his aviator glasses seemingly aimed in the direction of Charlie's windows, which he kept dark. Charlie knew he could not ask his parents for money. Such a request would serve as a crushing confirmation of his mother's pessimistic view of the world, her damning insinuations about Charlie's harebrained schemes for his place in it, her oft-repeated condemnations of Charlie's book project and his entire Brooklyn existence in which he flagrantly divested himself of the endowment his granny had spent decades clipping coupons and buying off-brand groceries to leave for him. And to ask his father? Even if he weren't penniless— Charlie knew the man was living on fumes, working the daytime shift at some new hotel in Lajitas—such was the state of things between them that Charlie would rather have taken his chances with Jimmy Giordano's "collections guy" than break the five-year vow of silence that was his relationship with that drink-clumsy depressive he used to call *Pa*. In panicked fugues, Charlie ran through mental lists of who else he might hit up for the cash. But nearly every other name in his phone's contact list fell in one of two categories: men he had slept with and then given the silent treatment, or friends from college he had neglected to write to since his arrival in Brooklyn. The fiction of his big city life was that he was not alone in it.

Charlie told himself that he was being ridiculous—that the money he owed wasn't so very much, after all—but the fact was that he had become too afraid to leave his apartment, and he went to absurd lengths to make it appear he was not home. When the need for the toilet forced him to pass the window, he bellied the floor beneath the frame. Trying to work at his computer, he tented himself under a fusty comforter, to hide the laptop's glow. Despite her yelping complaints, he made Edwina do her business on pages of *The Village Voice,* spread on the floor. And still he might have continued up there, subsisting on a jumbo box of granola, if Ma had not called.

Charlie had not answered. He couldn't foresee any way he could speak to her without admitting to his money problems. It had been a long while since they had talked; but then, from another perspective, in the arguments about his life choices he silently conducted with her in his mind several times a day, they talked all the time. Charlie hadn't answered, but then she called again. And then again. Her phone calls, over the past few years, had established a certain passive-aggressive pattern; she refused to call twice before Charlie called her back. But now she called once more. The last time they'd spoken, her list of Oliver's maladies had grown so long he'd stopped listening. *Bedsore infection, a blood clot in his leg, a chance of pneumonia, hypertension from the steroids—*

"Stop ringing!" Charlie yelled at the phone, but it rang once more.

"Stop it, please, stop it," he said, crying a little now.

She had called nine times and left four voice mails that evening; Charlie felt he had to do something, anything to get away from that apartment and the ringing of his phone. Charlie couldn't know what she had to tell him, did not yet know a thing about the fMRI his mother had scheduled for that day, but he understood this much, from the insistence of her calls: the likeliest news was that at last it had happened, that at last what remained of his brother was gone.

"Oliver," Charlie said, and shut the door behind him.

A half hour later, Charlie got off the subway at Second Avenue, then walked the six blocks of drunks, hobos, and mirthful hipsters toward Terrance's place. Terrance was not what Charlie would have called a boyfriend. Four months, and their time together still worked in weekend-long hangs, silences that could go on for whole weeks. In the muggy, agitated climate of Charlie's last months, he had always found reliable refreshment in the presence of Terrance and his moneyed degeneracy, but it remained a source of refreshment Charlie wasn't at all sure it was healthy to enjoy, like the cool, microbe-laced breezes that preceded a subway train's arrival through the filthy tunnels. And yet, at that moment, Terrance was the closest thing Charlie had to a relationship of any kind.

Like all the boys Charlie saw, it had only taken Terrance a little light googling to learn the only fact about Charlie anyone cared to know. Outside a Lower East Side dive, on their second meet-up, Terrance had greeted Charlie with the same giddy astonishment that was so wretchedly familiar to Charlie by now, the darkest brand of glamour that his own little part in a widening, nationwide crisis seemed to lend him. "My *God*," Terrance said, "I had no idea. You read about that kind of thing on the news, but to think it actually could happen to someone I know?" Charlie shrugged, felt his pockets for his gum. "I don't talk about that time," Charlie said later, when, awash in third-drink intimacy, Terrance inquired directly. Partially, Charlie would have admitted, this was just a technique. The trick to a convincing broodiness, he had learned, was to withhold the deepest horrors. To give those guys a feeling that they had to prove they were worthy of entering his quote unquote darkest chambers. And yet, this was a chamber that Charlie would never open for anyone; he had locked those first days *after* in a safe that he dropped to the bottom of the sea. And yet, from time to time the safe still released a bubble that popped into Charlie's awareness. Ma's eyes wild on the opposite side of the hospital's conference room, on that first night. Manuel Paz's hand on Charlie's shoulder, ushering him away from the image of weeping schoolchildren outside Bliss Township on the television screen. The thick, dimpled arms of the other mothers smothering him in the hallway of the hospital. The idiotic, cowboy-movie face of the state's governor, speaking platitudes at Charlie as he crouched to his level.

Charlie did not tell Terrance any of this. He even lied when Terrance asked him where he got Edwina. "A West Texas dog rescue," Charlie said, thinking of Edwina's true provenance: that morning, a few weeks *after,* the only time Rebekkah Sterling ever came to the hospital. Rebekkah Sterling, the girl he had met just that once at Zion's Pastures, the girl who had become to Charlie a kind of minor deity, the way she had walked out of that horror unharmed. Her presence in the hospital seemed to Charlie like some divination; he did not then think to ask her anything about what had happened that night. "I thought you could use a friend," Rebekkah said, piling the restive pup in Charlie's arms. "Her name is Edwina." "Thank you?" Charlie accepted the animal out of instinct, like another of the bundles of flowers that Oliver's old teachers and classmates were still delivering to the room. Ma had been down the hall, conducting one of her endless phone calls with the insurance company, and when she came back to the room, she only blinked at the dog in Charlie's arms. "A puppy?" Ma said. "Now they brought you a puppy." Charlie just nodded. There were too many unanswered questions back then, and they had no choice but to accept things as they came.

At the stoop for number 347 East Fourth Street, Charlie texted Terrance. *Feel like company? I'm in your neighborhood.* When a minute passed and Terrance had not replied, Charlie sent another: *Actually I'm right outside your building. Need to talk.*

The seconds passed like some kind of lecture delivered by time itself. But Charlie was also a little grateful to wait there, under a glaring lamp, the dull, municipal streetlight somehow making the potential horror contained in Ma's many voice mails just another of his exaggerations. And at least this conversation with Terrance was a thing he could do, a much lesser catastrophe he could put right.

But Terrance would not buzz him in. Five minutes later, wearing only pajama bottoms, the guy emerged from the graffiti-tagged door to speak to Charlie outside, where he could keep the conversation short.

"I'm desperate, Terrance. That's the reality here. You know I saw your bank statement? You left it on the desk, I'm sorry, but I saw."

Terrance, oddly, grinned at this admission. Charlie could feel him recording the details of this scene for later amusing retelling.

"And it's not even so much I'm asking for," Charlie added. "Say, five thousand, and I'll be able to finish. I'll pay you back, and more. You can even have partial ownership of what I'm working on, like, I don't know, shares of stock? I can show you the contract if you want."

"Right," Terrance said. "The book."

"Just hear me out. I've never even told you what it is I'm writing. You've never really asked."

"So tell me then."

Charlie tightened his lips, looked down at the sidewalk as he delivered a clumsy version of the pitch he'd long imagined making to some interested journalist. Charlie had rarely spoken the truth about his childhood, but now he held forth about the almost-poet Oliver had once been, the stories they had invented together, the thing Oliver had become, his paralysis, his hopeless diagnosis. Charlie cleared the phlegm from his throat and continued. "For a while I didn't know how I'd be able to carry on, and then the answer became clear to me. I had to tell our story."

But the pitch was not going as Charlie had long imagined it. He felt tears dagger into the corners of his eyes. How could Charlie tell Terrance that this so-called book was all that he might have left of his brother now, and even that was slipping away from him, day by day? That even still he had no real plan or organizational scheme for his work, only an unnamable boyhood hope that he still might find a kind of actual crossing place, some way back to Oliver deep in his own pages? That his act of literary necromancy had done just the opposite, that the more he wrote the farther Oliver seemed from him?

Terrance looked at Charlie with bemusement or else pity. "So how many pages do you have?" Terrance asked.

"I can feel this great energy? It's like something building up inside me that is just dying to get out. I'll bet you I bang out the whole thing in three months. Four months, tops. Maybe five. With revisions." Charlie looked down to see he was grasping Terrance's wrist.

"Right. Or maybe six or seven," Terrance said. "Or, quite possibly, never."

"Please." Terrance tried to liberate his hand, but Charlie dug in, renewing his sweaty grasp.

"I'm really sorry, I am." Terrance shook his head paternally. "But it's time to face facts, Charlie. You've brought all this on yourself. I must say that I don't see any particular reason to get myself involved in this little catastrophe you've made."

"You think I *wanted* all this to happen?"

"All those stories you tell about yourself. They're all a little— boom." Terrance made a gesture of an explosion with his free hand. "But I get it. Something truly, truly terrible happened to you, and so now you think terrible things are going to happen all the time. It must be a kind of paranoia, like some PTSD thing, right? And now you've invented a gangster who is out to break your kneecaps."

It was rare for Charlie to stay with any man long enough to allow him the requisite data collection for such a damning assessment, and with a sharp jab Charlie found himself missing another guy he'd known for a few weeks named Christopher, a slight, impassioned man with a head of sandy, luminous hair, who had left for the Calexico border crossing to fight for immigrant rights. And yet, when Charlie had been with Christopher he had missed others he'd been with, longed for men he hadn't yet met. The Loving Family Curse, Charlie called it, this damning belief that any place was far preferable to the present one.

"Invented?" Charlie asked Terrance. "If you want to meet Jimmy Giordano, you could just come to my apartment."

"No one's going to hurt you." Terrance took a deep sigh. "No one is going to risk going to jail to collect five thousand dollars. But, really, I get it, you *need* the drama."

"It's not just the rent. Poor Edwina, have you noticed? She has some bad breathing problem. Water in her lungs or something. But you know, the vet's office charges eighty dollars just to see the doctor."

"Poor pug," Terrance said. "Hitched her wagon to the wrong star."

"He's dead," Charlie said. "My brother has died. I didn't tell you that."

"What? Charlie. When did this happen?"

"Today." Charlie ran a spasming finger over his chin. "I just found out."

Terrance cocked his head, as if to a strange odor. "What are you talking about?"

Charlie couldn't answer. Maybe it was just that he needed to hear the words to prepare him for how his future would sound, in case it were true.

"I just needed to tell someone," Charlie said. "I just needed to tell you."

"Jesus, Charlie. Oh no." Terrance glanced back into his building. "Hey, listen, maybe there is someone I could call for you? Maybe your parents?"

"Please," Charlie said. "It's just a loan. Just a very temporary loan. Please."

Terrance put a hot hand on his shoulder. "Charlie. We have to call someone."

"Okay," Charlie said. "He's not really dead."

"What?"

"Or he might be. I haven't found the nerve to speak to my mother in a very long time."

"Fuck you, Charlie. I mean it. Fuck you."

"Please," Charlie said again. "You don't know what's in me."

"That's true," Terrance said, his eyebrows knitted. "Obviously I don't."

A miserable train ride back to Brooklyn, Charlie fretting over the sunk cost of his two-way subway fare. But out on Fourth Avenue, the humid, halal-scented air of Brooklyn helped bring Charlie back to himself. The New York City Charlie had found was a mostly antiseptic place, a glistening kingdom for the superambitious and the superrich, but a few corners still clung to the gritty charm Charlie had imagined he'd find. Across the street, a Hasidic man yelled at a team of construction workers; a flock of prepubescents hollered down the sidewalk on aluminum scooters; a spray-tanned woman said into her phone, "Honey, you ain't getting any more milk till you buy the cow." As Charlie passed an office with a red awning that brightly advertised ACCOUNTING, INVESTING, IMMIGRATION ASSISTANCE, LEGAL HELPS, AND CHECKS CASHED, he lit an American Spirit and commanded his legs to keep marching.

Charlie tried to keep his mind off the silenced phone in his pocket, entertaining instead a panicked arithmetic, doing the math to plot his New York ruination. The math wouldn't work out, he knew, but he had a desperate hope that if he drained his pitiful checking account and sold off his second- and third-hand furniture, he might be able to pay off enough of the back rent that he could throw himself on Jimmy Giordano's mercy before vacating the apartment. And then go—where? Somewhere.

And what was so great about New York City anyway? The throngs of New York, which Charlie had giddily imagined since that night in the hatchback, were sickening to him now. Nearly a decade *after,* Charlie's own reptilian brain—the instinctual fight-or-flight region that was impervious to reason—still maintained a threshold of a certain number of bodies it allowed into any room he occupied. And maybe, he thought, it was for the best that Pa only ever knew this city as an imagined escape. Charlie had come from his Big Bend childhood, from that state of strip malls and McMansions, with the usual Texan hunger for history, for a sense of a place with a past that went more than three or four generations back, but New York was mostly like any other placeless American place, only denser. Charlie saw that for the ways he spent his days—clicking around online, stopping by a Starbucks for a coffee, a Dunkin' Donuts for a snack—he might have been living anywhere. And so leaving wasn't such a failure after all, was it?

On Eighteenth Street, Charlie was profoundly relieved to find no landlord stalking the pavement as he staggered his way to the door. Back in his apartment, Edwina skittered across the floor as he lunged across the single room of his adulthood. He dragged a loose wicker chair beneath a chipped IKEA bookshelf, and he climbed up to reach the journal that he had banished to that high place weeks before. This journal still held the contents that it had for ten years, though its pages had begun to yellow at the edges and its ink had gone a little blurred from frequent exposure to the oils of Charlie's fingers. Charlie had liked to think about his project in the portentous terms of *fate*, but recently he had wondered what might have happened if he had never opened that book. Considering it now was unbearable, each vanished future he might have inhabited full of snow-dappled mountaintops, fragrant Asian cities, windblown cabanas on Latin American islands; he could have inserted himself into that self-photographing, backpacking milieu, his old college floor mates and drinking buddies, whom he often envied on Facebook. But, once more, Charlie now carried his brother's old journal to his kitchen table–cum–writing studio, where he set it next to his computer like some kind of talisman.

He flipped open his laptop. This dread, Charlie was trying to convince himself now, could be the necessary missing ingredient, the alchemical catalyst that might unite all his failed attempts to complete the book. This hopelessness, Ma's messages in his phone, and the imminent threat of eviction or physical harm would chase him, like a cartoon devil with his glowing hot poker, through an entire draft of a book. Charlie fleetingly pictured a Kerouacian fit, pounding for a couple weeks, arriving bleary eyed to midtown, where he would at last plop the bound carcass of the document on his publisher's desk.

"I did it," he now said out loud, like those words could make it true. "I have slain the beast."

And yet, even his laptop seemed to have grown listless under the years of revisions. The thing took a long time waking from its slumber, threw forth a few flashing glimpses of another moribund outline open on his word processor, and crashed.

"Edwina," he said, "I think we're fucked."

Charlie lowered himself to the floor. Sitting there in the darkness, atop the grayish fuzz that grew in the deep gaps between the cracked floorboards, he sobbed, producing bubbles of phlegm. His only true friend, his stubby black pug, licked the effluvia from his face. But all the activity triggered her lung problem, her breathing now sounding like a panicked snorkeler's, diving too deep.

"Edwina," Charlie said, hammering the wall with his fist. *He's gone,* his mother would gasp when at last he called her back, and what would he say to her? But how was it that even still he was infected by his mother's crazy, tired hope, that her news might be just the opposite? Even now, Charlie couldn't resist conjuring up an image of Oliver (somehow, impossibly) sitting up in bed, asking to speak to his brother.

In a single, thoughtless motion, Charlie did a crazy thing: he grasped his phone, and he pressed call on a number he'd found long ago in an online directory. The number of the only other person in his whole lousy city who might care about whatever his mother's voice mail contained. And yet, for quite possibly the hundredth time, a robot lady answered Rebekkah Sterling's phone, asked if he would like to leave a message.

Glancing around the kitchen, Charlie saw that his own upset had so upset Edwina that she had peed a little on the floor. And Charlie also saw this now: this room he was in—with its alcohol and nicotine refuse, its dashed and crumpled museum of misdirections—resembled nothing so clearly as his father's old shed. In the book he had imagined he'd write, it always seemed to Charlie that he could convert what had happened to his family into something else. Like unstable plutonium, he had thought he could take the annihilating power of it and transform it into an astonishing source of energy. But at last he knew better, that he was just like the rest of his family, still pounding at the walls of an instant, now many years past.

CHAPTER SEVEN

Charlie was fourteen years old on the day he first discovered Oliver's last journal, the same day Dr. Rumble gathered the Lovings in his western-themed office to inform them that, though Oliver's body might still be there, just down the hall, he was already gone. "Sometimes death doesn't look like what you'd expect," Dr. Rumble explained. "Liar," his mother said, and the truth was that word also burned in Charlie, there in Dr. Rumble's office. *Sometimes death doesn't look like what you'd expect*? The sight of the body in Bed Four might have been nearly inhuman—jaw gone slack, limbs snarled and strange—but the one thing Charlie could recognize—in the vibration of Oliver's eyes, the *ruh-ruh* sounds Oliver's throat made, the endless swatting of Oliver's arms—was *life*. Perhaps with its back to a dark corner, perhaps at the bottom of a deep crevasse, but still life, battling its way for light.

That night, when they got back to Zion's Pastures, Charlie tore through Oliver's things, as if he could find evidence that his brother still lived. He paged through the sloppy mess of Oliver's school binders, flipped through his various fantasy novels, felt the pockets of his pants. And there, in a bottom drawer of Oliver's desk, was the well-worn leather journal he'd seen Oliver toting around. Charlie slammed the drawer shut so loudly that his new pug barked from the next room. In those early months, Charlie's existence had become nothing but questions, the answers to which he was afraid of learning. Would his brother's eyes ever regain their focus? Would he ever go back to school? Would Ma and he ever learn to think of a future beyond the end of each day? Would Pa ever stop drinking in his shed? Would he forever wake to his brother's absence with the nightmarish sensation that somehow he had woken without all of his limbs?

Charlie went through Oliver's belongings, as if looking for some answer, but as they waited in vain for Oliver to speak actual words, the idea of setting his eyes on his brother's handwriting was too much. At the bottom of Charlie's closet was a small toy bank, fashioned to resemble an olden-timey safe from a Western, which Charlie had received as a gift one long-ago Christmas. This bank latched with a brass key; Charlie shoved Oliver's journal inside and locked it.

When at last he summoned the courage to unlock that safe, he was three years older, seventeen, a different boy. Three years, where did they go? Thinking back on them later, all those years would seem to Charlie a single smeary sameness, one very long overbright Tuesday afternoon. His so-called homeschooling? It was, he would have admitted, true what Ma later liked to claim about that time. "You chose it, Charlie! You told me you wanted to stay at home. It was what you wanted, in case you don't remember. So would you please stop acting like I was some tyrant?"

"Well. You are right. Technically speaking."

"Technically? What the hell does that mean, technically? These are basic facts."

Even still Charlie could not quite bring himself to tell her the truth that he folded inside the bland envelope of that word. But why couldn't she see it for herself? *Technically*, he did not see their "homeschooling" as a choice. Ma—the immutable icon, the implacable white colossus that had stood guard over his childhood—had been badly fissuring, and Charlie had known that only he could fill the gaps. After all, Pa had already crumbled.

Though Charlie had spent a good part of the first year or so of their "homeschooling" filling out the worksheets Ma ordered from Time4Learning, which issued curricula for the homeschool set, Ma soon lost her will to grade his assignments, and there was just something demonstrably unhealthy about a boy granting his own math exam a B minus. At last he quit this curriculum altogether. In truth, Charlie spent much of those months doing whatever Ma seemed to need, to which they retrofitted educational motive. Her occasional freak desire to go on manic shopping sprees in the concrete architectural atrocities of the new strip malls became "Home Ec." When Ma, considering what kind of sentence might await Hector Espina's father, threw herself into a month of library research into *aiding and abetting* and *felony arms possession,* she called it "U.S. Government," and when she told Charlie it was best that they try not to think of it, she called it "Behavioral Psychology." After Manuel Paz came by Zion's Pastures to deliver the news that Hector Sr. had simply vanished from the country, and Ma fell into a blackness Charlie couldn't do anything about, he called the following six months of novel reading and movie watching "Independent Study."

"A student-interest-led education," his mother one day named the endless lazy weekend that his high school years had become. "When a child takes his education into his own hands, that's when greatness is born."

"But don't you worry," Charlie asked, "that I couldn't tell you what the word trigonometry even *means*?"

"Neither could I," his mother distantly replied, "and I *went* to school."

His entire "homeschooling," Charlie perceived, was truly just an extended lecture on the distance between intentions and facts. Despite the fact that Charlie more than once beat at the cabin door until his fists were raw, Pa never stopped drinking out there. Despite Charlie's hopes that he might rescue Pa from the Marfa hovel to which he later decamped, Charlie could never get his father to summon any greater action than another fumbling apology. Despite

his attempts not to hate Pa, Charlie did come to hate him, refus-
ing his occasional offers for "a nice dinner out." Despite his efforts
to hold his mother together—boiling the brown rice and baking the
chicken breast as she continued to look upon even these wholesome
foodstuffs as if they were toxic substances, wiping down the dust
and grime that silently accumulated around them, pressing Edwina's
mouthy grin into her face in a futile attempt to lift her spirits—Ma
was lost to him, arriving each morning to the eggs Charlie had
scrambled as bleary and fazed as some mental patient. It was only at
Bed Four, with her son's vegetative body before her, that Ma groped
her way out of silence, reading to Oliver from his old paperbacks.
Charlie wanted to allow his mother whatever she needed to hold herself together, but a terrible anxiety, the strangeness of the scene he
was witnessing, the depth of Ma's—what? faith? delusion?—was an
alarm wailing inside him.

Of course Charlie also did his best to keep any of his own questions about that night's aftermath from his mother. He never once
spoke the name *Hector Espina* aloud. But Charlie himself couldn't
resist pilfering an occasional newspaper from the Crockett State
waiting room, and the stories he found there did little to explain
anything.

Like a tic in his brain, Charlie couldn't help but imagine and
imagine it, the impossible fact of it, what it would have felt like to be
Hector Espina on that night, the hate that aimed that weapon upon
children and fired. There was another kind of border there, a tow-
ering wall over which his imagination could not climb. *There is no
why:* Charlie was beginning to see the wisdom in his mother's motto.
"There is no why," Charlie told the dog that Rebekkah Sterling had
delivered to Oliver's room, as if Edwina might be in possession of
some knowledge to contradict him. But Edwina just licked his nose.

By the so-called *senior year* of their so-called *homeschooling*, student and teacher exchanged hardly a word. Ma spent her days like
an old lady, her movements gone slow and stooped, as she shuffled
clumsily through whole lightless seasons, lost in a kind of internal

arctic night. Somehow, Charlie managed to convince her to let him buy a used Suzuki motorbike, and he spent the better part of his senior year's first semester making a tour of the freaks, goths, gays, and other various castoffs of West Texas. He frequented Atomic Age Comics and Fantasy, where he met a twenty-eight-year-old named Antonio Mendoza, whose silver-riveted tongue at last put to bed any final doubts Charlie might have harbored about his inclinations. But Charlie was only seventeen then, his youth itself seemed a promise of something, and he began hatching a plan for a greater escape. Very late one sleepless night, he unlocked the toy safe. He opened Oliver's journal.

And what Charlie found there, in Oliver's chicken-scratch script, was a fitful record of his brother's attempts to become a poet. Many disembodied lines, dozens of abortive stanzas, a lot of rhymy, jangly nonsense, but also a few complete poems. Half of Oliver's reply to the world, cut off midsentence.

When Ma had shown Charlie Oliver's one published work, "Children of the Borderlands," which Oliver's old English teacher had sent to *The Big Bend Sentinel*, it had seemed so unlike the dreamy, fantastical stories they had imagined that it appeared to Charlie that it must have been written by another person entirely. The truth was that Charlie hadn't loved that poem when he first read it; the clipped language seemed disjointed and strange. But Oliver himself had seemed disjointed and strange to him in those last months *before,* when a nameless rift had opened between their upper and lower bunks. ("What are you thinking about?" Charlie once asked his brother, a full half hour after he had shut the lights. "You wouldn't understand," Oliver told him.)

But now, on the inky, chaotic, loosely bound pages of this journal, Charlie knew he had found the missing link in his brother's poetic evolution, from the lower-bunk storyteller he'd been to the almost-poet he'd become. Though the notebook lacked any sort of organizational scheme, Charlie identified the theme, announced on the fourth page.

I still can't explain it,
I could never find time,
For my words couldn't contain it,
And now I'm failing in rhyme.
Rebekkah.
I once heard of a land,
Where time bends its arrow,
Hours at our command
To widen or narrow.
So come away with me?
Through a hole in the sky?
Our little infinity,
To figure out why.

So overwhelmed was Charlie that he did not see any childlike clumsiness in Oliver's lines. To his own seventeen-year-old eyes, these lines were like a signpost, establishing the poetic journey to follow. The majority of the journal's poems fixated on the possibility of hidden, better realities, as borrowed from the stories they had told as children. *In another world / I might become anyone / an Oliver unfurled / with ten bodies in one / But sometimes at night, / in the darkness I'm freed / to thinking that I still might / become whatever you need,* one short poem read. *In my dreams time is frozen, / a universe of you / a single morning chosen / to be endlessly true,* another poem began. They were, Charlie saw, all love poems for the kind, vaguely sad girl he'd met once upon a time, on the night of the Perseid shower, the girl who had given Charlie his pug. Rebekkah Sterling, who clearly had not quite loved Oliver back. In one homage to his beloved Bob Dylan, Oliver had written, *Though a Rolling Stone / Might gather no moss / Like a complete unknown / I gather just loss.*

Charlie read patiently, staring down Oliver's cryptic scrawl until it yielded its words. By the time he reached the journal's conclusion, the dawn was beginning to gray the lechuguilla-dotted hills out the windows. The fantastical glee of their long-ago bunk bed sessions might have faded years before, but it was only now, seeing his brother's last words, that Charlie felt a draft of that long-ago magic swirling back into the room. And then a thought occurred to Charlie. It was a silly, nostalgic notion, he knew that. But how else to explain what had happened to Oliver—how else to make sense of the mysterious link- age between the stories of hidden lands they had invented and the actual buried earth where his brother now resided—than to believe, in a space beyond understanding, that something really had chosen Oliver?

It was after that morning that Charlie began to hear another voice, the word that his heart softly but persistently beat: *go, go, go.* He had to go. In the Marathon Public Library, at a battered old computer terminal, its beige keyboard yellowed with a long history of fingers, he did an Internet search for the words *homeschool* and *college,* and that is how he found out about a place called Henry David Thoreau College, in Merrymount, New Hampshire. "In the autodidactic spirit of our namesake, our aim is a diverse campus of independent think- ers." Thoreau College, the Web site informed him, was a school that "considers each student as an individual and bases admission deci- sions not on the common metrics but on the strength and originality of student writing." The Web page featured the grinning faces of im- migrants, reformed juvenile delinquents, and homeschoolers, all aglow in democratic New England light, autumnal sycamore leaves fanning over a Georgian colonial backdrop. The school's message seemed to be that all he needed to join that hearty cohort was a high school gradu- ation equivalency certificate and an original thought in his head.

In the way other boys his age might have lied about a club meet- ing or a sleepover at a friend's house to conceal recreational drug use, Charlie invented a comic book convention in El Paso, where he in fact tried his luck on the GED in a high school classroom that was that Saturday a room of adolescent outcasts: sallow-faced addicts, tattooed miscreants, moonfaced fundamentalist home- schoolers. Propped up by some eleventh-hour textbook reading he'd done, Charlie passed the exam by an unrespectable margin, and so he proceeded to compose an early application essay to Thoreau, in which he described the events of November fifteenth, the years of aftermath, his brother's vegetative condition. All the guilt, worry, and hope that he knew his mother could not bear to hear. Maybe Oliver was the real writer in the family, but it was as Charlie watched the unspoken truth of his last years transform into words on the page that he began to think that he might like to write, too. One afternoon, when Ma was off at Crockett State, he raided the bedside drawer where she kept her alarming bank statements and tax returns on her meager income. The next day, Charlie made Xeroxes, to apply for financial aid.

Ma, it is fair to say, did not take his announcement of admission and nearly full scholarship to a good liberal arts college the way most parents would. When Charlie passed her the thick envelope from Thoreau, the document fluttered in her suddenly convulsive hands. Her eyes began to fill, but before they spilled over, she excused herself for her bedroom. "Ma?" Charlie asked, by the door. She was so silent in there that he wondered if she might have suffered a medical event. "You just take care of yourself," she said at last, and Charlie would never be certain if she meant that as a cruel rebuke or a piece of motherly advice.

Charlie saw his brother just once more. It hadn't been so long since his last visit to Bed Four, but it felt to Charlie like a very long time since he had seen Oliver clearly. He saw now how his brother was aging too rapidly, his hands furrowed with veins, the tremble of his jaw like one of the geriatrics down the hall gumming his pudding, the scar where the bullet had entered like a gray nickel lodged just behind his right ear.

After his mother excused herself to the bathroom that afternoon, Charlie knelt over the bed. "Hi there," Charlie said. For a reply, Charlie received only the gurgle of an IV bag. Charlie was thinking of telling Oliver about his leaving for college; was it selfish or was he finally doing the right thing?

"Oliver, listen—" he said. But it was Ma's voice he heard in his throat. *Sometimes death doesn't look like what you'd expect.* And now

Charlie was considering Dr. Rumble's wisdom, which he had long ago raged against. Charlie knew he wasn't speaking to Oliver, just the vivified meat of his body. And it was occurring to Charlie that maybe the truest fantasy written by his family had nothing to do with parallel universes or spirit worlds. That maybe their grandest fiction was just Ma's faith that Oliver would come back to them. Charlie grasped for the paper sleeve in which Oliver's flesh was encased. "Oliver, I know, I should make her let you go, I just don't—" His voice fell silent in the softly humming room.

When Ma came back, she found Charlie still curled there, bucking with his sobs.

"Ma." And that, Charlie knew, was the moment he could have said it. His brother was gone, but they still might have had one another, as they had in those first weeks *after.* But he said nothing, and Ma's face tightened. She pulled him into the hallway.

"What the hell is the matter with you? Don't you know he can hear you? Wailing over him like he's already gone. What were you thinking?"

For a long beat, she assessed Charlie through squinted eyes, like some final exam for their homeschool years. "I truly don't understand how I raised such a selfish child," Ma said.

One day, a few weeks later, Charlie carried Edwina onto a bus without so much as a phone call to say good-bye to his father, and he rode for three days. Oliver's journal in his hand, Charlie stepped into a green, alien planet.

Thoreau! There weren't words to describe the joy Charlie knew when, after four years frozen in the ice of his family's grief, his affable, impish, truer self thawed to life. He became the kegger host, the campus gossip, the kid who'd do a naked lap around the quad on a dare. "You are *crazy,*" said all those charmed faces of his new friends, Nicole, Francesca, Juan, Michael—and too many more to name. And the wonder of snow, which fell and fell that first winter over the high pines and frozen lakes of New Hampshire. There at Thoreau, where even his gayness was not a liability but a kind of social currency—or maybe, he considered, his popularity was just an effect of the pranc-

ing pug he trailed behind him—Charlie found himself well liked in
the generalized way that meant he received enough invitations, saw
enough boys, that he never had to let any one person get to know
him well.

To Charlie's surprise, when he called home, Ma sounded—well,
still like Ma. "Oh, Charlie," she would say, her voice as flat and
empty as the Texan hardpan Charlie ached to remember. "I don't
have much time to talk, I'm sorry to say, but you should know not to
call so close to visiting hours."

Even if Ma never had patience for any stories of his collegiate
life, even if she treated his time at Thoreau like some indulgent
adolescent excursion she was forced to permit, Charlie was both
nicely reassured and a little appalled to find how unnecessary he had
been in holding her together. When she one day told Charlie that she
had sold off Zion's Pastures to cover medical expenses, he felt more
relieved than wistful.

Before Charlie knew it, the bright and blustery graduation day
arrived in Thoreau's quadrangle—springtime elms shooting their
ladybug buds, fat New England clouds dawdling through an outrageously blue sky—and where would he go now?

As his classmates stared off into the ambiguity of their futures that
afternoon, Charlie was thinking of the essay he'd written years before, which had earned him admission to that school. He was thinking of the lost poems of the lost boy who would have no place in the
future Charlie would now make for himself. The true purpose of his
education revealed itself to Charlie in an ephiphanic burst, the way
he'd always imagined artistic inspiration struck: before he could continue his own life, he would first put down his brother's story. It was
on that graduation stage that Charlie began to conceive of a book
that would use Oliver's poems like illustrations for the story of his
lost brother's life, his family's life, the life and death of the town
of Bliss, Texas, the blurring memory of November fifteenth in the
amnesiac awareness of his frenzied, trigger-happy nation, the great
and tragic love story of Oliver Loving and Rebekkah Sterling. A

book! The idea took shape with ever-greater dimensions in Charlie's imagination.

He would write, but where? The answer to that question, Charlie believed, was also in the journal he carried onto the commencement stage. Rebekkah Sterling and he had not spoken since the gift of Edwina, but Charlie had been conducting routine Internet searches for her name. She had made it to New York, where her name appeared in the listings for a few nightclub music shows. Charlie was proud of her. New York! Just like that long-ago night in the VW, New York seemed the very name of freedom, which Rebekkah had already found and Charlie would follow. He pictured them becoming friends. He would become friends with the girl who his brother had chased after until that last night, the only person who could tell Charlie the story he needed most, about his brother's last months *before.* He imagined long conversations with her in sidewalk cafés, Edwina panting at their feet, steam rising from their cappuccinos, Oliver regenerated in the mist. Never mind that Rebekkah had not yet replied to any of his e-mails. Charlie could convince her.

With the decent savings account Charlie had established, he and Edwina took over the Brooklyn studio apartment from a boy named Jared, who had graduated from his college the year before. What strangeness Charlie felt to find himself in a place so wholly the opposite of the one in which he'd been born, what loneliness he knew to stumble among the bustling millions, what dread he knew to watch his bank account dwindle: he resolved to overcome all these with work. *Once upon a time,* Charlie wrote fifty times over, *there was a boy who fell through a crack in time.*

Once upon a time, there was a boy who fell through a crack in time, and then what? The fact that Charlie had not yet completed a single showable page didn't stop him from setting up a meeting with a man named Lucas Levi, an editor at a small publishing house called Icarus, whose contact info Charlie found on the Thoreau alumni Web site.

Charlie liked Lucas immediately. The man was as compact and sleekly fashioned as a European sports car, and he was clearly gay, often touching a flirtatious hand to Charlie as he spoke. Lucas was just thirtyish, but he was prematurely gray, husky voiced, world-weary in a way that an older-brother-starved kid like Charlie craved. Over fifteen-dollar cocktails, Charlie hardly had to tell his story. Lucas had already read all about that worst night online, and the guy many times referenced his own fatally shot uncle (a gun range accident) like it lent them some kind of kinship. The conversation, it must be said, continued on to a second and then a third cocktail lounge, in whose rear garden, editor and author let their cigarettes burn to ash as they kissed in a patient and oddly tentative way, as if their flicking tongues needed to conduct a second interview of their own.

Three weeks later, Charlie sent Lucas a punchy, unsettled, forty-page document that included a few choice excerpts from Oliver's journals, an introductory chapter explaining how Charlie had come upon his brother's lost poems, and a seventeen-page speed-assisted "proposal" that amounted to a lot of fussy, sophomoric-academic meditations on the "reclamatory power of poetry and narrative forms." Charlie had spent two weeks fretting over this proposal's insufficiencies when Lucas Levi called to tell him that though he could not offer very much by way of an advance on royalties, this would be his "passion project."

"The poems, of course, aren't always great. Oliver was just a kid, after all, and what can you expect? But, framed by your brother's whole story, they could be beautiful," Lucas told him over the phone. "What you wrote about what has happened to him, to you all, it just broke my heart. The pages you sent me are rough, but I see a lot of talent here. And isn't that why we editors go into this biz? To find and, uh, nurture talent?"

A silence followed, as if Lucas really did expect Charlie to answer this question for him. "Sure," Charlie said.

"Plus," Lucas added, "these rampages are a national shame, an *international* shame, and we've got to do something, right?"

It seemed to Charlie, the next morning, that overnight he had grown an extra vertebra or two; he truly did walk a little taller. When

Charlie told Lucas Levi, "You won't be disappointed, I promise you I'll kill myself for this," he meant it. Charlie even declined Lucas's later drinks invitation, to keep things professional. Charlie would have walked three hundred miles in driving snow to chase the feeling Lucas Levi had just given Charlie with a single "yes," the magnificence of having been chosen.

Pa. Was Charlie also thinking of his father on that glorious morning? In the months that would follow, Charlie would come to see that more than one ghost was there with him in the cluttered hovel in which he clutched his constipated pen. A notion to keep the lights blazing on his blackest nights: the greatest revenge Charlie felt he could take was to succeed where Pa had failed. After witnessing Pa's years of thwarted visions in his cabin, Charlie could show his father what actual artistic triumph looked like, what it required. He would often fantasize his father's envy, Pa shaking the thinning stuff of his hair over the award-festooned paperback edition of his son's book in his hands. More than anything, however, what Charlie would imagine was his father's gaze rising tearily from his last page, on some distant afternoon when Charlie would sit with him again. "You did it," Pa would say.

Often, failing to write, Charlie set off with Edwina for long aimless jaunts through Brooklyn, and when he came upon some metaphorically pregnant detail—the way the pigeons congregated on the Islamic slaughterhouse on Hamilton Avenue, a team of workers soldering up on the suicidal heights of the Brooklyn Bridge, the annual twin columns of white shooting into the sky from where the towers had fallen, the subway sunrise of an F train writing its cursive of light along the grimed platform of the Seventh Avenue station—Charlie would think of his brother, all these sights Oliver once imagined he might see himself, and he'd rush back to the lousy 215 square feet he rented on the fourth floor of Jimmy Giordano's vinyl-sided monstrosity, hopeful that the especially potent symbol he'd found on the street would be the flip of the switch, the drop of the ball, which would set the marvelous Rube Goldberg device of his book into whirling motion. But when Charlie read back what he had written, he saw pages filled only with pitiable wish fulfillment—half-written scenes of Oliver walking with Charlie through his Brooklyn days.

"And what about that Rebekkah girl?" Lucas asked over the phone one March morning. Charlie had promised his first pages to Lucas by December, but he had just admitted that it could be another month or two until he had something he could share. "You are sure that she's willing to be a part of all this? I don't want to seem fretful, but what you have on your hands here is a love story, at its heart, and I worry that without Rebekkah's side of things, without showing just what Oliver and she both lost that night—well, what would this book really be?"

It was only now occurring to Charlie that it was a very strange thing indeed that Lucas had accepted Charlie's poor proposal, that Lucas's true motives might have been pity or else sex, and that in the months since they'd spoken, Lucas might have come to understand these were dubious reasons to issue a book contract.

"The way I see it, it's Oliver and Rebekkah's story, really, as much as your family's, your town's," Lucas said.

But Rebekkah still would not reply to Charlie's many e-mails. After the years by Bed Four, Charlie knew how grief was like flash flooding on a desert flat, cutting varied and permanent patterns, but why would Rebekkah not even explain her silence to Charlie?

He resolved to arrange a casual run-in on the street where, according to a public record database, she resided. More than occasionally, he would stroll up and down the same block of Eighth Street ten times in a row. At last, on one otherwise unremarkable Tuesday, Charlie found her down on Seventh Avenue, her arms laden with brown sacks of groceries. "Rebekkah."

She turned, and the click of recognition behind her eyes seemed to drain the blood from her skin. It was a strange and vertiginous moment, Rebekkah and Charlie, bound by a massacre two thousand miles and eight and a half years away, an open horror that still yawned so monstrously between them.

"Edwina," Rebekkah said, resting her bags on the sidewalk to kneel to the animal. Edwina did her happy snuffly dance, not so different from how she'd greet any attentive stranger, but Charlie was encouraged by the way Rebekkah tearily hoisted the dog to her chest, like some family reunion.

"I just want to know you," Charlie said. "Obviously you meant the world to him, and I just want to talk with you."

Poor Rebekkah. The way she looked between Edwina and Charlie reminded him of one of the dementia cases at Crockett State, suddenly baffled by the year in which she was living. Charlie considered that maybe he had been wrong, that maybe it wasn't freedom that Rebekkah had found in New York. Maybe it was just an attempted escape.

"I know what you want," Rebekkah said to Edwina's face. "I do read my e-mail."

"It's a noble endeavor," Charlie said, a phrase he had rehearsed.

But Rebekkah was right. Charlie did not "just want to know" her. The sight of her fazed, unreadable expression right there in front of him flooded Charlie with unanticipated fury. And it now felt to Charlie that the only true sentences he had composed over the last years were the same questions he never had the heart to raise with Ma, knowing what any mention of that night would do to her, the very questions that Charlie now understood had, in no small part, brought him to New York City in the first place, the same questions Charlie couldn't summon the courage to ask Rebekkah now. What had she seen? Why, really, had Oliver gone to the dance and why had he known to come find Rebekkah at the theater classroom? Though Rebekkah had become like a minor angel to the people of their town, might her survival that night have been no miracle at all? And now Charlie was wondering if maybe, all those years ago, Rebekkah had given the Lovings a pug in lieu of an explanation. "Rebekkah," he began.

"No," Rebekkah said. "I'm sorry, Charlie, I really am. But I'm just not interested in that sort of a thing." Rebekkah looked at Edwina with a hurt kind of disdain, as if the dog had somehow misled her. She stood, gathered her groceries, and walked away.

Back on Eighteenth Street, Charlie thought of Rebekkah the way a lover might. The thinness of her wrists, her soft ginger tints gone pallid, the way she'd made chewed gum of her lower lip. What were her days like now? *Absence might make the heart grow fond / but it's silence that sets the heart's cruel bond,* Oliver had once written about Rebekkah, and by denying him, Rebekkah had at least given Charlie this: he was learning what his brother had learned long ago. He had learned how Rebekkah's silence was a godlike force, in which she could take infinite forms.

....

CHAPTER EIGHT

Charlie's financial calamity and Ma's unanswered calls seemed to have worked on his nerves like a twice-struck bell; his hands vibrated clumsily as he lifted the journal from the table and slipped it into his patent leather bag. Edwina burbled curiously up at him. Charlie knelt to her, kissed her slimed nose, teared a little. Even then he wouldn't have admitted to the decision he was already making.

"Someone wants to go outside?" After days cooped up in his studio, Edwina expressed her relief at the idea of a walk in a frenzied jig, and it took him a minute to link the leash to her jostling rhinestone collar. "Just take it easy," Charlie told her. Her breathing had deepened to a frightening, sonorous register. "Okay, okay," he said, stroking her ears until she calmed a bit. Then Charlie went back out, with Edwina, into the Brooklyn midnight.

Edwina's claws clattered on the fractured pavement, past the storybook charms of the quarried brownstones, vintage lamps burning fashionably through the French shutters, and already Charlie was approaching 511 Eighth Street for the hundredth or two hundredth time. He looked up to the third floor, where he had looked many times for Rebekkah in the softly illuminated windows. She hadn't answered her phone, but Charlie was not at all surprised to find her windows lit tonight. "Cross your fingers, Weens," Charlie said.

Whatever it was his mother had called so many times to tell him, this much Charlie understood: that decade of waiting had come to an end, and at last Charlie was going to do with the journal what he should have done with it years ago, giving those poems to the girl Oliver had written them for. He mounted the stoop, and he pushed the buzzer for apartment number three.

His blood chiming in his veins, he pushed again, and waited. Pushed, waited. After a time, he descended, looked up into her lit window. Appalling but true: he saw Rebekkah's curtains part, caught a half-second glimpse of her face before the thick velvet snapped shut.

He pulled out his phone and dialed her number yet again. No answer, and so he worked the button once more. He stood like that for a while, fingertip pressed against the cracked ivory tab, Edwina pawing at the glass. A different man, a sane man, Charlie knew, would have turned away then. But Charlie felt Oliver's journal weighting his shoulder strap, and he couldn't just leave his brother's last words on her doorstep.

Later, Charlie would never be able to offer himself a satisfying answer for why he did what he did next. Maybe he *wanted* to scare her; maybe he just wanted to scream at her once, *Why won't you speak to me?* Or maybe, Charlie would admit, Terrance was right: maybe he just needed a dramatic scene, a climactic chapter made of the knotty stuff of his real life, in lieu of that other story he could not seem to write.

"I think," Charlie told Edwina, "that we'll have to find another way."

To the left of Rebekkah's building was a rare New York sight, a narrow alley, an undeveloped meter of space between her four-floor tenement and the long line of brownstones that shouldered into one another down the slope. This alley was guarded by an ungainly combo of hurricane fencing and a tall sheet of lime-colored plastic.

Edwina whined skeptically as Charlie tucked her in his bag, and he made his awkward one-handed vaulting of the fence. In the rear garden, Charlie stood beneath the black and rust-furred fire escape and leapt up to its retractable ladder.

Climbing the steps, Charlie saw that apartment three was a narrow duplex; a spiraling metal staircase led from the rooms downstairs to a little garden-view office above. He hurried past the light of the lower floor and was relieved to find the upper dark and empty. Cupping his eyes against the window, Charlie glimpsed a sight eerily close to the one he had so often imagined. A rutted library table, rows of books, albums, sundry ethnic knickknacks on floor-to-ceiling shelving. In a heap in a corner was a pile of musical instruments. Guitars with their strings snapped, a broken-necked cello, a mutilated banjo. He removed the spring-loaded insect screen and, pressing his palms into the glass, received the one lucky break in that luckless night. The window was unlocked.

Charlie origamied himself inside, and by the time he stood in Rebekkah's study, he stood also in sudden horror of what he had just done. But Edwina leapt from the bag, doing a rapid tour, smelling at the corners. "Shush, Weens, be quiet," Charlie was saying, when a horrible, heart-scorching pang split through him. He couldn't afford to take care of Edwina, and he understood now it wasn't only the poems he needed to return to Rebekkah.

And so the scheme, his last plan, this little climax he had contrived to cap off his failed New York existence, had come to its end. In this, at least, Charlie had succeeded, and now he needed only to place the journal on the desk, climb back out the window, down the fire escape, and into eviction, the menace of Jimmy Giordano, and whatever much, much worse horror Ma had to tell him, into his own whatever future. Careful not to make a sound, Charlie lifted the chair away from the desk and sat. He worked his fingers over the disembodied shapes of letters etched into the wood's soft surface.

Charlie knew now that he never could have followed his brother, not really. Not through the internal passage to the clamorous, brilliant otherworld of Oliver's imagination. The nearness of magic Charlie could sometimes perceive there, the plasmatic, brilliant surface of an internal, hidden sun he could sometimes find on the far side of a six-pack of Pabst Blue Ribbon and 3 A.M. until the actual sun would rise, exposing a clutter of beer cans, bagel wrappers, and a few pages holding the finger-smeared scribblings of an amateur.

Charlie wiped his face with the backs of his hands and stood. Very softly, he pulled open the door to the office, and he waited for a long while at the landing at the top of the stairs, looking down toward the glowing orange outline of the closed bedroom door. The air in the apartment was cool and musty with the smell of burned coffee. Clocks ticked and the refrigerator hummed. "I love you, Edwina," Charlie said, and turned for the window.

But then, behind the door, Rebekkah coughed, and at the sound of her long-ago human, Edwina flew from the office, so swiftly down the stairs it seemed her legs never contacted a single step. She pawed and burbled at Rebekkah's door. Charlie heard a muffled gasp. At last the door cracked open, spilling light. Edwina nosed forward, pushing the door wide and revealing Rebekkah, standing there with a hardcover book hoisted over her head, quaking so severely that the object nearly wobbled from her fist. Charlie could not make her face out against the brightness behind her, but he could feel their gazes meet. "Oh, fuck. Charlie?"

"Rebekkah," he said. Charlie took a too-long step forward then, losing track of the stairs.

Three hours later, on the fourth floor of New York Methodist Hospital, Charlie lay alone on the sheet-papered bed of an observation room. The doctor had told him that he would be back soon, once the cranial X-rays printed. Charlie had protested these X-rays, just as he protested the blood work and the resetting of a pinky finger he dislocated in the fall. Charlie's insurance plan was limited to superstitious knocking on wood and the weekly resolutions to eat better, abstain from smoking, and look both ways before crossing a street. But when Charlie tried to lift himself from the bed, a nurse held him back. "It's out of your hands," she said. Charlie's left forearm now resided in a mold of fiberglass, and he understood why people sometimes called a headache *splitting;* his swollen brain pushed so terribly against the jar of his skull, he had an image of hairline fissures racing across the bone.

"Jesus Christ, Charlie. What the fuck? Oh, Jesus. Don't you move," Rebekkah had told him when he came to rest at the bottom of the staircase. Her fright had still kept that book (an edition of Byron, he noticed) hoisted near her head. He watched her pull a phone from the embroidered pocket of her silk robe, juggling it for a second in her trembling hands.

"Rebekkah," Charlie said, his mind a grim montage of outcomes: a squad car, handcuffs, imprisonment, death. "Please. You don't have to call anyone."

"We—we need an ambulance," Rebekkah managed to tell the emergency operator, her voice weak with panic. "My friend has had a bad fall."

After ending the call, Rebekkah at last put the Byron on a table, and she squinted at him. Through the pain, Charlie worked to grin up to her, a twinkly rascalish expression he had perfected at Thoreau, a face he hoped translated into something along the lines of *This is very shameful, but aren't you, at some level, also charmed by my pluckiness?* Rebekkah, however, did not look charmed. From this angle, she hardly even looked like Rebekkah anymore, not the freckled girl who had seemed to draw a special sort of light as she passed through the halls of Bliss Township School, who could not fail to attract even the attentions of a ninth grader whose rudimentary love life was limited to the boys from his classes he'd conjure in his mind as he felt himself in his family's claw-foot tub. Rebekkah was only in her late twenties now, but Charlie saw more closely the face he had so often imagined, her lovely celtic features dulled a little by the years.

"What the hell is wrong with you?" Rebekkah said. "I could have you arrested, you know. You can't just break into people's fucking houses."

But Charlie sensed there were two Rebekkahs there: the frightened, angry woman with her wrinkle-webbed mouth and unruly threads of premature gray, and also a distant observer of these events, the younger Rebekkah for whom the horrors she'd seen that night had lowered a muted scrim of numbness between the world and her. His grin dropped.

"I can't take care of Edwina anymore. She's not well. She's really sick, do you hear how she's breathing? And I just can't afford to help her. And so I brought her back to you."

"You could have come in the front door, like a human being. I mean it. What were you—trying to *scare* me?"

"I tried the front door. I tried to call. You didn't answer. And you wouldn't have taken her. You wouldn't have spoken to me."

"Well. You've got that last part right."

"You could have talked to me, just once," Charlie said, without the fury he'd packed into those exact words in his many imaginings of this conversation. "That's all I've ever wanted."

"What *you* have wanted? Why does what you want count more? I think I've made it pretty clear what I want. What I need. Pretty abundantly fucking clear. So what is it? Huh? What is this thing you have to say to me? Just say it."

Charlie sucked a little groan down his throat. "I just wanted to talk about Oliver," Charlie said. "Just that. To talk."

Rebekkah knelt, as if to assess his wounds, but she was only greeting Edwina. "Edwina," Rebekkah whispered, and she used the pug's sable coat like a tissue. She carried Edwina from the room, and Charlie sat there for a long while on the bottom step, looking with muted horror at the wrong angle of his littlest finger. At last the erratic foghorn blare of the siren split the silence, and the ambulance lights turned the hallway into a discothèque. The doorbell rang, six or seven times over, and Rebekkah reappeared to open it.

"Rebekkah."

She paused but wouldn't turn. "What?"

It had always seemed to Charlie that he'd know just what to ask her if she would let him speak with her for only a minute. But that minute was ticking by now, and Charlie found that he couldn't remember.

Rebekkah shook her head, and went to let the ambulance men into her apartment. After they had led Charlie to a seat in the rear of the van (despite his vehement protests, affably ignored by one of the men, who told him, "Well, take a gander at that finger of yours. And you never know about head injuries, and not like we got anything else going on tonight"), Rebekkah appeared at the back doors, holding his bag, weighted again with the journal. "You forgot something," she said. "And Charlie? Next time, it's the police I'm calling. I mean it, I really do."

"Please," Charlie said.

"Please what?"

Edwina was still pressed to her chest. "Please take care of her for me?" Rebekkah nodded to one of the men, who shut the doors. The vehicle pulled away at a lazy speed. A case like Charlie's apparently did not warrant the emergency lights.

The clock in Charlie's room at New York Methodist now showed 4:15. He craned his head to see his doctor flirting with the night-shift nurse behind the counter. A young woman in a hijab paced the hall with a murmuring infant in one arm, a video-streaming phone in the other. No one seemed in any hurry at all.

With a miserable little gasp, Charlie lifted himself from the bed and went to the pile of clothes he had kicked to a corner when he changed into his paper gown. He grunted as he stooped to retrieve his phone from his jeans. Lighting its screen, he saw that he had missed one more call from his mother. Charlie inhaled sharply. He couldn't bear another second of not knowing, and so this room at New York Methodist—another hospital room not wholly unlike his brother's cell at Crockett State—would be where it would happen. At last he put the device to his ear and listened to the first of her many messages.

Later, Charlie would marvel at how he had done it. With a right arm mannequin-like in its cast, with his swelled brain pinging painfully in his ears, he tore away his hospital gown, buttoned himself back into his street clothes, slipped out of the room, and—when the nurse puttering in the hallway noticed him—"Mr. Loving?"—he ran.

Down the emergency stairs, through the hospital lobby, up Seventh Avenue to the subway station, where he took the first train into the city. At Port Authority, Charlie spent half his remaining cash on a Greyhound bus ticket, and as he waited in the deep-pocket smell of the station's basement, he vomited from pain, twice, into a garbage can that appeared, from its spattered stains, to have been put to that purpose more than once. But if there was one place where a battered, vomiting young man would not seem so out of the ordinary, it was The Port Authority Bus Terminal.

Still, when Charlie would later consider how he managed the dire forty-hour odyssey that followed, a transcontinental crawl, in which he slowly depleted a plastic barrel of pretzels as the pain and poor nutrition sometimes made his vision go dark and narrow, Charlie would think it was borderline miraculous that he made it all the way to the Big Bend without further medical assistance. But then he would play again Ma's first message, he would listen to the very simple and wholly impossible thing she hardly managed to choke through her tears, and he would know that it had been a night of miracles.

Many hours later, as the bus slammed through Midland and south into the desert, Charlie's exhaustion fluttered around the soft edges of a cozy dream: that he was back in his Zion's Pastures bed, that his brother was still there beneath him, in the bottom bunk of a bedroom in a house that was no longer theirs. Oliver was seventeen, and he was done conjuring spirit worlds with his brother. Oliver had just discovered a more marvelous hidden land, on a blanket just next to him, beneath the Perseid meteor shower. All it took was a single phone message from Ma: as on that morning with his brother's journal years before, Charlie could hear the spectral inhale of one of their ancient, magical portals torn open again, the feeling that their old bunk bed tales had in fact been a kind of prophecy, at last come true. Charlie looked down into that darkness, a hole in the land. Ten years. What words were there for it? "He's there," Ma said in her voice mail. "That's what I need to tell you. Oliver. They can see him now. On the computer screens? Charlie, he's there. He's here."

Oliver

·················

CHAPTER NINE

A portal torn open, but it would take more than your brother and
your mother and the latest medical technologies to see into that lost
place. It would take, also, the assistance of law enforcement professionals. It would take a man named Manuel Paz, Presidio County
captain of the Texas Rangers, a ranking officer in that antiquated
band of law keepers.

At dusk one evening, three or so years *after,* Manuel Paz was in the
evening-blued stillness of a far corner in Big Bend National Park, looking into a different sort of hole in the earth. He was standing in the ruins
of the Mariscal cinnabar mines, for which his grandfather and father
alike had worked themselves stooped. Among the wreckage of the old
mine camp and the rock-baking ovens that hadn't been stoked in half a
century, the warning signs loomed around him: these mines were still
gravid with the mercury his forebears had ored from the earth, the same
quicksilver that had engendered the cancer that had taken his father and
grandfather both. Manuel Paz twisted the wedding ring on his finger.

Once, ten years before, Manuel had taken his young bride, Lucinda,
for a visit to this same mine. Lucinda had just arrived to Texas then,
fleeing the narco warfare in the streets of Honduras, escaping with
her two sisters, and no small element of their early romance had been

Manuel's attempt to serve as a kind of tour guide to her life on this side of the river. This site seemed a particularly potent example of county history, a place where generations of Mexicans had toiled to an early grave at near slave wages, now just a ghost town, like so many others. "But they couldn't get rid of us that easy," Manuel had told Lucinda, and she grasped his hand. He'd brought a bottle of wine and a picnic basket, and he and Lucinda dined together in a roofless shed. An unusual spot for a romantic excursion, perhaps, but Manuel brought her here not only to tell the sad plight of his forebears but also because the national park, in whose far reaches the old mine was situated, held the promise of a more humane kind of border. Out in that park, there was no fence to demarcate Mexico. You could wade back and forth across the Rio Grande.

It was, after all, a new century, and Manuel had let himself believe that perhaps the ancient antipathies into which he had been born might ease. As a young man, he had signed up for the Rangers with the hope that, in his official capacity, he might make life a little easier for the Latinos coming over the river. Over the years, he had become friends with a number of Border Patrol officers, and they often let Manuel serve as first responder when a drone or concerned citizen spotted a figure hiking northward through the desert. Rather than cuffing these parched travelers, Manuel offered them maps, bottles of water, and the wrapped sandwiches that Lucinda had prepared, which he kept in a cooler in the trunk. And Manuel might have continued on like that for an entire career, glad to help in his own little ways, if not for the events of the night of November fifteenth.

Manuel had been in his Marfa office when the call came in, and once the impossible horror had sunk in—"three children?" he repeated several times over—he discovered there was yet another horror packed inside it. "Young Hispanic male," the arriving officer had described the shooter over the CB and even before he had learned the specifics, Manuel had a lucid, ominous foreboding of what was to come, a premonition that time would bear out. It wouldn't matter that Hector Espina had been an American-born citizen or that an Ecuadorian named Ernesto Ruiz stopped the kid that night. The fact was that Hector was a Latino with a firearm. He was a demon of white imaginings let loose.

Three dead children: Manuel Paz might have been only one of the many officers who had converged on the town of Bliss in the aftermath, but he carried that number like a mythical affliction, an itch he would forever scratch, the sting of it only growing more insistent, bothering his sleep. Three dead children. The itch asked for an explanation, and Manuel scratched and scratched. Manuel had spent hours playing wallflower in the meetings of the task force investigators. He had talked to all of those poor Theater Club kids. He had spoken to any person who had ever known the killer. And still the devilish irritant at the base of his affliction, a boy named Hector Espina, resided beneath his skin. Manuel could scratch himself raw and might never reach down to that boy's reasons.

And in the years that had followed, Manuel's worst fears had come to pass. Despite his peacekeeping entreaties to U.S. Representative Craig Armison, the deportations only ramped up. Despite his pleas to Otto Coop, superintendent of schools for Presidio County, the schoolhouse—the last reason anyone still came to the old town of Bliss—closed for good. "No one wants those memories," Otto told him.

But Otto was wrong. Manuel still had memories he wanted. He remembered his childhood in that same school; he remembered generations of his family scrapping for this spot of earth. "They can't get rid of us that easy, right?" Manuel said again to his wife one night.

"But don't you understand," Lucinda said with a sigh, "that there's nothing here worth staying for?"

Certainly Lucinda had a point. Their street, just west of Bliss, had nearly emptied. The few places of employment had long ago closed. Lucinda faced the ill will of the last residents, and she worried for her sisters, who had no green cards of their own. This, then, was how it happened: a few actual deportations, a generally hostile atmosphere, and a paucity of hope.

"You can't see," Lucinda had told him just a month ago, "that you are part of the problem. An old man, grasping at lofty ideals." The fact was that Lucinda's sisters were heading for better prospects to the north, and she had delivered what amounted to an ultimatum to Manuel: leave with me or I leave alone. But Manuel Paz was a man who didn't take well to ultimatums. She had departed for Chicago three weeks ago, and now, standing over the mine shaft, Manuel tugged the ring from his finger.

But he paused, even still thinking, *Why not follow Lucinda?* Certainly he could transfer to a different office. Leave the force for good, get some plum private security job. What was there to stay for? Manuel spent his days filling out paperwork, filing reports for violations of laws he hardly believed in. And yet, Lucinda must have known the man she had married, mustn't she?

Three years *after*, Manuel was still putting in after-hours bouts poring over the old task force dossiers, still speaking to the grief-sickened parents of the dead. Once, he had even driven down into Mexico, on a futile hunt to locate Hector's father. There had been a time, for the first year or so *after*, when Manuel had felt the only possible way he might forestall the unthreading of his old town was to locate some answer for what Hector had done that night, some very specific reason to ward off the vagueness of jingoistic nightmares. But still there was no explaining that madness, and it was already too late to make much of a difference, Manuel knew that. And yet, that was the nature of the itch: the more you scratched, the worse it grew. The very futility of his attempt was what made it into an obsession.

But as Manuel now held the wedding ring over an open mine shaft, it was poor Eve Loving that he was thinking of. Eve Loving, with her lovely, troubled dark eyes, the rare way that she, like Manuel himself, was able to blinker herself against all that had already been lost, limiting her view only to what each day required of her. They shared a stolidness, a kind of persistence that Lucinda never appreciated, though perhaps Lucinda had been right in her judgment, perhaps the brand of doggedness he and Eve Loving had in common had made them both a little unhinged, blinding them to the damage they wrought. Manuel, for example, had never once talked with Eve about that little sad habit of hers, never mentioned the several shopkeepers Manuel had talked out of filing charges against her. As with the immigrants he had helped, Manuel just did what he could and never spoke of it. Truth be told, Manuel would sometimes consider the woman's taut shape under the oversized clothes she wore, and he couldn't resist entertaining a fantasy or two.

And of course, Oliver, Manuel was also thinking of you. He was thinking of Oliver Loving, voiceless in his bed, a silence to answer the questions that even still bit at Manuel's skin. Often, perched over Bed Four, Manuel would put his hands to your shoulders, your forehead, and it could seem to him that he could nearly feel it: an explanation that was still somewhere out there, in that impassable otherworld of your memory, that place where you were still the same wholly whole Oliver, bumbling your way to the answer Manuel couldn't know. Manuel had only set eyes on you a few times *before,* but he often conjured an image of you as you must have been in those last weeks, the ordinariness of the life that had been taken from you. Just a seventeen-year-old boy, strolling down the streets of the doomed town of Bliss on a cool October morning. Manuel held his wedding ring over the mine shaft in his pinched fingers, and he let it loose. He turned his ear to the void, listening for the sound of its report.

It was October thirteenth, a Friday, just over a month before the beginning of your town's demise, but as you made slow laps up and down the streets, everything about Bliss seemed immutable and ancient to you. Your family's history in Bliss might have extended into the nineteenth century, but you felt no sense of belonging in the diminutive town your ancestors had helped to build. Those redbrick buildings, that flat of desert, the purple mountains in the distance— it all seemed alien.

Alien: that unfortunate word, often applied to half the school's population. Like some kind of bureaucratically veiled threat, the local chief of the border patrol, Officer Wallace Van Brunt, had been invited to speak at that month's school assembly, telling his dire work stories to the student body seated in the gymnasium's bleachers. Through a thick, woolly mustache, Officer Van Brunt employed that term often—not only *alien* but *illegal alien*—as he held forth about the many horrors and misfortunes he'd witnessed in his work. Children dying of thirst in the desert, women ODing from the erupted baggies of heroin they'd swallowed. The message of these grim tales: *Tell your families, Mexicans, to stay out!* The Latino half of the school sat quietly through that assembly, but just the next morning another big fight erupted when David Garza smashed Scotty Coltrane's head into a locker. Striving for fairness, Doyle Dixon suspended both boys for a week, but it did little to quiet the growing animosity. The Latino gathering on the schoolhouse steps had taken on a vaguely political air. That human wall of commotion near the front doors now stretched to the side door, too, forcing white students to enter the building from the back. You bypassed the whole scene that morning, ambling your way down Main Street.

Three buildings down from the school was a failing company called Made in Texas!, which used the long-defunct Bliss Hotel, a near perfect double to your schoolhouse, as a factory to manufacture little western tchotchkes, pewter longhorn key chains, bull scrotum coin purses. The kind of future garbage tourists pick up at the airport for their loved ones back home. Over those last weeks, the stale, manic, tense halls of Bliss Township had come to seem a sort of factory, too, the machinery through which you were daily processed, slowly rendered from a boy into a man-shaped sadness. It had been a month since Rebekkah had spoken more than a few words to you.

In your solitary walks at Zion's Pastures, in your days gazing unfocusedly at schoolhouse blackboards, in your nights beneath the grinning cow skulls that lined your bedroom walls, in the sad silence that had fallen over the bunks that you and Charlie once filled with your stories, you had addressed an imagined Rebekkah with a thousand variations on one same question: If she were only going to abandon you to your failed poems and the lonesome throb of your blood, why torture you with the hope of that kiss? "Rebekkah," you very often sighed to no one in those weeks, her name involuntarily escaping your mouth. Each day, after school, you couldn't resist turning a few extra hallways in the direction of Mr. Avalon's theater classroom, for the chance to glimpse Rebekkah through the little wire-veined window in the door as the club rehearsed its selections for the Homecoming Dance. And as you trailed Rebekkah, a word trailed you as well, the word for what you were making yourself into. *Stalker.*

And so, what did a lonesome speck of a boy have to lose? Back at school that morning, you were doing a sort of stakeout, waiting a few paces down the hall from Mrs. Schumacher's classroom. When Rebekkah brushed past, you surprised even yourself by the clarity of your anger, how forcefully you grabbed her shoulder.

"You have to at least explain it to me," you said. "At least once."

Rebekkah cocked her head. She did not seem just to be playing innocent; she looked truly innocent, as if she were oblivious to the devastation she could cause. "Explain what?"

"Explain what? How about the fact that you talk to me every morning for a *month*, that you even—and then, what? Nothing." You were dismayed that the speech didn't come out with the fury you intended. You said this with the full eyes, the cutely halting voice of a thwarted teen lover from some rom-com. All it took was one second of Rebekkah's attention to restore you to the feeling that had begun in those mornings before school in Mrs. Schumacher's literature class, brought to consummation, or at least your PG version of consummation, outside the football stadium.

"I'm sorry, Oliver." Rebekkah's eyes darted about, as if looking among the thinning crowds for someone to rescue her from this scene she couldn't quite tolerate. "I don't know what to say. I don't like you like that."

"You don't like me like what?"

"I have to go. We have to go to class. I'm sorry, okay? Sorry."

And how is this for foreshadowing? It was that very day that Mrs. Schumacher began a monthlong unit on Homer's *Odyssey*. "Does anyone know the secret about this gift that the Greeks gave the Trojans?" asked Mrs. Schumacher. "What was inside the horse?"

The class was silent. "It wasn't a gift at all," you said. "It was a trap."

"Bingo!" Mrs. Schumacher tossed, as was her custom, a Hershey's Kiss as a reward.

And it was then—your mouth pulverizing the stale chocolate, Rebekkah flushing under your gaze—that you saw it. Under the intense beam of your hard stare, Rebekkah shifted in her chair, a little movement like the ones that you had tracked so closely for weeks. This time, however, you noticed something strange there, just above the hemline of her skirt. A purplish mass, threaded with red. Very unlike her slight blue discolorations that you occasionally noticed, this was a severe bruise that ran halfway to her knee, its epicenter bound together by two Band-Aids, the cotton of which was stained a rusted brown.

By late third period, you were learning a new lesson about love, one that perhaps gave you a little sympathy for the mother whose worries so often agitated you. The sight of the bruise on Rebekkah's leg shot your veins with a very pleasing brand of upset. Heartsick boy that you were, you found, in that quick glimpse beneath Rebekkah's school desk, a merciful exit from your moody solitude. A new grim story, veering away from the ordinary dull one about your own rejection, a mystery you could pursue if you could no longer pursue her directly. Just one quick glimpse of a bad bruise, and you were conjuring monstrous abuse scenarios. Her father? You remembered her worry that night at the football game, her *fear* that the two of you would be seen together. Maybe her father was one of those jealous, faintly incestuous types familiar to West Texas, the kind of man who wielded his righteous morality like a bullwhip, disciplining his daughter like livestock, warning boys off what he believed belonged to him. Your dejection needed a face to clutch at, a reason, and here (or so you tried to convince yourself) was an answer for why Rebekkah would limit your company to your morning sessions, why she would steal a kiss, why she would be afraid to let it go any further. She must have been protecting you! But if her father was a hitter, why did she only ever speak of him like some obnoxious stranger in her house? Why—after all you said about your own parents—did she never tell you a thing about it?

You were silent as Pa drove you home that afternoon, silent at the dinner table as Charlie ran relays back to his backpack on an armchair to display the recent fruits of his labors, his marker- and sparkle-bedazzled report on Mount St. Helens, the A– paper on the construction of Versailles, the B+ on his math exam. You could only poke at Ma's "famous" macaroni casserole.

"How about you?" Ma asked. "Good day?"

"Great day. Actually, I was wondering if I could borrow the car tonight?"

"What for?"

"I have a study group."

"A study group? For what?"

"It's, ah, for this project on *The Odyssey.* Something I'm doing with Rebekkah, actually." Why did you mention her name? Perhaps just for the magic of the sound of it in your mouth.

"Rebekkah? Rebekkah Sterling? For real?" Pa asked. "Good for you. Good for her, too, of course. Lucky to have a, *ah,* study partner like you, huh?" Pa was grinning at you now, in his dumb-sly way.

"It's just random. We were randomly assigned, I mean."

"This study group, it's at her house?" Ma asked. "Can I at least speak with her parents first?"

"Speak with them about *what?*" you said. "What do you think will happen?"

"It's just a normal thing parents do, Oliver. They check to be sure there will be parental supervision."

"Ma," you said, loading an entire counterargument in that word. In another family, this might not have seemed such an unusual conversation, but in the history of your life as Eve Loving's son, this tense impasse represented a new escalation of the cold war of wills you and she had been conducting those last weeks.

"Fine," she said, waving her hands. "You do what you want."

Just after seven that night, you went ahead with your lie. It was ridiculous, you knew it, but the outrage of your heartache, funneling into the narrow trough of your worry, roared through you, and you needed to release it. As Goliath tore through the night, a Bob Dylan cassette wailing—*What drives me to you is what drives me insane*—the divider lines under the bright beams looked like stars at warp speed. Just after eight, you pulled up outside the address for Rebekkah Sterling that was printed in the spiral-bound school directory open on the passenger seat.

What would you say to her? You tried to convince yourself that the right words, the real poetry, came when they were needed, and you hadn't planned them. And yet, you wouldn't be needing them tonight. All the windows in Rebekkah's house, one of those new stucco McMansions metastasizing over the high plains, were lightless at 7:45 P.M. Only the foyer light was on, and just minutes after you arrived, it too went dark. Two adult bodies came from the front door, arguing over something you couldn't make out. The man was barreling unsteadily—drunkenly; a drunkard's son could recognize a drunk man even from fifty yards. He was a rotund, rook-shaped man, with no apparent genetic linkage to the girl you knew, but the rail-thin, birdish woman hovering behind him? You felt your heart click into higher gear, the sight of her parents like some secret your imagined, often-conjured Rebekkah was at last whispering into your ear. But where was the actual Rebekkah? You remained very still as they boarded the wine-dark Mercedes in the drive and drove away. You remained there for a long while, looking into those vacant, spotless panes of glass as you imagined Rebekkah's presence beatifying each sterilized room. You imagined what it might feel like for her to live in a gargantuan, automated museum of a house like that.

But no one was home now, or at least no lights were on, and so what else could you do but continue your *group project* for one? It would have been too shameful to return home so soon. You reclined in the seat, distantly hoping and also fearing Rebekkah might come if you waited long enough. You waited and waited, and you were trying again to play the lovesick poet; you tried to pass the time by composing a few lines. But you could not compose, that certain damning word was coming back to you with too much brutalizing force—a boy watching silently from a parked car outside a girl's house, what word for it but *stalker*? Still, you passed an hour that way.

You were startled by a dull thud. You flailed about, but fortunately you were at some distance, in a car shadowed beneath a stand of cottonwoods. And from that darkness, you saw that another vehicle had pulled up, a ways down Monte Grande Lane. A figure was marching across the pavement. This wasn't Rebekkah's father, come home—this man's gait was swift and youthful. This guy walked toward the front door, and it was there, in the dim and far-off light of the wall sconces, that you first glimpsed his face. The wide dome of a shaven head, the features beneath crowded and unreadable. A young man, who had the courage to do what you did not, to try the doorbell. When no light came on, when the door refused to budge, he knocked at it, so forcefully that the report reached your window. No response, so he knocked harder still. Was this, in fact, your imagined abuser? The violence with which he assaulted the door fit the monster you had been conjuring, but even from this distance he seemed an unlikely candidate. He seemed too old for Rebekkah, too forceful a presence to imagine a quiet-sad girl ever knowing him in a meaningful way.

At last, after repeated applications of fist to door, finger to doorbell, this man kicked the wall once, marched back to his old Ford pickup. And yet he paused there, the truck door halfway opened. He was not now looking at the darkened house; he was not looking at the door in his hands. He was looking at the car parked in the shadows. He was looking at you. Panicked, you started the engine, and Goliath's headlamps blinked on, casting him in the lurid brightness of a snapshot. This man did not cover his eyes; he squinted, as if challenging the light itself. There was just a moment there, a fractional second in measurable time, but also an oddly suspended duration, when you sat very still, staring back at him. And it was then that the fitful wattage of Goliath's lamps worked in parallel with your own memory, lighting up a certain recognition. The rounded slope of this person's forehead, the slight pronation of his feet, and—more than anything—that disquieting illegibility in his eyes: you couldn't name him, but you did feel you recognized him. An old student at your school, maybe? Or perhaps the recognition you knew in that moment was only a sense of what you and this stranger shared, two young men both on the same hopeless errand, trying to speak with the girl who was nowhere to be found.

It was just an odd bleak feeling of kinship you knew then—even Goliath's bright beams could not have shown you how much you truly shared with him, another boy who had wanted only to vanish into the crowds. Hector Espina, only three years ahead of you in school, whom you must have passed hundreds of times in the halls without even noticing. "Sometimes," your Pa had said, "there is a crack in this universe, where you can see into the next." And though you might have glimpsed the strangeness of the fissure that opened just a sliver that night, the unlikeliness that had brought you both to the Sterling residence, you couldn't have known then how your history and this young man's history were already entwined. You could not have known that the way he would escape his hell would be the same way yours would begin. You said nothing to Hector Espina, not then.

Much later, it would be easy to chide your younger self. *Speak!* You might have saved yourself, your town, your family if only you had rolled down your window and asked him a question or two. But that night, you just pulled a U-turn on Monte Grande Lane, wondering over this visitor to Rebekkah's house, this angry young man you would not see again until the night of November fifteenth. He was the black hole through which you'd fall. But just then he was only another question you wondered over as you puttered off for home.

Eve

· · · · · · · · · · · · · · · · · · ·

CHAPTER TEN

A lifetime before, when she was only nineteen, Eve herself had fallen into a different sort of chasm. Only two months prior, her father (just forty-six) had died of a heart attack on the floor of an El Paso dealership, and in the surreal, weightless months that followed, Eve found a job at a diner, Bliss Pies N' Stuff, rented an apartment in Marathon, bought a battered Jeep with doors that zippered off. She created a simulacrum of a life, then tried to believe it was her own. Eve was still hanging around West Texas only because, in the dislocation of her late teenage orphanhood, she couldn't think of anywhere else to go.

Eve's mother, a foster care graduate named Devorah, had died when Eve was just four (a stupid death, a brain infection from an abscessed tooth she had failed for months to bring to medical attention), and Eve's memories of the woman she once called *Mameleh* were now like impressions of some long-ago-jettisoned photo album, flashes that might have been true snapshots, might only have been Eve's later fabrications. That ringlet hair dangling over Eve's chubby, clutching fingers. Hands so white the mechanics of vein and joint were visible.

Unfortunately, in those first weeks after his death, Eve's memories of her father were still damningly vivid. The way Mortimer Frankl had lived his adult life: in his rumpled houndstooth coats and soup-stained

neckties, Eve's father had been fired or else walked out on car dealership jobs in Topeka, St. Louis, Crested Butte, Pasadena, Albuquer-
que. "I don't know why you whine so much," Morty often chastised
Eve. "At least, unlike me, you get to see something of the world. I
never got so many chances to start over when I was your age."

Start over? As the Frankls had cycled between frowsy, underpopu-
lated cities and sterile, soulless exurbs, Eve's father remained the same
glum, twitchy, cigar-puffing man, just becoming himself more and
more deeply. Morty's parents—a shrunken, Yiddish-speaking, blue-
collar Baltimore couple—seemed to want nothing to do with their
son or granddaughter. Solitude was what Eve's father and her wandering childhood had raised her to expect, and that was how she passed
the weeks after his death. Eve spent her off days in the great desert
that lay to the south, an infinity in which she could be alone. She fell
a little in love with that barbed, shattered, blazing desert, and she became its diligent tourist. She visited the Ernst Tinaja, hiked the South
Rim Trail in the national park, camped often in the Chisos Basin.

After a childhood in which her father had treated her the way
he treated his Cutlass Supreme—some onerous and cantankerous
contraption that he nevertheless was made to drive around and
maintain—Eve had just about come to believe it impossible that any
other man might one day choose to invite such a burden of a girl
into his life. Eve had never had a boyfriend, and it never would have
occurred to her to look for one now. Later, Eve would often wonder
what kind of muttering loner she might have become if she had not
one night made the trip to see the so-called Marfa Lights, a mysterious visual phenomenon on the scrub grass plains just east of town.

These luminous orbs were the source of considerable local lore. Supposedly they were inexplicable, balls of restive light that traveled the
desert at night. Some people called them reflections, some called them
electricity, most attributed them to supernatural influence. She arrived
to the observation spot, a parking lot off Route 90, just after midnight.
A little crowd was gathered there, but after an hour staring into the
dim plains as trains trundled past, the lights still had not come.

"There!" a man next to her said, very close to her ear. "Do you see that? Look just left of that mountain." Eve might not have seen the apocryphal lights, but she did notice something else: the waspishly handsome, wonder-struck face of the man pointing into the nothing of the desert night. The man was named Jed, and by that spring they would be married, and she would be a student at Sul Ross State University, a few miles east of where they stood. At the time, however, she only leaned closer to his outstretched arm, nearly resting her head on his shoulder so that she could follow the direction of his pointed finger. "I can't see it," she said. "Show me."

Almost thirty years had passed, and there Eve was now, just a few dozen miles away, waiting for another otherworldly phenomenon to appear on the desert plains. Three days after that morning in the fMRI-mobile, Eve was pacing outside a grimed glass cube—its windows showing sun-bleached posters of downtown Los Angeles's honeycomb of lights and the blanched sea green of the Mississippi coastline—that passed for the bus station in the town of Alpine. On a white square of pavement, Eve was staring down the perfect straight line of Farm-to-Market Route 28, waiting for the bus that carried Charlie to rise over the mirage-shaken curvature of the earth.

Over the last years, Eve had often harangued a conjured Charlie with scripted diatribes, but as she stood there now, peeling away a fingernail too close to the quick, Eve kept forgetting what it was she meant to tell him first. She hadn't yet told Jed about Charlie's imminent return, just as she hadn't mentioned to Charlie, in any of her numerous phone messages, that Jed had been there with her that day of the test. Like the Great Wall of Texas those crazed politicians had long wanted to build, an unclimbable barrier now stood between father and son. And even if Eve sometimes regretted that she herself had helped construct that partition, she felt that the map of her family had been drawn too long ago to revise the borders now.

At last the Greyhound bus materialized in the hazy suck of the distance and belched slowly toward her. At the station, it hissed to a stop, its flanks showing a dusty Texan brown over the deeper blackish grime of the East Coast. The windows were scratched with vandalism, the sides speckled with bleached-out spray paint, the whole thing like a lousy chunk of New York City, cut away and set on wheels. And there, the only passenger rising at the Alpine stop, was her own young New Yorker. Even through the puckering tint stickers of the bus windows, Eve could see how Charlie tried to keep up the air of an ordinary commuter, his posture a little theater of boredom. As if to tell her, before he said a thing, *my existence has become so interesting that my return home is only a station stop on the excellent journey of my life!* Like an oversized camel, the bus kneeled awkwardly to offload its rider, and Charlie stepped out, waving as if his mother were just some driver holding his name on a placard. But after the bus abandoned Charlie with a hiss, he was left to cross a field of asphalt, a tiny figure in the desert flat. Eve tried not to laugh to see him now, in his checkered poplin shirt, his painted-on jeans, his roguish mess of hair, buzzed at the sides. Charlie adjusted a pair of clunky tortoiseshell glasses—and since when did Charlie wear glasses?—with a self-consciousness that was almost touching.

"Ma!" he cried, his voice an ironic reenactment of some mawkish scene of return in a TV movie. "Your baby boy has come home to you, dear mother!"

"Oh, shut up." Charlie in Eve's arms: she could feel how his New York costume went deeper than his clothes. Charlie was now an anatomy lesson, bones and sinewy muscle. Charlie suppressed a little pained cry, and she noticed the swelling in his lip and his right cheek, the cast strapped over his left forearm.

"My Lord, what happened to you?"

"Oh, you mean this—appendage? Just took a bad stumble. Uneven sidewalks. Our mayor doesn't care about those of us out on the margins. That whole city is fucked."

"Your face!"

"I didn't quite catch myself in time."

Eve clicked her tongue. "Looks to me like you could use some good mothering."

"Couldn't we all?" The glare in Charlie's silly new glasses forbade a good view of his eyes, showing Eve only her own tired face, reflected with the mountains and low buildings in the last of the day's light.

"And where is your poor pup?" Eve asked. "Oh God, please don't tell me—"

"She's just fine," Charlie said. "I've got a friend looking after her until I go back."

"Until you go back. And when do you plan on doing that?"

Charlie sighed. "How about we take things one day at a time here?"

"Right."

Charlie pointed with his plaster mannequin's arm. "Holy shit. Is that Goliath?"

"Old faithful."

"Faithful? That is the only car I've ever known that literally farts."

The doors to Goliath whined open and Eve made a face as Charlie cackled at the old beast puttering to dyspeptic life. So it was a comedy to Charlie, the fact that her dire bank account balance kept her saddled with this heap. An angry argument on the topic of her finances took shape in her mind as they drove away. The vaporous ghosts of other arguments were there, too; all the nights she had spent alone, delivering those silent tirades to this boy for abandoning her, for believing he could turn the tragedy of their days into a titillating story for public consumption. But in the warm, close air of Goliath, Eve could still smell, beneath the seedy funk in Charlie's hair and the stink of his worn clothes, that old Charlie fragrance. That peanut-buttery scent, which cast an unfair effect, eliminating the last years and returning them, for a second, to the Zion's Pastures of her mind. For the last year, her imagination had tagged along with Charlie's days in New York, and her imagined city was filled with greater dangers than any actual ones. Her fretted-over Charlie had been beset by muggers, careening taxis, coins dropped from the top of the Empire State Building, air conditioners tipped from tenement windows, HIV-positive party boys. The relief that she could simply reach out a hand and feel for him now was irresistible. But then she felt the hard plaster of his cast and retreated, wrapping her fingers back around the cracked rubber grooves of the steering wheel.

"Did you get to sleep much on the bus?"

"Not really. I was too—awake?"

Eve nodded. It had been like that for her, too, in those three days since the test. As if Professor Nickell's fMRI had located also some inexhaustible new form of energy. Even now, unfocused with sleeplessness, she could plug back into it, the great wattage that morning still generated.

"Oliver," Eve had been saying into the microphone they had let her speak into, likely just to humor her. "Can you hear me? Oliver? It's Ma. I need you to focus now, they need you to focus. Can you do that for me?" Her pep talk was awkward at first, but escalating in its natural conviction.

Professor Nickell and his lazy-eyed underlings had been seated in front of their screens and gizmotic panels, dully performing their routine, but as for Eve? Even still, even then, she knew what every mother knows: despite whatever evidence, she knew her kid was different than the rest. And then? It was not as if anyone gasped or startled or even made much of a sound. But as she clutched Jed's arm and hunched over the microphone, it was unmistakable. Some power was building in the room, in the way she read once that static electricity accumulates on the ground where lightning is about to strike. "Oliver?"

One of the technicians, a goateed, potbellied guy, pulled away from his station and pressed the greenish crescent of a fingernail against the glass of the screen that showed her son's brain, the image wholly unlike the black-and-white printouts from that MRI Oliver had undergone years before. Eve could see the cerebral folds and crevices, neural activity lighting up the gray matter in real time. Professor Nickell and the other technician went silent then, and though after all her online research bouts, Eve's knowledge of human neurology may still have only qualified as amateur, she knew what she was looking at. She believed she knew. Just a human brain, lit up and pulsing with thought. "Oh, God," Professor Nickell said, turning to the Lovings as he considered this little window opened onto the cell where the prisoner had languished, all but forgotten. "Oh, no," Professor Nickell added.

"Oliver," Eve had continued into the coffee-scented microphone, trying to hold her voice steady, trying not to sob. "Oliver, brave boy, I always knew," she said—or something like that, because then she sort of lost track of herself. She flushed, cold fire spreading across her skin. And just then it somehow seemed to Eve that Oliver would complete the transformation. As if the effect of that machine on his body would work like a mother bird beaking at the hatchling's shell. As if Oliver might, right then, beat at the fragile eggshell his body had become, split right out of it, spread his wings. Though, of course, Oliver just lay there, beyond the window divider, shuddering as ever. But the beautiful bird was still beating its wings in the Technicolor display on the monitors, and in the three days that followed, Eve tried to accept it as miracle enough.

"The important thing to do here," Nickell had told Eve and Jed in an unscheduled post-test meeting back in Dr. Rumble's office, "is not to rush to any conclusions at all. We just can't know anything, not yet. For example, it's true, the structure is remarkably intact. Remarkable, truly, the kind of activity that we're seeing now. But we do also see some substantial degradation to the frontal cortex, dimness in the parietal. We're just doing brain measurements here, we aren't equipped to do any sort of cognitive assessment. Consciousness, it's not an all-or-nothing thing. There are degrees, and that's what we need to figure out now."

It seemed deliberately symbolic that as Professor Nickell delivered this opinion he occupied the armchair typically filled by Frank Rumble, the nice chesterfield by the sofa. Dr. Rumble, relegated to his distant desk, raised and lowered the slide of his bolo tie. "Degrees, right," Dr. Rumble lamely interjected. "And likely a very small degree. I really don't think we should be getting hopes up."

"I wouldn't say small and I wouldn't say large," Professor Nickell said. "I would say that we need to do some more extensive assessments here."

"So Oliver was *what*? Just misdiagnosed?" Eve asked. "Or did something change?"

"Hard to say if anything changed, though that is certainly possible. Dr. Rumble here showed me the old fMRI results, from nearly ten years back. I think we can see some of the activity I'm seeing clearly now, even back then. But the machines were cruder in those days, and it's hard to know for sure."

"I don't understand this then," Eve told Dr. Rumble. "You told me he was gone, Frank. Just his reptile brain, you said."

Dr. Rumble emitted a long sigh. "The fact is, we still just don't know."

Eve had to fold her hands to keep from choking the doctor with his ridiculous necktie. *Incompetence!* Did she actually say the word? *The evil of your incompetence!* And yet, even then Eve knew the true nature of the combustion happening in her chest: years ago, even Frank Rumble had brought up the idea of a second opinion, though in his dismissive, pandering tone. But Eve had never been able to bring herself to insist on other hospitals, other tests.

"Anyway," Professor Nickell added, "I've already put in a call to a neuroscientist in El Paso, a brilliant woman called Marissa Ginsberg, an expert with cases like these. Dr. Ginsberg, she's got a whole litany of tests she does, to assess just how conscious, how aware, a patient like Oliver might be. More brain scans, EEGs, a whole slew of stimulus tests. We've scheduled Oliver a long examination with her eight weeks from tomorrow, if you'll agree."

"Eight weeks?" Eve asked.

"It's a wait, I know it," the professor said. "Apparently, with Oliver's insurance plan, it's going to take that long for all the paperwork to go through."

"It's more than *a wait*," Eve said. "It's a *travesty*." And yet Eve was too overcome with hope even to maintain an appropriate rage for the negligent doctor pouting behind his desk. She understood that even this long-fretted-over test had not proven anything conclusively. But she couldn't help it; her hope was all that kept the blood moving through her veins.

"So what does all this even mean?" Charlie asked in the passenger seat now, after she filled him in on the basic details. "What do we do with these facts now? Eight weeks until the next test. What are we supposed to do in the meantime?"

"We celebrate. We celebrate this incredible news."

"And what about he who shall not be named?" Charlie said. "Does he know?"

"Your father knows," Eve said. And, okay, maybe it was just habit, how quickly the lie came fully formed to her lips, the very little lie that would confirm a really, truly true portrait of a father who had never been present for a family like a father ought to be. "Dr. Rumble told me your father seemed very happy when they spoke on the phone. But I don't think that 'happiness' can ever quite be the right word with that man," she said, because Charlie's return to her life was all the upheaval Eve could take right now, because she just couldn't bear to invite Jed back into the mix. And why not let Jed go on brooding in his Marfa bungalow if that was what he wanted?

The mountains were on fire with the sunset. With her son back in Goliath, some old impulse had misdirected Eve. She found that she had turned on the road not to Desert Splendor but to Zion's Pastures. They had been driving that way for ten minutes when she slapped at her head, as if to fix a wonky contraption.

"Don't be like that. Of course it's incredible," Charlie said. "I mean that. That we know now. Of course it is."

"He's back with us."

"Is he? We really don't know that for sure, it sounds like. And if he is, does that mean he's really been with us all along? Or did his brain, like, suddenly switch back on? Like a lightbulb or something?"

"I've spent the last three days wondering exactly the same. These are questions for the professionals, I guess. For that next test."

"But Ma? If he really has been there, every single day, I mean really hearing and seeing us—" Charlie hesitated.

"We didn't know."

"It would be hell. Maybe happy news for us, okay. But for Oliver? That would mean he has been in hell."

"Ah. I had forgotten," Eve said. "I had forgotten what it is like to have my son at home. This is good news, Charlie. The very, very best news. What about taking things one day at a time? Now that we know, we can help."

Determined not to let Charlie sense her directional error and so expound on its implications, Eve just kept on, toward Zion's Pastures. It was dim enough now that when a coyote crossed the highway its eyes flared blue in the headlights.

"Help?" Charlie asked. "How could we help?"

"Do you remember Margot Strout?"

"Doesn't ring a bell."

"That speech therapist woman. Usually she works with stroke patients, people with dementia. But starting tomorrow, she'll be working with Oliver every day. They say she's a miracle worker."

In that week of a great many reversals, not the least was the fact that—after all those years of shunning Margot in the halls, turning her head away as if the woman were nothing but an offensive smell with charging legs—Eve somehow now found herself in a position to extol Margot Strout's virtues. "It's a wonderful thing, ain't it?" Dr. Rumble had once mused, after Margot passed by the window. "A woman like that—everything she's been through, losing her daughter, and still she spends her life helping other people." Eve had paused from her combing of her son's thinning hair, turned to Dr. Rumble, and said, "What a hero." But then, just one day after the test, it was none other than Margot Strout who knocked at the door.

"How about this?" Margot said. "How about you and I try to start over?"

Margot's blue, thickly mascaraed eyes on Eve, so unafraid, so horribly, triumphantly *understanding*.

"So now you might be ready to listen to me. Now you think I might not be so crazy after all," Eve said.

"I never said you were crazy," Margot told her. "But you're right. You were right, Eve! You were right all along, about Oliver."

Eve couldn't resist letting the woman take her hands. She was so eager to share her joy with another human. Jed had walked away from that test as dazed as a man contemplating tax codes; Dr. Rumble and the nurses now tended to their patient like supplicants to a dying king. "I can't imagine it," Margot had added. "No, I can. If my daughter could suddenly come back to me? After all these years. Eve, Eve, dear woman. God is good, isn't he?"

"A miracle worker," Charlie said to his mother now. "Good. Well. A miracle is what we need."

"We've already had one."

"Sounds like we need another. Oliver does." Charlie sighed and shifted in that beleaguered way of his, as if the unfortunate truths of his life were weighty boxes she made him heft.

"You know what that Princeton professor told me?" Eve was strangling the steering wheel, twisting her wrists. "Turns out that it's more common than anyone knows. It's horrible, but apparently people like Oliver are misdiagnosed all the time. God. Imagine it. But people don't know this."

Charlie nodded, as though this fact dovetailed with the point he was trying to make. "We still just don't know. We can't know. What's in Oliver's head. What he might think of all this. What he might think of anything at all." Charlie was speaking to the dashboard, to no one, to the audience he convened in his mind. "Or even *how* he might think. Now it seems to me—" But Eve had stopped listening. She blinked and blinked at the cooling purple of nothing in all directions.

"What's up?" Charlie said. "You stopped the car."

"It's just too much. You are back here now. No. Not you, but a man with my little boy's face. And Oliver. And why can't we, just for one minute, why can't we just celebrate these facts? Why can't you let me have just one happy night in ten years?"

"C'mon, Ma. I'm really too tired for the martyr routine right now."

"Right. Because I'm just some hysterical, manipulative old shrew."

They were at the start of something, the same old thing. It had taken less than thirty minutes to arrive here. The thunder of the coming fight gathered behind the few words they'd spoken, but Eve was too exhausted to endure that storm now, too sore with the repetitive stress injury of her son's condemnations. Charlie, who was always insinuating in his pseudopsychological way that there was some deeper part of her that she was unwilling to consider, when Eve's entire mental life was just an endless spin cycle of consideration and reconsideration. Eve wanted to tear herself open, to let Charlie see all the way down to the deepest part of her where this self-fabricator, this manipulative shrew supposedly resided.

"Just please, Ma, calm down now, okay? Listen to me," Charlie reached for the back of her head, apparently forgetting the cast on his arm. Its corner slammed into Eve's face.

"Shit." Ridiculous: even with the fireworks blooming painfully in her eye, Eve regretted swearing in front of her son.

"Oh, no, Ma."

She clutched the injury, and Charlie reached with his good hand to pull her fingers away. Eve knew it was nothing serious—the pain had already passed—but she held on, making him suffer a little longer. Charlie lit Goliath's weak dome lamp, and at last she relented, displaying her face to him, blinking furiously. Charlie was so close, and his eyes were still his eyes. Gray and bright.

"We make quite a duo," Eve said. "A regular slapstick act."

Charlie chuckled, and so did Eve. Just moments ago they were walking a delicate line, the edge of something vast and deep, and these quick laughs tripped them, pitching mother and son over the cliff. They didn't just laugh then; they tumbled into laughter, down and down.

"Oh, oh! We have to stop this, we have to stop, I'm going to wet myself," Eve said, which only made them laugh harder still. They laughed until it seemed they arrived to the other side of something. Eve fired the colicky engine, put Goliath in drive, and pulled a whining U-turn across the asphalt.

"Where are we going?"

Eve grinned into the darkness to the east, the stars twitching to life. "To see your brother."

At eight thirty on a Sunday evening, the lampposts of the parking lot of Crockett State Assisted Care Facility were all dark. The building itself, illuminated by a few security lights, looked like a dinghy at sea. "We're way past visiting hours, so we'll have to take the back door. At night, the front is guarded by an Oompa-Loompa named Donny Franco."

Actually, of all the facility's workers, sad-eyed, shiftless Donny was one of the few Eve didn't despise, and she understood, in that bite of her tone, that she was already slipping back into the banter that was her relationship with Charlie at its most functional, that sardonic repartee.

"Not Donny Franco? That poor doof from my old class?"

"One and the same."

"Ha!" Apparently the fact that the people Charlie had left continued to live was some good joke. "What happens if good old Donny Franco finds us breaking and entering?"

"Let's be sure he doesn't find out." This was how they always worked best, she knew, as coconspirators. Even in those tense last years of homeschooling, Eve and Charlie would sometimes take Goliath on joyrides outside Marathon High School and jeer about the poor saps spending their days bedraggled and backpack strapped.

Charlie, creeping up to the dim building, did a cat burglar thing on his tiptoes. As she watched her son make a caper scene out of the place in which she had suffered all those years, Eve had to hold back another frenzy of laughter. But what about the Eve of three hours ago, the Eve of a silent decade, the Eve who had waited there as Charlie chased his fantasies in New Hampshire and New York City? Motherly love was no sentimental thing. It was irrefutable and unsparing, a squad of riot police mindlessly clubbing the protestor, no matter how righteous her cause.

"We do have fun, don't we?" Eve said. "When we get together, I mean."

"When do we get together?"

Inside, the same linoleum-floored, plastic-bumpered hallways Eve had walked six days a week for the last nine and a half years. But with the halls now dim, with Charlie flattening himself to the walls, it was both Crockett State and a funny dream of it. Three turns later, Eve paused to snicker at her own hand as she grasped the cool steel handle to the room that held Bed Four. She turned to Charlie, the humor of their little break-in vanished. Waiting for whatever Eve might say, Charlie looked very young. Down the hall, one of the dementia cases screamed at no one, "Happy birthday to you! Happy birthday to you!"

"He won't look like you remember. It's important that you know that. You have to picture the worst, okay? I need you to do that for me right now. Before we go in."

To her surprise, Charlie obeyed. He closed his eyes, and she could see them moving behind the lids. It occurred to Eve that she had never before seen someone so clearly, so self-seriously *imagining*, and she wondered if just maybe, some later day, she might ask Charlie if she could read some of the pages he had been writing.

"Okay," he said.

Eve turned the handle, pressed it open, and then there they were, all together again. Oliver's bed was silhouetted in the moonlight, making the body it held look like something from a myth, a mute oracle, some blind seer from a legend. That new bed that the facility had bought, a mechanized contraption that was supposed to ward off pressure sores, inhaled, sighed.

Eve felt along the metal rim of the bedside lamp and when she found the switch, she nearly gasped at what it revealed. Her son's face, the face she had seen each day, seen afresh through Charlie's eyes. Hair gone thin at the crown, jaw clenched and thick, skin like flaking parchment. But then, under the brightness of the warm bulb, Oliver's eyes did the one ordinary thing they could still do. His eyelids fluttered open—an instinctive reflex, the doctor had told her, reptile brain circuitry, but for the length of a single swift inhalation, it never seemed that way to Eve. Even this evening, it seemed that Oliver's gaze might at last fix on her own.

"Oliver," Charlie said. "It's me."

Over the last four days, Eve had slept maybe twelve hours, but after she showed Charlie to the bedroom she'd tried to throw together for him—not really a bedroom, just four walls with a shadeless lamp standing on a milk crate and an old mattress she had optimistically salvaged from Zion's Pastures in the unlikely case of such a visit—she willed herself to stay awake for a full hour after Charlie's shuffling, creaking noises down the hall fell silent. For the two waking hours he had spent in the house, half of Eve's thoughts had been on the bin in her attic, as if their contents might somehow suddenly come blurting out into the room. Her own telltale heart, beating overhead instead of from below. Not like she had any answer for what to do about the vexing throb of it, but she felt she must pay it a visit, double-check to make sure its padlocks were secure. And so she crept from bed to the bathroom, worrying over each creak and pop of the cheap floor-ing material beneath the balding Berber carpet. She pulled the cord, triggering the hidden door in the ceiling, and the collapsible staircase unfolded.

You don't keep your sanity amid the chaos of a family of boys without a good sense of order, and let Charlie say what he would about Eve now, but even he couldn't deny that she was always a dili-gent organizer. Her attic—a room bursting at the seams with Pink Panther insulation, funky with dry rot—she had neatly divided into two sections, subdivided into a great number of plastic bins. The room's left half: the Past, the boxes she had not opened once since her move, the boxes containing the remnants of Zion's Pastures she couldn't bear to throw away. Mostly the tired Texan heirlooms belonging to the Loving family—those rusting knives, sun-bleached photographs of Jed's nameless ancestors, and enough shellacked horns, skulls, femurs, and hooves to represent an entire herd. She'd never had any use for those boxes, but she was grateful for her decision to schlep all that junk to Desert Splendor so there was something up there to distract from the sight of the one great bin, sitting alone in the attic's other half, representing the Future.

Not the actual future. Eve knew that, she did. Only the future her hands still hoped for her son. For some reason, she was relieved to find that all of those objects—an avalanche of cheap electronic devices and DVDs, hardcover editions of sci-fi and fantasy masterpieces, shrink-wrapped desk sets, a hundred pens, several outfits growing outdated and unworn—just as she had left them, beneath a lid fastened with two padlocks. But then it occurred to her that rather than keeping anyone, keeping Charlie, from discovering her purloined bounty, the locks—along with the solitary prominence of the bin— would draw attention, should her snooping son go snooping once more. And so she silently strained to bury the Future beneath the Past. After ten minutes of this activity, when one of the boxes settled, it released a terrible bellow from the pressed wood floorboards, and she panicked. Like some girl past curfew, she raced back to her bedroom and shut the door softly, hoping that her son had not heard.

And there in bed, checking her phone before turning out the lights, Eve discovered a litany of messages waiting for her, the area codes unfamiliar. "Shit," Eve whispered, but she was hardly surprised. In a place like the Big Bend, where change is measured in geological time, any remarkable news spread over the dry, impermeable land like flash flooding. These foreign numbers might have confused Eve had she not already stood there once before, blindfolded before the firing line of journalistic inquiry. On the night of November fifteenth, Eve had gone from a woman few people thought to notice to some sort of spectacle; for a week or two *after,* she had become a kind of tragic actress, taking the stage each time she walked into the hospital parking lot, the electronic vultures descending, those news scavengers who fed on human tears. Eve couldn't know who might have spoken to the press about Oliver's latest test, and looking at those numbers, she still felt no kindness toward the reporters, whose curiosity this time was not about her family's tragedy but about the astounding news leaked by some gossipy Crockett State employee. The world was always happy to unveil a new cruelty, and here was one of the cruelest: Eve was so deeply alone where she needed help and so public in the parts of her life she wanted to keep to herself.

There were, in fact, a few things Eve had kept to herself, kept even from the one boy to whom she had otherwise granted almost unfiltered access to her inner life. She had not told Oliver, and certainly not Charlie, the glum report Margot Strout offered her after her first day of work at Bed Four, last Friday, just as she had not told anyone about a strange exchange she'd had with Dr. Frank Rumble.

"Can I speak with you for a minute? In my office?" Dr. Rumble had been hanging around just outside Oliver's door; it seemed that he had been waiting there for Eve to exit. He actually grasped the sleeve of Eve's blouse, as if he would drag her into his office if necessary. And there, among the potted cacti and vintage phrenology busts, Dr. Rumble did not even sit in his armchair. He spoke with Eve in a corner, in a hurried whisper, as though the place might be bugged.

"Just so that we're absolutely clear here, I did tell you that you should get a second opinion. Years ago. Remember? I did tell you. That's the truth."

"The truth?" Eve asked. "The truth is that you've spent nine and a half years telling me that there was no chance. That Oliver was gone. The truth is that I'm the only one who ever believed any differently."

Dr. Frank Rumble was the sort of windy old West Texan made for porch sitting, reflecting on the past with a tumbler of whiskey. A dull, circumspect man, as if the business of his life were already behind him. But just now Eve couldn't find the expected pleasure at seeing this outmoded incompetent, her son's chief jailer, so ruffled. His panic scared her.

"Jesus Christ, Frank, what's this all about, anyway? You worried you're going to lose your job or something?"

"Eve," Dr. Rumble said. "That officer. Manuel Paz. He came by this morning with a bunch of questions for me. Why not do the tests earlier? Why didn't you take him for another test? How could this have happened? He was talking to me like I was some criminal."

"Manuel Paz came to speak with you?" How long had it been since Eve had seen Manuel? Four months, maybe more. To think of Manuel's troubled, helpless gaze, trained so often on Oliver over the years: it now gave her a little jolt of panic.

"I mean," Dr. Rumble said, "what is the man possibly thinking?"

"I haven't the foggiest," Eve said, but the opposite was true.

Over that decade, in the absence of any real explanation for the events of that night, Manuel had related to Eve a number of the outlandish notions the townspeople had offered him, each more pathetically grasping than the last: supposedly Hector Espina was the nephew of some billionaire cartel boss in Juarez, and it was the cartel that had ordered the hit. Supposedly Hector Espina had been involved in a closeted romance with Roy Lopez, and he had aimed to silence Roy before anyone found out. "Just last week," Manuel once told her with a sigh, "I had Nicholas York's father in my office, swearing to me with a straight face that he had reason to believe that Hector had recently converted to Islam." Still, with that unbreakable patience of his, Manuel had always promised the people of Bliss that he would look into whatever crazed notion they presented him.

And yet, the truth was that one day, very long ago, Manuel had come to Oliver's room with a certain line of questions Eve couldn't discount entirely.

"I've got to ask you something," Manuel had told her that afternoon, just a few weeks *after*, when he had invited her to speak with him alone in the hospital conference room. "I'm just going to say it once, and then I'm hoping we can put it behind us. I know this must be the worst time for you."

"Say what once?" Eve had asked.

Manuel had nodded then, some hesitancy snagging in his throat. Manuel Paz, it was true, was not even a lead detective in the case, but—as the official Ranger captain assigned to Presidio County and a lifelong Bliss township resident—it was his glum face that was most often featured in the already waning news coverage that played on the waiting room television.

"I guess my question is about Rebekkah Sterling," Manuel said.

"Rebekkah?" Eve asked, as if that were a new word to her.

"Their teacher," Manuel said, "Mrs. Schumacher, she says Oliver and Rebekkah had a little friendship."

"So what is it you are saying?"

"I'm just wondering how well they knew each other. If their relationship might have been romantic in nature. Oliver and Rebekkah."

"And this is what you called me from his room to ask. This is what you needed to speak with me about in private."

Manuel shifted his weight in one of the hospital's lousy armchairs then, the thing squawking desperately, as if a small and displeased family of field mice lived in the hinges of the undercarriage.

"Eve," Manuel said. "Far as I'm concerned? Hector Espina was evil itself. Worse. Probably can't ever know his reasons, if you could even call them reasons. But it wasn't just those three kids, there also was poor Oliver, and doesn't that seem odd to you? That Oliver was there when it happened. I'm just trying to know why."

"I thought," Eve said, "that the story here was that this was some crazy kind of point Hector was making. For the way we had treated your people. That's what practically every other person is saying, anyway."

"*My people,*" Manuel said a little darkly. "Sure. That's what they're saying, but the thing just don't seem to add up for me. For example, what about the fact that Mr. Avalon himself was half-Mexican, that

Roy Lopez's folks came from Bolivia? Anyway, far as we can tell, that kid never raised a protesting word of any kind."

"So what's *your* theory then?"

"You know what one of those Marfa guys Hector dealt to told me? A young man, this burnout named Ken, he told me Hector got a little obsessed with Ken's girlfriend. The whole thing ended in some fistfight when Hector tried to make a move on the girl. Couldn't bear the rejection. And you know what they tell a detective on day one? Past behavior's the best predictor of the future. Jealousy seems to have been the kid's problem more than some sort of politics."

"And all of this has exactly what to do with Oliver?"

"Thing is, a couple students came to me, swearing they saw Hector Espina talking with Rebekkah out in the parking lot a couple weeks before. And then there's the fact that every other kid in the whole school was down in the gymnasium except for Oliver. Just the Theater Club kids, and also Oliver. And Rebekkah, coming out of that night without a scratch? And so it occurs to me that if Rebekkah and Hector really did know each other, then it also makes me wonder if just maybe there was some kind of, I don't know, love triangle situation there. With Oliver."

"So you are telling me that my son was *what*? That he was some kind of *reason*? A reason that a madman murdered those children?"

"I'm not telling you anything. I'm just asking a question," Manuel said.

"Oh," Eve said. "Oh," the strike of a match, the wind of her outrage blowing too hard for any coherent sentence to catch.

"Eve—"

"Manuel, I really don't have time for this. My son never did a single bad thing in his life, and he needs me, and so I'm going to go back to him now."

"Okay. That's fine. And I know. No one is saying anything bad about Oliver, of course not. But maybe if there's a chance to at least shed a bit more light—"

"Why don't you just ask Rebekkah if you have questions?" Eve asked. "Or Jed, for that matter?"

"We have. The girl doesn't want to talk with us much, can't say as I blame her. But she says she hardly knew Oliver. And she swears to us up and down that she'd never met Hector before, and truth is we don't got much evidence to the contrary. Just a couple kids claiming they saw the two of them together, but people are making all sorts of claims these days. And as for Jed, let's just say that conversation with you is a little more, um, fruitful. Can hardly understand the poor man, slurring so much."

"Rebekkah Sterling is practically a stranger to me. Jed invited her over to watch the meteorites once. Oliver knew her from class. I remember they had some study group they did together, but as far as I know that was it. End of story. There you have your answer."

Manuel rubbed his head like a crystal ball as he gazed at the tabletop. "I wish. An answer. I need it, the whole town does. You must've heard about those protests Donna Grass and her group are doing out at the school now? Jail the Mexicans, send us all back across the river, that sort of thing. All day long, my telephone rings, everybody has an opinion, some of them treat me like I myself was in cahoots with that monster. Me! Like I haven't been a neighbor to those folks their whole lives." Manuel concluded this monologue with his shoulders slung low, as if each word had been another pound piled onto his back.

"I wish I could help you, I do. Of course I do. But the town's business isn't exactly my foremost concern right now. Speaking of which, I really do have to get back to Oliver now."

Manuel snorted long and slow, a dispirited bull. He nodded into his hands.

"You're right. I'm sorry to bother you with all this. I am." Manuel reached across the table for Eve's arm then. His touch practically melted through her shirt material. "I couldn't be more sorry. I just need to find—I don't know, something. Those detective folks from Austin might not stick around long, but I won't ever stop. I promise you that. Follow every lead I can, even if they lead nowhere at all. I won't ever quit this thing, I promise you that."

Nearly ten years later, Eve couldn't now remember exactly what had followed that day at the hospital. Perhaps Manuel had asked her more questions; maybe she had wept on his shoulder. Eve knew she had not lied to Manuel—replaying this conversation in her mind, Eve could give herself a passing grade for technical correctness. But of course there was a reason that exchange had stained her memory so indelibly. Eve might have mentioned to Manuel those little "study group" meetings Oliver conducted with Rebekkah, but she had neglected to describe the way Oliver had spent whole weekends brooding in his cave fort, nor had she mentioned the splinter of ice that had lodged in Eve's heart when she had watched that girl disappear into the shadows that night on the television screen.

But her son, Eve knew, was a victim, an innocent, and she wouldn't let Manuel Paz make him into some character in Hector's demented story. Let Hector's story die with him, she had thought, why did that murderer deserve anyone's consideration, what quote unquote *closure* could it bring? Let the townspeople have their stories; there was only one story Eve believed, the one in which Oliver came back to her at last.

Over the years, when Eve had occasionally found her thoughts catching on snatches of that long-ago conversation she'd had with Manuel, she told herself: *Ancient history, what could it matter?* Any random detail from those worst weeks, she had learned, was the molehill that her decade of anxiety could make into a mountain. And yet, Eve knew there was another reason she hadn't told Manuel the whole truth that day in the conference room. The fact was that Oliver had tried to speak with her about Rebekkah, just once, in the last days *before*. "I don't even know where to begin to tell you about her," Oliver had said haltingly one night, as Eve sat in a motherly pose, resting one hand on his arm. And Eve's reply? "Believe me," she had told her son, "with certain people, it's better if you don't even try to understand."

At the time Eve had thought: *Let girls, heartbreak, all that fitful longing come later.* He was still just a boy, after all. Still, why hadn't she just shut her mouth for once and listened? What might her son have had to tell her?

But it wasn't really Eve who had ended that conversation with Oliver before it had even begun, just as it wasn't quite Eve who had not told the whole truth to Manuel that day in the conference room. It was that lesser, former version of herself that Eve still housed beneath her skin, a timid, needy, nutrient-deprived creature who had grown mothlike in the dimness and stuffiness of the cramped rooms of her childhood. That girl, gone frail with solitude, simply could not bear it, perhaps would not even survive the possibility that Manuel might come back to her with another kind of story, one in which she might have listened to Oliver that evening, one in which she might have done something that could have changed what happened.

But now, Eve knew, Manuel would believe he had some actual reason to hope the impossible questions of the years might find an explanation, as if all the answers for what happened that night really had been sleeping there with Oliver all this time and now he might finally make his reply. But of course Eve knew better. Eve had received a thorough schooling on the outlandish designs your futile hopes could spin, and she knew that this notion was just another fantasy Manuel was letting himself believe. And yet, the enormity of that possibility was like a pillow pressed over her face: a little writhing panic, and then she was asleep.

CHAPTER ELEVEN

She woke the next morning to the truckish noise of her vacuum cleaner whirring downstairs in the living room. Behind the stack of manuscript pages (already a week overdue, and she hadn't even started her copyedits) for The Holy Light's latest offering, *Jesus Is My BFF*, the glowing digits of her alarm clock showed 7:04.

After the visit to Crockett State, when at last they made it to Desert Splendor, Charlie had staggered around the rooms, drunk with exhaustion. But now Eve went downstairs to behold a borderline-fantastical vision. Charlie, down on his knees, a cowboy bandanna tied Rosie the Riveter–style over his head, his good hand working the undercarriage of a moldy love seat with the silver arm of the Eureka's attachment.

"This place, Ma . . ." Charlie was standing now, in front of the industrial-gray bricks of the fireplace, a vertical pavement that led up to a vault of fissures in the plaster above. The two second- or third-hand sofas sat with their spattered maroon pillows like the corpses of some monstrous species. The coffee table was a pane of dusty glass, holding a half-dozen mugs, their contents skinned with mold. It hadn't occurred to Eve to clean up for Charlie, so blinded was she by the miraculous brightness on the fMRI display.

"I know," Eve told Charlie. "Believe me. If there were any other choice."

"It's like a McMansion after the nuclear winter. Holocaust in the 'burbs."

"Well put, dear boy."

"It's full of dirt!" Charlie said cheerily. "It's coming in through the windows! And those big cracks in the ceiling? I had no idea you were living like this."

"You wouldn't."

"Well. I've been cleaning."

"I don't need you to clean."

"You're welcome. Oh, hey!" Charlie extracted his phone from his pocket, displayed its lit screen to his mother. NEW TEST SHOWS SHOOTING VICTIM—

"Apparently," he said with a big hungry grin, "word about Oliver has gotten out. I have a Google alert for his name, and my e-mail this morning? Jesus. A miracle, they're all saying. No one seems to mention the next test he's got coming, what we still don't know."

"I guess a miracle is what everyone around here needs."

"But it's not just around here! It was in the *Houston* fucking *Chronicle*! A short thing, but still."

"Tell me about it. When I checked my phone last night, you should have seen all the calls I'd missed."

"Are you going to return them?"

"Don't see why I would."

"Don't see why you would?" Charlie turned away, became an unreadable silhouette in the window. But the view out there, the lumber skeletons of the half-built neighboring McMansions, seemed to explain something to him.

"How about we go out for a breakfast?" Charlie said. "Something cheap. Obviously. Café Magnolia? Not so far from here, right?"

"I really don't see why it's worth the money. I have eggs."

It required an almost surgical effort for Charlie to reach into the pocket of his skintight jeans and extract a single battered twenty-dollar bill. Charlie held his crumpled twenty in a way that the Statue of Liberty holds her torch, as if his independence had just been affirmed by a foreign nation. "My treat," Charlie said.

An hour later, they were among the beaded curtains and half-blinded strands of Christmas lights inside Café Magnolia. They sat at opposite sides of the same wonky laminate table—with its chipped, beatific face of Our Lady of Guadalupe—which they'd claimed as their favorite fifteen years before. The same woman, Ana Maria, brought Charlie his huevos rancheros and tortilla soup. Eve could see Charlie's face relaxing, as if his smug, urbane mien were bound up by a series of internal ties, undone by the invisible fingers of chipotle spice and fatty queso that fluttered through Café Magnolia.

As Eve carefully shelled her boiled eggs and Charlie bolted his beans and tortillas, Charlie attempted to scandalize his mother with some of his New York tales. The boys he had dated. Terrance, Christopher, Bradley—on and on. Charlie was putting on a real show of his New York self, come alive once the cloistered dimness of Café Magnolia eliminated the desert outside, restoring him to a Brooklyn atmosphere. At one point, Charlie actually told Eve, "That boy has a body like forked lightning." Eve couldn't decide if Charlie was telling her these things to make a point, to try to squeeze a few vindicating drops of conservative disapproval from a mother who in truth had always enjoyed an outsider's pride at having a son whose unorthodox romantic inclinations she'd never once questioned. Or was this only the way he now told his stories to people he liked? She tracked his eyes, looking for the answer, but they were turned up and away, as he held forth into the mid-distance, as if his stories took place only in his mind (a mother could hope).

Eve was trying now to do the thing she knew a mother ought to do to a child's reports of his adult life. She tried to nod along encouragingly; she tried to remind herself of the perfectly rational conclusion she had come to over the years, that Charlie had no choice but to leave and make a life for himself away from the traumas of his late childhood. And yet, that insecure girl Eve still carried inside her wouldn't be persuaded. That needy teen even still worked the gears and pulleys of Eve's heart, manufacturing her own conclusions: that it was not the Big Bend that Charlie had needed to flee. Like Jed and Eve's own father, it was just Eve herself who Charlie had wanted to escape.

"Well, that's enough salaciousness for me," Eve said.

Charlie's face fell, as if, chastened, he might actually be ashamed. "There's something I haven't told you yet," he said.

"All right."

"It's not the hugest deal. Promise you won't make a huge deal about this, okay?"

"Tell me what it is first." Eve was feeling suddenly afraid.

"The thing is just that I need to borrow some money."

"Money?"

"The green stuff? With the presidents on it?"

"You need to borrow money for *what*?"

Charlie made his furniture-hefting sigh. "You have to know that things haven't been going so well. With the writing, I mean."

"And money figures into this how exactly?"

"I'm behind on rent. A few months. I owe some money, Ma. That's it. That's my whole story. So help me God."

Eve glanced at his arm in the cast, his lower lip, still as thick as a gherkin. She held a hand to her face. "You owe money to *who*?"

"Don't freak out. It's not even so much. It's only five thousand. Nothing next to what I'll get when I finish."

"Five thousand. Are you insane? I mean it, Charlie. I think you must be mentally ill to be asking me for five thousand dollars right now. Do you think I *choose* to drive that car? That I *choose* to live in that house?"

"All right."

"I'm sorry, but no. No! Why should I finance something I never wanted you to do in the first place?"

Charlie considered the plaster on his wrist and tucked his arm away, like an embarrassment.

"I don't know, Ma. Maybe you'd do it to support your son."

Honestly, she couldn't help pitying the boy a little, but Eve had thought and thought about it; she had even listened patiently to Charlie's many caffeinated diatribes about his "work," but all she had ever been able to register was the troubling possibility that Charlie had taken after the worst of his father, making of New York City his own profitless cabin. And she could locate no explainable reason for Charlie's project other than the obvious and appalling fact of his use of their family tragedy to kick-start a career.

"Typically," Eve told Charlie, "in financial negotiations, you don't berate the lender. Anyway, I don't have it. Even if I could, what, enable you, I don't have it. How about you ask your father for once?"

"Don't be cruel."

"I'm being realistic."

"Yeah, right. Like Pa would have the cash. It's a wonder he can keep himself fed." Charlie's face went a little purple. *Pa:* the first time he had said the word to his mother, possibly in years. "And, anyway," Charlie said, surprising her by grabbing her hand, "I'd never turn to the dark side, no matter how much dough Darth Vader offered me."

"He's not Darth Vader, Charlie. He's just a sad little man who can't help himself."

"So now it's Pa you are suddenly standing up for?"

"No," Eve said. "It's not."

As chance would have it, Eve did have the money. According to her last statement from West Texas Savings and Loan, her account contained $7,817, and she had another fifteen hundred headed her way, five hundred from the governor's fund, a thousand if she could only make her eyes focus on the absurdist parables of *Jesus Is My BFF*, in which the savior offered advice to the teenager contemplating an offered joint, a sweating can of beer, a racy post on social media. But Eve possessed other numbers, too, which she had so often felt for, like scabs. More than five years was how long Charlie had been gone. Nine times was how many times he had phoned her in the last twelve months. Nearly two thousand now: that was how many times she had visited Crockett State in Charlie's absence.

The next meeting with Margot Strout was scheduled for nine that morning, and by the time they left the café, Eve was horrified to find it was already 8:50. Outside, in the gathering heat, Goliath hacked and grunted, like a drifter prodded awake with a bully club. Eve was wondering if she should have told Jed about this meeting; she was more than a little furious at him for seeming to have no discernible interest in the aftermath of the wonderful thing he had witnessed with her. Out the windows, the dross chaparral and prickly pear studded the flat all the way to the end of the planet.

After a tetchy, silent twenty minutes, Charlie began to slither around in the passenger seat, contorting himself to reach for the phone vibrating in his pocket. He extracted it, looked at whatever flashed into its screen in the way he once looked, as a child, at a juice glass he had dropped and shattered. "What?" Eve asked, "Who is it?" In a trembling hand, Charlie turned its glowing face toward her, the name written in bright Arial font.

"*Rebekkah Sterling?*" Eve said. "Rebekkah Sterling is calling you *now*?" Charlie considered the phone for a moment, but the name vanished, the screen gone black. He shook the thing, as if it had malfunctioned.

"I guess she must have heard the news?" he said, as if to himself.

"How does she even have your number? You and Rebekkah are in touch?"

"Not really," Charlie said, his voice thin. "I called her up a couple times when I got to New York. Thought she might like to know she had another hometown kid in the city. But she didn't seem to want anything to do with me."

"So what could she want now?" was all Eve could think to ask. Eve glanced in the direction of her son, the stones and ocotillo outside blurred by Goliath's velocity and also by the face grease that Charlie, in his forlorn prison-yard stares, had already deposited on the passenger-side window. But Charlie did not reply, only shrugged timidly at the glass. She kept her eyes on Charlie for a dangerous duration, needing to see what this missed call had done to his face, but he wouldn't look at her. Rebekkah Sterling, or at least her name, back into Eve's life: horrible to think that the girl still existed, somehow galling that Rebekkah refused to remain what she had become to Eve, just a distant memory of a body walking off into the shadows, a hundred unanswered questions, sealed away in a past. Even now, she tried and failed to come up with a way to phrase the question thrumming inside her: What, exactly, had Charlie hoped to accomplish in speaking with Rebekkah Sterling? Eve reached for the radio, cranked up its staticky music: 93.3, The Golden Oldies. The station happened to be playing Bob Dylan, "Like a Rolling Stone." Eve and Charlie looked at one another at last, their gaze meeting for less than a second.

The sun was already high in the sky, pinning their shadows to the asphalt beneath their feet in the Crockett State parking lot. The oils and sour cream topping of Café Magnolia's tortilla soup, a few spoonfuls of which Eve insanely let herself eat at Charlie's urging, made magmatic progress through her belly as they paced down the Crockett State halls. At Oliver's room, Eve blinked rapidly at the sight of the open door.

"Manuel?"

"Eve. And is that Charlie? My Lord, get a look at you."

"Hiya. Look too long and it'll cost you."

"Har har," Manuel said.

Texas Ranger Captain Manuel Paz stood from the extra chair someone had deposited in the room. Eve sensed that their arrival had interrupted something. Margot flushed in her seat next to the bed as Manuel awkwardly rotated the ecru brim of his Stetson hat over the brass buttons of his uniform. The man now looked so different from the fleshy Ranger who had made his first reports at Bed Four all those years before. Like a blown dandelion, his final wisps of hair had vanished; Manuel had retracted to the hardened, denser form of himself. Frank Rumble, no surprise, was nowhere to be found.

"What are *you* doing here?" Eve asked, letting Manuel give her a little pat of a hug.

"Eve." Manuel pulled away, held her shoulders in his outstretched hands. "My God. I don't know what to tell you. This news."

"Margot Strout, I presume?" Charlie said. "I'm Oliver's brother. I'm Charlie."

"Oh, I remember you, Charlie." Margot brightened, rejected Charlie's offered hand to press his little scarecrow body against herself. "From way back when. And Captain Paz here sure is right. Wow! Now you're a man."

A West Texas conversation of course could not begin before the ritual preliminary niceties. Chatter ensued, mostly just talk of the weather—*can you believe this heat?*—a nonsensical and yet oddly beloved topic for this desert's inhabitants. At one point, Eve heard Margot say, with the adamant sincerity of original thought, "But, really, it's *humidity* that's even worse. At least we don't have *that* to worry about!"

Charlie smiled. "So," he said, "what did we miss?"

"Yes, to the business at hand. Well. I was just telling Captain Paz what I told you on Friday," Margot said to Eve.

"Friday?" Charlie asked his mother. "What did she tell you on Friday?"

Margot paused, felt her bangs, looking between mother and son. "I was just telling Captain Paz," Margot said. "I was just telling him about what I told you I learned in my training program. Over in Austin. About how we learned how people who have been locked in for a few years, how even if their brain function is normal they can still sometimes lose their language." Margot's voice, settling now into the substance of her training, gained confidence. "How language is sort of like a muscle. A use-it-or-lose-it kind of thing. Like we read about those feral children, the ones raised in the woods, and how no amount of civilization could teach them to speak well. But it's more complicated in cases like Oliver's. Sometimes, after a bunch of years, language goes away. But sometimes not. And of course there's still the physical brain damage, which we just can't know about yet, not until they do those next tests, at least."

Out the window, two Border Patrol SUVs blared through the silence that followed, the Doppler effect making whatever immigration emergency they were addressing sound a little silly, Keystone Kops material. Charlie made the furrowed expression of a man puzzling through a credit card statement.

"So what you're saying," Charlie said, "is that if someone had put Oliver in that fMRI thing earlier, it might not have been too late?"

"I'm not saying it's too late now. Only that, yes, if I'm going to be honest, that is a possibility."

"So then it makes me wonder again. Why didn't anyone do that test earlier? It must have been, what, eight years since his last MRI? Nine? Why wouldn't the doctors send him for another one? Get a few other opinions. What was the holdup?"

Margot shrugged, hunching her shoulders as if to diminish her substantial dimensions. But when she raised her head, her gaze on Eve was no longer that of the helpful professional she'd been playing those last days. She looked frank, accusatory. A little bitchy, Eve thought. Squinting at his mother, Charlie's mouth fell open a bit as he began to understand.

"Anyway," Margot said, "all this language stuff is pretty theoretical. Maybe we don't know yet if Oliver can even understand us, but I, for one, am not willing to let the boy wait another day. In cases like Oliver's, it usually takes a lot of fine measurements, a lot of data collection, and a whole lot of frustration. But mostly it takes faith, this sort of work. Faith for now, is what I'm saying, and we can worry about the rest later."

Eve watched the antibiotic liquid in an IV bag gather to a drop, release.

"Have you tried his hands again yet?" Eve asked. "I'm telling you, sometimes he can move the left one. Just a little, but I—"

"I just don't get this, Ma. I can't." Charlie made a broad gesture with his arms, as if to include Manuel Paz and Margot Strout in some group, as if they had all assembled there today to ask her the same question. "Why wouldn't you *insist* on another opinion? Was it too expensive to take Oliver somewhere else? We could have found the money."

"So now you are an expert on my finances."

"Ma."

Eve felt the trembling report of her soup-inflamed innards, but as her gaze met Charlie's, she strangely calmed, as if they were in some other room together, after this conversation was already long past. "I really don't know what to tell you, Charlie. This whole time, the doctors and nurses kept telling me about brain death, about the thing actually shrinking, withering away. Another opinion. I'm sure it all seems so reasonable to you now, what I should have done. It's a very easy thing to admonish me in retrospect, isn't it? But you are forgetting the days and weeks and months I've spent here. Not you, but me. And? And I just couldn't take any more opinions. All those opinions, those diagnoses, they were killing me. I mean that."

On the far side of the bed, Manuel Paz relaxed into his chair with an empathic sigh. "Of course we can understand that," Manuel said. "It's just like I've always been telling you over the years. Fact is, I can't imagine what I would've done if Oliver were my boy. But anyone could understand that. Ain't that right, Charlie?"

Charlie looked at Manuel for a long while, then nodded faintly, as if reminded of something. He grasped his airfoil of hair with his good hand, shook his head deeply.

"Jesus," Charlie said. "Jesus."

"Listen to me. Listen."

"Eve." A new voice at the door. "Good Lord. Eve!"

"Oh," Eve said. "Doyle. And you brought friends."

At the helm of a procession of the familiar crowd of flower-bearers, Bliss Township's erstwhile principal Doyle Dixon hobbled through the doorway, looking like Mr. Monopoly after a few years of bankruptcy, his mustache now blanched to the sullied whiteness of week-old snow. Donna Grass followed in Doyle's wake, smiling wearily behind piles of carnations. Four of the old teachers were there too, those handsome, blockish ladies, so alike in their sun-dried, earthy cheer that Eve always had a hard time keeping their names straight. Dawson, Henderson, Schumacher, and, yes, Abbie Wolcott. The casserole set who used to stop by Zion's Pastures, of-fering their chicken cacciatores and Tupperware tubs of enchiladas along with fistfuls of bromides: "God's plan for each of us reveals itself in time," and "The only way up is forward," and "What Charlie needs most is a little normalcy." Those women who spent their whole frumpish lives within a hundred miles of their birthplace and so could never understand the decisions of a woman like Eve, a woman from nowhere who made her own choices about what was best for her and her family. They were making a big display of it now, expos-ing their too-bright teeth as they laughed and hugged all the air out of the room.

"Can it really be true?" Doyle said, once he emancipated Eve from his marsupial grasp. "And Charlie? Could that be Charlie Loving?"

"Why does nobody believe it?"

"I believe it. But what a handsome young man you've become."

Oh, Eve could believe it, too. Here, after all, was inviolable evi-dence that Charlie was still Charlie. All it took was the simplest compliment to recalibrate his attitude entirely. Eve's cold-eyed accuser was presently grinning through a blush.

And now Eve watched Mrs. Dawson, Mrs. Wolcott, Mrs. Schu-macher, and Mrs. Henderson mass around the bed, arranging their cheap glass vases, reaching out their hands for Oliver's arms, greet-ing Manuel with overlong embraces. Eve really couldn't take it; she left her boys to the casserole set and drifted aimlessly through the hallways.

After long minutes, she found herself in the most distant wing of Crockett State, filled with teddy bears, cheery classroom poster encouragements (LIVE FOR THE DAY! HANG IN THERE!), and the Alzheimer's and Parkinson's cases making doodles of their spittle, swearing at nothing, yawning in the sanitized air. Above a stooped, wheelchair-bound lady, picking with great ardor at a scab on her thumb, a bulletin board showed a cartoon thermometer wiping his sweaty brow, his speech bubble saying, TODAY'S SEASON: SUMMER! TODAY'S TEMPERATURE: TOO HOT! The indignity that her son was made to live with these geriatrics was as fresh as ever.

She was hallways away now, but still the image was before her: Charlie grasping his head, his appalled face shaking. The life of a caregiver, Eve had learned, was built upon an unsteady earth, pocketed with many sinkholes. To keep the floor of your sanity from giving way, there were many places you must not step, many thoughts against which you must not rest your weight too heavily. But her rash, accusatory son had a knack for staving in that delicate material, showing her Rebekkah Sterling's name on his telephone screen, demanding on his very first morning back home for Eve to account for the decisions she'd made while he was gone. And now there was the worst thought again, opening beneath her. It was nothing but love and faith, nothing but goodness that guided her years by her son's hospital bed, Eve knew that. And yet, in all of Eve's fretful procrastination in scheduling a better test for her son at better hospitals, might she also have chosen her own hope over the results she couldn't bear to know? But what else, she wanted to yell at Charlie, could she have been expected to do?

Eve had made her way back to Oliver's room now, where she found the whole good-tidings party shuffling out into the hall, a noxious blast of floral-patterned dresses and toothsome grins. They continued to chat among themselves, their eyes ringed with happy tears. Doyle said something funny in a low voice, and the whole group guffawed, a laughter louder, Eve was sure, than those hallways had known for years. Charlie briefly turned back to the commotion.

"We have to leave Margot to do her work," Charlie said. "Principal Dixon was just telling me about this new path up at Lost Mine Mountain, offered to give me a ride there."

"The park?" Eve asked. "How will you get home?"

"Should be able to hitch a ride." Charlie shrugged jauntily. "I'll call if I need you. But I won't."

Maybe she and Charlie never would be able to understand each other. Her son was a boy so unlike her, a boy who could so easily engage in happy chatter with Doyle, the sort of conversation Eve herself had declined dozens of times over the years. Charlie was a boy who had found a way to transform himself into the dull, unbothered good cheer of the world's people, its seven billion Hendersons, Schumachers, Wolcotts, and Dawsons. In truth, Eve envied him. "You enjoy yourself," she said.

CHAPTER TWELVE

Hours later, when she stopped her car outside the Marathon electronics store, Eve told herself she would only look into a new set of headphones for Oliver to wear at night. And yet, inside the hangar hugeness, Roy Orbison's "Only the Lonely" burbling through the speakers, she found the good, pillow-ringed headphones were locked behind glass cases, each price tag another little obscenity. It seemed one too many cruelties. Was there anyone who needed such headphones more, anyone who could afford them less?

And soon Eve found herself drifting to the back of the place, following the circuit her boys used to make when she'd bring them there for an hour of consumerist envy. As if an antidote to the antediluvian way they lived at Zion's Pastures, Charlie and Oliver had always wanted to bathe themselves in the cool blue light of high-end electronics, run their hands over magical technologies that couldn't be theirs. "Just imagine how much more quickly I could write," Oliver once said, "If I had a computer like *this*." Oliver had pointed to things that didn't even look like computers to Eve, more like spacecraft for a race of diminutive aliens. She had always hoped to save enough money to present him one of these as a birthday present.

Today, when Eve put her hands on one of those portable computers, its cool curvilinear metal restored to her fingers that old feeling.
It began as the most pitiful sort of indignity, that the object that could
have made her son a little happier had been there in his hands but
wholly inaccessible to him. She was equal parts indignant and grateful that all the laptops were securely tethered to their display table by
those electronic ropes that Eve at least had the good sense never to
mess with. She left the computer section behind and walked back to
the front of the store. The brightness out the sliding doors was only
a few yards away.

But there, on the glass-top customer service counter, a computer
shone, in its cool silver promise, the exact model that she had just
been fingering in the back of the store. It was noon, and the red-
shirted employees were gathered behind an open door, eating their
brown-bagged sandwiches. No one was looking at her at all.

And so Eve had to wonder: How could it not have been a test? The
exact laptop she had been admiring, left for some reason unboxed
and without security tags at customer service, whose employees were
preoccupied by lunch. A part of her, of course, knew that it was no
test, only a coincidence. But as she fixed her gaze on the brushed
metal casing, it seemed to have come down to this, as it always did.
Did she believe in her son's future or not? Did she still believe in that
better future, the one she had never quite been able to give her boys,
in which they could have whatever it was they needed? Would she
take the plunge, follow her conviction, or obey the opinions of the
world and let Oliver rot? And could it have been a coincidence that
the present symbol of this dilemma, the object in question, was a
computer on which Oliver might someday begin the career he had
imagined? And would—

One of the red shirts in the break room stood, began to wad his
paper sack. Eve didn't have time to consider. She watched her hands
clutch the laptop by its perfect sculpted corner and slip it into the
wide maroon leather purse that, three years prior, she had selected

from a rack at Sears to assist in her thieving. She was already back in
the dense, hot air outside before she regained control of her body and
commanded it to take a breath.

"You're okay," she said.

Eve was driving, trembling, on the far side of the speed limit down
the sun-hammered highway. Her purse was on the passenger's seat,
some light embedded in the metallic casing glowing in the rhythm of
deep sleep. Eve knew enough about computers to know this meant
the machine was still on, in sleep mode, and she panicked as if it were
a living thing, a kidnapped child snatched from his crib who would
cry out when he woke in this strange car. She reached for the purse
straps and tossed the bag into the backseat. Down the highway, a
dust devil manically wrote its signature over the cracked concrete.

Eve's body registered the outward manifestations of shame for
what she'd just done—the fiery forehead, the excoriating blush—but
inwardly this shame went unacknowledged. How was it, even still,
that Jed was not present to keep her from becoming the kind of toxic
person who could swipe someone's computer? Oh, on a day like
today, she needed chaos, upheaval, a breach, and she wasn't done yet.
Forty minutes later, Eve found herself turning Goliath through the
streets of the town she most despised in the five thousand square
miles of the Big Bend.

And Eve soon discovered that the ironic smugness that was Marfa,
Texas, had only deepened in the years since she last visited. The old
derelict warehouses and big-rig filling stations were now done up
like urban lofts, all windows and poured concrete, a few meaningless
studies of geometric forms visible in their wide, otherwise empty innards. At lunchtime, some sort of hipster commissary, next to the old
train station, served the bearded, tattooed, hardware-studded populace
out of a battered taco truck. In front of the Victorian courthouse—a
limestone, cupola-festooned building out of a storybook of Old Time
Texas—stood a temporary sculpture park, the centerpiece of which

was a twenty-foot cast-iron statue, in the rough-hewn style of Auguste Rodin, of a human vagina. A man wearing a knit cap and a modish woman's librarian glasses presently emerged from the labial folds of this monstrosity, waving to a girl with a camera. The guy was shouting something as if there were an emergency. "It's a boy!"

So this was where her husband chose to live. In their few "dinners," Eve always brought Jed back with her to Desert Splendor, and she dreaded now to see how her husband might be living, a feral creature wallowing in the muck of his own wrecked life.

The Wild Man of the Navidad: one of her late mother-in-law's favorite stories. Nunu had liked to relate this hokey legend about a supposed monster born of the filth in the Navidad River. A giant made of mud, a kind of Texan golem who, according to Nunu, had haunted the first settlers of West Texas, lighting out on midnight pillagings, murdering livestock and children, conducting sexual abductions, setting homesteads ablaze. Eve was never as interested as her boys in this sort of hoary lore, and she might not have remembered this tale at all had Nunu not mentioned another name for this Wild Man, the name given to him by the old slaves of Texas. "They called him The Thing That Comes," Nunu said in her best spooky campfire voice, and that phrase had stuck. In Eve's life *before,* The Thing That Comes was the name she'd come to give it, the monster of mud that often came for Jed, stealing him off to some sodden blackness from which it could take him weeks to fight his way free. Eve called it The Thing That Comes just as Jed called it "art," just as a therapist might simply name it "clinical depression." The Thing That Comes, of course, was a creature she knew well, from a childhood spent in the passenger seat of Morty Frankl's Cutlass Supreme.

Indeed, after a past like hers, Eve had to consider that perhaps it was that same foul monster who had first delivered her to Jed. Even in their delirious first weeks together, in that space she had rented above a bank in Marathon, Eve had seen that there was something unpinnable, something aloof, something really quite sad about her new boyfriend; for whole hours, even in those best weeks, Jed would go mute, his eyes flitting about, as if spectating the harrowing day-long battle that took place in his mind. From the many similarly grim nights she had passed in her father's company, these silences were familiar to Eve, almost homey. And that was only a small part of what they shared. They had both been their parents' only children. Jed's gruff and punishing father, like Eve's, had died very young; Jed's grand-parents, like her own, were either absent or dead; like Eve, Jed didn't want to talk much about the past. "Every girl I've tried to be with, it was like none of them really saw me," Jed said. "Oh, I see you," Eve told him, slipping her tongue into his mouth. It turned out that she would not have to wander the world alone, after all.

It did not occur to Eve, at least not for a long while, to wonder if Jed's own sadnesses might be quite different from the brand with which she was familiar; she was young and grateful enough then not to consider that his history with the imperious mother he one night introduced her to, a lady dolled up in tulle who called herself Nunu, might be part of the cause. Well, she was only twenty.

But after three years in that far corner of America, her roots began to thread into the hardpan. She got pregnant, and though she wor-ried that a child might double her new mother-in-law's meddling—Eve had already, for example, agreed that if it were a boy, she'd name the child after the famous cattleman Oliver Loving, to whom Nunu claimed her husband had some distant ancestral linkage—when Nunu looked on her grandson for the first time, Eve saw the power had shifted, the crown passed.

"Meet Oliver Loving." Eve propped the infant on her chest. For the first time, Eve recognized the pleasing homophone. *All of Her Loving.*

"Praise be," Nunu said. "A king is born."

When Charles Goodnight Loving was born (yes, the name an-other concession to Nunu, but there was, after all, some folksy charm in giving her boys the names of their state's legendary cowboy part-ners), Nunu grew suddenly gaunt, prone to those monthlong "Nunu time" stays in the Thunderbird Hotel in Alpine, which became her permanent residence in the last years before her death. Back at Zion's Pastures, Eve and Jed, at last with a great topic in common, began to talk more. This, after a half decade of marriage, was how she learned something more of his childhood. "My goodness," Jed said, calming himself after his son emptied a jar of applesauce down his shirt, "they say when you have kids you become your father, but it turns out that having kids is all about trying not to be your father. Takes real oomph." Whatever it was that Jed had to muscle down into the garbage chute of his history, he kept it contained in a way that Eve, with her own bad stories, could still appreciate.

But somewhere down the line, the river monster rose to his beshitten haunches; The Thing That Comes came back for Jed. Jed's artistic voyages into his cabin became weeklong binges. Sometimes Eve pitied him, sometimes she upbraided him, always he nodded. By the time Charlie enrolled in kindergarten, she was raising their boys practically on her own.

And yet, even then, Eve still had something of the pioneer spirit, and she thought that they might find a way to battle The Thing, if only he agreed to try. Once, she brought home from Dr. Platz, their avuncular family physician, a pamphlet entitled *Overcoming Depression,* and she told Jed, "I think you should read this and give it some thought." Lunacy! As if she did not know just what her husband would do with that pamphlet—exactly what he did with any of her directives. He looked at it and nodded.

"I can't do all this alone," she told Jed. "I can't raise two boys by myself."

"You're right," Jed said. "And it's pathetic. I'm pathetic. You win."

"I win? I don't want to *win*. This isn't a competition," Eve said. "I don't even want to fight. I just want you to tell me. Why do you never tell me? What is it that makes this life so horrible to you? Help me understand it."

But there, once more, was that Jed face, almost-spoken confessions darkly clotting his eyes. "Please," Eve said.

Jed was nodding again, of course, as if to validate her need for an answer. But the actual answer Jed offered that night? "I can't understand it myself."

The years went by. The cottonwood tree in the front yard spread its arms, the ocotillo put forth its red flowers, the century plants shot their stems. Nature, too, stretched out her sons, elongating legs, cracking voices, darkening hair, ruddying cheeks. The lines around Eve's eyes deepened; silver threaded from her scalp. *Can't understand* what? She was still arguing with Jed, but only in her mind.

And even still she missed the shape of Jed's body when it failed to materialize next to her in bed. How was it that his distance from her only made her miss him more? Wasn't it pathetic how, even into her late thirties, she carried on like some nervous teen, taking Jed's disappearances as rejection, then wanting so badly to prove that she was worth staying with? She truly hated this thing in her, that attention-starved girl, for whom no closeness could ever disprove the intensive education in unlovableness her father had delivered to her.

For years, her sons—their tiffs, their homework assignments, their wounding by forces beyond her control—were enough to occupy her. Jed's noddings, his disappearances, she never forgave, but the cumulative effects of time and routine could feel not unlike forgiveness. Her boys were the shape of her days, and behind each hour was the impossible prayer that they never grow away from her.

Like some demonic genie, out to prove a cruel point, fate granted Eve her wish, in the most hideous way imaginable, on the night of November fifteenth. Eve clung, with both hands, to Bed Four, but Jed? His alcohol-shaky fists were powerless to battle the monster. He let The Thing carry him off into its mud. He no longer tried to fight his way home. Emptied bottles filled his shed.

"You're right," Jed told her one night. "I should go. I'll leave. Just for a little while, at least."

And even still she wanted to scream at him, *Leave? Why not fight? Why not fight for yourself? Why not fight to stay here with me?* But after half a life, after nineteen years of marriage, she knew her husband well, didn't understand him at all. This time, Eve had been the one to nod.

Eve couldn't remember exactly where Jed lived now. She had driven Charlie to Jed's miserable new place a few times in the first years *after*, and her memories were of a downtrodden ranch house, its chipped siding thronged by a snake nest of vines, somewhere on the west side of town. Eve turned Goliath up and down the same streets half a dozen times before she realized she had been passing it, again and again. It was easy to miss, hidden by a dense and terminal foliage. The vines had spread wildly and died, as if they had choked the house to death, leached all its vital nutrients, and expired. It was the sort of house whose doorbell young boys might dare one another to ring.

But when Eve herself pressed that doorbell, a dozen times over, she heard no report from within. Her knocking produced no reply. She could practically *hear* it echoing off the tired furniture, the stacks of unread magazines, the empty liquor bottles she imagined inside. Something twinkled in the blue sky overhead. A surveillance drone, bound south for the desert. Eve was turning back for the car when a great mechanical sound erupted from the shed ensconced in the dun tufts of grass that crowded the backyard.

"Jed, Jed! Hey there! Jed!"

Glimpsed through the open door of the shed, Jed appeared to be reenacting a scene from *The Texas Chain Saw Massacre*. An industrial ventilation mask covered his mouth like a muzzle; his goggles gave him the eyeless face of an automaton; he wore a thick headset over his ears. Jed drew back the roaring chain saw and drove it deep into whatever metallic material was before him, a swarm of sparks fireflying through the room. Eve had the irrational notion that she had to stop him before he did something drastic. She entered the dank, ferric space, black against the combustive glitter coming off his workbench. She pressed a hand between Jed's shoulders. He startled, and the chain saw slipped his grip, gnawing a few inches across the concrete floor. Jed stooped over it, flipped a kill switch and unmasked himself.

"Eve. What on earth are you doing *here*?"

Jed moved around awkwardly, as if trying to conceal with his body the contents of the shed.

"I don't know," she said. "I thought you might like an update."

Jed wiped his forehead with a filthy denim sleeve, slouched into the wrecked posture of the man she recognized. As her eyes adjusted to the grimed light seeping through the gaps in the shed's wooden slats, Eve received a glimpse of the actual art Jed had been working on. As it turned out, it was not at all like the glum abstract canvases she had imagined. Nothing like his old second-rate van Goghs and Munchs. Suspended from the rafters of the shed were human forms, rendered from strange materials. The rusted bumpers of cars, bones of dead desert animals, barbed wire, food containers. The sort of refuse that littered the region, what the Chihuahuan Desert left behind after the wind and sun, turkey vultures and hyenas all took whatever they could. And no, not just human forms, Eve saw. From the crushed, rotten scapulae Jed had fashioned, each body sprouted rusted wings.

"You're a sculptor now."

"Not really," Jed said. "I don't know what you'd call these things. Sculptures? I'm not so sure. Garbage."

"Garbage angels," Eve said.

"Couldn't have said it better myself."

"These are really quite beautiful. I had no idea."

"The seven archangels."

"It looks like you've got at least two more than that."

"I guess I couldn't stop," Jed said.

The mauled sheet of scrap Jed had been working at—it appeared to be the door to an old-fashioned refrigerator—emitted a strangled moan.

"What are you going to do with them?"

"Do? I don't know." Jed gave Eve a grateful look, full of sad knowledge. "I can't see how anyone would be interested."

"Hey, guess what? Heeee's baaack," Eve said Charlieishly, a line from some campy old horror film.

"Excuse me?"

"Charlie. I called to tell him the news. About the test. Would you believe it? The boy finally bought a bus ticket."

"My God." Jed looked at his angels, shook his head. "Charlie. How is he? I've been wondering and wondering."

"Why don't you go see for yourself?"

Jed didn't reply. The question just hung there for a while between them, like another strange object suspended from the ceiling, the meaning of which neither of them spoke aloud.

"This update," Jed said. "What is it? Something new? With Oliver."

She tried to come up with a few sentences to explain why she had come to Marfa. But Eve's thoughts flew sixty miles southeast, to Margot Strout's second day palpating Oliver for some sign. Words that were no longer words.

"I guess it's not really an update. They are working with him, trying to find a way for him to communicate. No update, really. But I thought I should tell you anyway."

As Jed returned his chain saw to a hook, an odd kind of nostalgia overtook Eve, a nostalgia unlike the usual, not for the sun-bright years when her whole family was with her at Zion's Pastures, but for the glum quietude of her life spent between Desert Splendor and Crockett State, her leftover life that the results of Professor Nickell's fMRI had just ended. That recent time when Eve hadn't had anything very specific to hope for and so her hopes could be vast, a life that was nothing but mother and son and the wild hopes that still bound them together. That time when Oliver had still been all her own. The wind outside the shed rose, whistled through the gaps between the walls' wooden planks. When it passed, the silence was immaculate.

"We've done everything we could for him, haven't we?" Eve heard herself say.

"What do you mean?"

"Oliver. Sometimes I just don't know. Sometimes I wonder if he might have been better off if we had just let him go. Do you ever wonder that? What it must be like for him. Even now."

Eve watched Jed pinch a loose corner of the metal on his table, bend it back. When he turned to her, his face was transformed with a beautiful kind of rage. But standing there with Jed, Eve understood that her question also held another question. The thought that had, from time to time, haunted her from the shadows of her days. Had Jed ever wished Crockett State would do to their son what Crockett State was built to do, to let some infection or act of medical incompetence free them of the decision, free them from the spiral of doubt, self-recrimination, and the arduous numbing grief that was their every day? "You can let go," Eve tried telling Oliver once, repeating that line she'd heard in dozens of movies, horrified to hear how the words sounded in her own mouth. But the part that truly shamed her, and shamed her still, was the corollary that came to her lips as this avowal's logical conclusion: she had added, "please."

"You've done everything you could." Jed made a gavel of his fist, disturbing the little metallic shards on his table. "What else could you have done? What choice did we have? Tell me. I'm all ears."

Eve shrugged. A part of her wanted to shout her agreement, the other part wanted to give him her own silent treatment, so that his rare anger would escalate further. How was this her husband? Was this at last what the bad years and heavy drinking had done to him? And now a very old tension ratcheted behind her face, like a sneeze that wouldn't quite come. She had an irrational, feverish sensation that Jed might hit her. But Jed loosened his fist, and in lieu of a fight, Eve chose the next best thing. She walked the three paces to him, pressed her fingertips against the grimed meat of his hand, the skin quite shockingly tough. She wove their hands together, and they both looked at them for a long while, like another sculpture they had just made. What was it they had made? Two boys, of course, but what was the strange form they had taken together, before their children even came along? Something abstract, not exactly beautiful but certainly what an art critic might call *arresting,* the unlikely transformations they both could undergo only in each other's presence. Those brief few years, at the start of their marriage, when their better selves prevailed, before their fugitive, hidden other halves—her need to have everyone near her, Jed's need to have no one near him at all—won out. And how was it that even still—even still!—she received a few seconds of Jed's unbroken attention like a precious gift? Even still, as soon as she saw Jed, her appropriate anger vanished and she found herself wanting only for Jed to tell her how very much he had missed her, how much he needed her still.

"I know I'm right, I know that," Eve said. "But why do you always let me be so alone in it all? Am I so horrible?"

"No," Jed said. "I am. *Me.*"

It started again as simply as that. Like the logical progression of the held hands in the fMRI wagon days before, like their few "dinners" in her barren house at Desert Splendor, pressed fingers became pressed bodies and mouths. It wasn't, at first, particularly sexual. Sex happened, but that seemed to be only the best way Eve could think to get Jed as close as she would have liked, and still he could never get quite close enough. The better part of her, after all, was far away, in the hands of Margot Strout.

With the moan of a man cracking a beer after a long day, Jed climbed on top of her. Eve would many times replay that particular instant. Her sigh carried both grief and relief, and also a pang of pity for using her husband this way. But he was, after all, still her husband. And his eyes, in the dimness of the shed, were not as red and swimming as they had appeared under Crockett State fluorescents. They were the eyes she knew, crystal gray and fixed on her, asking the same question they asked in her long-ago apartment above the bank in Marathon, as if decades and so much silence were not between them now, as if he were still only the hopeful stranger she had just met that night at the Marfa Lights. What was the question? Something having to do with beginnings but also (she had sensed, even way back then) with merciful endings. *Is it possible?*

But when it was all over, and they were lying there in the starlit purple of the evening that filtered through the roof cracks, it was Manuel Paz that Eve was thinking of. And now Eve was wondering whether her hands, which had always known her own needs better than herself, had in fact spent that day operating under a motive she hadn't considered. Perhaps the madness of the way her fingers had behaved over the last hours had only been an attempt to outrun the old memories brought on by the way Manuel had looked at her today at Crockett State, his expression as stolid and unblinking as the face of the moon. Over the years, in Manuel's many visits to Bed Four, in the most unlikely town theories that Manuel nevertheless "investigated," she'd come to see that Manuel really meant what he had said. He truly could not stop. There was something mechanical about Manuel, all old-fashioned gears and cogs, the Southern Pacific that wouldn't stop trundling down the tracks until it reached its destination.

There is no why: over the years, Eve had offered herself countless ritualistic recitations of that mantra, a spell to ward off the worst thoughts that still sometimes came back to her, of Rebekkah Sterling and of her son's broody last weeks *before,* of all she had never told Manuel. How many times had she convinced herself that she was wrong, that her grief had made her a little paranoid, that nothing she could have said to Manuel Paz could have made any difference? And yet, Eve had read Oliver's "Children of the Borderlands" a hundred times, her astonishment at it dimmed only by the *you* whom the poem addressed. And one day, near the end of his homeschooling, Charlie showed her a book he had found: Oliver's old journal, containing even more poems that she saw—in the few glimpses Charlie forced upon her, before the sight of the handwriting overwhelmed her completely—that in those rhymy, adolescent lines Oliver gave that *you* a name: *Rebekkah.* And so was it not also a kind of lie that she had failed to mention any of this to Manuel Paz, in his many Bed Four visits? Eve's dread set her back on her feet.

"I'd better get going," she told Jed. He nodded.

Back at Desert Splendor, Eve discovered that Charlie was already asleep, and she was touched to find he still dreamed in his profound boyish way, emitting a little "uh" sound before each exhale. Moving around silently, on the sides of her bare feet, Eve located Charlie's phone in the pocket of the jeans he'd heaped next to his bed.

Eve had been so certain that she was right on that long-ago day with Manuel in the conference room, that an explanation couldn't really change anything, that the only answer for the impossible affliction that the universe had handed to her son could never possibly lie with any one person or any rational accounting. If there was any meaning to be found, Eve had felt, it would forever hover beyond her, in the unknowable force that lay beneath forces, the mystery that birthed gravity and set the stars to spin. But time had proven that Manuel had been right, and that she had been wrong. *Why?* That silent cry into the scrubbed desert sky, the question that had become her life and Charlie's life, too, that terrible project of his, shuffling around the lightless rooms of the past, and what else might he find? Eve watched her fingers flip through the contacts in Charlie's phone until she located the name *Rebekkah Sterling*. She copied the girl's number into her own device.

In her bed, Eve held the phone to her face, listening to it ring and ring, until a computer answered and asked if she would like to leave a message. Like some reenactment of her many calls to Charlie, just a few days prior, Eve ended the call and then she called again. At last, on the fourth attempt, the ringing clicked to silence, and Eve could hear the faint stirring of breath. And then, for the first time in all those years, she heard the actual, still-living Rebekkah Sterling speak: too stunning for Eve to muster a reply before Rebekkah ended the call. "You have the wrong number, please stop calling me," a young woman's smoky voice told her. And now Eve was wishing for another, different conversation she had also held in silence all that time but needed badly. She was thinking how she might be able to explain any of this to Jed.

Oliver

CHAPTER THIRTEEN

Oliver, do you remember your father telling you about a phenomenon called Spooky Action at a Distance? That was how Einstein
described the troubling behavior of entangled particles. Those little
fuckers stumped Einstein; they broke down the equations with
which poor Albert tried to describe the universe. Apparently, once
two particles entangle, they move in tandem, even when separated
by light-years. One particle zips upward and, a million light-years
away, its partner zips in the same direction. What strange force
binds them together? Einstein couldn't make sense of it. But perhaps a similar force blind to the galactic distances was at work in the
years *after,* between your family and you. After all, you were not
the only one trapped in a sightless prison, vibrating against the narrow walls.

Your father. For years, he stayed at the periphery of your family's
story, out in that dim shed, beating away at his garbage. A painful
truth: he chose to exempt himself, as far as he could, from your tragedy. But the other truth is that, in measuring the effects of Spooky
Action at a Distance, its influence was perhaps strongest on Jed Loving. Perhaps no one shared more fully your imprisonment.

Take, for example, one random night from your father's life, a year or two into your confinement. His place was in a bad way, a house self-made into a jail cell. His little bungalow in Marfa had become like the home-sized version of his old painting shed, a collection of abandoned things: half-drunk bottles of soda, half-eaten carryout, a television set to mute. And yet there in Jed Loving's lousy house, this was a Sunday night to be celebrated.

Your father unbuttoned his denim shirt, threw himself gratefully onto the butt-cratered mold planet that passed for his sofa. On this particular Sunday, Jed had just completed his second full week of work as floor manager of a new gallery, Gotleib & Krav, which a German couple had established in Marfa's renovated abattoir. Jed did not understand all the galleries of Marfa—that whole strange art culture seemed somehow a sarcastic joke at the expense of the rubes of West Texas—and he did not care much for the pieces peddled by Gotleib & Krav, a series of wind chimes made from dismantled Nazi artillery. But he arrived to this sleekly modernized slaughterhouse sober and bright each morning. Your mother and your brother had not spoken to him (or was it he who had failed to speak to them?) for nearly three months, but your father had a plan.

Step one in the rehabilitation of Jed Loving was to prove himself a competent adult human, capable of holding down a decent position. With the first full month's paycheck in hand, Jed would venture into the terrifying, less certain territory of step two, returning home and proving himself a competent human father. But on that warm Sunday evening, he looked around his lousy bungalow as if it were a molted skin he might slough off. He envisioned dinners at the rutted table of Zion's Pastures. He imagined coming to your bed hand-in-hand with wife and son. Two more weeks.

Jed scratched his age-thinned belly, traced the widening circumference of his bald spot with a thumb. For almost a month, he had not once ventured out to the Marfa version of his art studio, a lean-to in his weed-choked backyard, but on this sober, electric night, he was feeling bold, capable of transformation, and he thought he might just take a peek out there, see if his last bout of work—a series of utopian seascapes he had painted onto scrap metal from the dump—had in fact turned out as miserably as he remembered.

It took less than five minutes for the sight of his work to rub the shine from his mood. He had initially thought the aesthetic juxtaposition would be interesting, a little romantic beauty atop the rust-pocked sheets of aluminum and steel. Instead, the stuff looked like Thomas Kinkade had fallen on very hard times.

Ridiculous. He knew it. Jed knew it was ridiculous that even still he thought he might make something valuable, something perhaps even sellable, something that was at the very least not shameful, from those last, worst years. And yet, for the one thousandth time in his life, your father told himself that it was now or never, that he was, perhaps, very close to making something he could proudly call his own, that to return in the way he must, he needed not only to play at being a functional adult, he needed to become one. Thus began, in the painting shed, the collapse of your father's latest step one. He blanked out the seascapes, painted strange biblical scenes (angels and demons, à la Bosch) until dawn, at which point he allowed himself a drink, just to steady his fingers. He downed the three inches of bourbon, the heat and head rush offering him five kind minutes. He poured himself another. What happened after? Jed could hardly remember when, on Monday afternoon, he blinked awake to a phone call from Michel Gotleib, informing him that he'd missed the private showing scheduled with a collector passing through town. "Just your third week on the job. Needless to say, this isn't going to work out."

The story of your father's thwarted plan at Gotleib & Krav was the story of his life in miniature. "On the verge of something," he really had believed what he'd told his family all those years. "Maybe a breakthrough." Even into his ruinous fifties, your father could hike out to the shut door of his "studio" and look at the building the way he once looked upon his marriage to Eve, imagining that within that chrysalis he really might break through his own leathering skin. Become a different man entirely.

And your father's transformation and self-improvement schemes were not only art related. In those first weeks at the hospital, Jed told himself that once the worst was over, once a single test result to hope upon came back, he would at last quit his long whiskey sessions out in the pickup, become the father his wife and son had watched him fail to be. When your mother expelled him from the property, he told himself it was only a temporary separation, that he would return very soon. Once the horrors of that night stopped playing on repeat on his closed eyelids, he would put down the bottle for a couple of weeks, regain the steadiness in his step, and then he could go home. Or he would write a long apologetic letter, an explanation of all the things he had never said, and then he could go home. Or he would wait until the worst of the summer heat passed, and then in the brisk mercy of autumn, he could go home. Or he would wait until Charlie was gone for college, when he could talk to Eve alone, and then he could go home. Or he would wait until Charlie came home from New England, when enough time had passed that his own failings were practically historic, and then he could go home.

Considering the specifics of the latest scheme, as he worked himself into a different spirit, it wouldn't seem so difficult. Home was just a forty-five-minute truck ride away. Yet each time he tried to take a few steps in that direction, the ground would go uncertain beneath him, and he'd allow himself the one quick drink. But the little finger of George Dickel rye Jed let himself imbibe did nothing to dim those memory flashes on his closed eyelids: the way the school cafeteria lights had suddenly blinked on over the Homecoming Dance that night, the crush of teenage bodies in sequins and oversize suits, the confusion of shouts, cresting in a wave of panic. The way Jed, baffled at the cause, had nevertheless done his duty as dance chaperone, throwing open the gymnasium doors, shouting at the emptying

room for the children to stay calm and make a line. But in the mass
of bodies and the chaos of vehicular emergency lights outside, his
son was nowhere to be found. A mad sprint back into the old schoolhouse, toward the distant corridor where the shouting escalated.
And then, splayed there in a spreading puddle, an unfurling red flag,
the body unseeable, crowded out by uniforms. At last Jed did see,
would always see. Oliver. Two, five, nine years later, Jed allowed
himself a second drink. Another drink led to others, to another ruined scheme, to another swollen-eyed, tooth-aching rebirth, to a
whole new plan.

And so, as you endured the desiccating sameness of days and
years in Bed Four, so too, in the prison of his Marfa bungalow, did
your father's life pass like a montage of decay, a time-lapse of a man
shriveling in his skin, passing images of his artwork morphing in its
futile directions. Landscapes became portraits, became clay busts,
became scrap metal fused by a secondhand blowtorch, became trash
left out at the end of the drive for the garbagemen to collect. A hundred
times, he staggered out into the purple kindness of a desert dawn,
looked in the direction of your mother's house. But he'd never make
it all the way. Because your father had come to understand this: the
walls of his prison were different than your own, but hardly less
confining. He might have walked the floor of the world, but it was
an illusion. Your prison was your own body, but your father's? It
was the unfillable, unforgiveable place that lay beneath. It was his
whole history, an unspoken and unspeakable force that cracked the
rock, swallowed the arid substratum, shook your father off his uncertain footing.

Jed marched out to the shed, began hammering apart his new
sculpture, as if the thing he made were a kind of Frankenstein, a
monster that might destroy him when it woke.

A lonesome, pitiable man, it's true, but even then, the effects of
Spooky Action at a Distance bound your father to you. Somewhere,
in a galaxy far away, in your last months *before*, you were still there
with him, in your own studio of failures, wondering over a silence of

your own. Somewhere, it was still just that overheated October morning, years before, your body still squirming beneath you.

It was October fourteenth, the morning after your stalker routine outside the Sterling house, and you had retreated to your solitude at Zion's Pastures, your secret lair. The weather inside your own head matched the day: a lazy, intolerable atmosphere, too hot for October even in West Texas. In your creekside cave, with its card table and folding chair, you were attempting to whittle down your worries, chipping away at their sharp edges. A bruise on Rebekkah's leg—it was true, it was much worse than the little faint bruises that often mottled her pale skin, but it was absurd, the stories you had let yourself spin. What evidence did you have that Rebekkah did not just take a hard fall? And what reason to believe that that strange bald guy who had shown up at her place had anything to do with her? Likely, you told yourself, he just worked for Rebekkah's father. And what could you really know about her father himself? Your sum total experience of the man was just a bumbling shape, arguing with his wife as he stumbled across the lawn. Yet the events of the last day, the last weeks, were stubborn materials, and your blade ran dull. You couldn't whittle away her vaguely pleading expression as you had held forth about your family, your astronomy, your tall tales. It was a sensation familiar to you from your faltering attempts at poetry: like some perfect, revelatory line whose existence you could sense but not quite fix into words, you could perceive the existence of some other unnamable, clarifying fact about Rebekkah just beyond reach. But why was it up to you to try to understand her, anyway? Wasn't *she* the one who had stopped talking to *you*? These were the excuses you gave yourself for not doing the obvious, scary thing, the one that would most likely subject you to further heartbreak, just to beg Rebekkah to speak with you again.

Outside, the upraised wire arms of a stand of ocotillo swayed, creaking like a ship at sea. Crickets made their ornery, orgasmic percussion, rising to a clicking fever and falling silent. You had not, as was customary, brought your Casio boom box to the cave; Bob Dylan had no mystical fate to sing to you that Saturday. Distantly, through the lifeless flat that lay beyond the ocotillo, you noticed the plodding, aggrieved movement of your family's one remaining long-horn, the steer your father named Moses. "Just like the real Moses," Pa had said. "A desert drifter, a survivor of a dying clan." Once upon a time, according to Granny Nunu, your ranch had thundered with the hoof falls of Moses's many ancestors. Moses turned to you now, and you shared a long stare. *Tell me about it.* The day smelled of skunk.

In the late afternoon, your father stopped by the cave. "Dinner in an hour," he said.

"I know."

"Your Ma has been cooking your favorite. Lasagna."

"That's great news."

"So," Pa said. "How was the big date?"

"It wasn't a date. It was a *study group.*"

Your father gave you an obnoxiously knowing grin, as if he recognized this sort of boyish ruse.

You turned away, studied your hands. It didn't take much to fight the urge to tell him the truth. The summery languor made all the words you would have to use feel too weighty and cumbersome. Instead, you offered a Moses-like shrug, slow and suffering, your head slung low.

"Welcome," he said, "to the world of women."

"Ha."

He put an inky and unsettled hand on your shoulder. "It's a very mysterious world, and believe me when I tell you that you can never hope to know all the answers."

"You mean with Ma?" you asked.

"Well," he said. "No, not with your mother, I guess. That particular woman will tell you all the answers herself, ha." You had never once before spoken with your father about his marriage, and this little conversation now seemed like a decent consolation prize for the loser in love. In your recent glum weeks, you had fallen far indeed from your hallowed place as your mother's most perfect boy. You had come to grunt monosyllabic replies to her questions, and she replied in kind, hardly asking you any questions at all. But as you now showed Pa a wondering look, your father thumbed his chin regretfully, as if remembering the order of things, this life in which he was able to carry on with his many failings in exchange for his silence on the topic of Ma's absolute authority on all matters Loving.

After he went, you leaned back in your chair, relaxing gratefully into your poor mood. Was this the nature of love? This lopsidedness, one always in the lead, the other always in pursuit? The light was dimming in the sky now, and the heat no longer dulled your foulness. Cooling, it came unsettled. You thought up a final stanza for a poem you had been trying to write, "The Endless Roundup." Nearly every poem you had ever written you had kept to yourself, but for this particular poem you had an outlandish idea: on Monday mornings, Mrs. Schumacher offered bonus points to any student willing to read out loud a short creative work. Thus far, the only takers to this offer had come from the class's collection of moody girls: plump Betty Greene, who wrote an ode to chocolate cake as if it were a devious lover to be spurned; Cara Stimson, whose five-page ode to her mother's needling Cara did not manage to complete before puddling into her own tears. Only one boy—Carlos Ramirez, your honors class's only Hispanic kid—had taken the bait, reading aloud an essay about his parents' entanglement with the cartels in Guadalajara, their abandonment of their little grocery, and their flight to America. "Ah-MARE-ee-ka!" The boys in your class mocked Carlos's accent for so long that they began to call him by that name. "Hey, Am-mare-ee-ka, you know where I could score some bud?"

But "The Endless Roundup," in your first blush of composition, seemed a thing that perhaps you might summon the courage to read for ears other than your own—to read, more specifically, for the ears of the one girl who otherwise now seemed wholly uninterested in what you had to say. "The Endless Roundup" was a riff on one of

Granny Nunu's favorite old tales, a little fable that the graying min-
ister had repeated at her tiny, December afternoon memorial service.
Nunu's story held that the booming reports of the very occasional
thunderstorms in the Big Bend were not thunder at all but the sounds
of ghost cowboys forever in pursuit of ghost cattle. You imagined
yourself in a world like that, a boy turned to a cloud. You wrote:

> *Sometimes I wonder,*
> *Will I live like that too?*
> *A body of thunder,*
> *Endlessly hunting for you?*

You furiously scratched away every word. Once complete, the
poem seemed suddenly pitiful to you. And what sort of poet could
the writer of those cornball lines ever hope to become? Your future,
you were fretting now, was bound to be just like Pa's. You would
inherit this land, you would marry a girl you did not quite love, you
would toil under the shadow of dead masters. The only difference
would be that you would produce bad poetry, not bad paintings.
You would work in the cave, not the shed.

And so you resolved to put the whole business to an end. Rebekkah, poetry, your future imaginings in Mrs. Schumacher's classroom. You would not be a poet, you told yourself, but you would be
something else. What? The only professions that came to you now
were just a child's trite replies to the question of grown-up plans: a
doctor, a lawyer, a fireman.

You were still trying to convince yourself, by very early Monday morning. But a resolution was not enough. Internal revelation,
everything outside unchanged: that was poet thinking, and what you
needed was action. And so, as the sky outside the bedroom window
grayed with the sunrise, you crept out of your lower bunk, careful not
to wake your brother. You stashed your journal of poems in a bottom
drawer of the old accountant's desk, buried it there. But a journal in a
closed drawer did not offer the closure you needed, so you found a

fresh sheet of paper, lifted a pen, and began to compose a closing coda to your failed future, a sort of epitaph to your young life as a poet. One last poem, about your factory of a school, your ruined future with Rebekkah, everything you would never be. Unfortunately, it was only as you wrote your retirement poem that you began to see what made all your other poems so lousy. Like the shape-shifting creatures of the fantastical worlds you had described, you were always trying to put on new skins, but in this last poem you wrote as yourself, unchained from rhyme scheme. This poem, in the end, would become the first and only poem of yours to be published. In fact, one year from that morning, its concluding lines would appear on that memorial billboard off Route 10. But at the moment of composition it was just a thing you dashed off in less than thirty minutes.

Two hours later and with no hope left in your heart, you arrived on time for Mrs. Schumacher's English class. Later, you would wonder at the boy who had shown up that day, who had looked directly at Rebekkah on the far side of the room, who had hoisted his arm when Mrs. Schumacher asked, "Any takers for this week's Bonus Point Salon?" Who had then—unbelievable!—stood before the assembled classmates, grasped a page in a shaking hand, and read aloud from the contents of his soul. Was it just exhaustion? Desperation? You became practically a different person then. You completed your reading. You dropped the page onto Mrs. Schumacher's desk. Fingers snapped sarcastically. You sat. As Mrs. Schumacher began her lecture on Odysseus's journey through the underworld, you returned to the Oliver Loving you had been, aflush with shame, watching Rebekkah, in her desk chair, straining not to look at you as she drummed her chin.

Like the cruelest kind of review, not only did Rebekkah fail to show up early to class the next day, she didn't show up at all. She was absent that day, and the next, and the one after that. At first you were embarrassed, then angry, then worried. By that Thursday, the stain you had seen on her Band-Aids seeped dangerously through your reconsiderations. Was she in real trouble? You decided to seek news from the one person at the school who you thought might be able to offer some explanation. You had never spoken with Mr. Avalon before, and it was no minor feat. A localized aura of fame surrounded Reginald Avalon, that former childhood demistar who had become a vaguely rebellious adult, eschewing teacherly chinos in favor of stylish theatrical blacks.

"Why look," Mr. Avalon said, dropping his lunchtime sandwich on his desk. "Jed Loving's boy."

"Oliver," you said.

"Oliver, right. You are looking for Rebekkah, I'm guessing."

Could she have mentioned to her theater teacher you were friends? A painful hope churned inside you.

"I haven't seen her around for a few days," you said. "I'm starting to get worried about her. I thought she might have told you why. Is she really sick or something?"

"You're wondering why?" Mr. Avalon looked at you like a housefly in the cake batter. "You and me both. My whole rehearsal schedule is falling apart, thanks to that girl."

"So you haven't heard anything?"

"Rebekkah is a flake," he said. "A flake! Can't stick with a single thing. She says a stomach bug. I think she just can't be bothered."

You tugged at the collar of your polo shirt, which suddenly irritated your neck. "Can't be bothered?"

"That's right," he said, resuming his lunch, taking an angry bite of sandwich. He spoke to you now through a mouthful of egg salad. "Take this under advisement, and do yourself a favor. Don't get yourself too involved with that girl."

But at last, the next morning, Rebekkah came back. It was Friday, a rare overcast dawn, the brown gray plain of desert doubled in the sky. The sun veiled, the desert was nearly cold as you paced nowhere in particular, killing those before-school hours strolling up and down the four blocks of Bliss. It was still a half hour until class began, and, unable to bear the heartache of waiting alone in Mrs. Schumacher's room, you were kicking around outside the modest redbrick castle of Bliss Township School. You were watching the fraying laces of your once-white Converses sweep the sidewalk when a hand pulled hard on your sleeve. As if your mind had suddenly developed wizardlike powers, when you looked up, your thoughts conjured their object.

"Rebekkah," you said.

She was slightly breathless. It seemed that she had run to find you, from the direction of the school. "You were looking for me?" you asked.

"I don't know," she said. "You wrote that poem. And I've been waiting there in the classroom, you know? So that I could say thank you, I guess."

"You're welcome," you said gruffly, your heart alight.

"I liked it. Really. I know that I might be biased. Ha. I had no idea how much—anyway. I just wanted to say thank you." Your eyes were back on your shoelaces; the vanilla seduction of her shampooed smell was a kind of cruelty. "You are a real poet," Rebekkah added, very seriously. "That much is crystal clear."

"I think I'm quitting poetry. For a while at least."

"That would be a mistake."

Did she know how poetry and she had become inseparable for you? Might this have been a sort of invitation? But you remembered your last silent weeks, and you hated her a little for this bit of hope. "Where have you been?" you said.

"Sick."

"You don't look good."

"Really sick."

"I was worried. I even asked Mr. Avalon about you."

"I know. He told me. You shouldn't have. Worried about me, I mean. You shouldn't."

"Sorry," you said gruffly. "But Rebekkah? It's not just that you've been gone."

"What do you mean?"

"Well, I know it's weird to say."

"What is?"

You looked at Rebekkah, tried to focus on the density of freckles at the bridge of her nose, but you found you couldn't say it to her face. You spoke to the sidewalk, the embarrassment of what you had to tell her, with its pitiful admission of how much you had been thinking of her, came out rapid fire, in a single breath. "It's just that I noticed something, this big bruise on your leg, and I guess, I guess I just let my imagination run away with me, like someone might have *hurt* you. Or something."

And yet Rebekkah did not reply. The word *hurt* seemed to hurt her afresh. Her eyes filled as if she'd just been slapped.

"I'm sorry," you said again, for some reason.

Rebekkah chewed her lip, looked at her palms, nodded.

"Technically speaking," Rebekkah said, "legally speaking, I mean— he hasn't done anything wrong. Believe me. I've researched it online. Corporal punishment seems to be one of your state's proud traditions. Perfectly legal, when it comes to your own kids."

"Your father?"

Rebekkah felt her hair.

"And it's not so bad," she said. "Not like it used to be."

"You're not a child, and that wasn't a spanking. God, Rebekkah."

Rebekkah shrugged. The sight of her slim shoulders, pressed up to her neck, made you a little breathless. "I'll tell you something I know for sure," she said. "It will only get worse if I say anything. If you do. Promise me you won't."

"You have to talk to someone."

"I can't, like I said. But you shouldn't worry. It really has gotten better. We're moving in a better direction, I think. I promise."

You nodded, puffing your chest out, feeling perversely wonderful in this role. "If it happens again, I'll have to say something."

"Well," she said, "I believe you."

For a second, you could feel the lovely glow of those many before-school chats stoking back to life, still bright and hot beneath the ash.

"I'm messed up, Oliver," Rebekkah said. "I don't do the right things. I'm sorry if I led you on, I know that's a thing I do. But you don't want a mean girl like me anyway, right?"

"Don't tell me what I want." And then, to your mutual astonishment, you just left Rebekkah standing there as you began to trudge back to the schoolhouse to serve your daily seven hours of silence.

A minute later and just a few paces outside Bliss Township School, you came upon the group that congregated, as ever, just beyond the gates. David Garza, a dozen kids whose names you didn't know, and Carlos "Ah-mare-ee-ka" Ramirez, whose mocking faces registered what you had not, how your own face was slimed with tears, how you were working a fist into an open hand. "Oh, look, it's Willy Shakespeare," Carlos said, now not at all the awkward, heavily sighing boy he was in your Honors Literature classroom. "What happened to you this time?"

What happened? Even you couldn't have said. Even you couldn't have known what that conversation with Rebekkah had meant; in that day's unfinished puzzle, you only had your own unplaceable fragment. But at last, years later, the particles of two distant universes began to draw together again. After a very long while away, your father began to visit you at Bed Four.

It wasn't often, and when he came to see you, his skin exuded hard living, armpit stink and nicotine, the sweetened heat of whiskey pluming from his sighing nostrils. Your father's visits were very different from the others'. No recounting of the day's events, no updates on the news, no memories described, no conversations with you, playing both the parts. Your pa watched you in the way he'd sometimes sat with an easel, squinting at a desert valley, his overcast eyes waiting for the vista to reveal some new aspect. When he did speak, he spoke in the way of quiet men, no niceties or small talk to diffuse the crucial content. *How could I let this happen?* he'd ask, sitting in the silence that was your only reply. *How could you ever forgive me? Please, Oliver . . .*

But then your father stood away from the bed. He left. He left you there for another night at Bed Four—no, he only left your body. As for you? You were still someplace immeasurably far away, still just the boy you'd been *before*, trapped in ancient history.

Charlie

. . . .

CHAPTER FOURTEEN

One Thursday morning, a few weeks after his return to West Texas, Charlie was out stalking the plains. He was cruising the asphalt on his old neon-pink Suzuki motorbike.

Despite the outsized hopes of his mother and the people of his lost town, that motorbike's resuscitation had been the only certifiable miracle that Charlie had witnessed since his return. Within forty-eight hours of his arrival to the Big Bend, Charlie had felt himself quickly falling into a kind of adult education version of his old homeschooler's curriculum, reading his novels and magazines in his room, writing his moody musings he'd share with no one, silently trudging out of any room his mother tried to share with him, glumly staring out the passenger window on the rides to visit his brother's ruined body at Crockett State. Having failed to pack a single change of clothes, Charlie was even dressed in his old teenage getups, the cringe-inducing cargo shorts and ironic Hawaiian short-sleeves that his mother, for some reason, had held onto. And so Charlie had been enormously relieved when the Suzuki came back to puttering life with a bit of oil and a fresh tank of gas. Its tremble resounded pleasingly in Charlie's groin now as a high hot wind chased a single cloud over the shabby gasoline-scented tourist settlement of Study Butte. He gassed the throttle.

Charlie arrived early that morning to the beige monstrosity that was Crockett State. Beyond the magazines she had just fanned on the coffee table, Peggy the receptionist waved at him with giddy, Bob Fosse hands. Long ago, Peggy used to work the counter at Bliss Pies N' Stuff, and though they'd never really spoken in that *before*, Peggy seemed to lay the same cheery claim on Charlie as the rest of his old town's people, always flashing her tinsel teeth when Charlie passed. He nodded at Peggy now, turned to the familiar halls, flexing the joints of his left pinky finger, still worryingly tender days after he sawed the cast off with a steak knife. Charlie entered the room to find the wide apricot shape of Margot Strout hunched over Bed Four. The machines made their endless whirs and pings. Margot was whispering something softly into her patient's ear.

"Mrs. Strout," Charlie said, and the woman turned lazily.

"Margot," she said. "I told you to call me Margot. Haven't been a missus for almost fifteen years now."

"Margot, hi."

"It's a little early for visiting hours, no?"

"Sorry." The intensity of Margot's annoyance made Charlie's pulse quicken a little. "I was just heading out to meet some friends for breakfast, and I had to pass by here. It felt wrong not to drop by, check in."

Margot shrugged in an aggrieved way. "Same story, different day."

Over the last weeks, Charlie had watched Margot Strout's patience with him drop as a nearly visible phenomenon, the falling mercury of a thermometer. But in their first proper conversation, after the bad scene with Manuel Paz when Charlie had proven his willingness to say to his mother what no one else would, Margot had presented herself as a different sort of woman—an affable, solicitous lady, so forthcoming she could make him blush.

"The Lord is giving, isn't he?" Margot had mused that first day. "I go into this work because I lost a child, and now here I am, working with a boy like Oliver." Charlie had nodded. He'd grown up in close proximity to Margot's brand of rosy Christian notions, and he could still find them homey if a little cloying, like a slice of Apple Spice from Bliss Pies N' Stuff.

"Well," Charlie had said, "if there's one right woman for the job, seems like it's you." He'd meant it. In that first conversation, Margot revealed herself to be a big toucher, always grasping for his wrist, his shoulder, his knee, in the manner of the Bliss Township teachers, when they had sometimes come by to check up on him in his homeschooled years. "Thank you," Margot said. "Really. I hope you're right."

The sensation of Margot's fingers in Charlie's palm had been enormous and unsettling; his relationship with mothers, and not just his own, wasn't right. When his Brooklyn and Thoreau friends used to tell Charlie of their mothers' offenses, he would enthusiastically encourage their filial laments. But when reading novels or watching movies, Charlie would find that it was always the mothers for whom he wept. And here, in that perfumed, jowly woman, was another mother who had lost another child; her power overwhelmed him. "Tell me about you," Charlie said.

And Margot had gladly offered up her whole horrible tale. About her husband's third-term abandonment of his pregnant wife, and about the terrible genetic condition with which her daughter Cora had been born: Cora's four years of bronchitic, wordless life before the poor girl at last suffocated. About Margot's year of listlessness, speaking to her daughter's memory, and also about Margot's "rebirth," her two-year-long-training program in Austin, where her work had been divided between the university lecture hall and the stroke, muscular dystrophy, Parkinson's, cerebral palsy, and autism sufferers she assisted in the public hospital on Austin's east side. About how Margot and her classmates had conducted with the enthusiasm of neophytes even their most onerous labors: helping the geriatrics of Austin type out their pervy comments to their nurses, using the medium of hand puppets to help autistic children voice their complaints that they were not allowed enough video game time, displaying vocab flash cards to the stroke-numbed nonagenarians who were able only to roll their eyes at the chatty cheer of their speech pathologists. About how everyone in her modest cohort had shared an ambition to work with a locked-in patient. "Patients like Oliver," Margot had told Charlie with a rueful smile. "For us speech pathologists, it's like getting a chance to paint a Sistine Chapel, build a cathedral."

"I'll bet," Charlie had said and gestured toward the bed. "So where do you put the first stone in this particular cathedral?"

"There was this incredible professor there at Austin. Professor Brooks. An amazing lady, really. I could go on and on about her. Professor Brooks, she liked to say that working with the locked-in patient is a bit like being an old-fashioned radio operator. Your fingers and the EEG are the antennas, but at first they receive only static. Your job is to make small adjustments, to listen very closely, until you start to receive a signal."

Charlie recognized Margot Strout as a type he had known at Thoreau, one of those anxious-antsy students, so grateful their college had not demanded to see their pitiful or nonexistent high school transcripts, so eager to prove themselves in that wondrous second chance. "With a brain injury like Oliver's, the most likely place to locate purposeful movement is from the neck up, and that's where I'm starting," Margot explained, and then she'd let Charlie watch, as he had tried not to scoff at the crude simplicity of her so-called techniques.

"Blink twice for yes, once for no," Charlie heard Margot say, a hundred times over, speaking to Oliver like some bound and gagged prisoner of war, as she placed the antennae of her fingers near Oliver's eyes and kept her own gaze on the readouts from the EEG sensors she had taped to Oliver's head. Oliver's eyes, of course, only continued their erratic involuntary flutter, like lightbulbs faultily installed. As the days passed, Margot repeated the procedure on the hinge of Oliver's jaw, the pad of Oliver's tongue, the length of his throat, each eyebrow. She flashed colors, pictures, words, sound tones at Oliver from her electronic devices. She paused often to recalibrate the EEG analysis software.

"I know it might not look like much," Margot told Charlie and his mother after a few days of work. "But there is a method to this madness. A whole system for exactly where to test, and how. And maybe what I need most right now is just to be alone with him. I hate to say it, but it's a little distracting to do this for an audience."

Message received. Often, Margot was only able to squeeze in half days at Bed Four; some days she couldn't come at all. But Charlie and his mother knew that even her limited pro bono work with Oliver meant the other neurologically impaired people of West Texas went voiceless, and they didn't want to do anything that might discourage her, remind her of her other obligations.

But Charlie hadn't been able to help himself. At the end of each morning, when they arrived for visiting hours, Charlie asked Margot for updates, as if instead of signal divination, he thought Margot was slowly laying a landline between the world and Oliver. Charlie's questions plainly annoyed her; the cheery woman, with her former talk of miracles, had become a heavy sigher. But Ma, Charlie suspected, bothered her even more, never able to bear to meet Margot's gaze for fear of registering the disappointing results.

"Believe me," Margot told Charlie now. "When I have something to tell you, I'll tell you."

"Right," Charlie said, rubbing at his hand as if to encourage Margot to take it once more. "I guess if I'm going to be totally honest here? I really have another question."

"Oh?"

"Well. It occurs to me I've never asked you. How long is normal? Like, is there any sort of time frame to expect here? How long does it usually take with patients like Oliver? If there's anything to find at all."

"Unfortunately, there is no such thing as normal. It's a case-by-case thing. It takes patience. Sometimes a lot of it. And the truth is that we just don't know yet how much Oliver can even understand. It's important that we're all very clear on that point. When they finally do that next test, that will be very useful information."

Charlie heard a close, croaking noise; it took him whole seconds to recognize it came from his own nasal cavity. The round head of the woman seated before him softened impressionistically. "Ah," Charlie said, slapping at his tears. "God, I'm sorry."

And yet here, apparently, was the secret pass code to Margot's fortified heart. She now took Charlie's hand again, then his shoulders and torso, too. Charlie was drowning, gulping in the perfumed crevice of the woman's considerable bosom. "No," she said. "Don't you apologize to me. Don't you say sorry, dear boy. *I'm* so sorry if I've gotten a little gruff, but we're all on the same team here, right? We all want the same thing."

Charlie clambered free of the woman's cleavage, braced himself on her shoulder. And now he was wondering about the empty house Margot must have returned to each day after work, the bravery or else child-simple belief that kept up her Christian cheer in those bleak rooms. "Here's what I've learned," Margot said. "You have to have faith. That is what the Lord asks of you."

"The Lord?" Charlie said. "I'm afraid me and the big guy aren't really on speaking terms these days."

Margot smiled, almost nostalgically, as if Charlie's faithlessness were a kind of developmental stage to be passed through, one she herself had long ago outgrown. "He's all any of us really have, I think you'll come to see."

Charlie shrugged.

Certainly it was true that the miraculous resurrection of the Suzuki suggested the hand of the divine, but the bike could go fifty, tops: not at all fast enough—Charlie had learned in his first grim weeks back home—to outrun the anxieties that had pursued him halfway across the continent.

Since his arrival in the Big Bend, Jimmy Giordano had phoned Charlie sixteen times, and Charlie had answered zero times. Why, Charlie wondered, did he even keep his phone turned on when it was just his landlord who called him now? Even Terrance had given up on Charlie, his intermittent string of texts (*You there? Everything okay? What's going on? I'm worried about you*) terminating the same way Charlie had ended every friendship and romance, into his own dithering indecision that became his nonreply. Over the last weeks, Charlie had received only one call he wanted to answer, but Rebekkah Sterling had hung up before he could put the phone to his ear. Why, after all the months of willful silence toward Charlie, had she suddenly decided to call? That next morning, Charlie had spent a long while on the spring-mottled mattress at Desert Splendor, Rebekkah's number on his screen, as he contemplated the call button. In the end, Charlie settled on a jaunty little text message, which he regretted immediately after pressing *send*.

You rang? Charlie had watched the text message dialogue screen for a long while, applying the forces of mental telepathy to will her to reply. After ten minutes or so, the screen at last showed a pulsing ellipsis, indicating Rebekkah's typing. *Dot dot dot.* Only three mysterious periods, but enough, or so Charlie felt, to transmit the whole scene through the skies. Rebekkah, once more in her silk robe, her phone casting the only light in the dimness of her bedroom. Edwina dozing throatily on a pillow. Rebekkah considering, reconsidering. In the end, however, that ellipsis apparently was the most that Rebekkah was willing to offer Charlie. Charlie's fingertips went white against the telephone screen then, as he fumingly forwarded to Rebekkah the several recent news articles that Google had delivered to his phone, those substantially inaccurate, overly optimistic reports of the fMRI test results. No surprise: in the days that followed Rebekkah never replied.

But, of course, Jimmy Giordano kept on calling, and even when his phone was not actually ringing, Charlie's dread had become like a second device that wouldn't stop going off. A measure of his desperation: one afternoon, a week after his return, Charlie scrolled through his phone, drew his breath, pressed *call* on the name Lucas Levi.

"Well, well, well, Charlie Loving," Lucas answered. "My favorite author."

"Your favorite author. Hard at work!"

"So, uh, Charlie, what can I do you for?"

"A couple fancy cocktails. Maybe dinner."

"Oh?"

"Kidding. Actually, I wanted to tell you about some good progress I've been making."

"Really. And what sort of progress might this be?" Lucas asked.

Though the wave of articles that followed the news of "A 'Miracle' in the Big Bend" had quickly subsided, before dialing Lucas, Charlie tried to embolden himself with thoughts of his own privileged angle. The world—or at least some fraction of the world beyond their narrow slice of Presidio County—was paying attention again, and only Charlie had the inside scoop. He freshly imagined a whole book that would incorporate, in swiftly readable, emotionally riveting fashion, all the elements of his last weeks that, in truth, made Charlie go numb and nauseous to consider. Still, Charlie felt the possibility of relief, like a toe testing cool water, as he convinced himself that, in light of the remarkable developments, Lucas might be able to advance the rest of the cash owed to Charlie on completion.

"God," Lucas Levi said, after Charlie had offered a manic, clumsy summary of his recent weeks: the results of Oliver's latest test, Margot Strout's work, the several news items about his brother that had appeared in the local papers.

"But you still don't know if he'll ever be able to communicate?" Lucas added.

"No," Charlie said, and the line went silent for a few seconds.

"And so this progress?"

"That's just the thing," Charlie said. "The story is changing so quickly that I'm just going to have to start over, and that's where I'm hoping you could help me."

"Help you?"

"It's just that I need a little more of my contract money. Whatever you can give."

"Charlie."

"I promise you! I'm moving quickly now."

"Right."

"Listen—"

"No," Lucas said, "you listen. I hate to tell you this, but there's no way around it. My boss? I have to tell you that he's been talking about canceling this contract."

"*Canceling* it?"

"Are you really so surprised? We agreed that you'd show me some pages by last December, and now it's August. August! And every time we speak you tell me you are starting over."

"But what about what you said? About the national shame?"

"Well, that's true. It's a tragedy, what happened to your brother, a great shame, like I said, but these shoutings are at like what, one a month now. Honestly? Can't blame people for getting fatigued on the whole topic."

Charlie bowed his head, nodded. According to the loud and brief burst of press that had desultorily followed the night of November fifteenth, Hector Espina's motive might have been some misty conflation of mental illness, gun violence in the media, white xenophobia, and drug troubles, but in Charlie's many feverish considerations of Hector Espina's unknowable reason, the truest answer he had been able to offer himself was that Hector—a boy who hadn't been able to pull his life together after he graduated from Bliss Township School—had hoped to make the whole unlistening world learn his name, that Hector had thought he might use the weapon in his hand like a different kind of machine, one that could convert his lonesome agony into the blackest kind of public fame, detonating private misery into public bloodshed. But it had gotten crowded, that wicked pantheon. Those lonely, hormonal, zealous, and demented young men, unleashing hell in classrooms, military bases, churches, night-

clubs, movie theaters, shopping malls, and airports. His town's tragedy had become a relatively small statistic, just a data point on the
updated infographics to which liberal Congresspeople angrily gestured each time another demented young man attempted to outdo
his predecessors. Over the years, a great number of friends and boy-
friends had kindly suggested Charlie give his rage its appropriate
outlet, joining the poster-waving set on the steps of state legislatures
to fight for stricter gun laws. But, Texan that he was, Charlie knew
how each catastrophe was just another excuse for the crazed citizenry to weaponize more elaborately.

"I'm not saying you are hopeless, Charlie," Lucas added. "I do
believe you probably will have a good book in you someday, when
you are a little more, uh, mature as a writer. But editors can make
mistakes. I'm starting to see that I made one myself."

A dreadful pause. "But . . ." Charlie said, desperately wishing
upon a dependent clause.

"How about this," Lucas said. "How about you send me—I don't
know—say a hundred pages or so. By the end of the month. I'll do
what I can. But you should know, it ain't looking good."

And yet, even then, Charlie had been able to dam his panic. He
reasoned that he would simply write those pages, and his work would
speak for itself. "Speak for itself," Ma said when, with the false confidence of too much coffee two days later, Charlie tried to deliver to
her a self-rallying account of his quote unquote *incredible progress.*
"An interesting choice of words," she added.

"Interesting?"

"You mean speak for us. You mean speak for your brother. And
what about what he might have to say?"

"Exactly. What about it? That's my whole point here—"

"I'm really too tired to argue. If you need a hobby, have a hobby.
But maybe, if you are interested in actually contributing, you could
poke around for some job."

"I have a job. I have a contract, if you'd like to see it."

"And how much money have you made at this job?"

"I've already made money! And there is more coming, but, see, I was going in the wrong direction all along. My job is really just starting right now."

"Right," Ma said.

"Yes," Charlie said. *"Right."*

Charlie had been enormously relieved to return to his mother's rent-free household, but he was beginning to see the true, hidden cost of his tenancy. And Charlie also saw this now: his back rent aside, the only way out of a permanent return to his mother's home would be to write himself to freedom. "So I'm setting up shop down the street," he told Ma, "where I can get a little space and distance to work."

"What do you mean down the street?"

"I just think it's important that we set up boundaries here."

"Okay, but where down the street?" Ma fairly asked.

Charlie had spent the better part of that afternoon exploring the half-constructed houses of Ma's failed neighborhood, and when he happened to come upon that rare Texan thing, a basement, beneath a house that would never rise, he knew he had found his next studio. This *studio* might only have been a lightless cement cube, but Charlie had visions of William Faulkner dashing out his tour de force, *As I Lay Dying,* on a jury-rigged writing table Faulkner had made out of a wheelbarrow he found in his night shifts as a power plant supervisor. When Charlie happened to find a similar wheelbarrow of his own, a behemoth of a cart made of rusting iron, the coincidence couldn't be ignored. He kicked open the metal hatch to his new basement studio, rolled his worktable down the stairs, and laid a square of particleboard on top of it. On the first piece of paper Charlie placed before himself, he wrote a new dictum, the guiding thesis statement of his revised future. *Tell the TRUTH.* He looked at that cliché as if it were some revelation.

At that wondrous wheelbarrow, a night's solitary work spreading before him like a promise, Charlie felt it again: the spine-tingle of the old bunk bed tales, the ancient magi's incantation to raise the dead from the earth, the same giddy electricity that had pulsed over him the first time he had held Ma's news to his ear at New York Methodist. *He's there,* she'd said. *He's here.*

But Ma had not told him the whole truth then, only her desperate version of it. It was not by chance, Charlie understood, that she hadn't offered him a full report of those fMRI results until he was safely back home. *He's there,* Ma had said, but it was still entirely possible that Oliver was not there at all, or not completely. Or maybe he had been there all along? *Tell the TRUTH:* but already, his marvelous new dictum hit a snag. What truth? A miracle, as Ma and the whole town said? Maybe. Maybe for them. But Charlie was also thinking that from a certain perspective—from the perspective that mattered most, from Oliver's perspective—that even if the next exams Ma had scheduled in El Paso came back with the best, most miraculous results, even if this Dr. Ginsberg found that Oliver was still as awake and aware as anyone, couldn't one also say that such a miracle wouldn't be miraculous at all, but exactly the opposite? A confirmation of an unthinkable horror, perhaps the most hideous form of solitary confinement humankind had ever created, concocted by a gun-mad nation, twenty-first-century medical technology, and a mother's smothering love? Or had Ma been right, on that last afternoon before Charlie left for Thoreau—had he committed the most selfish act of all, mourning the death of a brother who had lain just inches from him, listening to his farewell sobs? How, how, how could Ma have not insisted on another test over all the years? Worse: How could Charlie himself not have made her insist? Charlie had spent the first four years of aftermath tending to his mother's needs, proudly polishing his Man of the House crown each morning, but with a painful lurching sensation in his esophagus, he wondered now if all those years of labor had summed only to his enabling of his mother's ruinous delusions. Was he, in fact, as guilty as she? Charlie felt desperately alone in these questions.

Since his arrival, Charlie hadn't gone anywhere near Marfa, but he sensed Pa's presence in the way a body feels the years, a gentle but accumulating sway, something insidious and intractable, bending him toward the ground. But what would he possibly say to the man? *How's tricks, Pops?*

On the wheelbarrow Charlie wrote, *Faulkner said the past isn't over, it isn't even past. But out in West Texas, it's something worse. It's the future.* He excited himself with the clarity of his anger, as if the meaning of things could reveal itself on the page before him, like the floating message in one of those novelty Magic 8 Balls. And yet, sitting each night at that wheelbarrow, he found himself scrawling only more aimless pages. As the days passed, Charlie lost the thread of his latest idea; he lost even the conviction of his anger. On his phone, Charlie spent hours clicking through his social media profiles, his obsession fixated on the anarchist guy he'd known for a week in Brooklyn. Christopher, whose many shirtless pics Charlie often enlarged, gazing upon his extraordinary stomach musculature like the map of some better land, a reassurance that Charlie's life had, at least for a short interval, taken place somewhere beyond this desiccated and fissured country. Christopher was living in Austin now, and though that city might have sat eight hours from his mother's crumbling house, Charlie several times looked up driving directions, contemplating the bluely highlighted routes in his phone.

"So, Charlie Dickens," Ma said on a Friday, on another drive back from Crockett State, "how goes the writing?"

"Hard to write," Charlie said, "when the story is still ongoing. But I'm sticking to it." He looked for a long time at his mother then, took in the wrinkling around her eyes, her lips thinned by age to near nothingness, the gauntness of her neck, the way her gaze could never seem to land on his, as if in all those years alone she'd become just a little touched, a little unwell in ways not immediately apparent. She was halfway on a journey to become the kind of tiny, cranky old lady Charlie had often encountered on Brooklyn streets, elbowing her lonely way through the crush of her days. And so wasn't it pathetic, what he still wanted from her? From his mother, teacher, principal, only friend, and loving jailer of his high school years—from that Supreme Being of his neuroses—he still wanted, needed, validation.

"It's not a story, Charlie. It's our lives. This is real life. And please stop making that face at me."

A half hour after leaving Margot and his brother at Crockett State, Charlie was straddling his motorbike, speeding through the desert, its veins of fossilized flooding, its million stones showing their blank, sunny faces, a geriatric audience. Charlie was on his way to a brunch.

"A brunch in your honor," his old principal, Doyle Dixon, had said, the city word *brunch* sounding silly in his mouth over the phone.

"Brunch?" Charlie had asked.

"A bunch of people would love to see you," Principal Dixon told him. "If you'd be willing. I know it'd make their day. Their whole month, really."

"What people?"

"A few of my dear old teachers. Manuel Paz, too. We all were hoping for a better chance to talk. And I thought a brunch would maybe be a nice occasion to shame me into straightening up my place."

"Manuel Paz?"

"That's right."

Charlie had paused, thinking of that balding, old-Texas holdover he'd seen at Crockett State. The idea of a brunch with Manuel Paz and those gossipy teachers was unsettling in the extreme, but Charlie thought of his directive to himself. *Tell the TRUTH.* A brunch, he decided, might be endurable, but only as *research*.

"I'd like that," Charlie had said.

Doyle's house was just beyond the western edge of the park, and Charlie chose the scenic route. He passed beyond the Austin-stone gates into the twelve hundred square miles of immaculate desert, alpine mountains, and Rio Grande–gorged canyons that constitute Big Bend National Park. Just beyond the ranger station, Charlie passed a grim gathering: a couple of Minutemen conferring with a police officer near a Hispanic guy seated on the curb, bowing his head over his handcuffs. And beyond this forlorn scene, the view before Charlie could have been a sepia-tinted photograph of Mars. It was no surprise, he thought, that this desert spawned so many amateur astronomers, that it made telescope people out of his father and brother. Nowhere more than in this desert had Charlie ever felt himself so clearly on a sphere of rock hurtling through the cosmos.

Charlie arrived at the address Doyle had given him to find a gathering of parked cars, one police cruiser. Even from the outside, Charlie saw that Doyle was right to warn Charlie about his place. Slabs of the stucco façade had fallen away in mangy patches, and the leaking AC units had made pouches beneath the windows, like heavily bagged eyes. "Charlie!" Doyle greeted him, and in the bright morning light, Charlie noticed how aged Doyle looked, his skin gone a little loose in the jowls.

In a flurry of hugs, shoulder squeezes, handshakes, and cheap perfume, Charlie entered. Manuel Paz extended a thick, chapped hand. "Welcome to your arraignment," he said.

"Ha," Charlie grunted, already starting to like the man a little.

The state of Doyle's domestic existence, inside that house, was dire, like its own little ghost town, cramped ruins amid the empty infinity of the plains. The word for what Doyle had become, Charlie sadly recognized, was *hoarder.* Some of his things were quite nice—Charlie noticed a mint-condition frame to an Eames chair, an intricate kilim rug that could have fetched a few hundred dollars at the Brooklyn Flea, a fanciful mantel made entirely of interlocked longhorns—but Doyle piled these fantastic objects in unruly heaps. Charlie had to swallow hard to hide his shock when, hanging directly over Doyle's many-quilted sofa, he noticed Pa's painting, which they had secretly helped Doyle purchase in that other life *before.*

"I know, I know, this place. I can't seem to stop buying things. It's like I think I'm shopping for the mansion I'll someday inhabit," Doyle said, waving his cane.

Doyle had made for his visitors a big egg casserole. After years of witnessing Ma turn away the flotilla of casserole trays that had once sailed for the front door of Zion's Pastures, Charlie downed the sodden, half-cooked stuff like a kind of victory. As they ate on the space Doyle had cleared on a Georgian Colonial dining room table, the school's former faculty had many questions about Charlie's Brooklyn life. "And is there anyone special?" Mrs. Schumacher asked. "Can you explain to me how any couple ever stays together in a place like that, with so many options?" added Mrs. Henderson.

Charlie was relieved by their questions, then delighted, then a little regretful. He had spent the last ten years carrying around this persuasive story that a willowy, sway-gaited boy like himself had never belonged in a school like his anyway, that his "homeschooling," whatever its questionable motives, had provided a kind of merciful escape. Of course, Charlie had never felt too much familial danger because of his romantic life, that much he could say for his parents. Charlie merely grew up, and the fact of his inclination became as apparent as his taller-than-average height, his thinner-than-average frame. But the citizens of West Texas were not all as progressively minded. At thirteen, when the boys in his classes had begun to perform their bellicose swagger, mocking the most obviously mockable as if denigration itself lent them some manly cred, Charlie had sensed that he was at a steep precipice, the end of his easy popularity as a younger kid. By the time Charlie left Bliss Township for the Zion's Pastures Homeschool for Lovings, a certain group of loutish, zit-stricken boys had begun to infiltrate the packed lunchroom table where Charlie sat with his many friends. Trying out the bitter flavor of the trite slurs they'd learned from their older brothers, these boys rechristened Charlie "twinkle-toes," "gaywad," "fudge packer," "queergayhomo," and plain old "fag," on a near daily basis. Charlie had been relieved not to have to descend into the hormonal inferno of the ninth and tenth grades. And yet, maybe Charlie had underestimated the people of his hometown? Or perhaps the cities' rainbow-flagged protests had at last crashed upon these shores?

"And please," Mrs. Dawson added, "tell us about the food. I want to know what a New Yorker eats."

Even Manuel Paz looked on with a grin as Charlie obliged the teachers' questions, extolling a New York existence substantially more glamorous than his own. He described a successful young writer, the object of a glut of professional and romantic attentions. Playing the part of hometown hero, Charlie looked upon those women's heavily blushered, wetly lipsticked faces as if they were some kind of authentic article he had forgotten.

"So what is it you are working on up there now?" asked the pleasantly wrinkled Mrs. Henderson.

"Actually," Charlie said, "I'm trying to write something about all of this. Oliver. Our town. The whole story."

The room fell silent as Charlie pushed around a limp white mushroom.

"Wow," Mrs. Schumacher said after a time. "I don't know how you could bear to think about it every day. Must be a brave boy."

Charlie shrugged. "Writing things down, writing it all out, it's about the only way I can have some sense of control in this world. Though, of course, I know it's likely an illusion."

Doyle Dixon looked at him pityingly, pressing his lips together.

"Actually," Charlie said, "while we're on the topic, I do have a few questions I'd like to ask."

Charlie strained to face Manuel Paz, feeling profoundly fraudulent. *Big hat, no cattle,* an old Texan like Manuel would say. "Really?" Manuel asked. "Like an interview? You gonna make me famous?"

"Hardly. But it's hard to imagine telling Oliver's story without you in it. I mean, you are definitely a character in this. An honest-to-goodness Texas Ranger."

"Har. Can't argue with that," Manuel said.

"How does a person even become a Ranger in the first place?"

An awkward moment ensued, Charlie's biographical question disrupting the chatty flow over Doyle's table. But Manuel just tipped back in his chair, crossed his boots, striking the atavistic Texan storytelling posture, an old man recalling youthful days by a fire at dusk. "We Rangers like to say it's a calling, like the priesthood or something, though I've come to suspect that we all just watched too many episodes of *Gunsmoke* as boys." Manuel then offered a short version of his own story, telling the assembled brunchers how joining the Texas Rangers, the legendary band of dragoons that had kept safe—from invasion, thievery, and the maraudings of bandits—the West Texan expanse, now struck him as a childish, ridiculous dream. "People want drugs," Manuel said. "The Latinos want a better life in America. I'm just the rule keeper. My job is to enforce the law insisted upon by the hundreds of millions to the north, who couldn't know the first thing about the truth of life down here on the border. Hardly more than a glorified paper pusher."

Manuel frowned, his whole bad story written in his face. Over the years, as November fifteenth had become just more waterlogged jetsam deposited by the ghastly tide working its way back and forth across the continent, Manuel's life had stalled, and not only in his career. Charlie knew, from Ma's gossip, that his wife had left him long ago.

"You must be more than that," Charlie offered. "Back when it happened? You were all over the news."

"The news. Suppose that's true." The man grimaced, mined his teeth with a fingernail. "Just over nine and a half years ago, but feels like a lifetime now and also just like yesterday."

"Preach," said Mrs. Dawson. "Truth."

"You know, those poor kids' parents still show up," he added. "A few times a year, they still drop by the office, to check in. To howl at me, really, instead of at their own empty rooms. And I just sit there and take it. I get it. It's like the assassination of JFK, impossible for folks to believe that a tragedy like that could be caused by nothing but one twisted young man. Honestly, it almost made me quit altogether. I used to think that all it took was a good strong mind, a Sherlock-type person, and every answer could be known. But to think that fellows like that exist, that maybe for some things there could be no reason—"

"That's just it," said Mrs. Dawson. "No reason! You know, I had that boy in my class?"

"You did?" Charlie asked.

"Sure. So did Mrs. Henderson here." Mrs. Dawson gestured to her grimly nodding colleague. "And I think your pa taught him, too, right? In his art class."

"He *what*?" Charlie slapped at his arm, like he'd been stung.

"Ah." Mrs. Dawson touched her mouth. "Well, could be that I'm misremembering. Anyway, that was all years before, and how could anyone have known? What was there to say about a boy like that? All mumbly and angry. I, for one, never believed any of that political talk. He wasn't some freedom fighter. He was just, I don't know—*off*."

"I have to say," Manuel said, "I'm inclined to agree with you." When Manuel paused, Charlie could perceive the charged oxygen in the room, Doyle and his former staff hanging on the officer's words. Manuel put two fingers to his lips, as if sucking at the memory of a cigarette. "But I suppose I'm like all those parents, too, in the end. This thing sometimes still keeps me up at night, honestly. All these questions. Why Hector, why that particular room, why Reg Avalon. Or even, for example, why on earth your poor brother was down there, too. Why, why, why. The detective itch, I like to call it, it only gets worse the more you scratch at it."

"Reg!" Doyle cried. "I can hardly bear to hear his name, even still. Dear man."

As Mrs. Henderson rubbed a hand along Doyle's spine, Charlie felt himself giving up his reporter act. It wasn't an alleged writer who blurted out his next words; it was just a brother. "I always thought he must have been there for Rebekkah," Charlie said. "That night. Oliver must have been looking for her. Did you know he used to go see her? A couple of times. A study group or something. And has my ma ever told you about the journal I found?"

"The journal," Manuel echoed.

"Yeah, that journal where Oliver wrote a whole bunch of these—I'd guess you'd call them love poems. For her."

Manuel nodded, but in the distant way he looked at Charlie now, Charlie wondered whether this journal's existence might have been a new fact for Manuel. The Ranger was silent for a moment, considering Charlie, considering the teachers. "These questions," he said at last, "truth is, there probably is no bottom to them. And sometimes I wonder why the *why* even matters anymore. But, sure, I'm just like anyone else. More so, even. It's crazy, I know it, but when I heard about that test in the fancy new machine, and Mrs. Strout working with your brother—well, I don't got much left to hope upon."

Mrs. Schumacher's breathing began to strain. "Do you really think they'll find a way to let him speak?"

Charlie shrugged. "Miracles can happen."

"They sure can," Doyle said. "They already have, sounds like."

"Yeah, it sounds like," Charlie said.

"Did the doctors say what the chances are?" Mrs. Dawson asked.

"I don't know that I'd be likely to believe the doctors anyway."

"But they wouldn't even say? If there really is a chance?" added Mrs. Schumacher. "If that Strout woman is really making any sort of headway?"

"Honestly, I have no idea."

"What do you think he'd say?" Mrs. Schumacher's voice was thin, as if trying to speak into a driving wind. "I've been wondering and wondering."

"Me, too." Charlie nodded.

Something faintly tightened in Manuel's face. "And how's your ma doing with all this?" he said. "I worry about her."

"Oh, I wouldn't do that."

"You're probably right," Manuel said. "But that's my job now. Professional, deputized worrywart."

"Ha."

"And what about your father?" Doyle asked. "How is he these days? Still working at that new hotel over in Lajitas? Haven't seen him around much."

Charlie shook his head, as if to a bad flavor in his mouth.

"Look," Doyle added, in a tone to suggest that this line of conversation had been planned in advance. "I can guess how things are between you. But the man is hurting. Won't even hardly talk to us. We're worried about him. He's not as strong as you or your ma."

"There's the understatement of the year."

"See him when you're ready," Doyle said, showing Charlie his palms.

"Easier said than done."

Manuel scraped his plate with a knife. "I'm sure you're right." Manuel bent forward to rest his elbows on his knees. "But take my advice, Charlie, and here's a quote for that book of yours. When it comes to family, that's a mystery no detective in the world, not Mister Sherlock Holmes himself, could hope to crack."

CHAPTER FIFTEEN

"Where were you last night?" Charlie asked idly the next morning, just after dawn, when he found Ma combing through a mound of walnuts at the kitchen table. "I didn't hear you come in until—it must have been near midnight."

"Peggy gave me a few more hours with Oliver. They've been nicer to me lately. All those nurses and doctors, just wanting to shuffle into Oliver's little halo of fame. It's twisted, but that's people for you."

Charlie wasn't too exhausted to miss that Ma likely intended *twisted* as a dig, but he was too exhausted to muster a comeback. Charlie had hardly slept, had spent the greater part of the night watching a blue square of moonlight scroll across the cheap drywall, spotlighting delicate fissures and a perfectly still scorpion. The old Navajo blanket smelling of mothballs, his brain a monstrous contraption, thumping, grinding, beating away, unable to process what Mrs. Dawson had told him. Hector had been one of his father's students? Even now, at the kitchen table, Charlie was wondering how he might relay this information to Ma. But this new variable seemed, in some calculus Charlie couldn't quite grasp, bound up with something unspoken between his mother and him.

Ma consulted her plate, pulverized the meat of a nut. "Hey, where are your glasses? I thought you wore glasses now."

"Oh, right. Thanks. I forgot." Charlie did not really need the glasses he now retrieved from his milk carton nightstand. He was only a tiny bit nearsighted. In his solitary Brooklyn days, the glasses often stayed on the secondhand bookshelf for whole weeks. Charlie knew his mother suspected the truth, that he wore them mostly for the professorial air of legitimacy their thick tortoiseshell frames lent him.

"Big plans for this morning?" Ma asked. "I hope you are being careful out there. And, I hope you won't feel—what was your word for it? *Infantilized*. I hope you won't feel *infantilized* when I tell you that I really don't love the idea of you riding around on that ridiculous motorbike."

"Actually, I was thinking I might go for another hike today."

"Oh?"

Last night, Charlie had powered down his phone, shoved it into a drawer, but now he was imagining Jimmy Giordano's many calls going straight to voice mail, imagining the man in his grimy Gowanus office, plotting his Plan B. Charlie swallowed, nodded, wondered if he really could do the thing he had in mind.

Lajitas, when Charlie was a kid, had been home to a *bona fide* national celebrity: the town mayor, the Honorable Clay Henry, who was a goat who drank beer. "A beer-drinking goat!" The friends Charlie made at Thoreau had always said this at some point in the first day or two of their acquaintance. It was a story to dine out on in preppy New England, that folksy, yokelish charm. "Hand to God, I'm telling the truth," Charlie would say, his voice slipping a little Texan for effect. Charlie never mentioned the sad fact that a town could elect an alcoholic goat for mayor because it was no longer technically considered a town, an unincorporated municipality, and that the half-ghosted settlement's primary economy came in the form of the bottles of beer tourists bought from the Lajitas Trading Post, feeding the booze to staggering, gaseous Clay Henry, before they headed down into the park. But many years had passed since Charlie had been to Lajitas, and, even with Ma's warnings, Charlie couldn't quite believe what he found.

Like so many of the county's Mexican-owned businesses and an entire Hispanic neighborhood of trailers that once sat west of Bliss, whole streets had been razed. Where Clay Henry's pen once stood was now a manicured cactus garden. And, across the street: an astonishing, fantastical sight. Behind a laser-etched placard that read LAJITAS GOLF RESORT spread a compound arranged as a faux–Wild West street scene, complete with a bank that advertised Texan trinkets, a corral that ran with chlorinated water, a swing-door saloon. A sort of Texas theme park.

Pa, Charlie thought. As Ma had instructed him to do at his first return to Bed Four, Charlie tried to imagine the worst. Cheeks of exploded capillaries, skin gone slack, eyes blinking and red. But the only image of his father that Charlie could hold in his mind belonged to the last time he'd seen him in Marfa, in that tuna-can-and-bottle-cluttered archive of sorrows Pa called "the new place," when the man had run a hand through the matted shag of his hair as they said good-bye at the front door. "What I want to say?" Pa had told Charlie then. "All I really want to say is that I promise you. There is fight in the old beast yet, right? I just need to find my way back to—"

"To what?" Charlie had asked.

"I don't know. You. All of you."

Good luck with that: the last words Charlie had spoken to him.

Six years had passed, and now Charlie straightened his spine, steeling himself for a performance of faked confidence. Charlie walked into the main entrance of the complex's largest structure, a grand replica of a Wild West brothel, its lobby all mahogany and stained glass, the sort of place where a poker winner might blow his wad in a Hollywood western. It smelled of Lysol and the new-house zip of fresh plaster. A player piano banged out a staccato barroom jig, but the lobby was empty except for a slumped janitor in coveralls, sweeping the glistening marble floor.

"Charlie."

Charlie knew to look for Pa behind the desk, but the man who spoke his name was not his father. This was a no one, like one of those any-men you could see smoking outside a public rehab facility, with their wiry bodies and shot nerves, their drinking and cigarette habits having cured their faces into uniformly shiny, textured masks. Charlie took a few steps closer, needing a clear view of Pa's eyes to convince him. They were, after all, Charlie's own eyes, if diluted; Charlie's own eyes reflected back to him in day-old rainwater.

"Pa."

Pa's hair had abandoned his crown, established survival colonies on his neck and chin. This hard-times stranger, this fazed drunk with Charlie's grayish eyes, was as still as statuary behind the counter. Then, as if forgetting the desk, he lunged in Charlie's direction, the marble top striking his ribs. The man looked so delicate that Charlie listened for a popping sound. The player piano silenced for a beat, then resumed with that classic of vaudeville madness, playing "Flight of the Bumblebee" along with Charlie's thumping heart.

"Here I am," Charlie said.

He was just a few paces away now. Pa. The same man Charlie had vilified, longed for, counted as dead, now only stood there as this ordinary and weathered person, costumed in the purple-collared shirt of his work uniform. This was just another minute, and its ordinariness struck Charlie as the most desperate fact of all.

"Your ma told me you were back in town," Pa said.

"She did?" Only one sentence between them and already Charlie was appalled. He had come to Lajitas, still playing the part of his mother's dutiful son, showing his father the firewall of contempt she had taught Charlie to erect, but apparently she herself had already broken it?

"How *are* you?" Pa asked.

"Oh, just swell."

Charlie crossed his arms, hugged himself as if to give some silent lecture on how he'd had to become his own father. It didn't take long to collapse the false smile Pa was trying to work into his hollowed cheeks.

"Charlie. Jesus. You. You look so great. Grown-up. Handsome."

"What the hell happened here?" Charlie said. "What is this place?"

"What do you mean?"

"Last time I was here it was a one-horse town. Now, voilà, it's Disneyland. And where is old Clay Henry?"

"The goat?" Pa scratched his widened bald swatch, looking sorry, as if of course his son would demand to see the old mayor, and he had somehow failed to anticipate that request.

"What the fuck is this music? Listen, uh . . . can we please just find somewhere quiet to talk? Just for a few minutes? It's important."

Pa considered for a moment. He glanced furtively in the direction of a woman typing at a computer in the back office. Then, as if they had just completed check-in paperwork, he turned back to the desk in a businesslike way and grabbed a room key in a trembling fist.

Pa was silent as he led Charlie up the grand wooden staircase, down a long, velvet-trimmed hall to a door labeled THE BIGFOOT WALLACE SUITE. Inside, Charlie found an anonymous corporate hotel room, with a few "Texan" touches. A bronze cowboy riding a bucking bronco on the coffee table, a plaster replica of a longhorn skull over the bathroom transom. Double doors led out onto a terrace, with a view of the improbable rolling greens of a golf course. Distantly, a man in a cliché of a cabbie hat swung a golf club.

"But seriously." Charlie turned. Pa was holding his hands together in the dim of the room. "This place."

"Some telecom tycoon bought the whole damned town, put up all this."

"Of which you are a faithful employee."

Pa shrugged heavily, as if straining against the silly starched shirt he was made to wear. "Believe me, I looked for other work. But I guess a job like this, it's all I deserve."

Charlie felt his lungs constrict. Was this what Pa deserved, or was that idea just some kind of guilt trick he was playing? But Charlie knew now that this scene was what *he* deserved, breaking their six-year silence in the hope that his father might lend him some cash. Charlie stepped back into the room.

"You don't have to worry, I'll spare you a big scene." Charlie wanted, very much, for his father to make a big scene. "I just came to ask you a question."

"A question," he said.

"That's right. About Hector Espina."

Pa shook his head in fast, startled turns.

"He was your student."

"What?"

"Please don't play dumb with me. That's all I'm asking you to do right now, is to be honest with me. I know he was a student of yours. I know it. Mrs. Dawson told me so."

"Mrs. Dawson? What were you doing speaking with Mrs. Dawson for?"

"Why didn't you ever tell us?"

Charlie noticed that a dew of sweat had broken out on his father's forehead. Even from a few paces away, Charlie could smell the familiar toxins, nicotine and ethyl alcohol, pushing out of his pores. "What was there to say?" Pa said. "That miserable little speck of a person I hardly even knew. A boy I could have killed myself, before it was too late."

"Okay, fine. So you know nothing. Big surprise! Jed Loving knows nothing at all."

Pa's shoulders had lost their heft, but he could still work them into the *what-can-I-do* shrug Charlie remembered. "He was just another strange kid in my art class, Charlie. There were a lot of kids like him who passed through over the years."

"Right," Charlie said.

Pa's shaking escalated a tick, and it seemed to Charlie that if he listened closely, he might have heard the man's bones rattle, like seeds in a dried pomegranate.

"How about we try to start over here?" Pa said. "How about we try to just talk? I mean really talk. I want you to say whatever is on your mind. Doesn't matter what."

Pa had always been the head-nodder; Charlie had become the head-shaker.

"I'm still your father," he said.

"I'm not so sure about that." Charlie turned, lifted the statue of the bucking bronco, felt its heft, as if he might use it to brain this stranger who wore his father's petrified face, and so liberate them both from this miserable reunion.

"Charlie . . ."

"My father was too sick to live with us," Charlie said, repeating the lie that he'd told to so many strangers, the lie that, he'd learned from dozens of movies and novels, was practically expected of an angry, abandoned young man like himself. "And then he died."

Charlie was feeling lit up now with the old righteous fury, the meaningless howl of the adolescent monster he'd gestated in all those silent years of homeschooling, all those years Oliver had spent in Bed Four, all those years when Pa never told Ma once, *This is wrong, we can't let things go on like this.* Charlie didn't mean to say what he said next, and yet out it all came. "What the hell is wrong with you?" he said. "How could you let yourself become like *this*? And never, not once do you even try to talk with me? For years. *Years!* Haven't you been at all curious about where I've been living? What I've been doing? What it's been like for me? And aren't you curious about Oliver? About what is happening now?"

Pa nodded, oddly brightening a little to this tirade, as if Charlie had just conceded something. "Of course I've wanted to know," he said. "You wouldn't talk to me."

"I wouldn't talk to you? I think maybe you've got that backwards."

"Okay, you're right."

"I never really knew my father at all," Charlie said.

"Okay."

"For fuck's sake." Charlie walked into the bathroom, for the relief of its sterilized closeness. After a time, the ghost of his father darkened the doorway.

"Look," Pa said, and Charlie waited for him to say something more, he really did. But after tense, silent seconds, Charlie lowered himself to the closed lid of the toilet.

"At least my father taught me one good lesson," Charlie said. "When it comes to my family, you have to get out when you can."

To Charlie's surprise, Pa raised a strict finger then, carried it into the bathroom, where he pointed it at his own chest.

"I'm the one who messed up. I'm the mess-up. Me. Me. Someday you'll see it. Your mother has only done the best she could."

"You really, truly have no idea what you are talking about."

"I think I might."

"I mean it." As if Pa's DTs were a genetic affliction, Charlie was also vibrating now. "Who is this stranger who talks about my family like he knows us? No one I recognize. The best she could? Did you know that Ma never once got a good second opinion on Oliver? Did it ever occur to you that this so-called miracle everyone is going on about is really just a test that no one fought for, years and years ago? We buried him. Ma did. We all did."

"We did what now?"

"Just what I said. But of course Ma probably would have made a different choice if she'd had a husband around." Pa pushed his palms hard into his deeply socketed eyes. A few months before, Charlie had seen a news item about some nonagenarian Nazi they had rounded up to face his seventy-year-old crime. Half of him thinking, *Let the devil burn;* the other half thinking, *Just let the old man die in peace.*

"I'm sorry," Pa said.

"Oh, right. The MO of Jed Loving: when angry, apologize. Please, Pa. Leave. Just leave me alone."

"Leave you alone? Wasn't it you who came here to see me?"

"I just need a minute to myself. I mean it. I really, really, really do."

Pa shrugged again, even more heavily than before. "All right," he said. "If that's what you need. "

"If that's what you need." Charlie snorted. "You should get that printed on a business card. Chiseled onto your headstone."

Charlie closed his eyes, and after a moment, he could hear Pa's tentative footsteps, the door latching behind him. He emerged at last from the bathroom, paced the Bigfoot Wallace Suite, returned to the baronial balcony for a while, surveying the brown ancient mountains, reframed by the rolling fields, a few acres of Welsh heather transposed onto the great Chihuahuan.

Back on the Suzuki, Charlie tore down the tarmac, hot wind screaming over his face. He thought of returning to Lajitas, and the Suzuki dithered with his indecision, listing a little dangerously now. But then he balanced himself and picked up speed. Charlie was taking the long way home.

He'd had the scene in mind for weeks. Perhaps, Charlie had considered, his book would open not with the night of November fifteenth, but with this: the wayward son, walking the tumbleweed streets of his ancestral hometown. It all would look diminished, of course, and Charlie knew that the whole town, deprived of the primary economy of the old school, had fallen on hard times. The young man from the city would see that the center point of his boyhood universe was now just another town withering on the high plains.

And yet, Charlie now felt that he had another to add to the considerable list of his imagination's failures. As the Suzuki made a dusty progress, Charlie saw that Bliss, Texas, was more than diminished. The half-shuttered Main Street he remembered, under the harshness of sun and wind, had already made significant progress toward joining all those various miners' camps, those myriad ghost towns that dotted the desert. Bliss Pies N' Stuff was now an oversized tin can with pimples of rust, plywood for windows. The frontage of the only other business in Bliss—the Made in Texas! factory, which had once turned out those kitschy Old West knickknacks—was half busted in, its walls grayed and buckling. Charlie slowed for a better view of some movement he glimpsed within. A family of javelinas, it turned out, those wild hogs of West Texas, his country's attempt to offer up an archetype of ugly. Their tusked, anal snouts snuffled through the shattered ceramics that littered a rotted field of carpeting.

This was the town generations of his ancestors had built; the twenty-odd structures of Main Street were the setting for the lore, the ancient rivalries and romances, that had formed Charlie and his brother, or at least their paternal halves. But the only living citizens of Bliss that Charlie could locate now were the javelinas and a couple of mohawked roadrunners, zigzagging manically across the cracked asphalt of Main Street as if they too had just returned from a long time away and had gone a little crazed with grief.

And so Charlie could not bear to do what he had imagined; he did not dismount the Suzuki for the mythic hometown stroll. He rode on, as slowly as he could without tipping. And, at last, there it was. The redbrick husk of Bliss Township School, each pane of window methodically shattered, the western portion of the roof staved in, as if from aerial strike. Charlie could see a slice of the Bliss Mountain Lions football stadium. Zombie grass, high and dead at the fifty-yard line. The flagpole was gut-punched, doubled over. The only traces of the flowers and wreaths and tributes once attached to the rust-furred bars of the gates were little bits of wire, gathered near the ground, and a badly faded, laminated sheet of paper with a couple of cursively scrawled, English-version lyrics from "Besame Mucho," a song Mr. Avalon's theater club never got to sing that night: *Oh, dearest one, if you should leave me, my little heart would take flight and this life would be through.* All it had taken to end the town of Bliss, Texas, was one demented boy's decision. Manuel Paz was right: the horror was absolute and unacceptable. Someone else must be accountable. Someone must still be made to pay. And yet, Charlie knew his Texas history. He was thinking of the ancient Mogollon, the Apache, the

Comanche, the Spanish, and the Mexicans, the hundreds who had perished on all fours, crawling to America. All those history-crushed people. His own ancestors, trying to establish human time in the eternity of a desert that so quickly brushed it away. A wind rose from the west, a ghostly abstraction of dust lifting through the air, depositing itself over Bliss, sanding a few more grains from the façades of Main Street. Then the dust sucked up into the immaculate blue overhead, sighed off into the nothing to the east.

······················

CHAPTER SIXTEEN

Back at Desert Splendor that evening, Charlie spent a whole hour hiding out from his mother in the bathroom, his legs going numb on the toilet seat. Just now, he couldn't stand to be in a room with Ma, not for another minute.

Over the cool hollow of the porcelain bowl, Charlie was thinking about his father, from long before. The hard scrape of his shoes, chasing him up the dirt road of Zion's Pastures. The callused weight of his father's hands, ink stained. Sitting there together, on a special "boys only" trip to the rodeo in El Paso, Pa pinching sprayed bits of cow patty from Charlie's nacho cheese. Pa making the whistling sound of artillery falling as his fingers soared through the air to Charlie in bed.

"Every story in the Western canon is, in one way or another, the story of the fall from paradise," Professor Waters once told Charlie's Masterpieces of English Literature class at Thoreau. "But isn't the loss of the garden just a metaphor?" Charlie had asked. "That we all feel we lost something in childhood, some thoughtless, innocent state before we knew better?" Of course Charlie knew that the Lovings of *before* had never been a paradise, but Charlie felt that they had at least lost an *idea* of paradise, the other family that they still might have been. The family that suggested itself in a wad of gathered money at the Bliss Township Jamboree, in the exhilarated darkness of the many bunk bed stories his brother had begun, in the vertiginous view on a family hike to the top of the Window waterfall, its limestone-framed image of a tan and lavender expanse looking like a doorway to another country entirely. It wasn't only those five people who died that night. It was also the other future that could have been theirs that Hector Espina had murdered at a school dance when Charlie was thirteen years old. Ten years had passed, and despite his best efforts Charlie was exactly who he'd been in those first days *after*, a disgruntled son, accompanying his mother each day to Crockett State, hardly saying a word. What had changed? Only the year.

How to explain the rash decision that Charlie crafted that night on the toilet? He knew he had no real excuse, even then. He had only the hours and days ahead with a family there that he could not bear, the incalculable burden of all the debts each of them could never repay. *Why?* "The detective itch," the question that knocked at the walls of all their days, Ma's, Charlie's, the town's. With no way to open that door, some had shouted at the sound, others had tried to speak back to it. Charlie had locked the door, covered his ears, pretended not to hear. But the knocking came at irregular intervals, loud, then soft, then vanished, then loud again; there was no way to ignore it. Charlie thought of the next test, the one in El Paso. He thought of everything he still did not know, might know. There was much Charlie couldn't bear about his homecoming, but nothing was as horrible as that hope. The nearness of his brother's voice to at last answer that rapping. Hope: Charlie had watched his mother waste a decade inside of it, and so he resolved again to banish the word.

A few hours later, Charlie was back in the unhoused basement down the street, surveying the grim scene in the dim luminance of an old kerosene lantern. From the look of the febrile, halting notes Charlie had scratched onto printer paper and scattered across the room, it appeared that he had bludgeoned a manuscript to death. Hefting his bag over his shoulder, Charlie paused for a long while, trying to take it all in. As if he had deliberately arranged to offer himself a little piece of dispiriting symbolism, Charlie found, trampled and ash-stained on the floor, the very page on which he had written the words *Tell the TRUTH!*

"That's it, Weens," he said—Charlie still found himself, in certain dark moments, speaking out loud to his pug. He thought of Edwina there with Rebekkah, on Eighth Street, the answers to everything that would always be beyond him. Edwina's warm potato of a body, curled against the crook of Charlie's leg all through his one New York winter. "The end," he really did say out loud, and he tried to believe it this time.

Dear Mother, Charlie began on a page plucked from one of his journals. *I think we both know that this arrangement of ours isn't working for either of us.*

But that struck Charlie as too passive-aggressive, with a vaguely Oedipal note. He wadded it.

Dear Mother, I've come to see that it is impossible for me to be my own person in this place, where the past and its horrors and confusion are like cobwebs growing over my body, not letting me move. I know how selfish that must sound.

True enough, perhaps, but to Charlie it did sound selfish indeed. And he imagined the red ink of Lucas Levi's handwriting in the margins: *Overwrought.* Was it possible, Charlie wondered, that he could not even write so much as a decent runaway note?

Dear Ma,
I think it will not come as a surprise to tell you that I couldn't bear it here another day longer, and I've left. Someday, I'll be in touch again. I'll be thinking of you and Oliver every minute of every day.

Love,
Charlie

He saw that this note was a failure, too, but he marched back to his mother's house and magneted it to the refrigerator, like the final book report he had written for the Zion's Pastures Homeschool for Lovings. And at least there was this consolation: at last he had done it. With this note, he would at last thoroughly break Ma's heart, end her last hope that Charlie might ever be the sort of son she needed him to be. *Knock, knock, knock:* Charlie's thoughts were running back to what might still happen, the next test, more tests. *No.* He freshly reconvinced himself he had to go.

At five thirty, with a backpack holding four of his teenage outfits, Oliver's journal, and the $142 that represented his entire estate, Charlie left his Suzuki in the drive, hiked out the forsaken stone perimeter of Desert Splendor, made his way to the tidal whooshing of big rigs barreling down FM Route 28. The dawn had just begun to make the headlights of passing traffic unnecessary, and right when he reached the ribbon of asphalt, the sun crested the eastern horizon, throwing his long shadow into the soft, diesel-hazed redness to the west. Charlie crossed to the far side of the road, to the side that represented the country's ancient myth of rebirth and transformation, the westbound lane. Like a thousand hard-luck poets before him, he extended a thumb and pointed it in the general direction of the Pacific Ocean. He was now entertaining a vague fantasy of San Francisco, a few nights in a YMCA, a resuming of his barback career.

But the thing that happened was that nothing happened. There was a very suggestive lull in the traffic. He waited five minutes and still the road was silent. The land to the east was a perfect flatness, but in the west it rose in disturbed waves, the farthest southern incursions of the Rocky Mountains. Over one of those distant hills, headlights winked at him, from the eastbound lane. With his preternatural susceptibility to signs and portents, Charlie lowered his thumb and made a decision then, a way to put a final and conclusive period on the sad ending of his youth he was that morning trying to contrive. Or maybe he was just looking for an excuse to delay the criminal selfishness of his scheme. Charlie took the eight paces to cross the street and once more extended his thumb, now pointing eastward.

After fifteen minutes and one very strange conversation—about polygamy, with a big-rig trucker improbably named François from Butte, Montana—Charlie was standing just a couple hundred feet from Bed Four, in the back corner of the parking lot. He would only need a few minutes inside, he told himself, and a half hour later he'd be off in the passenger seat of some unknowable future. He tugged open the back door.

Inside, the same sterile hallways he had walked each day with Ma. His footsteps chased the greenish reflection of fluorescent tubes across the linoleum. In case Donny Franco or one of the night shift spotted him, so long before visiting hours, Charlie tried to affect a gait that was at once swift, purposeful, and nonchalant, and when he arrived to the room, he pushed confidently through, then paused to catch his breath. The bed was around the corner, and to be sure he wouldn't lose his nerve when the grim, snarled sight of his brother confronted him, Charlie prepared what he had come there to do, which was the exact thing he had tried to do in Rebekkah's Eighth Street apartment weeks ago. From his bag, Charlie produced the albatross that had hung around his last years. Oliver's journal in his hand, Charlie's only plan was to deposit it on the bedside table, perhaps say a word or two to his brother, and go.

If Charlie had been asked to pick a single word that best summarized his existence on this planet at the age of twenty-three, the choice would have been simple: *however*. The History of Charlie Loving, he felt, was nothing but twenty-three years of *however*, his expectations and reality forever a dizzying double vision, the image never quite coming into focus. And here was the latest *however*: from the space beyond the corner in which he slouched, Charlie heard something curious. A high-pitched computerish sound, animated like some canned politician's voice delivering good news. A robotic voice, saying the word *yes*. And when he glanced around the corner, Charlie discovered, bent once more over Bed Four, the floral-patterned shape of Margot Strout.

"Margot?" This time the woman startled so severely she nearly fell off her stool. Pivoting, her eyes looked something more than surprised, a touch manic and oddly naked. It was the first time that Charlie had seen her face without the dressing of her makeup. Un-feminized, Margot looked nearly butch. Over the bed, Charlie saw that Margot had rigged a touch screen on the swivel arm of a metal stand.

"Charlie. So early again. Very early, in fact. What is it, six? I couldn't sleep, so thought I might as well get to work."

Hoping to avoid Margot's questions about just what *he* was doing there at that hour, hoping also to distract her attention from the book Charlie was presently slipping back into his bag, he asked, "What's with that weird roboty sound?"

Margot and Charlie looked at one another for a strangely long moment. Apparently, all it had taken for Margot to recategorize him as a "dear boy" had been his teary little outburst the morning before. The woman smiled at him now, snapped her fingers in Charlie's direction, held out her hand for him to take it. He did as instructed. "I was going to tell you both about it today."

"Tell us what?"

"Charlie, sweetie," she said, touching his cheek, blinking very quickly.

"Excuse me?"

"I've finally made some, uh, progress?" Margot seemed to choose that deliberately vague word for the pleasure of loading it with implication.

"You don't mean . . ." Charlie paused, feeling the simultaneous tremendous weight and helium lightness attached to the second half of that sentence.

"Like I told you," Margot said, "with a head injury like Oliver's, if there's anything to be found, it's usually neck up." Margot's lips curled then, the sly look of a great secret in the offing. "But I finally decided to listen to your mother. I tried his hands, like she's always been saying."

"His hands."

"His left hand, more specifically. The thenar muscles. This little band of muscle between the thumb and the wrist."

Charlie felt for his own thenar muscles, as if for a pulse.

"At first, it seemed like the same tremble as the rest. Just involuntary muscle contractions. But there was maybe something else there. It's weird but purposeful movement, you sort of develop a sixth sense for it. Well, I stayed with it. All day long. I stayed with it, and I kept tracking his neurofeedback on the EEG." She gestured to the little wired stickers that made an electronic Medusa of Oliver's scalp. "That info alone couldn't tell us much, of course, but when I matched it with what I started to feel—"

"Started to feel *what*?"

"Here," she said, pulling Charlie's hand toward Oliver. Over the last weeks, Charlie had spent a great deal of time over Oliver's searching eyes, his jaw forever chewing at nothing, his skin borderline jaundiced. Charlie had made good use of his teenage self-training, taking in the sight in only nanosecond glimpses. When Ma had kissed Oliver's forehead before they left each evening, Charlie offered no more than a brotherly pat of his shoulder. But now, as Margot guided Charlie's fingers into Oliver's palm, he did not resist. Charlie could smell the coffee on Margot's breath, see the pores on her nose, the wetness around her eyes, those little unsettling intimacies. "Just like that, do you feel that muscle?"

But what Charlie felt was not, at least not at first, this muscle Margot described. What he felt, what overwhelmed him, was the simple meaty fact of Oliver's hand in his. It was like—just like an ordinary hand, like the hands of any of the men he had held in his coat pocket like lucky rabbits' feet as he staggered out of some New Hampshire or New York dive. Instead of whatever little movement Margot expected him to locate pulsing under Oliver's skin, Charlie received only another reminder of his wrongness, felt that all his reading and writing and imagining had been wrong. All that work seemed nothing next to the damp warm truth of his brother's hand.

"I'm not so sure. What should I be feeling for?"

"It took me a while to find it. But if you just stay like that, just keep your fingers there until you start to ignore the tremble, it's . . . well. It's there."

And then Margot turned to Bed Four and asked, "Isn't that right, Oliver?"

As if holding to a cliff face to keep from sliding, Charlie dug his fingers tightly into the rough nap of Oliver's skin.

"Same as before," Margot was saying. "Twice for yes."

And then it was as if the connection between hands became a live wire, sparking Charlie away. He dropped Oliver's hand and grasped his own, nursed it. In Charlie's fingers: the muscle memory of quick, twinned pulses. He could feel it still, as if, even now that they were apart, Oliver's thenar muscles were still beating against him.

"And he can—"

"Seems he can understand just fine." And now Margot completed the show of her technological sorcery. She returned to the work she'd been at when Charlie had come in and distracted her. She swung toward the bed a touch-screen monitor, its image divided in two. On the left, in a bright field of springtime green, was the word YES, and on the right, over stop-sign red, the word NO. "When the EEG reading spikes and he flexes twice," Margot said. "I guide his hand to press YES, and when he flexes once, I have him press NO."

Charlie was breathing through his gaping mouth.

"Oliver," Margot said, "do you know who is standing here with me?"

"Wait—"

Margot turned to flash Charlie a frustrated look—or maybe that was just the resting state of her wattled face? She spun back to observe the neurofeedback monitor, pointing at the screen with her free hand. "There," she said, and she guided Oliver's limp fingers to the green panel. "Yes," said the sprightly computer voice.

"Would you like to say hi to your brother?" Margot asked.

"Yes," the robot voice replied.

In the quiet that followed, Charlie stumbled over the bag he had dropped, nearly fell into his brother's lap.

"Oliver," he said. Or did not say. Charlie could hardly shape the name out of the air.

"Yes," the computer replied.

"You can really hear me?"

"Yes."

"It's still, I mean inside, it's still really—" Charlie did not quite know how to finish the question.

"Yes."

It was twenty minutes later when Charlie came back to himself and remembered why he had come early to Crockett State that morning. "Hey," Margot interrupted his barrage of questions. "Maybe we should give your ma a call? I have the feeling she might be interested in asking your brother a few questions of her own."

Charlie nodded frantically, clumsily grasped for the phone in his pocket.

"Ma?" Charlie asked the phone. "Ma?"

"Charlie? Where *are* you? What is it?"

Later, Charlie wouldn't be able to remember how he explained any of this to her; at the time, he was too busy replaying in his mind his first conversation with Oliver in a decade. No, not the first conversation, just the first in which Oliver could reply.

"Yes," Charlie had heard Oliver say, via his left hand's thenar muscles, via Margot Strout, via a computer's idiotic cheer.

"You can really understand every word?" Charlie asked.

"Yes."

"I—what can I even ask you? What is it that I could even say?"

"Yes."

"Ha. Ha ha!" There were tears in Charlie's eyes then, as the sentences begat more sentences. *And could you understand this entire time? Did you ever think no one would know? Do you know that Rebekkah is okay? I've seen her—she misses you still, she's never been the same, I'm sure you must know that?*

"Yes," the computer speaker answered.

But it was not all yeses—to a number of questions, Margot had piloted his brother's hand to the red panel for NO. "Are you in a lot of pain?" "No." "Have we done everything we can to make you comfortable?" "No." "Is it the bed?" "No." "Oh! Is it the window? Do you want it open?" "Yes."

After all those years, Charlie knew his questions were insufficient. Given only binary replies, he couldn't find the right things to say. But as Charlie cracked the window and so allowed Oliver to breathe possibly his first unfiltered air in years, Charlie understood that whether the robot voice said *yes* or *no,* it was truly just one question he had asked.

Yes. Though he had never told his mother in so many words, Charlie had always felt certain that if she turned out to be right, that if some part of Oliver really were awake inside his body, then his only answer to the question of that most pitiable life could be *no.* And yet, *Yes.* All of Charlie's despair, all his ruined ambition, all the things he thought he could not bear—what was any of that, when Oliver, in the least form of life that was possible, still beat his thenar muscles, twice for yes?

"What are you telling me?" Ma asked, many times over, on the phone.

"The truth!" Charlie said. "The truth!"

The truth shall set you free. Charlie's friend Christopher had liked to quote that adage from his AA program. Fifteen minutes later, Charlie was in an expansive, forgiving spirit, thinking about Rebekkah and Pa, thinking that he might call to tell them the wondrous news, thinking it might free them, too, thinking that he would at last tell Ma the whole shameful, dangerous truth about Jimmy Giordano and his "collections guy" and beg for her help, because wasn't that what family was for?

A decade prior, on the steps outside Bliss Township School, Hector Espina had liberated himself from this world, and at last Charlie knew that his brother had found a chink in his own jail walls, a brightness between the bricks, a starter tunnel, an actual crossing place from his nebulous spirit world. *Why?* Now that the rapping fist had found a door, it was louder than ever, but maybe they could finally turn the dead bolt, twist the knob, and at last . . .

Charlie would later remember grinning at a canyon lizard sprinting giddily across the parking lot. It would be difficult to forgive himself that morning's unquestioning optimism, his old pluckiness kicking back to life, his immense anticipation like some promise that his life's vexing conjunction was at last done with him. *However.* It did not occur to Charlie then, not at all, that the coincidence of Margot's eleventh-hour miracle work might have been no coincidence, only a scene Charlie himself had set in motion.

Oliver

....

CHAPTER SEVENTEEN

Spooky Action at a Distance: it wasn't only your family or the people of your town that were tangled up with you in that vexing physics. Thousands of miles away, in an apartment on Eighth Street, Brooklyn, sat another of your entangled bodies, in a very different sort of prison. Ah, that apartment, lost tenancy of your future! Dark mahogany bookcases, gingko trees filling the window greenishly, a spit of sunshine angling between the buildings. And there she was, Rebekkah Sterling, on another unremarkable afternoon, sitting alone in an upstairs room, plucking something tuneless from a guitar, tossing aside the guitar, grabbing a coat, and stepping out into the day.

Rebekkah Sterling, in her mid-twenties now: another prisoner of that night, setting the reel for another montage of miseries. Her guitar noodlings, her thousand meals of hummus and crackers, her two thousand pots of coffee. Her many abortive careers (an editorial assistant at a magazine: six months, a junior real estate broker: three months, a yoga instructor: abandoned before she had even completed her training at an ashram upstate), the retinue of strangers she brought back to her bed and quickly expelled ("A meeting in the morning," Rebekkah would say, or just "I'm not so good at sleeping with another person"), countless sobering 3 A.M.s, alone again in her bed. Miserable scenes, but maybe they would have been a kind of solace to you, Oliver? Years had passed, miles stood between you, but Spooky Action didn't care about these metrics. The long-lost love of your teenage years might have been thousands of miles away, might have grown into a future in which you'd have no place, but she was also still there with you in your bed, bound by that mysterious force. Bound, like you, in silence.

And yet, sometimes there at 511 Eighth Street, she would begin to type some confession into her computer; she would lift her phone and consider your brother's name. But always, in the end, when it came to the only story that mattered, she was as voiceless as you.

Of course, you would have envied those many men in Rebekkah's bed, but at least there was this comfort: not a one of them, no one Rebekkah knew there in Brooklyn, could know what you knew. The bad fact that turned the lock on apartment three, set the security chain. The sight you'd witnessed one October night.

October fifteenth. The sun had burned off the cloud cover by late that afternoon, when you were once more hanging outside the school. You had a half hour to kill as your father conducted an after-hours detention session, and you were sitting in Goliath, wanting the intensity of the summery warmth still in the car's interior to make your thoughts go fuzzy. Even the Hispanic kids' gathering out front had suffered from the heat. Like water, it had vanished into the afternoon haze, leaving behind only a couple doughy boys silently sipping cans of Dr Pepper.

An irony: when you had your first glimpse of the truth of things, you were trying very hard not to think of anything at all. But it was then, in the hazy distance, in the hellfire of four thirty on another West Texan afternoon, that you saw two figures exit the side door of Bliss Township School. They were just mirage-blurred abstractions, but you could recognize them both. The slightly hunched shuffle of Mr. Avalon, and the tentative half tiptoe of Rebekkah. It was just over a week now until the homecoming performance, and you knew that she had after-school rehearsals with Mr. Avalon. And yet there was something odd in the way they left the school at that slightly hurried pace, odder still that they then climbed, together, into the fancy vintage Cadillac Mr. Avalon drove. The engine fired, and they motored away, leaving behind a thick cloud of exhaust.

Two hours later, after a wearingly silent drive in your father's truck: the too-bright dining room at Zion's Pastures, your family taking forks to meat loaf, your brother smirking into his lap as he reread some lengthy letter from a friend. Another request of car keys from your father, another display of your mother's anxiety, the way she interrogated her ground beef with the business end of her knife. "Rebekkah Sterling again, huh?" your mother said. "Another one of your study groups."

You shrugged. "We just have more work to do. Why are you acting like that?"

A tense second, gathering energy, Ma shifting around in her chair, like she didn't want to tell you what she had to tell you next, but she was powerless to stop its rise to the surface. "What about how *you* have been acting? Suddenly we hardly even talk anymore, and you treat my basic questions like—" Her voice broke off before she arrived to the true substance of what she had to tell you, which her better reason kept quiet. But you didn't need your mother to explain her frustration; you were your mother's favorite, an invisible umbilical still connected you, and you knew that the defeated way she had often looked at you across the dinner table those last weeks was just a result of accumulating evidence that vast and vital parts of your life would take place beyond the two hundred acres of home.

And so, by a little after seven thirty that evening, half-sick with filial guilt, you were once more behind the wheel of Goliath, out on another fake study date. The fuchsia blush of sunset; a coyote singing his lonesome song over the plains. After years of citizenship in the teenage tyrannical state imposed by your West Texan classmates, you knew the official condemnation for a boy like yourself at this moment. "Loser," you said. But you couldn't help yourself. That evening, you were back to playing private investigator, conducting a stakeout on behalf of your demanding and unreasonable client, your jilted, baffled heart. The oddness of seeing Rebekkah getting a ride from Mr. Avalon, compounded by the strangeness of Mr. Avalon's anger when you came to ask him about her that day—understanding nothing, you felt you had to do *something*. These were questions that drove you through another desert night. Not eastward, to the Sterling McMansion, but to the north, past your school, to the address listed in the directory for Reginald Avalon. You clicked off Goliath's headlights as you approached the house.

It was dark now, and the last of the daylight made the night sky look electronic, lit bluely from behind. The thickly piled stucco of Mr. Avalon's pueblo looked like melted candle, or else scarred, burnt skin. All you could make out inside was a single light, the orange rectangle of a lit window against the cooling purple of the evening.

You told yourself you were being ridiculous, a boy stalking a teacher's house in his parents' hatchback. *Ha!* And yet. You opened Goliath's door and stepped into the chalky air of the Chihuahuan night.

But what were you going to do now? Creep up to the one lit window like some Peeping Tom? Crouch down low, beneath the sash, press your fingers to its frame, and slowly hoist your head into the light? Pathetic. But that is what you did anyway.

You made slow, trespasser progress to the house, testing each step as if the earth might suddenly give way. The remains of a long-abandoned flowerbed crunched and popped. But as you crept closer still, a sound overtook the quiet. Much louder than your own footsteps. The loose music of a guitar emanating from the window. And you were beneath that window now. Your fingertips shook on the stucco frame. You lifted your face into the light.

You were a silent and pitiable creature, a desert animal crouching in the moonlight, and what you saw inside the window was like a perfect tableau of what would never be yours. Rebekkah Sterling was just sitting there in the living room with her teacher. The music came from Rebekkah's own hands, as she sat on a kitchen chair, plucking a pretty tune from a guitar. You had no idea she played guitar. Her eyes were sealed now, as if she were becoming the music itself, sweet, simple, melancholic. A wind rose, Rebekkah opened her mouth, and her song drifted out.

I was living in a devil town, didn't know it was a devil town. Rebekkah's voice lifted—*Oh, Lord, it really brings me down about the devil town*—a voice to break apart your skin, to burst the glass from the window, to atomize the thick stucco wall between you and blow it out into the desert night. Your lanky body might still have been bent there on the other side of the window, but now you were with Mr. Avalon in his living room. You *were* Mr. Avalon, when Rebekkah struck the final chords. It was your hands that clapped, your body that hoisted itself from the sofa, you who stumbled a bit over the coffee table.

No, not you. Not anymore. Something bright and furious bursting. Before you could comprehend, before you could measure the meaning, you knew only the lover's ancient lament, the cruelty of hands that weren't yours wrapped around her. Rebekkah tilted her head in Mr. Avalon's direction.

You were outside the window, and you were also very far away, blinking into the scope of your father's Celestron. You began to understand in the way that Galileo had cracked the mystery of Earth's third-class place in the solar system—first, he had to patiently measure shadows moving on the faces of distant planets. You, too, had been measuring. The warm grin Mr. Avalon showed her in the halls. The gloom in Rebekkah's face when you brought up the man's name. It was those observations, and just the closeness of your attention to Rebekkah, that let you begin to comprehend what you were seeing. But an amateur astronomer like yourself could not have understood, not at all, the full truth.

Mr. Avalon stooped to Rebekkah and your world undid itself. Were you wrong? And yet, what was there not to comprehend?

Mr. Avalon pressed his lips against her. And not as you had, in your bashful, fumbling way. He held her cheeks and applied his mouth. Rebekkah did not fight, nor did she do much to return the kiss. She just offered her face and received him in an untroubled, routine way.

You did not speak or cry out. You were careful not to make a rustling sound against the wall. You made a silent plea into the night, which at last Rebekkah's face answered. Technically, her gaze met yours, but it looked very far away. Light-years.

A snapping. *Snap spap:* a dry branch in Mr. Avalon's dead garden. He turned. You dropped to the ground. Had he seen? What had he seen? What had you?

Light years: but Spooky Action, the mysterious understitching of our universe, renders our ordinary ideas of time and distance moot. And so, as you looked into Mr. Avalon's window, so too, ten years later, in the distant world over your bed, did your family look into another kind of opening. Seeing, but not understanding, not yet.

Eve

·················

CHAPTER EIGHTEEN

"Yes."

In the five days that Margot Strout had been translating her son's replies into the world, her son's *yes* flexed on inside of Eve, even alone in her bed at Desert Splendor. *Yes,* Eve had come to see, could also be a negation. Eve had quit her secretive little visits to her husband in Marfa. The attic stockpile she had been amassing for her son's future had not grown by a single hardcover. The day before, she'd even resisted the nice fountain pen someone left on the reception counter.

Yes: the word in her son's left hand, exactly where Eve had claimed. More specifically, the thenar muscles, just beneath his thumb. "I should have listened to you earlier," Margot Strout admitted, in what surely counted as one of the top ten most gratifying moments of Eve's life. Eve shrugged. "A mother knows these things."

It might have taken Margot Strout—with her EEG feedback software, her communication gear, and her training—to translate those twitches into anything legible, but it belonged to her, Eve felt, this second miracle. She had been very adamant on that point, lecturing Charlie and even Peggy to say nothing to the Fifteenth of November set, the Wolcott/Henderson/Dawson/Schumacher cadre who had dropped by again with a plate of oatmeal cookies, the larger set of politicized mourners led by Donna Grass who had sent carnations, or the reporters who still sporadically phoned her. Harder to ignore, though ignore she had for three days now, were the phone calls from Manuel Paz, asking her to stop by the station. "I know what a time this must be for you," Manuel said in one of his several voice mails that she let herself play, "but it's very important we talk." Even if Hector Espina was ten years in the earth, Eve knew how much the former citizenry of Bliss might make of it. The lost boy, the most inexplicable victim of an inexplicable catastrophe in a vanished town, a nearly forgotten tragedy's only living memorial, at last able to reply for himself.

"I think we have a right to know what Oliver has to tell us before we invite the whole world to come crowding in," she told Charlie. "I think Oliver has that right. I think he deserves a little space here. We all do."

"But what about Pa?" Charlie asked. "Shouldn't we at least tell him? Put the man out of his misery?"

"Soon," Eve said, and meant it. "I'll tell him myself." But something had thus far kept her from sharing this news with her husband. Perhaps it was only the old vindictive streak, or perhaps something else, something about the dark, silent place she occupied with Jed when she went to see him in Marfa. A warm-sad safe room, securely sealed off from the unsettled atmosphere of her present life.

It had only been five times with Jed, and each time Eve told herself she was only going to "update" him, offer a little kindness to the leathery old depressive. And yet, each time on the drive over, she felt her whole body swelling with the promise of a quick lance of relief, in the way she could feel her hands trembling to act out another theft. Except this particular need was not about the future, of course it was not. It wasn't about some shallow and sentimental idea of partnership in her fraught days, certainly not about any hope (*God forbid!*) that they might actually get together again. Though he lamely claimed it was only turned apple cider, Eve found on one visit two jars of Jed's urine stashed beneath his bed! But she had been able to ignore the piss jars; the whole thing seemed not quite real, a few crazy, stolen hours in some place so far beyond the boundaries of her daily reality that Eve knew she would never have to acknowledge any of it. Also, no denying it: for all of Charlie's smug condemnations, his twenty-three-year-old's certainty that he must know much more than she, there was more than a little pleasure in this one thing he didn't know. What would Charlie think of *that*? Often, Eve had failed to keep the grin from her cheeks.

The morning that Charlie had tearily called from Crockett State to tell her the news, Eve had already discovered his little runaway note fixed to the fridge. "To be honest, Ma," Charlie later admitted, in the rare bout of honesty the newest development had apparently inspired, "I'm in trouble, real trouble." Charlie had sobbed, Eve had rocked him quiet in the kitchen chair. "I'll pay it. Of course I'll take care of you," she told him. "I know you sometimes forget this but I'm not only the dictator you think you've escaped, I'm also your mother who loves you." A victorious moment, no doubt, more victorious still when Charlie freshly crumpled into her arms. And so she had no choice but to pay as promised, and now the combined life savings of the family Loving was at $962 and falling. The night before, Eve had felt that the pages of *Jesus Is My BFF* were radiating moral condemnation from her nightstand—as if her own life were the cautionary epilogue for Christians who denied Christ's good counsel—and she gathered the papers and slammed them into the stand's bottom drawer.

And so the dreaded financial scenario had arrived at last. Eve was falling to the red side of the money line now. The Lovings would have to live on credit, Eve on her shiny blue Visa, Charlie on his mother's overstrained generosity, her threadbare patience. A question she told herself that she really must stop asking: How could she have raised a son to do something so stupid as to fall three months behind on rent to that gangsterishly accented landlord she'd spoken with on the phone? "Family," Jimmy Giordano—his actual name!—had told Eve over the phone, "it's a merciful thing. Glad to know that kid is with a mother who loves him."

"Well, for the record, I think we should have already told Pa, but I'll let you call the shots," Charlie said.

"You'll *let* me. How decent of you," Eve said.

And yet, in the Big Bend, news never stays private for long. Eve didn't know who summoned her—she suspected Peggy, or Dr. Rumble, or perhaps even Margot—but on that Friday an M.D.-Ph.D. (or, in her own words, "a grief and trauma specialist") named Linda Finfrock showed up, all the way from Midland, to "help you and Oliver through this exciting but also very complicated time." Linda Finfrock's idea of "help" was apparently the lengthy lecture she delivered to Eve and Charlie on the topic of post-traumatic stress, about not prying the lid too soon.

"It is like the lid on Pandora's box," Dr. Finfrock said in her pedantic, lounge singer's dark-smooth voice. A streak of white rose through the lady's hairdo like a semicolon. "Of course you'll have questions for Oliver, I know that everyone will, but we need to move slowly. None of us can possibly even imagine what all this might feel like for him now. And from what Mrs. Strout tells me, Oliver is still struggling to work out basic words. The point here is that we have to give him time, a lot of time, before you force any hard questions. We don't, you know, want to let out all the ghosts at once."

Eve nodded. "I couldn't agree with you more," she said.

"And how are you doing?" the doctor asked Eve, pointing her pen toward Eve's baggy, reddened eyes. "Everything okay? This is no small thing for you, either."

"Never been more wonderful," Eve said.

"The alphabet," Margot Strout was saying, after Eve and Charlie had settled into their chairs by Bed Four that Saturday afternoon. "It's far from perfect. But we're making progress."

"The alphabet?"

Margot grinned, sucked audibly at a butterscotch candy. Indulging her dramatic streak that Eve had noticed over the last week, Margot declined to explain anything more, leaving her demonstration to do the explaining.

"Hey, Oliver, do you know who just walked in here? Who I'm talking to?" Margot resumed her work posture, pressing her index and middle fingers in to the meat of Oliver's left thenar muscles. The EEG wires trembled.

Eve anticipated the bright, robot cheer of the familiar "Yes." Instead, Margot did something new.

"A? B? C? D? E? F?" Keeping her gaze on the biofeedback reading, Margot recited the alphabet until its middle, pausing at M, at which point Margot pressed a key on the screen mounted over the bed and started the alphabet anew. "A?" she asked, but this time she made it no further. And when Margot now pressed another button, the computer spoke Oliver's name for Eve—not *Mother* or *Mom* but the Texan endearment, "Ma."

"Oliver." *Ma:* like a sharp blow to her back. Eve was breathless, straining. Dr. Finfrock was right, but Pandora's box did not only belong to her son. It was all screaming out of her now. Years, terror, stolen goods, a disintegrating house, a lost and reckless son, a prayer offered for genuflecting hours each day. It rushed down her cheeks, rose in her throat. She was very nearly sick.

"Holy shit," Charlie said. "I mean, shit!"

"You said it." Margot laughed.

"We can ask him whatever we want?" Charlie asked. "We can just say whatever we want, and he can talk back to us?"

"I'd steer clear of asking his opinion on politics. Ha! It's slow for now, one letter at a time." Margot's voice trembled, quavering away from professional neutrality. "But there are techniques to pick up speed. And we'll get to all that soon. We'll start using another kind of alphabet, with the letters arranged by frequency—"

But then words seemed to abandon the speech pathologist, too. The woman's skin had gone splotchy, red continents lighting up all over the globe of her head. She was, after all, a mother as well, another mother who had lost a part of her own body. She was another mother with her heart torn out, who had tried to make for herself this second or third life pulling words from the aphasic in the forlorn clinics and hospitals of the West Texas desert. Watching the wetness pool and roll over the blush of her cheeks, it was the first time that Eve let herself consider that Dr. Rumble and the rest might have had a point about Margot. Eve and Margot had never spoken, at least not directly, about the events of that night or about the daughter Margot lost, the husband who had walked out on her, but just now it seemed to Eve that the woman's story might really have been quietly heroic all along, sublimating all that sorrow into this vital work. To Eve's considerable surprise, she saw her own arms reaching for Margot Strout, pulling the woman's heft against her, their mingled tears making a sloppy sound where their necks touched. Even Charlie tried to get in on the act, gently patting both women between their shoulder blades.

They disentangled and inhaled. Eve cupped a hand over Oliver's cheek as his eyes carried on their frantic search. Margot lifted his left hand, bored into the meat of his palm.

What words does one say when one can, after a decade-long silence, speak with a lost son? What are the first words and the second? The first thing Eve came up with might have been the most overused sentence in the English language, the language's oldest recipe, served again and again to the verge of blandness, but what else was there for her to tell Oliver but "I love you"?

"A? B? C? D?"

"L," Margot announced when she felt the twinned pressure of Oliver's thenars at that letter. Then O, V, and E.

"Love," the robot voice said. And though the intent was already clear, Margot worked to give the full weight of the phrase. A minute later, the computer added, "You."

In the last hours of that day, before they broke for a Sunday off, Margot translated eighty-six words from her patient's thumb into the robot voice. All these words on Finfrock-approved topics. To the question of comfort, "G-tube tight." To the question of entertainment, "Tolkien" and "Dylan." To the question of loneliness, "Some-times." To the question of boredom, "Sometimes." To the question of desired visitors, "Dad."

"Dad?" Charlie said, glancing up to Margot, who squinted at her neurofeedback screen.

"A? B? C?" Margot asked.

"Want to see Pa," the computer eventually pronounced.

That evening, after Eve had customarily kissed Oliver's cheek and gathered her things, she looked for a long while at Margot, unbur-dening her hand, flexing at its stiffness. When Charlie ran off to the bathroom, Eve spoke the woman's name.

"Yeah?" Margot looked up from the packing of her gear, sniffed wetly.

"I don't know," Eve said. "It's kind of ironic, right? That I don't have words to tell you how—grateful? Thankful. I am."

"Just my job," Margot said. "Just a very lucky part of my job."

"The thing is, what I want to say to you—I want to say that I know it can't be easy. If I had lost a child, and then had to do what you are doing for Oliver now? I don't think I could quite bear it. Or maybe I don't know anything. But I want to say thank you."

Eve, after the fashion of the Loving family, had long ago learned to make her skin into stone, fortifying herself against the outside, bulwarking what was within. The way Margot took her hands was not merely surprising, it was existentially jarring, to be reminded that a human could respond to another human so nakedly. "No," Margot said. "Thank *you*."

········ ············

CHAPTER NINETEEN

Sunday morning. Charlie had left at dawn, depositing on the kitchen table a note that read only "Working. Be back later." And so Eve, in retaliation, decided to offer no further explanation for her own day's plans than a retaliatory missive that read, "Went out." She looked at it for a while, penned onto a paper towel, and—deciding to take the higher road—added, "Hugs and Kisses, Ma."

An hour later, Eve pulled onto Paisano Lane in Marfa. She did a cursory inspection of the property, but Jed could not be found beneath the garbage angels strung up in his shed. Cupping her hands to a bit of filthy glass behind the dead circuitry of vines, Eve couldn't find any sign of him among the frowzy furniture and grayed light of his living room. In the week since she had last visited, it seemed that the stage for their absurd trystings had gone dark, and the wistful nostalgia of romance they'd moaned about on the dun weave of that tired sofa shamed her now. It was Sunday, and she remembered Jed telling her that he got the weekends off, but where was he? Eve thought of the place he once told her about, where he went to "recover" his artistic materials. An industrial waste dumping ground, a pit dug into Tusk Mountain, to be filled in at the end of the year.

She found the dump a dozen miles south of Marfa, a place so desperate as to be a little beautiful in a soulful way. A great crater in the desert, a bowl of West Texan refuse, as if an asteroid had perfectly struck and demolished a little town that once stood at the mountain's base. Eve parked Goliath at the pit's rim, and among the glinting metal, the visual cacophony of colors slowly coordinating themselves into brown-red rust and brown-gray rot, she saw a man in denim coveralls crouching in the trash, a cigarette fuming in his face, as he attempted to dislodge some object. In the direction of the sole survivor of an Armageddon, Eve waved both her arms, the motion of her scapulae igniting the fuse of her spinal cord.

"Jed!"

He stood. In lieu of a wave, Jed flicked his cigarette into the scrap, and Eve, for a breathtaking moment, had the apprehension the whole thing might explode.

The way down into the pit was a ladder, bolted into the limestone edge. "You shouldn't be here." Jed reached to help lower her onto the spongy, creaking surface.

"Maybe not. But here I am."

"No, I mean that it's dangerous. This place used to *glow*. At night. Honest to God."

"Then what are *you* doing here?"

As if to demonstrate, Jed plugged another Pall Mall into his sun-pleated face. He grimaced there, irradiating himself triply: the carcinogenic torching of his lungs, the penetrating UVs of the sun on his skin, the unstable nuclei of the waste beneath spinning off their beta particles and gamma rays.

"Sweetie." Eve recognized Charlie's condescending voice in her own mouth. "You don't need to play the martyr for me."

Jed nodded, turned back to the work she had interrupted, pulling at some protruding wooden knob as the fresh cigarette puffed tractorishly from his head. He lost his purchase on his grasp, fell drunkishly on his ass.

"Will you at least let me help you with that?" Eve went to Jed and crouched as she tried to heft the sheet of corrugated asbestos that covered whatever he was tugging at. She passingly wondered at the strangeness of it all, that this was her life at this moment on earth, grunting and wheezing with her rumpled husband–cum–secret lover to deliver a garbage child. With their combined effort, Jed at last pulled the object free. An old tailor's dummy.

"The fifth one of these I've found," he said admiringly. "I think I might do another series."

"Your mother was a seamstress, wasn't she? During the war."

Jed didn't answer. He gave Eve his cigarette to hold, then pulled away a brown crust of something stuck to the dummy's armpit.

"He's speaking," Eve said.

Jed turned to her, pleated the leather of his forehead.

"Remember Margot Strout? That speech therapist. She found some movement, in his hand. Just like I always said." Eve described Margot's palpating and her EEGs, the first yeses and nos, the alphabet. "It's him, Jed," she concluded in a low, exhilarated voice. "It's *Oliver*."

"I know, I heard. Dr. Rumble called to tell me." Jed looked at her, seeming to conduct some private tabulation.

"So I don't understand this then. My God, Jed! We should be celebrating. Why didn't you come running over when you heard?"

Jed eyed the headless mannequin, shook his head. "I don't know."

"You don't know *what*?"

Jed pinched the cigarette from Eve's fingers, sucked at its trembling end. "Did you know that Charlie came to see me?" Jed said gently.

"He didn't."

Eve watched Jed rub his arm, the old posture of his silence, as if he literally had to hold his opinion in. "Well, he did."

"You didn't tell him about—about us, did you?"

Jed shook his head. "Eve? He asked me something."

"Oh, good."

"He asked me why we never fought them for more tests, second opinions. For Oliver. He asked why we didn't know. Sooner. Years ago."

"And what did you tell him?"

"I didn't know what to tell him."

"No one thought . . ." Eve said.

"Why didn't we make them?" Jed said meekly. "Why didn't you?"

"Why didn't *I*? Why didn't *you* ever stop me? If what I was doing was so wrong, why didn't you tell me? I'll tell you why. It's because you were nowhere to be found. You were curled up at the bottom of a whiskey bottle."

Even now Jed didn't speak. He gasped, the cigarette tumbling out, burning his arm. "Shit!" Jed clasped at his wrist, a fury in his eyes.

"You want to know why I haven't come?" Jed seethed. "I didn't come because I really just can't bear it. Because I really have no idea what to believe anymore."

"Meaning what?"

"Meaning," Jed said, "that I've been thinking of what that professor told us, how we just can't know if Oliver can even understand us. And Margot Strout tried once with Oliver before, right? She tried, and she failed. And you said you didn't trust her, remember? One of those fanatic Christian types, off in some world of her own. And suddenly she's found something? Look. Maybe you're right. But I just can't let myself get my hopes up until I know for sure. Not anymore."

"Until you know? It's him, Jed. Come to the place and see. It's *him*."

"Okay. I'm only speaking for myself. I'm not saying you're wrong."

"So what are you saying?"

Jed shook his head. "I'm sorry. Don't listen to me. What do I know? Nothing."

"So it's finally happened," Eve said. "You have completely lost the ability to believe good things. It's very sad, really."

"Maybe you're right," Jed said. "You usually are."

A cloud of some unspeakable decay, arsenic and death and something like yogurt, hit Eve's nostrils. Whatever further reply Eve wanted to make was like a book from a dream, the words vanishing just as she tried to read them. But at least Eve understood now why she had waited to share the news with the walking five-foot-nine mood disorder that was her husband. His disbelief in any good news, the helplessness he'd learned over thirty years of false escapes in his painting shed.

"Good luck with your dummies," Eve said. "I hope they're better company than us." She made creaking, popping progress back toward the ladder.

"You want to know what we're doing here?" Jed spoke to her back, and she turned. "This whole thing of ours. We're both just looking for an excuse."

"An excuse? An excuse for *what* exactly?"

He retrieved the dropped cigarette, and what he said next he said in a practiced way, a sentence that he had scripted long ago. "For what we've let him become."

Eve looked at this sad-eyed drunk, his teeth going gray. Her anger burned on her neck, white-hot and consuming.

"If you can sober up enough to drive over," Eve said, "you might want to hear what Oliver has to tell you."

"I hope you're right. I mean that." His tone condescended in a way that even Eve could never have mustered. The sorrow of an old man, an aging priest, addressing a little girl.

"You hope I'm right? This isn't a matter of opinion. Really, truly, I can never understand you. Not at all."

On the way home, Eve panicked a little as the traffic slamming up the westbound lane warped and blurred with the tears that were coming. But Eve focused on the yellow and white lines of the pavement, a textbook lesson on vanishing point, and she managed to make it back to Desert Splendor. Parked in the driveway, Eve dabbed furiously at her leaking nose. She jammed the heel of her palm into her eyes until her vision sparked and exploded. But, pulling her hands away, she could smell it: beneath the oily funk of the garbage she had handled, the acrid, nicotine scent of Jed Loving.

Eve had never had any patience for smoking. Even when he claimed to have quit, her father still often smoked his cigars in motel bathrooms, the fumes leaking out underneath the door, an excellent example of his noxious decisions, their pernicious, secondhand effect on his daughter. Eve could never imagine the utter stupidity required to put death into your mouth and light it up. But that hated smell, the chemical tang of self-destruction, she furiously sniffed at now. The smell that had, in the haywire circuitry of her exhaustion, become inseparable from the warmth that cracked open when she was in close proximity to Jed. What was it about Jed's sorrow that always overthrew her fury? Maybe it was her father, leaving some ruinous stain on her psychic life, setting a pattern she couldn't break? Maybe she—Eve let the thought go when she located the odor's epicenter, the knuckles of her left hand, and shoved them halfway into her tear-prickled nostrils. She inhaled and thought of turning the car around. She thought, also, *This will be the last time I will smell him.* A part of her knew she was being melodramatic, scoffed silently at that knuckle-sniffing Eve. The other part of her sniffed away, miserably.

When Eve unbuttoned her jeans and worked the free hand beneath the elastic, the sensation was curiously like her megastore purloinings, the glee of appalling herself, this demonstrable if peculiar evidence that she was giving herself what the world refused her. Eve had not touched herself like this in a very, very long time; the lost Eve, the younger Eve, now communicated with the present aging knuckle-sniffer via her pressed fingers. She moaned loudly, obliviously, and so did not hear the sound of the car's approach up her drive. She could not, however, miss the *thump* of a car door slamming. She startled, retracted her hand, did not quite manage to button her pants before Manuel Paz was tapping at the window.

"Manuel?"

Looming over her car, Manuel did not quite look like the man she knew, her occasional Bed Four visitor with his hangdog grimace. Now he was Ranger Captain Paz, making a gun shape of his hand, his stubby index finger for a barrel, which he pointed at Eve. She rolled her window down with a few angry cranks.

"Look who came to drop by," Eve said.

"You really should have returned my call," Manuel told her. "Why didn't you just call me back?"

"I've been busy."

"Well," Manuel said sadly, "next time you should probably call back when an officer phones you. Because now this conversation isn't exactly optional."

Eve looked for a while at this bald Ranger, halfheartedly playacting the part of a serious law enforcement professional. Beyond Manuel, the land shimmered with heat in all directions, the sky bluely doubled in the earth. They could have been alone together, Manuel and Eve, in the middle of the ocean.

"Okay, then," Eve said.

Ten minutes later, on the peeling veneer of Eve's kitchen table, Manuel Paz had placed a fuzzy, still image from a camera at the electronics store, a grainy picture of Eve dropping a laptop computer into her purse. Eve oddly accepted this police evidence of her own larceny like a development that had happened long before, eyeing the five-by-seven glossy as if the woman in the picture were not quite she. Eve's initial reaction to this image bothered her only in its suggestion of how unhealthy—how gaunt and mildly deranged—the woman in the picture looked to her. Even now, the fact that her son was communicating was like a velocity that could keep Eve running over any canyon, like Wile E. Coyote before he looks down. "The security guy sent some tape of a certain lady in a business suit," Manuel explained. "Local cops couldn't figure the thing out, though it didn't take me but a second to recognize you."

Eve nodded, received this news philosophically. She was thinking of the glowing light, the computer's electronic slumber. It seemed that she had been right; the laptop really had been a test. Though of what she couldn't exactly say now. "I'll give it back," she said. "Of course I will."

Manuel squinted at her, worked a thumbnail between two upper bicuspids. "Right."

At last, Eve did look down. She was thinking of the irrefutable argument her fingers spoke to her just before they made their many petty thefts. Those same fingers, feeling a black chip in the surface of her tabletop: in this room they now seemed the hands of a madwoman.

"I don't know what to tell you," Eve said. The sight of Manuel's familiar, age-pocked face was going a little fuzzy. "I'm sorry."

"You know what that thing costs?" Manuel asked with a paternal kind of disappointment. "Two thousand dollars. *Two thousand.*"

Eve hung her head. "And I never even would have turned it on, honestly. I can't explain it."

Manuel felt for Eve's fingers, gave them a squeeze. "Try," he said, not entirely kindly.

Eve nodded again, because hadn't something in her, a wild something that began in her fingers, always thrilled at the thought of being caught, the very private crisis that was her life forced into public view, when she would at last be made to speak the unspeakable? Had a scene like this, in fact, been the secret plot her fingers had been contriving for years? "It was for Oliver," Eve found herself instantaneously relieved to admit. "I know how crazy that might sound. And I know it's wrong, I know that. It's hard to explain. But sometimes? I see something he would want. And it's like—it's like I'm a bad mother if I don't. I think that you of all people might be able to understand that."

Manuel's gentle demeanor broke now. He pulled away from Eve, and the frustration in the fist he made around a pen seemed oddly husbandly, resentment petrified to stone. "For your information," Manuel said, "this ain't the first time that one of those stores has sent pictures of you. For your information, you've given me some explaining to do over the years. The poor woman lost her son, she ain't thinking straight. Just leave her be, don't let her back in the store. I've even lied for you. Don't know that person in the picture from Adam. This ain't the first time I've had to lie for you, Eve."

Eve truly was appalled by herself, but only for three or four ticks of the wall clock. "I never asked you to lie," Eve said.

Manuel thinned his lips. "Though I think you might be a little grateful. You've really given me quite a burden to shoulder, you know."

"I've given *you* a burden, have I?"

Manuel waved a blank sheet of paper, as if to show he was already so tired of this nonsense.

"So arrest me now, if that's what you want," Eve said. "But maybe first you could do me the favor of explaining why it is then that you have chosen *now*, of all times, to have this particular conversation."

Manuel loosened his hand, puffed his cheeks, blew. "Maybe I'm here," Manuel said, "because when this particular tape landed on my desk, I got to thinking that after all this covering I've done for you, I'm starting to feel like I just don't want to do it anymore. Not when it turns out you weren't straight with me from the get-go."

"Meaning *what* exactly?"

Manuel held his stubble-white chin with three fingers, the posture of a man in distant theoretic discourse with himself. "Eve," Manuel said, "why did you lie to me?"

"*Excuse* me?" A wasp alighted on the table, then flew across the kitchen and hurled itself futilely against a window. "And what was it that I supposedly lied to you about?"

"Charlie told me something interesting the other day. Says that Oliver wrote a bunch of love poems for that Sterling girl."

"Charlie told you that?" Eve managed to say these words as a question, pressing her fingertips to the desk to keep the shriek of betrayal in her chest. What did Charlie have—some list of people he might visit to inflict maximum agony upon her? "And so what? So what if Oliver wrote a few moony love poems years and years ago? What difference could that fact have possibly made? For God's sake, Manuel."

"Sure," Manuel said. "Maybe you're right, maybe it couldn't make any difference now. But if it didn't matter at all, why not tell me about it? Doesn't that seem strange?" Manuel renewed his grasp on his face, covering his mouth for a long moment, looking like the speak-no-evil monkey. "I'll tell you what," he added. "For years, I've been saying it to myself, that if I couldn't ever offer you any real answers, the least I could do, after all y'all have been through, was to help you where I could. But maybe I've let that guilt of mine make me a little blind. Maybe I should have pressed you a little harder on this particular topic, all that time ago. Look. Maybe there's no explaining Hector, or maybe all those folks are right, maybe he really was just trying to make some sort of point. But I still can't believe it. I can't believe there is simply no reason why a boy would just suddenly turn into a monster without warning."

"And so," Eve spoke levelly, at the table, "what you believe is that some love poems my son wrote a decade ago are somehow going to explain away three dead children?"

"My question, if you recollect," Manuel said, "is why Oliver was at that classroom that night. And also why Hector let Rebekkah just walk away. That maybe Hector was jealous of what Oliver and Rebekkah—"

"Oliver and Rebekkah! Oliver and Rebekkah, you keep saying, like they were some couple. They weren't. They weren't! Wouldn't I have known about that?"

"Apparently," Manuel said, "there's no telling what you might know."

Eve wouldn't reply; she wouldn't even shake her head.

"You know that we have a term for lying to an officer don't you?" Manuel said. "It's called obstruction of justice."

"So you should really do it, then. You should arrest me! And while you're at it, you should probably arrest Jed, too. Or was it apparently only up to me to describe every little detail of how Oliver used to spend his time?"

Manuel pushed the end of his pen against his finger, twirled it as he spoke. "It's been almost ten years now, Eve, and I've followed more dead ends than I care to admit, heard so much craziness. A good number of people dear to me have left town, treated like criminals because their folks came from the other side of the river. But still I can't bring myself to quit this place. I just need to know how it happened. Whatever there is to know. Anything. I need to know. Don't *you*?"

Eve inhaled deeply. The image before her, that security photo of a rail-thin middle-aged lady dropping a computer into her bag, was like a vivid medical exhibit on the pathology of her own secret-keeping, so why not just tell Manuel at last? Between the moment Eve gathered her next thought and actually, finally spoke the oft-imagined admission out loud, there was just a single free-fall second of terror. "He tried to talk to me about her once," Eve heard herself say.

"Oliver? He tried to talk with you about Rebekkah?"

Eve tipped her head slowly, up and down. "He tried to tell me something about her once, how he was worried about her, but I never let him explain it to me."

Manuel tilted back in the kitchen chair, its vinyl moaning. "I see," he said.

"But do you?" Eve looked up at Manuel now, as she had looked pleadingly at many security guys before him. "Do you see what it would be like, to spend ten years wondering what might have happened if only you'd listened one night? Do you see why I couldn't, just could not, bear to talk about something like that?"

Manuel didn't answer. He only studied her, as if each word, the twitch in her nose, the way she felt for her bun of hair, might have suggested another conversation entirely.

"He's speaking!" Eve blurted. "Did you know that? If you have so many questions, you can just ask Oliver yourself."

"Speaking?"

Eve did her best to calm herself and explain again about the thenar muscles, the alphabet. The latest miracle, which just now sounded, in Eve's trembling voice, like some dubious lie she was inventing on the spot. Manuel certainly squinted at her that way, as if she was only telling more stories of the sort he'd learned better than to believe. "Well." Manuel drew his mouth into a sideways pucker. "That *is* interesting."

"Interesting?" Eve asked. "It's more than interesting. It's the truth. It's the wonderful truth."

"But didn't it occur to you," Manuel said, "that if this *wonderful* thing has suddenly happened, then that might also be a fact I'd be interested in knowing?"

"I didn't think it was any of your business. I mean, what do you have in mind now? You're going to carry on some kind of interrogation with a boy who has to spend five minutes to type out a single word?" Eve was choking on her tears.

"I really am sorry for you," Manuel said. "I am." And the horrible part was how truly sorry he really did look, the patronizing expression of a man speaking to an insane person. He reached across the table again, but this time she jerked her hands away. "I'll tell you what," he added. "How about I just go to Crockett State in the morning to see for myself?"

"See for yourself what?"

"I suppose," Manuel said, with a wistful half grin, "to see for myself if we've got an honest-to-goodness miracle on our hands."

Eve did not look up at Manuel as he patted her shoulder twice in parting. She leaned forward in her chair and pressed her face to the cool of the table as the squeak of Manuel's footsteps retreated.

Eve had long ago learned how to make her anger a steadier, more dependable substance, how to smelt and recast it into a thin barbed wire she strung around her life. And yet, just now the perimeter did not hold. As the sound of Manuel's squad car rumbled away, Eve was not thinking about that shameful security glossy or even about the fact she had at last admitted to Manuel. She was thinking, instead, of the uncertainty that had come into her voice when she related Margot's work with Oliver. She was thinking, also, of Jed standing there in the crater at Tusk Mountain, the way he'd spoken Margot Strout's name like some kind of curse. And she now let herself consider it, her one spot of bother, which her gleeful relief had happily skipped over. "Is there anyone you want to see? Anyone you want me to bring here?" Eve had asked Oliver. When the computer answered, it had said not her son's name for his father, not *Pa,* but *Dad.*

Eve clenched her fist, beat the table with a few quick raps, but it was still there, that worrisome little syllable from the computer speaker. Like that long-ago conversation she'd never let Oliver have with her, a tiny red stain on her certainty. *Dad.*

And look: this day had one last indignity in store for her. Eve startled at the whine of a body shifting its weight on the floorboards. Apparently, there had been a witness to the scene she had just endured. A room away, Charlie sat in the dimness of the stairwell, palming his stubbled jaw. "We need to talk," Charlie said.

Oliver

· · · · · · · · · · · · · · · · · ·

CHAPTER TWENTY

Oliver, the events of your final walking weeks might have become the defining details in the story of your life, but why suffer needlessly, dwelling solely on those last days of your upright existence? There were more than a few happy memories there, in that distant ether on the far side of Bed Four, and before setting you back down amid the worst of your memories, why not first pause to return you to one of the best? Memories of hazy summer light, an inky paperback in your hand, a lingering smell of sandwich condiments. Your family.

July in West Texas was a lot like deep February in four-season country. When you were locked inside for unending days, time became a slack, amorphous substance, the chiming of the clock like some hourly repeated sardonic quip. Truth be told, despite your complaints, Bliss Township's early-August start to the school year was a relief. The air-conditioning at the schoolhouse was vastly superior to the single little wheezing window unit at Zion's Pastures.

But on that particular summer day, when you were fourteen, it was still blazing July, a drab 2 P.M. You were all there together in the living room. Lethargic from lunch, huddled around the AC, you hid behind your books. Often, you'd complain about the grunty rustle of your father's breathing, your brother's picking at his nose, the weird video

game sounds he hummed. Your mother always seemed the least bothered by these forced confinements. When you could bear it no longer
and would set off for a dip in the tepid, brackish Loving Creek, she
would complain, "But we were having family time!"

But those days were not, in the end, endless. Later, you would all
do anything for another.

"I have an idea!" Ma said, cueing the collective groaning that often
greeted her inexplicable afternoon inspirations. "Let's all draw a picture."

"A picture?"

"Yes!" she said. "We'll each draw one picture of Zion's Pastures.
The thing that we think about first when we think about home."

"Ugh," you said. Yet you were too lazy from the heat to put up a
protest when she came back to the living room with a box of col-
ored pencils and four sheets of paper on schoolhouse clipboards.
The effort of this activity would be taxing, but worse would be Ma's
silent-treatment punishment for not cooperating. You picked up a
brown pencil and began to sketch.

You were never much of a drawer, but the image materializing
onto your sheet of printer paper didn't look so bad to you. You hadn't
chosen a subject, you had only started to doodle an arching shape
that, as the line extended, revealed itself to be the wide horns of your
ranch's last steer, Moses.

You weren't trying to make any sort of point to your mother that
your one image of home was not of the meandering and ramshackle
house, not the four of you standing portrait style on the lawn, but of
your lonesome, wandering beast. It was simply what your hand
wanted to draw, and the more you drew, the more surprised you
were at the detail you could remember. You could call forth the exact
pattern of Moses's brown patches, the touch of mange on his rear
haunches, and you thought you quite expertly captured your longhorn's
eyes, as Zen wise as an infant's. "Okay," your mother said. "Let's
compare. On three. One, two, three!"

Laughter split the heat-thickened silence of the living room of Zion's
Pastures. It echoed off the bones hung on the walls, agitated the porce-

lain figurines of cowboys and stallions in the china cabinet. All four of your pages showed the figure of Moses, wandering the hills. Charlie's was a crude, grinning stick figure, your mother's was a hirsute and frenetic squiggle, your father's was done up in his van Goghian eddying style, and yours looked less like a cow than some sort of cow-hybrid monster. But you were still laughing in bellyful gasps. Laughing and laughing because, in the drowning July heat, when the warmth had pooled between you like deep water, making you each an island, you still all shared the same unlikely idea of what was home.

And yet, Oliver, it is unavoidable now: that pulled drain plug at the bottom of your story, that black hole into which time itself bends, that immeasurable heaviness to which all your memories return. No use in trying to fight its intractable sway. The night of November fifteenth.

November fifteenth: it was just after 7 P.M., and there you were, looking at those portraits of Moses, cheaply framed on your bedroom wall, when the phone rang in the kitchen. Annoyed, you did not so much as turn from the pillow, and at last it fell silent before ringing again. The Homecoming Dance was a supposed privilege for juniors and seniors only, but even your freshman brother had big plans for the evening, another one of his massive friend gatherings, at the Alpine Cinemas. Your mother was off driving Charlie to the movie, which she had agreed to do only with Charlie's dubious reassurance that he'd find some other friend's mom to give him a ride home. You plodded into the kitchen, plucked the wireless phone from its cradle, and marched back to your bed.

"Why don't you just come?" Pa asked over the phone. He was serving as a school dance chaperone, and behind him you could hear the crowd noise, the bass line of some familiar but unplaceable pop hit. "You only get two homecomings."

"As if it's not pathetic enough," you told him, in an imitation of his own defeated voice, "that I have no date, now you want me to show up alone."

The fact of your datelessness had been on full display that day at Bliss Township School, a result of the miserable statewide homecoming tradition in which your school proudly took part. On the night before the dance, your school's juniors and seniors had met in living rooms across Presidio County for the well-photographed exchange of mums and garters. Mums for the girls, garters for the boys. Both were bouquets of gaudy ribbons and silk flowers—lighting or sound effects often included—handmade by a special someone, to be worn at school the next day. And so, on November fifteenth, the divisions had become clear: the beloved strolling the halls, their dates' names spelled in sparkling stickers, their toy cowbells ringing. The dateless made to wander undecorated and bereft.

You were a little disgusted by yourself, wallowing in these teeny dramas. But a week had passed since the night at Mr. Avalon's window, and the fact of what you'd witnessed was too big for you to know what to do with it. The monster wasn't her father or some other boy. But was Rebekkah right, that your telling would only make it worse for her? And what did you know of romance, sex, love? It was not as if Mr. Avalon had pinned her down; she had lifted her head to meet his. But then why that bruise on her leg? Your muscles were too weak to make a fist around these combustive facts. The only action you had taken was to resume your pathetic stalker routine, stopping by the theater classroom after school to watch Mr. Avalon play the piano as Rebekkah and the other students sang their familiar tunes, "Besame Mucho," "Amigo," "Oye Como Va," "Mambo No. 5." Through the window, it all had looked so like an ordinary rehearsal, you could almost convince yourself you'd made up that night outside the teacher's house. You were always a consternated boy, but even Ma had noticed this new register of your worry. "Can we just try to have an actual conversation?" she had asked you a couple of nights before, finding you alone on the porch. "It's time."

"Time?"

"I'm worried about you."

You shrugged.

"All this moping of yours. The way you've been slumping around. I can't just act like I don't know who is the cause of it. Your new study friend."

"Ma—"

"Don't worry. I'm not going to give you the third degree. All I want to tell you is that—just that obviously you are suffering, and I just want to say that you really shouldn't let a girl like that make you so blue."

"Okay," you said.

"I, for one, took one look at her the night she came over," Ma told you, "and I knew she was trouble." You couldn't fail to notice that your mother used only pronouns, *she* and *her,* as if Ma wasn't even willing to grant Rebekkah a name.

"Trouble?" you said.

"Just something in her eyes. That certain broody way she carries herself. Maybe not trouble, but *troubled,* at least."

"Troubled." You felt for your neck, where the possibility of admitting the whole story to your mother broke coolly over your skin. "Rebekkah," you said. "She just seems, I don't know. Ma? I don't even know where to begin to tell you about her."

"Then maybe don't," she said. "Believe me. With certain people in this world, it's better if you don't even try to understand."

"But—" The firmness in Ma's face warned you off telling her more. This conversation, you knew, was not really about Rebekkah, or even about you. It was about the untenable faith in which she had tried to raise you: that all you had ever needed was right there, in the very cramped but infinitely loving planet she could enfold in her arms, and that the world beyond could only corrupt that simple, beautiful vision.

"I guess you're right," you had told her, because that was the easier resolution to that conversation. It had been easier not to say anything. It was still easier tonight. Easier to pity yourself, easier to hide out in your room, behind your tattered copy of *Childhood's End,* when Pa had left for the Homecoming Dance.

"I think there are lots of people here without dates," Pa now told you over the phone. "Take, for example, that Rebekkah Sterling of yours. Didn't see her wearing any mum today. But here she is, looking quite good in a little red number, I might add. Rebekkah was asking me about you, actually. If you were coming."

"No. Are you serious?"

"As a heart attack." You could nearly *hear* your father's grin.

"What's all this?" your mother said, an hour later, when she came into the house to find you buttoning yourself into one of your father's ill-fitting suits.

"I just thought I'd like to be there," you said.

"Really?" she asked. "Is that really a good idea? Going to a dance without a date? Maybe times have changed, but in my day that was a recipe for a truly bad night."

You shrugged. "I don't know about that," you said. "I think I could still have fun." You didn't mention your father's phone call; you knew how angry your mother would be with him if she knew that it was he who had spurred you to this potential humiliation. Ma shook her head, and she made her protest known by remaining silent the whole drive, clicking her tongue at the windshield.

A half hour later, there was Bliss Township School, the hundred-year-old, redbrick behemoth on its last night of life, its heart still beating, that season's popular Beyoncé song thumping into the warm night. You grasped the car door handle, pushed it open, and stood.

"Oliver?"

"Yeah?"

"Oh, I don't know," Ma said in the driver's seat, her eyes still begging you to spare yourself from embarrassment, her body shifting around awkwardly as if her motherly obligation to let you make your own mistakes was a kind of internal jujitsu move she was presently performing, to outmuscle what she really wanted to tell you.

And then your mother said the last thing she would ever say to you on that side of Bed Four. "Try to have some fun, I guess?"

The school's gymnasium was nearly unrecognizable, festooned in ribbons and velvet curtains, lit by the whirling sparkles thrown off by the disco ball. As Sarah McLachlan sang her weepy song about the angel and his beautiful arms, teenage bodies in cheap satins and silks swayed softly—white teenage bodies; a school dance, like a football game, was a decidedly white activity. The room's few Latino kids, a tiny sampling of the boys and girls you recognized from your honors classes, made a small cluster near the snack table, watching on like children at a lake's edge, looking diffident as they considered a jump in. For a long while, you just stood there near the doors, terrifically uncomfortable in your stained sack of a business suit.

"You made it." Pa tossed a jolly arm over your shoulder. "I'm proud of you."

"I'm not so sure this was a good idea," you said.

"Mm-hm, mm-hm." He pressed one faux-thoughtful finger over his mouth as he nodded. "She's right over there."

And it was then that the rental lighting kit, rigged into the gymnasium's rafters, came into perfect synchronicity with your teenage heart. A parting of darkness, as if from the heavens. A single slant of brightness, eliminating the masses from the room, landing on Rebekkah, a dream of Rebekkah, the dream of Rebekkah you would carry with you, her maroon dress like a second, silken skin as she rocked gently in the seraphic light. Somewhere, a DJ pressed a button, a lightning storm of strobe effects erupted, Salt-N-Pepa's "Whatta Man" blasting forth. At the precise moment Rebekkah's gaze landed on you, your father gave you a hard nudge from behind, like a shove into cold waters.

You turned to show him a glare. You turned, also, to receive your last view of Jed Loving in that *before*. "Be bold," Pa recited his favorite Goethe quote with a goofy, bemused smirk, "and mighty forces will come to your aid."

But you were not bold, not then, and no forces came to aid you. For a long while, it could have been fifteen minutes, you slouched against a corner, striking the posture of a boy having a meaningful conversation with the scuffed leather of his loafers. At last, when you could bear it no more, you lifted your eyes, and they seemed to know just where to find her.

Rebekkah Sterling was at the room's far side now, walking in the direction of the snack table. You did not so much follow Rebekkah as you were pulled into the gravity of her sway. Contact, your first in days, was made at the start of an empty hallway, lit dimly by a fluorescent panel at the gymnasium's edge.

"Rebekkah," you said.

"Oh, Oliver! Hi." The joy of your proximity to Rebekkah nearly threw you. But, up close, you noticed a little flaw in that disco-lit vision of beauty you'd seen from the gymnasium's edge, her eyelids ringed with teary swelling. In the story of yourself you were trying again to contrive, you stuck to your new character, Rebekkah's 120-pound protector.

"What did he do?" you said.

"Excuse me?"

"You've been crying."

"Oh, that? It's nothing. Just this, uh, new makeup I was trying? Must be allergic."

"Right, allergic."

"It's just that. I mean it."

You scanned the party daddishly, as if everyone in the room bore some responsibility.

"God, Rebekkah. We've got to tell someone. You can't let him hurt you any more." *Him*, you said, not at all sure if you meant her father or Mr. Avalon.

Even then you doubted that you'd really find the courage to do anything, but you feinted a few steps in the general direction of— who? Someone. Shameful: what you wanted most was for Rebekkah to pull you back, for this little dramatic theater, starring yourself, to continue. For a single grateful second, you were very happy Rebekkah played her part, gripping your wrist.

"What has he done to you?" you asked again.

"What has who done?"

"Who? Mr. Avalon. How long have you—" You paused. The freckles dotting Rebekkah's cheeks had become suddenly vivid as the color behind them drained away. But Rebekkah never answered you. Because now another boy had come jangling over, in full mariachi regalia. This boy was Ray Lopez, a kid you didn't know, a boy who himself couldn't know that he was walking through the last moments of his life. "What are you doing?" Roy Lopez asked Rebekkah. "We're all waiting for you in the theater room. You have to get into costume. We start in thirty minutes!"

"I have to go," Rebekkah told you. "I really have to go."

"But—" But the moment passed. Before you could think of what else to say, Rebekkah turned her back to you, as if wishing you out of the room. And yet you did not leave, not just yet. You stood there, eyeing Mr. Avalon, beneath the upraised basketball hoop, waving his arms in Rebekkah's direction as she slowly began to cross the gymnasium. And when Mr. Avalon's gaze locked on yours, you learned that the corollary to the six-second hypothesis was also true. You did not blink for much longer than six seconds.

On a Young Astronomers Club trip to the McDonald Observatory, a docent had told you that when you view any darker spot in the sky through the great telescope, thousands of galaxies become visible in the ambient luminescence. A hidden starscape whose pattern bore the record of the universe's fourteen-billion-year-old explosion, the secret of the Big Bang. On the night of November fifteenth, you were just starting to see that pattern, but you didn't have the equations to make sense of it. At the time, you just watched as Mr. Avalon followed Rebekkah toward the theater classroom. You turned, set off down a different hall.

And so: it was sometime before 9 P.M. on November fifteenth, and you were wandering Bliss Township School. The hallways after hours were surreal and lovely, without the alienating crowds, a nice reminder that time went on there in those stale corridors, and you were only passing through. You ran your fingers along the tattered lines of lockers, over the poster board displays and the many hand-painted encouragements for the Bliss Township Mountain Lions football team, along the cheaply ornamented crenulations of the frame that held Pa's cheery, wind-warped vision of your school. Distantly, the deep cardiac rhythm of dance music throbbed through the walls.

In a far wing, you could just make out the familiar chord progression of "Baby Got Back" as you drifted along—*lonely as a cloud,* you thought in a tragic, poetic mood, remembering a poem you'd read in ninth grade. You were as lonely as a cloud in the West Texan sky, and like condensation, you fell back into the place where that particular lonesomeness first rose up, your desk in Mrs. Schumacher's empty classroom. The whiteboard said, THE ODYSSEY: HOW IS IT RELEVANT TODAY? You hardly even heard it, that first fractured noise.

And yet, you stood up from the desk and walked back into the hall. You were feeling afraid, but you couldn't name why. You crept past the slumbering lockers, the shoe-leather, municipal smell of the library. The polished wood floorboards squeaked under the loafers you'd borrowed from your father. You had nearly convinced yourself that the only thing that could be wrong was bound in your own thwarted heart. The flooring popped, then moaned. Then, an unmistakable sound: a high trill, very different from the ordinary girl-screams that filled Bliss Township. A scream that registered in some primitive part of your brain, panic washing any clear thought away from you, and you were running now.

For weeks, you had stolen glances through the window to the theater room, trying to understand, or else trying just to see Rebekkah. Why would she talk with you, kiss you, then leave you to silence? Why would she do what you had seen her do with Mr. Avalon? Your heart churning inside you, you once more turned to the long plank hallway that led to the theater classroom, where the screaming began again, and in your last moments of walking life, the questions only multiplied inside you.

The sound of firecrackers, rapid, crackling bursts. You turned the final corner, and there he was. The person you had only seen from a distance, that night outside Rebekkah's house, the same boy you must have shuffled by in the halls for years without noticing, both of you training your eyes on your shoes. A young man who, in your many lovelorn contemplations, you had all but forgotten. You had only ever seen him from the distance of your own bounded story; you couldn't have known all that you shared. Even up close you oddly could not quite see him clearly. He was shaking so severely, his features seemed to blur. You smelled a sharp, sulfuric tang. *Something bad,* the primitive part of your brain was saying to you sharply now, but it didn't offer answers. You never even saw what this person held at his side. Your panic kept you from understanding. His arms moved like unhinged things, jointless and strange. His eyes were extinguished, unreadable. If still you failed to understand, it was only because you, like the 736 other people of your school, could not have imagined, until that night, that something like that was possible, not there.

"It's over," this man told you, his voice a dim echo off canyon walls.

"Okay," you said.

His oil-dark eyes went wide and emphatic, as though he were trying to convince you of an argument. "I had to."

"Okay," you said again.

"He bought me a dog," he said.

Appropriately, your last word was a question. "Who?" And then there was a blinding violence, a terrible whiteness, a crack in time.

And then what? That is where your family lost you, to that place like the one your father had described that night in his painting cabin. A black hole, in which no telescope could ever locate you. A place of pulverized years, an infinitely heavy blindness, a forsaken desert island in the pooling vastness, and where could your family find you now? Perhaps only in another unlikely idea. Only in the stories they still tried to believe.

Charlie

....

CHAPTER TWENTY-ONE

Once upon a time, there was a boy who fell through a crack in time. After Manuel Paz left their house that Sunday afternoon and Charlie stood from his shadowed spot on the stairs, that oft-written sentence of his was feeling autobiographical. With the lid pulled back on his mother's long-sealed secret, Charlie was swamped by his old teenage guilt, his powerlessness to keep Ma from becoming the kind of person she had apparently become. He felt he wore his lean six feet like the costume of an adult as he timidly marched toward his mother at the kitchen table.

"Shoplifting, Ma? Seriously? How much are we talking about here?"

"I don't know."

"No I-don't-knows. How much did you take?"

"You mean this time, or altogether?"

"Christ."

But after twenty-three years under the tyranny of Ma's certitude, wasn't there also something a little wonderful about being in this position with his mother, in the sudden and wholly unexpected position of moral authority? Charlie had to concentrate now not to let a smile into his face.

"It was all for Oliver," Ma said.

"Of course it was," Charlie said. "Show me."

Without complaint, as if she had anticipated this demand as fair punishment, Ma pushed away from the table, led the way back up the whining, thinly carpeted stairs. In an unused bathroom on the second level, she pointed to a string dangling from a ceiling panel. Like a teased cat, Charlie hopped and pulled at it. A collapsible staircase yawned open. And up those stairs, when Ma punched the switch on an old Coleman lantern and unlatched a giant plastic bin, Charlie was frankly astonished by what the light revealed, that little hillock of shrink-wrapped plunder.

"Ma," he said. "Jesus Christ."

"I know," she said. "It's horrible."

"That's one word for it."

Charlie felt his skull for a long while then, as if trying to divine his own thoughts.

"But I'll tell you what," Charlie said. "If I'm being honest? What I'm thinking right now is that it reminds me of my book, only in stuff instead of useless pages."

He lifted a DVD of *2001: A Space Odyssey*, tossed it back into the bin.

"So," Charlie said. "About that other thing Manuel mentioned."

Ma nodded, her exhaustion vibrating through her. But she held herself together long enough to recount the whole awful scene with Manuel in the hospital conference room, years ago. His questions about Hector and Rebekkah and Oliver, about what she hadn't told him then, her guilt ("like a sickness I carry in me") at Oliver's long-ago conversation about Rebekkah Sterling that she had ended before he could explain anything to her. "I don't know. This whole thing, Charlie. I just don't know."

"Well," Charlie said, dusting off his old Man of the House crown, "I'm not saying you shouldn't feel bad about that, what you never said to us. And as for being less than honest with the police? Probably not your best course of action."

"Tell me about it."

"But Ma?" Charlie said. "Do you know that I've wondered the same? About Rebekkah. Wondered so much, in fact, that I practically stalked her out there in Brooklyn, so that she'd just talk to me."

She turned away from Charlie, unwilling to show her son what this confession did to her face.

"Did she?" Ma asked softly. "Talk to you, I mean."

"Not really," Charlie said. "But now I'm wondering. Why didn't I just tell you about all that business? Why did I keep it to myself like some big secret? It was like I thought—like I didn't ever want to put you through the pain of talking about what happened that night. But now I'm wondering if maybe that was very wrong of me. If maybe the very, very painful part was *not* talking about it."

"We're talking now, aren't we?" Ma said, but the old combativeness in her words was wholly at odds with the way she nodded at the Tupperware bin, touching her mouth with the back of her hand as if the piled mass of her shameful habit was a sickness she had at last expelled.

"So what do we do now?"

"Now?" Ma asked. "Now I guess we have to ignore the advice of that Finfrock lady. Tomorrow we'll just have to ask Oliver all these old questions, right in front of Manuel Paz. Put all this business behind us so we can focus on what really matters here. Focus on helping Oliver."

"Right."

Charlie hardly slept again that night. By 6 A.M., when he gave up on bed, exhaustion was sanding his eyes. His gut was roiling. The revelation of Ma's shoplifting: all night, he had kept probing that truly shocking fact, and once the astonishment passed, he quickly lost the sweet flavor of moral superiority. What sort of a woman, Charlie was wondering, could go around stealing other peoples' things, as if her own crazy needs mattered more than the laws of the world? What sort of a woman, presented with questions from a police officer, could allow herself to reach for such a pathetically false nostrum for her own guilt, when the truth might have led to some sort of explanation? The same sort of woman, he supposed, who decides to pull her child out of school to comfort her in her grief. The sort of woman who chooses to outsource her own suffering onto those nearest at hand.

Charlie had spent a good part of the night stewing in a noxious memory, a certain day from the first years *after,* which had left him so furious with his mother, whose emergence from bed he heard in the creaking plywood, that he chose not to wait for her. He deposited a note, telling his mother that he had left early for Crockett State on the Suzuki. He snarfed an English muffin and moved swiftly through the rooms of the cracked McMansion, silently latched the front door.

The sun looked bald and gentle as it rose over the distant mountains that morning, its cheery light throwing the etched shadow of Charlie's motorbike across the asphalt expanse. But, even at top speed, the memory was still holding on there, in Charlie's wind-lashed head.

Charlie must have been fifteen, maybe sixteen. Oliver had been gone long enough that Charlie had begun to glimpse the futility of his efforts to keep his mother sane, to engage her in any activity beyond her daily visits to Bed Four. Still, that morning he had been trying.

"A five-letter word, beginning with T, that means a dance," Charlie had said, tapping a pencil against the book of crossword puzzles spread over his legs. On the far end of the sofa, his mother hardly flinched, apparently engaged in a staring contest with the wall. "Okay," Charlie said, "how about a three-letter word that means family?" And when still she did not reply, Charlie scooted next to her, rested the book in her own lap. As if woken from a deep sleep, her hands startled, slapping the book away, the edge of a page slicing her finger, which she sucked at furiously.

"I don't know why you can't just leave me be," she said. "Why you are always asking me these *questions*. Why you can't just be *quiet* for a while."

Ma pulled the wounded finger from her mouth, smacked her hand on the tired cowhide of the sofa. "That's the difference between your brother and you," Ma told Charlie then. "You always need all the attention in the room." And then she stood, leaving Charlie alone in the silence he had disturbed.

This was one of his mother's condemnations of Charlie that he had heard before, in many forms. "There are those people who can be alone together, and those people who don't know the value of listening to their own thoughts," ran a common variation on her theory. This was, in fact, one of a great many ways his mother had always divided the world into two types of people: the virtuous, contemplative, amenable people like Oliver and Ma herself, and the unsettled, disruptive people like Charlie and his father. In the now mostly unacknowledged prehistory of the Lovings, in the family they had been before the night of November fifteenth, Ma had come to use "like Oliver" as a shorthand to mean *good* and "like Charlie" to mean *bad*. But Charlie knew the truth: "like Oliver" just meant someone who would always be what she needed: a timid, ever attentive and agreeable boy.

And after that worst night, Charlie had still tried. He had tried and at last utterly failed to enter into the tacit agreement with Ma that had been made by his brother before him: that he would always be present and that he would consign any hard truths to silence. "There are those people who can be alone together," Ma had said, and here was the darkest thought of all, the awareness Charlie glimpsed that day on the sofa but understood clearly now, as he ripped down the highway: a quietly receptive, forever present son was all Ma had ever wanted, and in the worst tragedy of her life, she'd had her insane prayer answered.

. . .

A half hour later, with the pleasing hiss of automated doors, Charlie was back in the deep time, the placeless place of Crockett State Assisted Care Facility. He waved at Peggy, who showed him the usual jazz hands.

Once more at Bed Four, he followed his familiar routine, clicking on the Bob Dylan, pulling up the plastic chair, trying and failing to avoid the panicked sight of the eyes beneath him, awake, searching as ever. The crossed tin bowie knives of the wall clock showed 6:45. Charlie had at least an hour to fill, and he knew now it had been a mistake to come early.

"Why didn't you ever stand up for me?" Charlie heard himself say. The words opened a courage or rage, and Charlie found that he now wanted to look Oliver right in the eyes. He clutched his brother's face by the ears, and in quick birdlike snatches, his gaze met Oliver's. "Stand up to Ma, I mean."

Part of Charlie felt he was being ridiculous, cruel, maudlin. The other part thought, *This is why I'm here now.* "Why didn't you ever once tell her it was wrong? To treat me like your lousy shadow." This anger was very old; it had done erosion's slow work, carving ancient fissures to conduct that fury. It sluiced through him, bearing the rotten things he was saying now. "Why did you always let me be her big disappointment?"

There was a pack of American Spirits in the pocket of his jeans, and he jostled a smoke free, lit it, exhaled gray plumes into the room. "And then you just leave me there," he said. "Leave us there, to rot. And you know what? I tried, I did. I've tried to give her another you, to let my whole life become nothing but you, you, you. Do you know what it was like? What it is still like?"

The cigarette grew a crooked finger of ash that self-amputated, falling on the pillow. Like a little streak of excrement against the starched whiteness of the linens. He brushed the ash away, unlatched the window, tossed the butt outside.

Charlie slumped back into the plastic chair, said nothing more to his brother for the half hour that followed. Bob Dylan sang and moaned his way through another spinning of *Blonde on Blonde*. The heat and smell of baked creosote cleaned the last tang of the cigarette from the room.

"Charlie," Margot said, arriving at the door just shy of seven fifteen. "Always the early bird."

Charlie saw, as soon as Margot passed the door, that something had shifted, as if the cheery bright curtains of Margot's God-fearing manner had parted just a bit, showing some illegible darkness behind. "Couldn't stand to wait," Charlie said.

Margot nodded. "Your ma told me everyone wouldn't be here till eight. What's this all about, anyway? I thought your ma said mum's the word, and now all of a sudden we have another meeting with Manuel Paz."

"I'm not so sure myself."

She smacked her fresh maroon lipstick. "Well. I guess we're gonna find out." The hand-holder, the fast-talking, buxom-smothering Margot seemed wholly absent now, spooked off perhaps, given way to this second Margot, the sort of Texan ma whom Charlie knew very well, with that long hard stare into the country's emptiness, something lofty and possessive and damningly maternal in her eyes, as if she'd already told the world how to behave and she wouldn't tell it again.

Margot grunted as she pulled her equipment from her pack. Her wish that Charlie leave her alone with her patient was palpable, a risen temperature in the room. *Mothers*, Charlie thought. Mothers, always staking their claims. The voice of his brother—and not just Oliver's voice, it now seemed to Charlie, but also the story of their family, the whole story of Bliss, Texas—belonged now to another clinging, imperious, grief-wracked mom. It struck Charlie, for some reason, as hilarious. He tried not to laugh, but the attempt at suppression only made the laugh come out in an audible, hiccupping way.

Margot, clamping a touch screen to a swivel arm, turned to scowl at Charlie. "What could possibly be so funny?"

"Nothing. I was thinking of something else."

"Um." Margot had the touch pad in position now. "I don't mean to be rude, but it could take a while to finish setting up. Maybe you could go somewhere to wait?"

"I'll be quiet."

Charlie was very patient there, in the chair beside Bed Four. As Margot attached the EEG sensors, Charlie could feel her straining to ignore him, like a hand pressing his face away. Ten minutes passed, and the displays were glowing as Margot coordinated her fingers into the place where she did her palm reading.

"Good morning, Oliver. A? B? C? D?"

"Good," the robot voice eventually said. "Morning."

"Look who came to visit you early today." Margot gestured toward Charlie. "A? B? C?"

"Hi Charlie," the computer spoke.

Hi Charlie, as if he had not been there for an hour, as if he had only just arrived. *Hi Charlie:* but that strangeness was only the final nudge, the little upsetting breeze that brought the whole rotten roof of things crashing down on him.

"Oliver," Charlie said, "what did I just do?"

"What do you mean?" Margot asked.

"What did I do after I woke you up?" Charlie leaned over the bed to speak into Oliver's face. "What was I doing until I stopped and opened the window?"

"What were you doing?"

"I'm asking Oliver a question."

"This is ridiculous."

"Why ridiculous?"

Margot relinquished Oliver's palm. "What is this, some sort of a *test?*" She looked down her nose at Charlie, with the sourest glare of disappointment.

"It's just a simple question."

"Please leave us alone." Margot's voice was proprietary, not unlike Ma's voice, as if Margot and her patient shared a love the world couldn't possibly comprehend.

"Oliver," Charlie said again, his voice crackling now. "What was I doing before Margot came in here?"

"Charlie—"

Oliver's face was just inches away. His breath fogged Charlie's glasses. "Please tell me. Tell me something. Anything. I don't know, our cow. What was the name of our steer at home?"

Charlie turned to Margot, who just kept her trembling hands folded in her lap. "Let him answer," Charlie told her. "Pick up his hand and let him answer."

Margot shook her head in slow, sorrowful turns. "I can't," she said. "I won't. Not like this, with you yelling at me."

"Please," Charlie said. The devastation of an understanding collapsing upon him, Charlie perceived now what a truly shoddy, desperate house it had been. The poverty of Charlie's pages, Ma speaking to this shell of a son, all he and his mother had never said about the events of that night. "Faith," Margot had often said, as she fingered the cross on her chest. "We must have faith." Faith: maybe that was the name for it, the cheap, cracking adhesive that bound their desperate lives together. A ridiculous, outrageous, and unending faith. Like one of those holy rollers pitifully babbling away their sorrowful past under the sway of pure illusion, might Margot have pressed her fingers to her patient's left thumb and believed that she found what she needed to find? Might Charlie and Ma have, too?

"Listen to me," Margot said.

But Charlie bolted from his seat, spent a while staring into the framed vintage poster for *Calamity Jane*. "You know I have to tell them."

Margot wouldn't look at him, but Charlie could see her panic, flushing into her neck. She was still for a moment, then she scooted her chair right up to the bed, planted her fingers firmly to their spot.

Charlie still had some reckless, careering hope that he might be wrong. And yet, a moment passed and another. Margot stared intensely at the neurofeedback monitor, readjusted her grip several times, an EMT searching for a flatlined pulse. From down the hall, Charlie could hear Peggy shrieking with laughter at someone's joke.

"I can't find anything," she said, "just now."

"No."

"It's not perfect!" Margot's expression was fierce, which only made the fact more apparent: the furious, pent-up denial of someone who expects accusation. "It's not a perfect science, but I promise you."

"Did you really think no one would find out?" Looking at the woman, Charlie really did now feel a kind of pity for her. "How long did you think you could go on like this?"

The heat out the window plumed into the room. "Please," Margot said. "Please just leave us alone."

Ma was climbing from Goliath when Charlie stepped back outside. Manuel Paz was out there, too, sipping at a coffee against his squad car at the far side of the lot, the Ranger's right boot hitched up against the fender. It was not even eight, but Charlie could already feel the heat penetrating his skull. Manuel, eyeing Charlie, sauntered up in his roomy, West Texan amble, arrived in time to hear the substance of the short exchange between mother and son.

"Where are you going?" Ma asked. "Are you *leaving*?"

Later, Charlie's guilt for how he acted that morning would drive him half-mad. That he would ask her right there, in front of Manuel Paz. That he did not consider the repercussions, that if he had just pulled Ma aside to speak with her alone, Charlie might have spared her a world of hurt. But, just then, Charlie felt avid, canny, powerful as Shiva with the destructive power of the truth. As if with one act of truth telling in the parking lot of Crockett State Assisted Care Facility, he might have unveiled the chimera, the cheap smoke and mirrors of faith and delusion, under which they had been laboring all those years. "You knew, didn't you?" Even then, Charlie could hear how aggrieved, how vindictive his own voice sounded. "Some part of you must have known."

"Known what exactly?"

"Known that it wasn't really Oliver we've been speaking to."

"What the hell are you talking about?" But Ma looked at Charlie as though, at long last, they had arrived to the point.

"What I'm talking about? I'm talking about Margot Strout," Charlie said. "I'm talking about the fact that neither of us ever once stopped to ask whether this magic trick of hers could actually be true."

"Excuse me?"

"My God," Charlie said. "And here I thought we'd finally gotten somewhere, like we were starting to be honest with each other. But, no no no, because you never could listen, could you?"

"Oh, screw you, Charlie. I mean it. Just leave, then, if that's what you want." Ma's voice was quaking, but hers wasn't a very convincing brand of outrage—at least not to one who had grown up under its various tones. This, like so much of Ma's Oliver-related fury, Charlie saw, was her anger in its porous mode, her doubt seeping through.

Charlie glanced at Manuel, read his tight sad grimace as a kind of solidarity. "I'll tell you what," Charlie told his mother. "Why don't you just let me know when you are ready to tell me the truth for once?"

"I have no idea what you could possibly mean."

"Oh, Ma," Charlie said.

The sun ended that day with none of its false morning timidity, igniting a firestorm of reds and oranges. Charlie had one last plan for his day, but he'd had the good sense to wait until the evening, hiding out in his basement "studio" with a bottle of rotgut whiskey he'd bought, trying hard not to think of the scene he had initiated back at Crockett State. Less than sober at sunset, Charlie took the roads slowly, and when he kicked the Suzuki's stand, he paused to let the twilight dim a few clicks deeper. At last, he was alone in the pale blue of a gibbous moon, in a stand of grama grass a quarter mile outside the gates of Zion's Pastures.

The air out there, tangy with the mesquite and cedar that grew along Loving Creek, his family's tributary of the Rio Grande, was the same air Charlie's lungs had first learned to breathe. A deep inhalation of this healing stuff of his home planet, and he was feeling sharp, bright, a little brilliant. If he had at all doubted this last excursion, he knew now that he would see it to the end. He followed the loony song of whippoorwills to the gates of Zion's Pastures.

Charlie knew now how badly he would have tolerated any change to the place, and he was relieved to find the old gate, that same lattice of wrought iron with its sprays of rust, standing there as it was the last time he closed it, more than five years before. The same sign, too, the one his great-grandfather had made, the words ZION'S PASTURES written in a bumpy Olde English font, an arrow pointing up the pot-holed stretch of road. The gate was held shut with a new length of chain and a padlock, and so Charlie took a look around, percussively tiptoed over the bars of the cattle grate, and hopped the fence. Then, serene as a pilgrim, he began to walk. A mule deer shuddered through a thicket of agave. A milk snake crossed his path.

A long, eulogistic stroll into the valley. Charlie understood that the gnarly live oak by the road, the battered shed of his father's studio, the squat cliff faces into which Oliver and he once scratched crude cave art had existed very long before his family and would outlast them to take on new meanings. But so thoroughly had Charlie and his brother mythologized every inch of that land that even a leonine-looking boulder or a particularly cartoonish patch of prickly pear still seemed symbolic, portentous. He passed over the low-water crossing at Loving Creek. Just a droughty, sluggish trickle now, but it was also a deluge of memory, of crawdad hunts, of fishing trips, of water moccasin evasions, of occasional floods that kept them happily stranded for long days of movie watching and book reading at the house just over the rise. Of Oliver and he running thoughtless and giddy, to present the gift of the fistfuls of thistle heads and Indian paintbrushes they had just picked for Ma.

Charlie knew, of course, that his early childhood was not the little utopia that this return visit was now urging him to edit it into. His parents, after all, were mostly silent with each other; Pa suffered gray nights, blinded by the inimitable gleam of dead artists' masterworks; Oliver was a pimply teen, hopeless in love; Ma was anxious and obsessive, as if she alone could invent a cure for the disease of time and the trip wires it sprung in her family's genes and keep her children with her forever. It was true, what Charlie had told Oliver at the hospital. For their mother's benefit, Oliver had gladly donned the role that Ma had brought him into this world to play, offering his daily performances of unquestioning devotion in exchange for the bouquets and plaudits of Ma's favoritism. But hadn't Oliver offered something to Charlie, too? An escape, and not only in the stories they had told together. As Oliver had given himself as the silent receiver of Ma's worry, as he had made himself the heir to Pa's thwarted hopes, Charlie had, in the theater of his family, been able to costume himself for a role of his own choosing. The cheery one, the jokester, the clown. And maybe that was the real reason Charlie needed to keep Oliver's story, his poems, close to him. Charlie's own existence without Oliver felt like too sorrowful a thing to live in alone.

Under the shade of the cottonwoods that lined the road, Charlie did a little reenactment of his nice memory, sprinting up the last turns to the house. He almost stumbled on the ruts, made a loud bang on the second cattle grate, the one installed by some ancestor to keep cows from wandering into the front yard.

But now he halted, frozen by an impossible vision. So impossible, in fact, that he did a couple of spins, certain that somehow he must have gotten lost. It was disorienting to the verge of nausea; it was like a door from a dream, which you open not onto another room but an entirely different time.

The house of his childhood had been demolished and replaced. Was it even a house that stood there now? It seemed less an actual home than a magazine spread of a design concept in which it was hard to imagine actual people spending their days. Spotless squares for windows, white stucco for walls, something between a house and a work of minimalist sculpture.

"Whoa there." A man's voice.

The voice drew Charlie's attention to the people he hadn't noticed in his bafflement at the rectilinear architecture behind them. Four shadows, a mother and father, two children, looking like an old-fashioned silhouette portrait of a family, black against the decidedly new-fashioned blaze of halogen porch lights.

"This is private property," the man called. "You're trespassing here."

"I'm sorry, I'm sorry," Charlie said.

The man took a few steps toward him, but Charlie seemed to be screwed to the spot.

"You have to leave now," the man said across the new, chemical-lush lawn. "Joyce, call the police and get me my gun."

"No. I—"

"I advise you to go back where you came from," the man said, and at last Charlie flinched and bounded away, like a startled deer.

In his panic, his lostness in time, Charlie thought of the ancient escape route his brother and he once mapped "in case of invasion." Now Charlie was the invader, but he took this trail anyway, sliding into the dense grasses that had overgrown their old machete work. By the time the lights of the impossible house had vanished from view, his arms were nicked and bleeding from the thorns and abrasive branches of the flimsy mesquites. He continued, through the sludge of Loving Creek, and pressed his way forward until he came to a clearing, a little swatch of knee-high bunch grass, where he caught his breath.

According to Granny Nunu, when their family first established Zion's Pastures, more than a century before, the descriptor "pastures"

was more fitting. In the few uncommonly wet years that had followed the founding of their ranch, that property had been mostly
such scrubby, low-lying grassland, assiduously mowed by their once-
great herd. Even in Charlie's earliest memories, the land was much
grassier than now, its wide, reedy pitches wandered by their last feral,
sentimental longhorn.

The mesquites, as fragrant as Christmas trees, formed a sort of
natural wall around this final pasture, giving the little field the atmosphere of an outdoor theater, the sharp half moon contributing a
suitable spotlight. And just as Charlie's breathing quieted enough to
hear the insectival droning, the mythic protagonist of many of their
long-ago bunk bed stories took the stage, so still that at first Charlie
doubted his eyes.

Charlie took a step forward. When the gigantic parentheses of the
beast's horns lowered, he gulped at the air. Even in the moonlight,
Charlie could make out the patterns of brown and white, that bovine
inkblot that still he could have drawn from memory.

"Moses?" Charlie called, and began to move for the steer. Once
upon a time, Moses would let Charlie and Oliver put their stubby
fingers on his El Greco skull, would lick hay and salt out of their
hands with his viscous and sentient tongue. Now, however, Moses
flinched at Charlie's approach and seemed about to dart off for the
bramble and scree downhill. It would, Charlie saw, have been a pitiful darting. The longhorn was thin from rough living. He carried on
his skeleton no more meat than a man. His joints bulged, the legs
shaking arthritically.

"Moses," Charlie said more softly, from five yards or so. Close
enough to smell his familiar tangy hay and mud odor. Close enough,
also, that Charlie could see the wide oily globes of the animal's eyes.
The last of his family's ancient herd, Moses had always seemed to
carry the opposite of a cow's lazy stupidity in his eyes. A rub of his
nose was a blessing.

But, of course, Moses was only a steer. Zion's Pastures—with its
little creek and romantically craggy landscape—was only a choice

two-hundred-acre patch of desert real estate. Their house no longer existed. Charlie understood that the new owners likely were letting Moses end his days there for the touristy charm of a longhorn on the property, that a cow's average lifespan made Moses no holy manifestation, just a tough old beast. And yet, even if he understood that no divine hand, no fate had wrangled poor old Moses to meet him there, Charlie was still powerless before this four-legged symbol, this last survivor of the old Zion's Pastures, locking eyes with him in a clearing.

In the moonlit meadow, he produced his phone from his pocket, pushed its single button, and the brightness of the screen blanked away the grasses, the stars, Moses. Charlie hit *call* on the same number he had called so many times before, to no answer. *However.*

"Charlie."

"Please don't hang up."

The line was silent for a long while, and Charlie expected to hear a click that would end the call.

"Is it really true?" Rebekkah asked. "That e-mail you sent. All those articles. Is he really—"

"Yes, it is," Charlie said, as if his severe tone could in fact make that claim true. But if Oliver couldn't twitch out a single word, how could anyone know what was left of him now? It had been weeks since that fMRI, and still all they knew of Oliver's mind was just that mysterious plasmatic pulsation Ma had seen that day in July. Just a suggestion of thought whose depth and extent they could only guess at. In truth, Oliver's present hour was as unknowable to Charlie as that night, a decade past. "Or anyway," Charlie added. "that's what they're saying."

And what Rebekkah said next she said so softly that Charlie might have mistaken it for his own sigh. "How is he?"

"How is *he*?" Charlie felt his anger bursting outward, but he breathed, and Moses's gaze was still on him. Moses, starved from neglect, but still treading this last patch of pasture all along. "If you wanted to know, then why is it me who is calling you? Why is it always me who is begging you to talk, if you care so much?"

"Well," Rebekkah said, "I'm talking to you now."

"Not really," Charlie said. "You're just listening. Congratulations, Rebekkah! You've picked up your phone for once in your life."

"So, here I am, listening, as you say. And what is it you want to tell me?"

Charlie pressed the rounded edges of his phone into his cheek, but for a long beat he couldn't think of any words to add. A few lines came back to him then, from Oliver's journal. In a poem musing upon the silence that had fallen over his life's only romance, Oliver had written, *Is there anything worse / than the torture of lost time?/ Death would be kinder / than a lifetime this blind.* Charlie looked into the blue-black night of Moses's cataracts as he at last told Rebekkah the thing he had made out of this strange encounter, the lie that was Margot's work, and his family's horrible faith, too. That bounded little world the Lovings had made, where they couldn't see the truth about each other at all. "It's wrong," Charlie said. "It's so, so selfish, Rebekkah. That's what I'm calling to tell you. That some part of him is still there, he just keeps going on and on, all alone. And never once have you come to visit him. Never once have you come to talk with us."

"To tell you what, exactly?" It sounded as if the tight weave of Rebekkah's familiar contempt was coming looser now, distressed. "What is it you think that I could have told you?"

"I don't know. Something. I believe there is something. I believe that."

"Right. That's what *you* believe," Rebekkah said.

"And I'm not saying I'm innocent, either," Charlie told her. "I didn't see him for five years, did you know that? Five years I left him there, rotting in his bed, with only our crazy mother for company. And you know what? I still can't take it here. I can't take it here another day."

"I'm sorry. I am."

"Okay. Then why don't you do something about it?"

"But now you think you somehow get to tell me what I'm sup-posed to do?" Rebekkah's voice was rising. "And now you think you know about *me*, what *I've* been through?"

"So *tell* me."

"Oh, fuck off."

"Right." For years, Charlie had wanted just one conversation with her, but now he thumbed his phone to end it.

Later, as he climbed back onto the Suzuki, tearing away from Zion's Pastures, and from the Big Bend, too, Charlie was still thinking of Moses; he was still thinking of Oliver, wandering the barbed-wired desert of all those years, the locks on the gates set by his own family. The moon had sunk behind the Chisos, and the dark of the night hardly relented against the Suzuki's fitful headlight. What lay be-yond? Just the torment of everything Charlie still couldn't see.

And yet, even then, with the wind bearing into his throat, Charlie found his own old words in his mouth, the spell to conjure a story that had never materialized on his word processor; a spell to conjure, too, his brother back into this world. Just a dream of Oliver waking in his bed, an idea of what might have happened that Charlie still could not quit. *Once upon a time there was a boy who fell through a crack in time.* Even now, all the answers unknown, Charlie couldn't help but imagine it: some hidden, mythic version of his brother, even still waiting in some unseeable place, to tell Charlie the answers. Even still, Charlie was drafting his way into the dark.

Oliver

. . . .

CHAPTER TWENTY-TWO

Once upon a time there was a boy who fell through a crack in time, and then what?

Once upon a time there was a boy who fell through a crack in time, but the truth is that he didn't fall all the way. Half of the boy remained there, on either side.

Oliver, what were they like, those first seconds after you woke? You must have believed that you were still dreaming. How long, you wondered, would you have to wait in this blank sleep? But in this dream, time was indistinct. You had been mouthing the polyurethane sealant of the schoolhouse's plank floorboards on the night of November fifteenth, each second a gravely sharp thing in your throat. But then time drew out like cotton, in that gauzy, white-laced sleep.

And then? Eventually your bright white dream took on the air-conditioned, Sheetrock-paneled confines of a hospital room. A downy translucence hung over everything, but after a time it began to pull away. Now faces were not just their fuzzy shapes. You could see their wrinkles and moles. These faces passed over like designs stitched into gossamer. Doctors, nurses, your mother, your father and brother, ministers, a rabbi, reporters, teachers, anonymous visitors. Never Rebekkah. You were still dreaming.

But then the distant groan in your ears resolved into a clock's ticking. Your mother's face was above you. She was telling you something. What? A story about your brother, and her tone struck you as odd. She had complained about Charlie before, of course, but never so honestly. Never, at least not with you, had she used this tone, the one that in your childhood she typically reserved for your father.

"And, to tell you the truth, I even understand why a kid like Charlie could start to feel a little—cramped. Cabin feverish. At home all day. But can't he see what would have happened to someone like him in the Texas public school system—"

You couldn't say why it happened then, but that's when you woke, from your deep white sleep. And now you were just your mother's son, in a hospital room, in an afternoon.

"Huh?" you said. And yet, could not say.

"Ma?" you said. And yet, could not say.

"Ma," you shouted, but your face held some nostril-interfaced tubing. You reached up to swat that tube away. But could not reach.

"Honestly, it's like he thinks he's some sort of therapist or something. He just loves to tell me how we need to quote unquote *learn to cope*. What I can't get is how anyone, and especially a son of mine, could be so *selfish*."

You gathered your strength; you pressed together all your panic. And yet.

Your mouth was still. Your arms were silent. Your body slept soundly beneath you. But your mind? It was a leashed monster, a jailed dragon, thrashing furiously and futilely at its chains. And as you steeled yourself for another assault on your invisible, inexplicable tethers, you felt a word gather deep in your stomach. It rose with a gag in your chest. It passed by the useless orifice of your mouth. And then it burst in your brain. *Rebekkah.*

As the clock had begun to tick, as your mother's face had become legible, your memory, too, had resolved, and terribly. And now you lay there, gaping up at one of the last things you remembered. The thing you'd understood, only too late. The name you tried to yell, and yet—

Those losses, they were too mighty and too foreign for you to comprehend. They were the hordes of war-costumed barbarians at your gates, and so you went to battle against them. You couldn't holler or swing your actual fists, but your trapped brain swung a ghost's fists, screamed a ghost's empty battle cry. You were only yelling into the wind, but for each day that followed, you yelled and yelled until you had exhausted yourself, fell asleep and woke up, rejuvenated for another day's muted warfare.

You couldn't direct your eyes where to look; they were like separate, skittish creatures inhabiting your skull. But still you became as familiar with the constellations in the foam ceiling of your room as with the freckles of your own hands. For company, when your mother left each day, you had only the western-themed artwork on the room's walls. Desert landscapes, old poster advertisements for Buffalo Bill's Wild West Show, Warner Bros.' production of *Calamity Jane,* all yellowing in cracked wooden frames. Counting off time in this hellish predicament was a chintzy keepsake, a wood-rimmed clock, its hour and minute hands two tin bowie knives.

If you could have spoken, your first words would have been *What about Rebekkah?* So desperate was your need to know that one day, when none other than your former English teacher came to your bed to offer a prayer for the dead—Keith Larsen, Vera Grass, Roy Lopez, and Mr. Avalon, too, gone forever now—whatever grief you might have known was outshone by the wild relief that Rebekkah Sterling's name was not among them. And yet, even there, even then, you were still the lovesick kid wondering why she didn't visit you.

At last, one morning, you awoke defeated. You were too exhausted to muster the day's counterattack against the past, so your mind fell silent, as silent as your mouth. All you wanted then was to draw that silence over you, like a blanket. And you found, at least for a while, that you could make yourself quite snug, wrapped up in that nothingness. The strongest feeling you let pass through yourself then was a horrible, interminable craving for any bite of actual food. You would have been delighted by the simplest saltine, any palatable alternative to the nutrient packs piped into your veins and into your digestive system's obscene new aperture. But it was a vision of a particular burger from Café Magnolia that tormented you most. For a long while, as your body spasmed ceaselessly beneath you, your mind held nothing but numbed silence and a torture of fantastical cheeseburgers.

Your mind. After many months adrift in some immeasurable, white, insubstantial place, it had at last landed back on solid earth, the soft shore of Bed Four at Crockett State Assisted Care Facility. Didn't that mean that someday your arms and legs and hands and voice would also return to you? You waited. They did not return.

Doctors strapped sensors to you. They shined flashlights into your eyes. They tested your reflexes with little rubber hammers. And still these alleged doctors spoke about you as if you weren't there in the room with them. Sometimes, you convinced yourself you could still twitch your muscles, and so you strained, trying to produce a series of SOS signals. When your mother felt something in your left hand, she called for a doctor, who sighed and named it *involuntary muscular contraction.*

"I'm sorry to tell you again, Mrs. Loving . . ."

As ever, your mouth and your body were silent. The doctor believed your skull was silent, too. All you wanted then was to be equal to everyone's expectations. And to answer the question plainly: yes. Many times, in those first months, you did resolve to join those theater students and Mr. Avalon, to end your own life by sheer force of will. You pictured the white hole of death and tried to force yourself through. But the machines stubbornly circulated the business of your heart, bladder, and bowels. You had no choice. Oliver, you had no choice but to live.

In the first months *after,* your mother always arrived to your room in makeup, like an obstinate hopefulness she had painted onto her face. One day—you couldn't say why it was different from the dozens that had preceded it—she wore no makeup. Her graying hair tangled away from her at strange angles, looking like something her anxiety had pressed out of her narrow skull, like the fraying by-product of her exhausted hopes. This was the same day that she mentioned Hector's name. Only now did you realize that she had never mentioned him before, not once in that room. That name, you understood, served as the cap that had bottled her grief. "Hector." When she cracked it open, her grief poured forth. She tried to wipe away her tears, but they rained down on you nevertheless. Unable ever to weep on your own, those tears on your face were a kind of relief.

She asked the questions she knew you could never answer. But no, she did not *ask:* these questions came out as a grave, breathy chant, sentences she had recited to herself over and over again, for however long you had already been in that bed.

"What happened?" she began.

Questions sparked questions, which rose and spread into more and more: about Hector Espina, about what you had seen that night, about why you had been there in the first place, and *did you feel any pain?* Her interrogation had the logic of a house fire. It wouldn't cease until it furied its way through all available material.

You tried, you did. To each of her questions, you formed your answer, and you tried your best to hurl your replies all the way across the vast chasm to your throat. But your explanations, your apologies, your assurances, and your confusion, they never reached the other side. The answers were all between you, in your mind's eye. In your mind's hand, you felt the reply, a single *no* or *yes* or *maybe.* You put your mind back into it. The answers your mother needed were six inches from her ear, but they might as well have been miles away, falling to dust on the desert floor.

And so what was left for you now? In your bed, you thought often of one of your granny's tales, this one about Saynday, the great trickster in the stories shared among the Kiowa tribe. "According to the Kiowa," your granny had once told you, "we humans were originally an underground species. We were down there, in the underworld, until the day Saynday turned us small as ants and then led us through a hole in a felled cottonwood tree. The humans climbed out, but at last there was a snag. A certain pregnant lady, she got lodged there like Pooh Bear in that opening. One half above, one half below. The Kiowa say that she's still stuck there, half the people of the world trapped beneath."

You were like the woman from that Kiowa creation tale, jammed in your own passageway, but it wasn't a pregnancy that had pinned you there. It was the story of your last days, thousands of words, knotted and dense, swelling inside you.

"Half the world's population on this side of the earth, the other half still trapped beneath," your grandmother had added. "And sometimes, if you are real quiet, you can hear the humans beneath us knocking at the ceiling of the underworld. Just as those down beneath, from time to time, can hear the clunking of our footsteps. The poor pregnant lady, she split us in two, and all we can do is wonder about what life is like for the people on the other side of things. But listen now. Saynday is a trickster, and here is his greatest trick of all. He left the pregnant lady there, sure, but the thing about a pregnant lady, someday she's gonna give birth."

Oh, you could hear all right: on certain nights, green with your room's nauseating light, you could hear their muffled murmuring beneath the bed. *What is it?* you'd ask. *Tell me.*

You could never make out an answer, but through the floor you could hear the familiar timbres and inflections. You knew whose muffled screams resounded in your room, shook your hospital bed. *Pa!* you shouted and yet did not shout at the floor. *Rebekkah!* Worse, you knew that it was your hospital bed that stood over the passage, trapping your father and Rebekkah in their own sealed dimensions. *Tell me!* you tried to scream at the linoleum. *Can you hear me?* They never could.

Once upon a time there was a boy who fell through a crack in time, and even that boy tried to think of his fate as if it belonged to someone else. And yet each passing day was another cruel confirmation. Oliver, that boy was you. In a fraction of a second, one long ago night, you had been plucked out of an ordinary life and been given the life of a myth. But plucked by who or by what? You asked and yet could not ask the same question as everyone who visited your bed. "Why?"

But you felt that maybe, if only you could have pulled just a word out of yourself and passed it to the woman bent over your bed, then she might be able to tug on that single thread and unravel the whole tangled mass. Maybe, you could feel, your mother really might pull all those words free, and so free you, too. You tried again to speak her name.

Eve

· · · · · · · · · · · · · · · · · ·

CHAPTER TWENTY-THREE

"Eve."

"Who is this?"

Eve knew who it was, of course. Even without caller ID, she would have known in the caller's first syllable, or before that. The unmistakable quality of his breathing; even that silence seemed softened with a little sigh of apology. Still, for some reason, Eve felt she needed to play dumb.

"It's me."

"It's you who?"

"It's Jed."

"Ah."

It was late morning at Desert Splendor. Eve was still wearing the same business suit, the gray, shoulder-padded number, the uniform she donned for thieving and for doctors' meetings. She hadn't eaten anything in the last twenty-four hours, as if her body, like Tinker Bell, had begun to dematerialize along with her belief. But the voice of her husband cruelly brought Eve back into her own fetid skin, the quaking toll of her spine, the cranky reports of her thoughts pounding back inside of her. It was eleven fifteen, but she wouldn't be arriving for visiting hours today. For nearly a decade, Eve had volubly played both sides of their conversation, but she just couldn't imagine what she might tell Oliver now, how she might explain any of it. And Jed's voice on the phone seemed like some fitting vengeance he had contrived, in the same way that Charlie always seemed to know that abandoning her, as he had once again, would hurt her most. This was the first time Eve had spoken to Jed since the dump at Tusk Mountain, and she could hear him smoking as he tried to gather his thoughts.

"Dr. Rumble called to tell me about what happened with Margot," Jed said.

"He did?"

"Eve, I'm so, so sorry."

"I thought you had officially decided not to get your hopes up," she said.

"I don't know that's a decision I could ever make."

Another conversation, one Eve and her husband had without saying a thing, conducted itself over the line.

"Listen. Look," Jed sputtered. "It's just that—Dr. Rumble mentioned that Manuel Paz was there, too. And I'm wondering, why? Please tell me what's happening."

"So now suddenly you want to know. Now you want to help."

"I know—"

"What do you know?" Eve said, without exactly meaning it, just a bit of the decade-old harangue script on rerun in her brain. A moment later, her telephone screen was black on her kitchen table. Had they said anything else? Had she hung up on him? She couldn't remember; her panic blotted away whole minutes at a time. She tried to breathe.

But every time Eve let her thoughts settle, they fell, like a neurotic tic, back into an obsessive loop of the same terrible minutes from the morning before. It was, really, an absurdly simple test. A simple test, whose failure robbed Eve of every hope, pulled the air from her lungs, the oxygenated blood from her arteries. The test that had been prompted by her own son's parking lot accusations. Manuel and

Dr. Rumble had plotted it in a corner, enacted the whole exam in less than ten minutes. They sent Margot Strout to wait in a conference room down the hall, subjecting her to a sort of makeshift Cone of Silence as Dr. Rumble told Oliver the story of Hansel and Gretel, showed him a blue plastic cup, sang "Deep in the Heart of Texas." When Margot returned, Dr. Rumble asked Oliver what story he had told, what object, what song. The EEG wires adhered to her son's skull now looked to Eve like they were draining some vital substance from him.

"This is ridiculous," Margot said, before even attempting to feel for an answer. "This isn't how it works."

"How does it work, then?" Manuel asked.

Margot, seated on her perch by Bed Four, ran her hands over her slacks, spoke calmly at her lap, as if reading from a manual. "It's like tuning a radio. Sometimes all you get is static. But then the weather is good and you get a signal."

"And let me guess," Dr. Rumble said, his accusatory tone some lame attempt to compensate for the embarrassment that he'd let Margot's untested work get as far as it had. "Static on every channel this morning."

Margot shrugged her heavy shoulders to suggest that, sadly, this was the case.

"How about you just give it a try? Just to humor us," Manuel said.

Margot shrugged again, as casually as she could, as if all her work— her career as a speech pathologist, her future by Bed Four, the sense she had tried to make of the senselessness of her daughter's death— were not being put to the test. As if she were only indulging the whims of ignorant men. Eve watched Margot click on her EEG software, plug her fingers back into her patient's palm. And if, as Margot Strout claimed, her brand of speech therapy was like operating a radio, now it was like tuning a cheap transistor model in a rainstorm. Eve could see beads of sweat pearling in the place where Margot's hand met Oliver's.

Margot closed her eyes then, and Eve could sense how ridiculous, how perverse the whole tableau would appear to Manuel: the twenty-

first-century medical version of an ancient palm reader or a necro-
mancer channeling the dead. Seconds passed, and Eve felt the
straining—not just Margot Strout, not just the suspicions accumulating around her. The thing that tightened to the verge of popping, it
seemed, was whatever it was that kept Eve upright in this world.
Oliver's left leg spasmed for a moment, stilled.

"Like I said," Margot told her observers. "All static. Right now."

All Manuel had offered, at this second theft of Oliver's voice, was
a windy Texan "Oh, Lord."

"Is this what you wanted?" Eve snapped at Manuel. "Are you
happy now?"

"No, Eve. Not happy. Of course not. No."

A moment of silence had followed then, a collective aphasia. The
air-conditioning groaned throatily, the clock clicked. But Margot's
face was blazing, certain, fixed, as if the only failure on display here
was her audience's galling lack of faith. It was a ministerial Dr. Rumble who made the first noise, his throat grunting with his low,
eponymous sound. "Mrs. Strout?" he asked. "Have you ever heard of
something called the ideomotor effect? I've just been reading about it
myself."

Behind the tarantula legs of her plumped lashes, Margot rolled her
eyes deeply. But Eve, too, had read about this ideomotor effect. In all
her research, there were certain facts that Eve had long ago learned to
banish from consideration. Like the diminishing chances of her son
ever regaining neurological function, Eve had excommunicated from
her awareness the conclusions of a few articles she had read about a
controversial form of speech therapy called facilitated communication, sometimes misused with vegetative patients. According to a
skeptical breed of researchers, that sort of labor was vulnerable to
this ideomotor effect, a.k.a. the Ouija board effect: speech pathologists were known, sometimes, to attribute the subconscious hopes
of their own minds to the bodies they palpated for a reply. It was not
that these poor therapists were liars but that they were perhaps something worse, so desperate to believe that they convinced themselves

of their own illusions. Writing, like authors, in the voices of the characters whom they imagined to be real. A thought to sentence to the far Siberia of Eve's mental life: like Eve, those deluded professionals could hear the lost voice speaking, beyond all evidence. With all Margot's machinery—with those neurofeedback monitors and the fancy word processing and waveform analysis software she employed—Eve hadn't believed that what she saw Margot perform at Bed Four had anything to do with Ouija boards. But now, as Margot's haughty, dismissive condemnation of this notion burned hotly in her plump and painted cheeks, Eve saw the hideously obvious conclusion, the thought she had occasionally felt brushing at her neck but had never allowed herself to turn and see. Who more than another grieving mother might want to use her son's hand to write her own little fantasy?

"The ideomotor effect. You can't be serious. Feel his hand if you don't believe me. Feel it!" Margot had truly shouted. "It's him."

"Okay, okay," Dr. Rumble said in a tight, paternal voice. "I think the thing we have to do now is just wait. The fact is that we still can't even know just how aware poor Oliver might even be. Those diagnostic exams in El Paso aren't far off, and we just need to wait and see what happens."

Manuel Paz sighed windily then, a desert gale stirring the dead grass. "Eve," he said, "truth is, we all let this thing get our hopes up too far. We all did. To think there might finally be some kind of change. Some kind of answer. Something. Wishful thinking, I'm guilty of that, too."

Eleven fifteen, twelve fifteen, twelve thirty. Time had become restive, punchy, whole minutes elided, her thoughts darting about sparrow-like, swerving off into the sky just as soon as they landed. Eve looked around the grimed brightness of her living room. The wicked black cracks fissured through her ceiling like petrified lightning. The dust had already made new brown pillows on her window sashes. She hadn't seen Charlie since that scene in the parking lot, and he hadn't come home last night. Had he, what, *slept* in that basement he'd found down the street?

And then a thought, a sharp blast from above that drove her hard back down to earth. An idea she was distressed to realize she should have had long ago, a thought to rewind time, return her to the question she should have asked in front of Manuel Paz and Dr. Rumble yesterday morning. Eve followed this line of thinking, this backward movement of time, back out of her house, back into the hot fug of Goliath's interior, down forty miles of asphalt, through fields of abandoned oil derricks, their steel heads bowed in frozen prayer.

Eve didn't have Margot Strout's address, but she knew the woman resided somewhere in an apartment complex called Vista de Chihuahua, a mass of eighty identical units erected a few years prior, just outside Study Butte. The buildings in Vista de Chihuahua were the same sort of anonymous homes her father had shuttled her among in her migrant childhood. Domestic cubicles, stacked atop one another, all fronted with desert-colored stucco. The immaculate sidewalks and central chlorine-blue swimming pool were empty on a Tuesday afternoon. There was so much Eve had never bothered to learn about Margot Strout, but she did know the woman's car. And when she found the familiar white Corolla on another identical street, Eve parked, climbed a flight of metal stairs to the nearest door. A sticker affixed to the tin mailbox encased in the stucco read STROUT. Eve took a breath and worked the faux-brass knocker.

"Oh. Eve."

Oddly, Margot seemed unsurprised to find Eve there on her doorstep. She poked her dumpling of a head from the dim space of apartment 15 out into the brightness of the day. Margot's hair, untamed, rose in frizzy curtains, caught the sunlight like a blondish fire. Apparently satisfied that Eve had come alone, Margot waved her in.

Eve walked a pace ahead, examining the living room as if for some detail that might explain something more about Margot Strout. But apartment 15, like Vista de Chihuahua in its entirety, was an austerely appointed no place. The furniture was blocky and cheap, as though mass-ordered from a catalog. No suggestive magazines or books on the coffee table. The artwork all hotel art, canyons and cordilleras honeyed in the ocher light of sentimentalized sunsets, a few of those vistas de Chihuahua unavailable through the sliding glass door, which gave a view onto an identical apartment module. Too horrible to think of all Margot's hours alone in that boxed noth-ingness of a home, what on earth Margot might do with them. But then, what did Eve do with her own solitary hours? Eve gulped a breath and asked the question she should have asked days before. She spoke to the closed blinds of the neighboring unit.

"How could you have known all that? About Oliver. How did you know about Rebekkah? Or even, I don't know, about how he loved Tolkien? Or Bob Dylan? And so what? You just learned all this stuff about Oliver from what people told you?"

"I don't know what to tell you," Margot said. "People told me things, of course they did. But you're right. I couldn't have known everything. I didn't."

"Then it's impossible."

"Yes. It would be impossible. You're right about that."

When Eve turned, she found Margot nodding at her, the way Eve once nodded at her sons as they puzzled through a math problem. *You're almost there.*

"Eve," Margot said. "In our classes, when I was training in Aus-tin, the professors used to say that being a speech pathologist is not just about helping patients speak. It's about opening a mind to the world. But it's an imperfect art. And I've always said this. I've never claimed to get it right every time. I don't know why Dr. Rumble can't understand that."

"You didn't say that. You didn't! My God, I should have been making a transcript, if I'd known how you would lie. I should have been recording you. You never said that." Eve's back seized and fal-tered; she was fortunate that there was a sofa to catch her fall.

Margot pulled a clunky wooden chair away from a table in the corner, dragged it close. She made that same concentrated face she had always shown her patient—brow furrowed, mouth a pinprick of careful attention—as if she were now facilitating another mind, the one locked behind the aching musculature of Eve's aging body.

"Listen. Listen," Margot said. "After I lost Cora—have I ever told you this?"

"What on earth does your daughter have to do with anything now?"

"I'm just trying to explain something. I wish you would just let me explain."

Margot patted Eve's hand twice, and Eve sharply retrieved it, as if bitten. "Okay, fine," Eve said. "So I'm listening."

Margot sealed her eyes then, inhaled deeply, as if she were about to dive into cold water. "For a year or so after. Eve? The truth is, I just couldn't believe it. I was still living in my old place, out near Terlingua. I was still living in the house, and I couldn't change a thing about my daughter's room. I kept her tiny bed just as she had left it the morning I drove her to the hospital. I never made the bed. No. It's worse than that. Honestly, I'd still make her a breakfast sometimes. I even spoke to her picture, I did. I did that. Talking to her like she was still with me. But there was just my silent house."

"And so?" Eve said. Every little instant now was a battle, and Eve was furious that she couldn't quite stanch her tears.

"And so eventually I tried to start over. I went back to school. I got this job. I worked. I tried to spend each day acting like I believed my daughter was really gone forever. And the truth is, I still can't believe it. Where do all your words go when there is no ear left to hear them? And so you believe in an ear, because what choice do you have? I know you think I'm some Jesus freak, but it isn't a choice, my faith. It's faith or death. For me, at least, but maybe for you, too?"

Somewhere in the apartment complex, an engine turned a few grunting times, wouldn't catch. "And so you are telling me that this is what you've done," Eve said. "You've come back here to use my son to act out some ridiculous fantasy."

"No." Margot spread her hands like a supplicant, or else a woman comparing two invisible weights. "All I'm trying to tell you is that like everything else in this world, in the end it comes down to faith. For me, I know the truth. I know it. It's imperfect, what I do. I'll be the first to admit it, but that doesn't mean I'm *lying*."

"I don't understand this." Eve shook her head. "I don't understand all this garbage you are telling me now about faith. You are a medical professional, Margot. Or at least I thought you were."

"But it's just like you said, isn't it? How could I have known all that, everything about Oliver? And so all I'm saying is that, well, what choice do you have? What I'm saying is that even if those next tests turn out good, and we know that Oliver can still hear and understand, how could we help him if he can't speak back to us?" Margot's voice had shifted into something more breathless, popping with phlegm. "And so? And so if you think there's any chance at all that I might be right, then you really don't have a choice, and no one could blame you for that."

"Easy for you to say," Eve said as she stood.

"Eve. There's a reason you came here to see me. Seems to me that you've already chosen and you're just hoping that I'll tell you what you want to hear. But I can only tell you what I know. It's up to you if you want to believe it."

The larger part of Eve was still incredulous, lectured by this woman. Eve knew things about this world that this simple, Christ-loving lady, whatever her own losses, could never know. But there was also another part of Eve, a little vulnerable piece of her, who sighed and asked, "How could you even go back? I thought Dr. Rumble told you to keep away."

Margot picked at the flaking maroon edge of her left thumbnail, tore a crescent free. "They can't stop me from coming to visiting hours. If I'm invited."

"And so now you are out to prove some point."

"You think I care about proving anything to anyone? Then you really don't know anything about me. There were a hundred careers

I could have chosen, but this is the path I went down. Something put me here, with you, for a reason. I know that now. What else could matter to me?"

Eve felt for her eyes, gave a lash a firm tug. "Please stop," Margot said, pulling Eve's hands away from her face. "Be nice to yourself."

Eve crossed her arms, as if to show she couldn't be persuaded. Yet she found herself checking the time on Margot's knockoff Rolex to see if they might make it to the end of the day's visiting hours. And what she said next she said in a voice she saved only for the hard canyon floor of her worst days, the voice displaying its own brokenness, which she had employed with Charlie just a couple of nights before as he stood with her in the attic, looking at her shoplifted booty, her own shameful enterprise to outshame even her son's dealings with his landlord. "Do you promise?" Eve fairly pleaded with Margot now.

Eve didn't care that Margot saw her this way. Eve *wanted* Margot to see her like this. Eve wanted to remember Margot Strout seeing her like this. Eve wanted to store this moment for later, when Charlie came back, when Manuel Paz or Dr. Rumble or Jed berated her for inviting this shyster palm reader back into her family. She wanted to remember her brokenness in that woman's blank apartment. *I was broken. I was vulnerable. I was out of choices.*

"Of course I do," Margot said. "And haven't you learned by now? You can't always listen to the doctors. There are certain things only mothers like us can understand."

Except it wasn't true, not exactly. Eve would have one more choice to make. Forcing her head to a high and confident angle as she led Margot down the retinal-frying brightness of Crockett State's halls, Eve was trailed by that same shadow, the same decision that had always waited there around Bed Four, stalking her in the dark, just beyond the ring of fire that her insistence had thrown. If all those brain scans and cognition assessments Eve had scheduled in El Paso found no evidence that Oliver was still aware, then Eve, with medical power of attorney, could allow the inevitable conclusion. That Oliver would never speak, that he was lost in his body, that no suffering could be worse.

Eve would have a choice, a choice you couldn't ask a mother to make. Soon, as on any of the thirty-five hundred days behind her, it would take nothing more than a bit of paperwork, the disconnection of a feeding tube. But what did Oliver want? She knew the only way to answer the question she had asked—in silence, in whispers, occasionally in tearful pleading to Oliver's quaking body—he might or might not hold in the palm of his hand. Margot had reassembled her gear over the bed, and she pressed so hard into that hand that the woman's knuckles protruded whitely.

"Oliver?" Margot asked. "Guess who has come back? A? B? C? D?"

"Ma," the machine replied.

"See?" Eve told her son. "I'm not going anywhere."

Four days followed that afternoon at Crockett State. There still had been no word from Charlie—where could he have possibly gone this time? But nothing impressed Eve more than her ability not to care much. She ignored the fact that Jed did not even call. She practically shoved Manuel Paz aside when he appeared at the doors of Oliver's room one morning, asking Eve, "Are you sure you're thinking straight? I know you're hurting, but you can't just carry on like nothing's changed."

"This isn't over," Eve told him, trying to angle her way around his solid shape.

"Well," Manuel said, pausing her with an outstretched hand. "Sadly, I have to agree with you there."

Eve impatiently shifted her weight from foot to foot. "Meaning what?"

"Just that I think you should know," he said, palming the nape of his neck, "that I felt I had to mention the conversation we had about that Rebekkah business to one of those old task force guys. I'd suspect you'll be hearing from them soon."

"Thank you so much for that, Manuel." Eve said. "Really."

Manuel rested his hand on Eve's raised shoulder. "All you have to do," Manuel said, "is tell them the truth."

And yet, the next day, when an ominous Austin area code rang Eve's phone, she ignored that call, too. Once more, Eve found she could narrow the radius of her concern to the body before her.

Outside, high cumulus clouds nearly gathered to rain, then tore apart in the wind. Soon, they would have to take the ambulance to El Paso and her world would change once again. And so why not just a few more days talking with her son? Or even a few weeks? Why not even push back those next exams at El Paso another month or so, until things settled down just a bit?

"Back again," Eve told her son on her last morning with Margot at Bed Four. "We're both back again."

But, for once, the world would not permit Eve her desperate procrastinations. Soon, Eve would be made to understand: how, for years, she had forced Oliver to listen to his mother lovingly converse with nothing more than her own hope's echo, deaf to the true story beneath, how ready she still was to let that God-fearing woman convince her to allow the one-way conversation to go on and on. *An excuse,* Jed had said, *for what we've let him become.*

"A? B? C? D?" Margot asked.

The robot voice made its reply; the oldest recipe, served afresh. "Love you," the computer said.

Oliver

· · · · · · · · · · · · · · · · · · · ·

CHAPTER TWENTY-FOUR

Oliver, almost ten years trapped in that in-between, and what, exactly, had you become? But how to describe a place like yours, where even words at last lost their shapes?

For a very long time, you tried your best to stay on the right side of sanity. As the voices and faces over Bed Four began to bleed their specificity, as the whiteness in which you had been lost began to fade its way back into your days, you tried to remain diligent. Before the truer madness came, you invited minor illusion as the key to sanity. You learned how much a human body needs movement, how much you missed it. And so you devised a fiction of another place, your old house at Zion's Pastures, in which you tried to believe. When Nurse Helen woke you under your purple felt blanket in the morning, you called the cell in which you found yourself your bedroom. The morning ablutions—the salving of your bedsores, the shaving of your face, the emptying of a foil sack of Jevity into your G-tube— you thought of as your old home's bathroom. Ma's daily visit was the front door thrown open, and as she spoke to you, you were strolling among the cacti and ocotillo, the bluffs and the buzzards. The occasional trip to the physical therapy room—where assistants tied your limbs to machines to spin, gyrate, flex the rot out—you thought of as a rare trip to town. Alone at lights-out, left with not even the company of the radio, only the endless electronic percussion of the machines that kept you alive—well, it took great effort to think of it as a dinner at your old dining room table. And yet, you tried to believe.

A few months before your own imprisonment in Bed Four, you had read a story about a prisoner locked in the lightless cell of solitary confinement at Alcatraz. Denied light, a view, any material thing to focus his attention, this prisoner developed a blind game of solitaire. It was a very simple game. He tore a button from the thick wool of his uniform, chucked that button to ricochet against the black walls, and spent a long while on all fours, feeling for the metal tab. Victory was short-lived; just as soon as the button was in hand, the prisoner tossed it off again.

In your own prison, you were not so lucky as to possess a button, nor could you lift a hand to throw, nor were you able to crawl around to search. But when your horror blunted to boredom, the boredom became unbearable. And so, in lieu of a button, you plucked a date at random, tossed it through the locked hallways of your awareness, then went fumbling around to see what you could find.

Your last Fourth of July: you sent that date skittering, and after a good long search, you felt its shape. The abrasive zest of gunpowder in the air of Bliss Stadium. Your father's hands, sticky with the runoff of a Popsicle. A child puking something electric green on his Dallas Cowboys T-shirt. The image fizzing to black, you grabbed for another, your thirteenth birthday: the high bright sun over the national park. A picnic on the bald summit of the Lost Mine Trail. Charlie extending his arms as if he might attempt flight off the steep overhang. *No, wait.* That was your twelfth. Thirteen was laser tag in Midland: screaming with weapon in hand, Fatboy Slim thumping through the darkness. Dr Pepper, Doritos, and sheet cake in the linoleum-dull party room.

You clutched these little facts in your palm until your solitude came crushing back down upon you, and then you plucked another, throwing it as far as you could. And after a great many tossings, when you pressed your fingers around a day and held it up to your mind's eye, the madness of your solitude transmuted it with a desperate kind of magic. A December fourth in your fist was no longer just some shining bundle of facts, trapped beneath the enamel. Your brother's birthday—a horseback ride to the Window pour-off, your mother snapping photos of the wedge of sky over the canyon, your father smoking cheerily atop a boulder—now that memory cast bright light, like a single rip in a black window shade, filling the walls of your confinement with high Texan daytime. You poked at that light, and its edges crumbled, fell away. September third, less than ten weeks *before:* a paddle of prickly pear, the pinkened skin on your arms, the weedy scent of creosote, the morning sun slanting brightly into Rebekkah's eyes as you found her there, outside Bliss Township School. "Oliver," she said, your name in her mouth sounding, to your hopeful, prelapsarian heart, like an invitation. "There she is," you found that you could reply, as you had not on the actual day. Because now your buttons worked like little wormholes to the lost universe of your memories; they worked like the great wooden doors to the school in front of you: an opening through which, for a time, you could escape the smoldering hell outside.

And yet, of course, hell always came back to you, the bowie knife clock setting the metronome, parceling out your suffering in a series of ticks. Your body only lay there, enduring your mother's attentions—her changing of your socks, her reading aloud of magazines, her shaving of your clenched jaw. What was left for you now? Someday you would tell your story: that was the only sense you could make of what your life had become. You told yourself that you were trapped there so that someday you could come back to the living and tell what you had seen. And so, for a long while, you spent your time retracing your steps back to that placeless place, feeling for your last days, searching for what they had shown you, if only you had known to look: the actual reason Rebekkah tossed away your hand outside the football stadium that night, the truth about the man you'd seen outside her door, the exquisite ache of the dozens of early-morning conversations with Rebekkah, when you had never pressed her to explain just a little bit more. And, of course, the greatest torment of all, that one button you sought more than any other. It caused you great pain, but that memory became an obsession, an infection in your palm. November fifteenth. The unblemished starscape over West Texas, Rebekkah swaying softly in a column of light. An understanding that had come too late.

But there were only so many times you could relive those last tormenting days, and for whole weeks at a time, you set your buttons aside. And as Dr. Rumble, Nurse Helen, Peggy, your mother, and occasionally your brother and father continued to speak, their voices began to run together into a meaningless sound, distant thunder. You at last lost yourself into some dreamy, hazy state, the endless daydream of your life just a mirage of heat thrown off the baked Chihuahuan. You were nothing; you were vapor. Whole months passed that way, in your wordless place. There are no words for it.

And yet, sometimes, a charge gathered in the atmosphere, and you felt yourself sharpening to a thunderbolt. The meteorological sciences are notoriously tricky; it could be hard to know what confluence of conditions churn the thunderstorm. A Bob Dylan song on the boom box, a nurse's cool hand cupped to your jaw, the familiar smell of some foodstuff from the cafeteria. All those things, together, would strike you back to awareness, writing your whole sad predicament in lightning: Ma's eyes, your empty throat, the giggle of the machine circulating the business of your bladder and bowels, your mechanized bed, breathing beneath you. Sometimes, however, the conditions were more obvious, a major new front sweeping into your room. One day, for example, after a very long time away, your brother's face—or not exactly his face, but a stylish, bespectacled, adult rendition—returned to your bed. "It's me," Charlie said, and you could hear him perfectly. And in the weeks that followed, you continued to hear, too well.

Another very unexpected arrival at Bed Four. You recognized something familiar in her doughty face, her intensive cheer. Once, very long before, she had spent a day whispering into your ear, palpating you. From time to time, in the months afterward, she came to your bed and wept, like so many others. "Hello, Oliver, remember me?" she said now. "I'm Margot Strout. I'm here to work with you again."

And it was true, she did work, or at least she tried. She interrogated your body, laboring all day. "Twice for yes, once for no." And yet, it was also true that when her hands cramped up against your cheeks, your eyelids, your throat, she'd rub at the pain and tell you other things, not strictly related to work. "Oliver, you are the reason, the reason for everything that has happened to me. It's clear as day to me now," she said, as if it were a compliment. "Do you know that? Twice for yes, once for no."

To be kind, you did try to flinch, twice for yes. "Love you," you heard the computer tell your mother a dozen times over, and sometimes you could nearly convince yourself it really was you speaking.

In fact, you were not as troubled by all this as people might assume. Why not let your family believe whatever they needed? As the border between waking and sleep had grown ever more porous, you let yourself dream up stories of your own. You weren't Oliver Loving at all, you decided, only a ghost who had taken possession of a vegetative patient named Oliver Loving. When your brother rubbed his hands against your hands that couldn't rub back, when your mother embraced a body that could not embrace in reply, you would think that this Oliver Loving, this family, that past, none of it was actually yours. That you were, in truth, only a ghost subletting this skull, pitying the original owner. Soaking up that family's heartache as if it were your own. In this story, you found you could even forgive your father for failing to come see you for so long. Divorced from yourself, you saw what torture it would have been to visit the body that once belonged to his son. As a ghost, you were the better form of yourself, copasetic, generous, accepting.

All of that you could bear, but what you could not bear was to witness your mother lose the last hope that bound her to your bed. *What object did we show you? What story? What song?* your doctor asked you one day. *Please,* you tried to shout, and yet could not shout. Heartbroken, Ma left you there, alone in Bed Four. *Please,* you were still shouting that night, when at last a voice answered you.

"Okay, okay. Quiet down now." It was that night, almost ten years *after,* that a ghost visited you at Bed Four.

But this ghost was very different from the kind you had nearly convinced yourself that you'd become. This was the sort of ghost that perhaps can only exist in a place like yours, where time is jumbled, where the dead can take on all the qualities of the living. His footfalls against the linoleum sounded just like any ordinary living person's. And you could smell this ghost, piney marijuana and the locker-room tang of a depressive's weak hygiene. You tried to ignore this reek and focus on your music, Bob Dylan's *Blonde on Blonde,* playing softly on your stereo, but the volume clicked off. *No,* you thought, wanting to close your eyes to sleep. But your eyelids were pulled shut only by the tide of your drowsiness, not something you could choose to close at will. You were very awake and so you had to see. Hands grasped your ears and turned your head. Your gaze stuttered over the last face you had seen in the final instants of your walking life.

"There's a sight for sore eyes," Hector Espina said.

Hector Espina was a ghoulish rendition of the boy you had vaguely noticed around the school halls, the young man whose shape you had lit up with Goliath's headlights one night outside Rebek-kah's house. But something was wrong with his face now. A third, unseeing eye, just over his brow, the wound of his suicide still faintly leaking. For a long while, you only looked at each other, Hector trying to gauge something in your eyes, which fluttered over the bleak wreckage of his face. You might never have spoken with Hector when you had your one chance, out there in front of the Sterling residence that night, but at last he was speaking to you now.

"And so what," he finally said, his voice a harsh whisper. A tone that suggested a certain black camaraderie, as if you were colleagues in wickedness, two gang bosses breaking from street warfare to renegotiate terms. "So now you thought you'd found a way out of here, is that it? And I'll bet you think you have quite a story to tell."

Under the pressure of Hector's proximity, you felt the magmatic force of your rage, which had, at the beginning of your stay in Bed Four, incinerated whole months. You had a senseless hope, burbling angrily inside you, that you might still find a way to say what you had never said. But then something struck you. Hector's brimstone tears, sizzling on the skin of your arm.

"You and I, Oliver, we're more alike than you could know."

And Hector was right: when your gaze now met his, what you saw, in his weary and death-fogged eyes and in the small abyss in his brow, was something of yourself.

And so, in the Legend of Oliver Loving, you had at last arrived to the monster in your labyrinth. But your monster was much more terrifying than that burnt-out, bald-headed kid your town had vilified. Your true monster was just an aspect of yourself, in Hector's face. Years had passed; you had fallen asleep a boy and woken as an aging man. You had not yet seen your face in a mirror, but Hector's face suggested what you might find. Something deformed by death and time. Hector Espina: another boy your town had turned into a myth, ignorant of his true story.

Only you could see that history now. He was with you in that black hole, and his eyes showed his own skewed dimensions, displaying his memories to you like some grim cinema. The son of a sanitation worker, a punishing hiss of a father, whose limbs were heavy with the violence of his own youth. A boy whose mother was cuffed and sent back across the river when he was just five, evanescing into a vague memory of abandonment, a scar in his life that was visible to everyone. A kid who had grown up on the west side of town, in a community treated like itinerant labor, a community that itself treated him—a quiet, stammering boy—like a punch line to some joke; schoolyard couplets had been written about Hector's pussyness, his supposed fartlike smell. A young man whose only comfort was his unspeakable dream of escape through the songs he'd learned to sing to himself when no one was around. One day, outside the schoolhouse, Hector had been crooning along to a track by Boyz

II Men on his Walkman when a heavy palm fell on his shoulder. Wincing, Hector tugged the headphones off to find a mustached face grinning down upon him. "Get a load of that voice!" the theater teacher, Mr. Avalon, said. The next day, under the promise of singing lessons, Hector climbed into Mr. Avalon's nice Cadillac.

All of this, in the jumbled time of your black hole, you could see at last. And now you understood that the kinship you'd known that night on Rebekkah's lawn had a deeper cause. Hector was, in fact, a lot like you, but an Oliver of another, much darker planet. He was a stammering, angry creature, what your own awkwardness might have turned you into if not for your mother's constant bolstering. He was another boy with thwarted artistic dreams, but whereas you could imagine many alternate futures, Hector was not so lucky. When Hector gazed down the forlorn tracks of his future, he could see only his father's trailer, a blighted career in manual labor, a fate so much worse for the brief hope Mr. Avalon had given him, all the ways Mr. Avalon had used the hope to do with Hector whatever he liked, before losing interest in the boy completely. And no matter the exact events of November fifteenth, they were the sickness that you shared, the particular disease that had transformed you both, the curse that had turned you into some tall tale, shackling you together in that in-between.

Once upon a time there was a boy who fell through a crack in time, but he didn't fall all the way. Like the woman in the cottonwood tree from his granny's stories, his torment was to remain there, half of him on either side, pinning a desperate populace below, a cacophony that rattled his every night. But now, at last, hands were reaching to pull him free.

In a swift motion, Hector stooped over you. Ten years prior, he had found his own escape from the hell of his doomed hope, and now he had come back to deliver you the same mercy. Fear pounded in your temples as you waited for Hector to drag you off into his unknowable region, not heaven or hell, not the past or the future, just a relieving nothingness. You could see it: the placeless white place opening its bright, mute crevice. A benevolent eye cracking open. The endlessness that was the truth of time, a great blind sea that would mercifully sweep away the little dark mote of your few years on earth.

Hector reached to your neck, but just as his hands touched your skin, they turned vaporous. *No, please, not yet,* because now another morning had come to Bed Four, because even after you had failed that last test, your mother had returned.

"See?" Ma said. "I'm not going anywhere."

"Someday she's gonna give birth," your granny had told you, and now, at the sight of your mother, even still hunched over your body, the story that pinned you there had begun to beat back to life inside you, kicking and clawing its way toward daylight.

Your story. After years of rehearsing the tale of your last days, it had come to seem hardly a story at all, just a life fractured by the bad coincidence of where you had stood at a certain moment in time. *Why?:* like your family, you had shouted that word, even when you couldn't shout, and then you had turned an ear to the silence, even still believing that an explanation might come. It never had, at least not in any words you could hear. And yet, you had learned well from your father the cosmological mysteries forever tipped in life's favor: the invisible and unending battle between matter and antimatter in which matter just slightly won out; the way that a few lifeless molecules, sparked in the right conditions, become a living chain of organic material. For reasons no scientist can name, the universe forever chooses something over nothing, and so why could it not also have chosen something for you? Maybe you had never needed to ask what the days and years in your bed had meant; maybe your survival *was* the answer. Locked in that space between one world and the next, your body was all that had held open the only passage to a place that no one else could see or know.

And yet, yours was a story you could never have delivered on your own. Those hands—your mother's hands, Margot Strout's hands—even still you could feel that they were reaching down to help you. They were still there today, pulling and pulling. But your liberation would also take other hands, hands at last pushing from below, from that hell of silenced voices beneath your bed, that lost dimension, where you had trapped them. You could feel them there now, those two hundred trillion particles entangled with your own, pushing at your feet, allowing little gaps in the seal. Just tiny slits hissing apart, but you paused to look down into those openings. And at last, after nearly ten years, there they were. Rebekkah and your father, coming home.

Rebekkah and Jed

....

CHAPTER TWENTY-FIVE

Halfway down the jet bridge of gate six of the Midland International
Airport, Rebekkah Sterling understood she had made a terrible mistake.
She flashed on the feverish, chain-smoking image of herself from just
two days ago in her apartment on Eighth Street, the self-chastising,
resolution-making Rebekkah that Charlie's condemning voice in her
telephone had briefly let loose in her. But she found that this prior
Rebekkah was a completely different person than the timid girl who
emerged into the dull regional terminal. What could she possibly have
been thinking to so impulsively buy a plane ticket? Rebekkah walked
up to a woman wearing a silly sailor's cap, fashioned in the corporate red
and blue of her airline. "When is the next flight back to New York?"

"But you've just landed," the airline woman pointed out.

Rebekkah nodded. "You've got me there. But when is the next
one?"

There was one direct flight to New York a day, and the woman
informed Rebekkah it was not until the next morning. Progressing
toward baggage claim, Rebekkah hefted a mesh duffel, and through
its screening, she spoke to the smushed face of its contents. After the
heavy course of expectorants a vet had prescribed, Edwina could
once more whine at guilt-inducing volumes.

"Don't cry, pupster, we only have to be here for eighteen hours."

One night on the phone, a few years before, when her mother had tried again tentatively to raise the topic of Rebekkah's "plans," Rebekkah had sighed and said that, with her alleged music career going nowhere, she might quite like to be a triage nurse, a wartime Red Cross worker, a stitcher of shrapnel wounds. "Fixing up the war wounded," her mother replied theoretically. "Don't have to think too hard about what a shrink might tell you." Rebekkah's mother didn't push the point. Rebekkah's father had long ago absconded to an early "retirement" in Thailand, and Rebekkah knew that her mother now needed Rebekkah much more than Rebekkah needed her. "I'm being honest," Rebekkah told her mother. "I think it would be nice to give yourself over to something like that." The appeal of such employment, or so Rebekkah believed, was not in the mending of shattered history, but in the surrender to a force much greater than herself. Since November fifteenth—no, even before that, really—Rebekkah had always sought irrefutable directives from the world, and now she received the flight schedule of American Airlines like its own airtight argument. A half hour later, as she and Edwina climbed into a rental Ford Fiesta and emerged from the garage into that impossible blue sphere of Texan sky she remembered, Rebekkah tried to believe that this return wasn't exactly her choice any longer, that the schedule of things had taken her choice away from her.

Of course it was Charlie's phone call—his call and the terrible, astonishing things she had read about Oliver online—that had brought her back here, but even as Rebekkah piloted her Fiesta in the southwestern direction of the Big Bend, it was hard to imagine how she could really do it, how she could possibly do the thing she had come back to do, say the thing she had come back to say.

And as for visiting Oliver in his hospital bed? Too horrible for her even to consider just now. When Rebekkah still dreamed of Oliver, his skin was painted the vicious red-black of dried blood, studded with the pebbles and dust Oliver accumulated as he dragged his body toward her across a Chihuahuan flat.

The hugeness of the blue above her, the strewn material of desert earth; where, in this sky-blasted land, could Rebekkah go to try to reconstitute any of the resolve she had known two nights ago on Eighth Street? She pushed a lever, signaling a left turn to no one.

Rebekkah, whose family had only landed in Bliss for a three-year stopover on her fracking engineer father's world-tour plunder of the earth's petroleum resources, did not know any homecoming feeling or any tragic sense of lapsed time as she drove, two hours later, through the broken, decomposing stuff of Bliss. The town was in reality just what it had become in her memory, a rotting exoskeleton, harmful only if you got too close and inhaled its toxic spores. Rebekkah aimed the Fiesta and half closed her eyes as she passed by Bliss Township School.

And on the far side of Bliss was the end of the earth, or at least the end of human civilization. Not so much a landscape but a minimalist study, perfect cerulean dome above, perfect brown plane below. It was five in the afternoon and the sun went on and on.

Rebekkah continued through the Chihuahuan, in the general direction of the distant blue shapes of the mountains just gnawing their way over the horizon now. Edwina lolled on her back in the passenger seat, luxuriating in a slant of sunlight. This place had never been Rebekkah's home. Rebekkah's home was nowhere and everywhere. It was a string of McMansions, in Scotland, Singapore, Rio de Janeiro, Dubai, Norwalk. Then again, Rebekkah felt that West Texas was also exactly the place she was from, nowhere at all. She was a no one from a nowhere. She felt she was a dabbler, a failed musician, a dilettante, a bum who had made her hovel beneath the bridge of a trust fund—a kind of end-of-childhood bonus her grandmother had established for the successful survival of her first eighteen years. Her life was like an organism in a laboratory cage, and Rebekkah was the scientist studying it through a two-way mirror. What happens to a human after unchanging years, what was the smallest amount of human connection a person needed to live, what was the least that was necessary? She made music and shared it with no one. Her past, and the lost future, all of it belonged inside the cheap drywall, particle board, and chintzy masonry that constituted her family's abandoned house in the Big Bend, alone on Monte Grande Lane, where Rebekkah now put the Fiesta in park.

Oliver. She was not so far from him now, but in the desert distances deceived. She was fifty miles from the actual Oliver in his bed at Crockett State, but the bland house standing on its gray patch of lawn was just like the boy she'd known. The doors locked, the rooms empty. But, no, not empty. It had, Rebekkah knew, been so much easier to believe that Oliver was only an empty house, too, devoid of animating life. And yet, when at last she found out the truth, it seemed to Rebekkah that she had already known, all along.

For nearly a decade, Rebekkah had practiced the words to tell her true story. Often, walking alone in the silent streets of Brooklyn, beneath another stranger's body in the Lower East Side, burning through an insomnia in the bright lights of midtown, Rebekkah had sickened herself with the plain fact that she could have just told it to anyone. Any police officer, her mother, a therapist, a woman on the street, Charlie. But the words were still there, boxed up and filming with dust inside her.

Rebekkah cracked the car door and the immense heat outside crashed over her, a wave of memory, washing years away. The ache of acne was back on her teenage chin, her stomach cramped in the way it always had in those months. The unwashed body smell of her secret covered her. Rebekkah reached for the handle to reseal the door, but it was too late. Edwina had torpedoed out and was presently doing a manic relay race on the brown front lawn. Rebekkah inhaled a sorcery of dust. She was twenty-seven years old when she lifted a foot out of the rental car and put it on the combed cement. She was seventeen years old by the time she stood.

. . . .

CHAPTER TWENTY-SIX

On a sofa fifty-five miles to the northwest, at 14 Paisano Lane in Marfa, Jed blinked from his nap, looked at his piebald hands, his grimy fingernails. For six nights straight, Jed had been battling angels. The archangels, the garbage angels, his latest so-called *series.*

Last night, fueled with a liter of Dickel and two orange Adderall pills he had scored off Francisco, the fifty-year-old hotel bellhop, the battle had raged beyond reason. Jed vs. the angels, and the angels had won. He had taken chain saw and blowtorch to the metal scraps of a great winged behemoth, but the angel's face only grew more damning, his wings spreading more gloriously. Moonlight on rusting metal; a burn in his throat; steel and wood and plastic taking strange shape. His fight with Eve at the dump, all he had said and had never said. Metal filings burst into his goggles. He had burned through the night, the next day, too.

At 5 P.M., Jed was extinguished. The substances had made their gloomy exit, and his gums were bleeding from the clenching of jaws on dental negligence. Jed was nearly asleep again when some alarm cut through his fog, like a sharp smell in the air. His phone, screaming him back to the late afternoon in his Marfa bungalow. The state of Jed's house: he had to search his phone acoustically, waiting for the next ring to suggest its location. The thing was beneath a wadded grease-stained sack, atop a pile of old newspaper he was saving for poor man's drop cloth. On the seventh ring, he found the cheap purple plastic, lifted the receiver. He tried to collect himself, mask his exhaustion with volume. His voice ended up coming out like some television announcer. "Hello!"

"Jed? You're there. Good. This is Manuel Paz speaking."

Jed could hear, in the voice of this officer, a strange tone competing with Manuel's old Texan formality. An unsteady undertow pulling at the vowels, drawing them out. Why had Jed answered? For days now, since Dr. Rumble called with the news of the bad test with Margot, Jed hadn't turned up to work. He'd played possum both times that he had heard Manuel's car in the drive.

"What? What is it now?" Jed was catastrophically sober, his eyes not working in parallel.

"I wanted to talk to you about this in person," Manuel said, "but I couldn't find you at the hotel, and nobody answered the door when I came by."

"Doorbell's busted."

"Ah."

Silence. Jed, a man who had lived inside of silence for fifty-seven years, felt all this particular silence might hold, all he still might not know. He thought of Manuel Paz, the boy he'd grown up with, the men they'd become.

"Manuel. Speak," Jed said.

Sometime later. Jed was driving his pickup against the sunset, to the east. He didn't know where he was going, but the need for movement was the first clear thought his wobbling sobriety could shape after Manuel had told him too much: Eve's shoplifting, Margot still at work with Oliver, questions and questions about Hector, Rebekkah, and his son, those weeks, that night. "I know what you've been going through, and I've been trying to keep you out of it to spare you the agony, but I just can't get my mind off it, and I need to know," Manuel had said.

"I don't know," Jed had told him, several times over. As if, even now, even still, he could plug the black groundswell by pretending. By pretending that he could not still hear the ice river sloshing beneath every hour of his life, a time and place he had tried so hard to cover with flimsy material, with George Dickel No. 8, Pall Malls, white canvas, garbage. It hadn't worked, not for long. Down there, Jed was still years younger. Seeing, not speaking.

CHAPTER TWENTY-SEVEN

Rebekkah was seventeen years old, standing outside her family's house that August. Her third-period theater teacher, Mr. Avalon, had given her a ride home. Oddly, when Rebekkah stepped from his Cadillac, he exited, too, as if she had invited him into the house. This was how it began.

"They're gone a lot, aren't they?" Mr. Avalon asked. "I've seen you walking home a few times."

Rebekkah shrugged. She tried to project the confidence she affected at school, the up-for-anything girl, but a half pint of her mother's gin, which she had been rationing through the school day in her thermos, had gone to her head. The act of trying to straighten her spine was exhausting, and Rebekkah was chagrined at the sound of her own childish, teary sniffles.

"Poor thing," Mr. Avalon said. He slung an arm over her shoulder as if this were how teacher and student were supposed to touch. What did Rebekkah know? Maybe it was. "I know how that goes, my folks were the same way. But listen, if you ever need anyone to talk to . . ." Mr. Avalon said, and Rebekkah nodded.

No denying it, when Rebekkah was near Mr. Avalon the air felt glamorized. Twenty years had passed since Mr. Avalon had found and lost a little fame playing Latino standards on the Tejano circuit, but still a strange halo of renown hung around the lean, aloof, olive-skinned man. "He *looks* like a rock star, doesn't he?" the girls in her class asked, and Rebekkah had to agree. Mr. Avalon must have been near fifty now, but still some kind of feckless teenageness clung to him, in his lank, shining hair, his unbuttoned black shirts, the school-boyish way he'd kick back at his teaching desk, sneakers crossed on the tabletop. Reginald Avalon's Theater Club had an aura unknown to other school clubs. People treated a spot in his biannual *Bliss Township Tejano Espectacular* like a Broadway casting. His club offered only two performances a year, at the Homecoming Dance and at Prom, and the tryouts for this fall's show had been a big drama. Even a newcomer like Rebekkah couldn't fail to notice the deep antipathy in the way the school self-segregated, the gibberish Spanish that the showoff white boys barked at their Hispanic classmates, the menacing jocularity of the Latino guys who hung around the front gates, the occasional shoving matches that broke out in the halls. But, apparently, to get your heart broken by Mr. Avalon was one of the few activities for which the Hispanic and white students would line up together. Rebekkah couldn't blame her fellow classmates for hating her a little. Rebekkah had a spot in the show, and she hadn't even tried out. Mr. Avalon had just heard her sing a selection from *Les Misérables* in his theater class and simply insisted that she join.

On the doorstep to her family's house, Mr. Avalon now handed her a CD. "Listen to track four. 'Historia de un Amor.' It takes huge range, a real virtuosa, and I've never found a singer strong enough to put it in the show, but I have a feeling that maybe I have this year." Mr. Avalon winked.

Rebekkah listened to the track over and over that night, and the next day, at rehearsals, she offered an a cappella rendition. Even as she squinted her eyes to belt out the high notes, Rebekkah could see her fellow club members gaping, could also see the bright, slightly bent way Mr. Avalon watched on. Was there anything in this world that had ever made her happier than the way Mr. Avalon listened to her sing? He leaned into her voice like a houseplant to a window, as if her lungs were shedding some life-giving sustenance. When rehearsals were over, Mr. Avalon snagged her by her blouse. "That was marvelous," Mr. Avalon said. "You are a very, very special creature."

"Thank you," Rebekkah said.

"But you know, I was worrying about you the whole night. And I got something for you, but I can't give it to you here."

Rebekkah cocked her head, and what Mr. Avalon told her next hit her bloodstream like sickness, an infection of gratitude replicating itself. "I don't want to make any of the other kiddos jealous," he said. "I've got some paperwork to do. Find me outside in a few?"

Less tipsy than the day before, Rebekkah waited for Mr. Avalon in the parking lot outside the school. And it was there, as she was trying to strike a cross-legged sophisticated-looking pose on the hot grill of a bench, that Rebekkah saw him for the first time: a young man who found Mr. Avalon as he came out of the school, his briefcase swinging. This guy marched up to Rebekkah's teacher, as if they might hug or at least shake hands, but they did neither. A brown patch of schoolyard lay between Rebekkah and the two curtly speaking men, and she had trouble getting a read on this new person. He carried himself in the self-conscious way of a teenager, but his boyish face was incongruous beneath a shaved head. She couldn't hear a word of what he and Mr. Avalon said, but from the tight way they carried their shoulders, from the way Mr. Avalon kept flinching as if he might march away, she sensed that the conversation was an unpleasant one.

"An old student," Mr. Avalon explained when he at last came to Rebekkah. "Dropped by to say hi."

"Oh," Rebekkah said, her gaze drifting back to this *old student*, who had not budged from his spot near the school's side door. He still just stood there, watching Rebekkah and Mr. Avalon speak. Rebekkah was relieved to climb onto the cool leather bench seat of his vintage Cadillac. But, after an awkwardly silent drive, when they arrived at his house, Rebekkah hesitated. She had seen how her father was with the world—jovial, generous, attentive—an identity he seemed to take off with his business suit at home. At home, Rebekkah's father was afflicted by "nerves." "Nerves" was her father's term for the undetonated minefield of his personality, a wrong step in any direction triggering a charge. Anything Rebekkah said might set him off, and an hour later, Rebekkah would be tending to a fresh welt as her mother persuaded her to apologize to him.

Mr. Avalon, however, seemed just the opposite; in his cluttered pueblo, he came more fully into his kindness.

"So!" Mr. Avalon clapped his hands. "Are you ready for your surprise?"

The surprise was waiting in an outbuilding, a little wood and asbestos shed across a flat. The surprise bounded out as soon as Mr. Avalon opened the door. "How?" Rebekkah said breathlessly. How could Mr. Avalon have known exactly what she had wanted since her ninth birthday? A little black fur ball, a squirming pug, twelve inches of adorable that was all hers. She hoisted the whining dog, pressed it against her face. A realization, both wonderful and also horrible: not all adults were like her parents. Easier to believe in a world in which everyone dealt with secrets, bruises to cover, a memory of a mother asleep in her own sick to wash away with daytime gin. Sorrowful to think that she might have been Mr. Avalon's daughter, that another life could have existed with a father like him.

"Oh, geez, did I do something wrong? Why are you crying?"

Rebekkah bit her lip and shook her head. "We'll have to keep her here. My parents would never let me have her at home."

"Of course, we'll do that. You can visit her every day. The only thing you have to worry about is what you'll name her."

The next weeks were very happy. Each day, after rehearsals, Rebekkah visited Mr. Avalon and Edwina, and she ate four-compartment frozen dinners, after which her teacher helped her with her homework, his own theater assignments and otherwise. As for payment, Mr. Avalon would just tap at his own rough cheek on parting, and

Rebekkah would give it a quick little kiss. The first term ended, and her report card became one less trigger to her father's "nerves." She hadn't yet told Mr. Avalon about what it was like with her parents, but sometimes, as they hunched together over her geometry text-book, he ran his fingers near a furious Ping-Pong ball of a bruise on her shoulder, and his eyes watered. She wouldn't have known how to explain it, and she was glad Mr. Avalon didn't make her try. And yet, one day, on another ride to his house, Mr. Avalon's mood had shifted like her dad's daily arrival at the doorstep. When she asked about his day, he sniffed the Cadillac's leathery air, as if she had just filled it with a fart.

"What were you talking to Oliver Loving for?" Mr. Avalon asked later, over a pepperoni pizza dinner.

"Oliver?" She thought of the kind, nerdish boy she chatted with before first period literature, the boy who had nudged a nervous hand toward her that one night when his father had invited her to the meteor showers. The truth was that when Rebekkah talked with Oliver, she thought often about Mr. Avalon's kindness to her, how she should pay it forward.

"He seems lonely, but he's really nice."

"Don't play stupid. I saw you acting all—" Mr. Avalon did a grotesque imitation of girlish flirting, batting at his hair and gig-gling. "His family is not like yours or mine. For your information, they couldn't know one thing about what it's like to be like us."

Mr. Avalon was standing now, a posture very much like her father's, gathering a dark charge.

"To be special, you have to be broken. It's the trade-off. A boy like Oliver Loving couldn't understand that."

Rebekkah was so afraid of losing Mr. Avalon's attention that she did not ask him, "Why?" She nodded, regretfully.

"I won't let anyone ever hold you back from what you could become," he said, as if that was what this conversation had been about, as if that sweet-shy, scrawny eleventh grade boy held some claim on her. But Rebekkah could tell that Mr. Avalon expected this proclamation to elicit a hug, and it was then, when she stood from the table to let him receive her, that he kissed her for the first time, a kiss quite unlike the dozens of pecks she'd planted on his cheek. She now tasted his sweet, musty flavor. She tried to measure what this kiss meant, and she wasn't sure except that she knew it would repair the blackness of his mood, so she kissed him back.

"Who's there?" her mother called from the study when she came home, just before midnight.

"No one," Rebekkah said. She took the steps two at a time. Alone in bed, Rebekkah was lit up with her secret, her skin glowing in the dark.

CHAPTER TWENTY-EIGHT

Jed's secret, poorly kept: it was true. Once upon a very different time, Hector Espina had been only another student of his.

Jed was in his early forties then, at what would prove to be a kind of zenith in his life, though he couldn't have known it. Jed Loving, local art instructor, with his dreams of succeeding as an artist in his own right not yet entirely crumpled, his whiskey sessions still limited to the weekends. Jed had never wanted to be a teacher, but he liked his job well enough. Things hadn't been right in Jed's own childhood, and those kids—sketching miserable scenes of their family lives alongside the usual dragons and flowers and pretty sunsets—were like some daily lesson for Jed, suggesting that he might even still paint his way free of his own past.

But Jed saw it, even back then: Hector Espina had been more troubled than most kids. A slight and awkward boy, all elbows, who chose to work at an easel near the back of the room, just as, in the halls, Jed had watched Hector move through his days like the shadow of his classmates. A flitting, furtive, shaking boy, whose first drawings were grim indeed. "Is that your father?" Jed would later remember asking Hector Espina one day.

"It is a nightmare," Hector said. "My nightmare."

Jed looked at the blobby blue corpse Hector had etched, maggot eaten and nude. "It sure is," Jed said.

Hector shrugged at the mess he'd made on the page. "It's ugly," Hector said.

"But isn't ugliness the point?"

"Not in the way I wanted."

Jed nodded. "Well, how about you try to do something a little happier next time? Maybe your ma?"

Hector clenched his eyes, shook his head. "My mother? She went back to Mexico when I was five."

Jed took this fact the way he took many similar admissions from his students; he couldn't quite bear to look at the poor kid. He looked, instead, at the drawing. The horror aside, it really was crude. Hector was no artist. Still, if ever there was a boy who needed a gold star, it was he. "You are really making some improvements there, Hector. Your only problem," Jed said, "is that you need to *shade*."

Behind Jed, other boys were hardly trying to stifle their snickering. From day one of the semester, Jed had seen that Hector was the un- luckiest kind of target for adolescent tormentors; Hector was the kind who fought back. "Fuck you," Hector now hissed at these boys, to their considerable delight.

"Don't listen to them," Jed told Hector in a close voice. "And maybe chill it with the language?" Hector nodded, and Jed patted his shoulder, feeling no small sympathy for the kid. Every day, in front of his class, Jed delivered the same timeworn lectures. Perspective, the color wheel, the tricks to diagramming the human face. But some- times it could seem that his class work was more therapy than art.

And drawings like Hector's were hardly unusual among a cer- tain set of Jed's moody boy students. In fact, Jed often encouraged these boys in their catharsis through painted gore. Near the start of each semester, to make a display of the fact that art should not only be about prettiness, Jed offered his class a slide show of a time- tested student favorite: details from *The Garden of Earthly Delights* by Hieronymus Bosch, its fancifully macabre depictions of hell, the demons delighting in the grotesque punishments of the writhing, naked bodies consigned to their damnation. This slide show was Jed's little rebellion against the banalities of the state-issued curriculum. More than that, Jed hoped his students might feel encouraged to draw away their own demons.

But perhaps Jed had made a mistake; Hector took to Bosch in a way no boy before him had. Every six weeks, each student was assigned to present a completed painting, to be presented at a "gallery show," a Friday morning event to which Jed brought decaf coffee and croissants, trying to create a cultured atmosphere. And on that first "viewing" Hector revealed to his teacher and classmates a truly appalling work, a kid's ode to Bosch that might have dismayed Bosch himself. Hector's painting was divided into three sections. In the bottom area, Hector's hell, was a clumsy Boschian display of miseries. In Hector's rendition, the demons supped at steaks made of human thigh, they luxuriated on a throw rug made of flayed human skin, they bludgeoned the poor humans with a variety of implements: a rolling pin, a golf club, a baseball bat. In the center panel, perhaps representing purgatory, was a clumsy, overcast depiction of the town of Bliss. At the top, Hector's heaven showed a malformed version of Hector himself on a cloud, while below, a crowd of similarly misshapen audience members, rendered with heartbreaking intricacy, threw up their arms in Hector's direction. But there was a different, less adoring kind of crowd gathered around Hector now: his fellow art students, who were scoffing quite openly. Jed raised his voice, trying to speak over them.

"Is that you? What are you doing onstage there? Is that some sort of play?"

"I'm *singing*," Hector said in a grumpy whisper, bristling at the mocking attention of his classmates.

"Really? You sing? I had no idea."

"You will," Hector said, glancing around with a little defiant glare. "Someday everyone will. I'm very, very good."

Jed cringed a little, on Hector's behalf. In his own childhood and in his years at the front of the classroom, Jed had learned well that the one piece of truly irresistible bait to a bully was a claim of specialness.

"Yeah, right," a voice said from behind. "Hector Espina, rock star!"

Hector stiffened, turned to face the speaker. "Now, Henry," Jed was saying, but he was useless with discipline, and his students knew it. Henry pushed his way forward, just a few inches from Hector. "Want to know where you'll be in ten years? Eh, *maricón*?" Henry pointed to a detail in Hector's deepest hell, where a demon probed a kneeling man with what appeared to be the barrel of a handgun.

The suddenness of Hector's violence: it was as if Jed could *hear* the sound of a leash being ripped. Hector was on top of Henry now, pinning the boy with his knees. He had already landed two punches to the kid's face before Jed could lunge to pull him away. And then Jed did try, but he wasn't much use. In the bear hug he had on Hector's back, Jed could feel the relentlessness of Hector's swinging arms, a thrashing machine that would not stop running until its job was done. Thankfully, Henry's friends came to Jed's aid, jarring Hector away, pinning him to the blackboard. Ten minutes later, after the classroom had emptied, Jed was looking at Henry's fat lip, the knot rising on the side of Hector's head. And what did Jed do? A lifelong nonconfronter, he handled this fight as he always handled the little skirmishes that broke out in his classroom. No boy wanted a trip to Doyle Dixon's office, with its inevitable call home to explain the specifics. He made the kids shake hands, and no one ever spoke of it again. Weeks passed, at last the semester tipped to its end, and then the problem of Hector was no longer Jed's to worry over.

Hector was, in fact, only one of a great many disturbed kids who had filtered through Jed's room over the years—if not for what happened years later, these memories would likely have vanished, not taken on their crushing tonnage. But Jed would remember too well the fury he had felt in Hector as he hooked his arms around the boy's shoulders, a machine set into frantic motion, a violence that only the muscular effort of other bodies could put to a stop.

········

CHAPTER TWENTY-NINE

One day, in the midst of another quiet evening of homework at Mr. Avalon's kitchen table, Rebekkah perked her head to a knock at the door. Rebekkah would not yet have admitted to any feelings of shame about their evenings together, but she panicked a little, not wanting to reveal her presence there to whoever had dropped by.

"Oh," Mr. Avalon said to the dark figure at the door.

"Forget about me? You *said* I should drop by sometime," the voice said, in an odd way that brought Rebekkah away from her books, made her creep up behind for a better glimpse. This visitor's face was mostly shadowed in the porch light, but she identified his shaven head from that afternoon, outside the school.

"Her again?"

Something in this guy's tone had an odd effect on Rebekkah. She could only name herself in a near-whisper. "Rebekkah," she said. "I'm Rebekkah."

"What can I do for you, Hector?" Mr. Avalon felt for his mustache.

"It's been a while, aren't you happy to see me?"

"It's just not a good time. Right now. We're in the middle of some work." Mr. Avalon was already closing the door a few inches. "If you'd like to come visit some other time, I'd be happy to talk."

"Right. Work." This young man now craned his head past Mr. Avalon. "And so what did he tell you—Rebekkah, you said it was? That you're gonna be some rock star? I should tell you," he said. "He lies."

"Hector."

"He lies! You know, he never even let me sing in that stupid club of his? He wouldn't even let me join his class! 'First you have to hone your craft,' he says. Hone my craft! Ha ha!"

Mr. Avalon jerked back his arm, as if he might shove the kid to the ground. Instead, he slammed the door shut into Hector's grinning face.

"I'm sorry about that," Mr. Avalon said after the sound of the car had grumbled away. He cleared his throat a couple of times, shook his shoulders like a wet dog. "Hector. Truth is the boy was very talented. Another kid from a broken home. I thought I could help him, but sometimes boys like Hector just go in the wrong direction."

"Wrong direction?"

"Last I heard he's got himself involved in some bad business. Selling drugs around town. It's such a shame, really, all that wasted talent, what he could have been."

Mr. Avalon made a boyish display of pouting, sticking out a shining lower lip. "But maybe, in a way, I'm just like him, aren't I? What I might have been, too."

Rebekkah could see that Mr. Avalon needed reassuring, but she couldn't think of the right words.

"It's different for a girl like you," Mr. Avalon added, a little viciously. "You couldn't understand."

"What do you mean?"

"You probably can't even see it, can you? The gifts you've been given in this world. Hate to think how far I myself might've gone if I'd been born to some rich white folks like yours."

Rebekkah nodded awkwardly. "You've given your life to help kids like me. And that isn't nothing," Rebekkah said. She did not ask, *How many of us have there been?*

Rebekkah hated the thought of other super special students before her; she hated the threat of Mr. Avalon pulling his attention away. Someday, when he was through with her. But mostly Rebekkah was afraid, at all times, that she would do something wrong with Mr. Avalon, and she'd have to go back to the way things were before. Everything had gotten better, including her stomach. Even her father, who noticed nothing, had noticed the difference. "Look at you, finally brightening up a bit!" Rebekkah had kindness to spare. Despite Mr. Avalon's admonishment, Rebekkah still showed up each day for a nice, warm hour of Oliver Loving's attention.

·····················

CHAPTER THIRTY

Hector's painting scenes of his father as a feast for insects, a mumbling kid who had suddenly become a machine, an instrument of punishment that day in Jed's classroom: Why didn't Jed ever say a thing about it?

Silence: Jed had learned it from his father. When Jed was a boy, his pa, Henry Loving, had conversed with his family in grunts, sighs, coughs, throat clearings. Silence: Jed had learned it from his mother, too. After a stroke ended his father's life, Jed and his mother hardly spoke of him again—his ma had a knack for twangy chatter that never touched on any subject that mattered. Like some sort of compensation, in the very room where his pa had expired, Jed had spent the balance of his teenage years filling the settler's cabin with better visions, his paint piled thick. Jed hatched a plot to apply to art school, sketched mental images of himself in New York galleries, paint-spattered in a bathrobe on a European balcony—a life so unlike West Texas, he might forget home entirely. And yet, there he was now, almost thirty years later, just an art teacher at his old school, time still scrolling by, and at last Jed understood. That image of himself painting in New York or Paris? False hope. Jed's assumption of his own father's fate, his up-all-night drinking sessions, his brooding? Reality. He was his father's son. No, except for the lame paintings he still dabbled at, he was his father. A silence in the shape of a man, a family he disappointed daily, worries he never spoke of to anyone.

The years just kept passing, but time was also a salve for a schoolteacher, easing away his students and the concerns they brought to Jed's room. Hector Espina left Jed's art class, and Jed never spoke to the boy again. New bodies came into the room with their new problems. Only the teachers remained.

Reginald Avalon. At the time, he was just another faculty member, a man whom Jed had known since they were boys together in that same school; soon he'd become a kind of local deity to the town of Bliss, his sun-scrubbed image singing out from the high billboard over Señor Buddy's. Reginald Avalon: Jed would later wonder at the man's remarkable capacity for transformation. At seventeen, Reg had already been on his way to his brief local fame, playing fandangos and honky-tonks, doing performances at the school assemblies. As a kid, Reg had been nearly as friendless as Jed. Half Mexican, half white, Reg had seemed a boy welcomed by no one. From a distance Jed had admired the way Reg seemed to put his own aloneness to artistic use. What had made his performances so arresting was a certain wizened melancholy in his voice. Watching from the audience, Jed had thought he recognized his own outsider's sadness, but Jed had never spoken more than a few words to Reg. And he had hardly ever spoken to the man Reg had become. After a few years out in Los Angeles, Reg had come back to West Texas to play his old Spanish songs to diminishing crowds at county fairs until he stopped playing and became a teacher. *Those who can't do*—Reg and Jed, the town's two failed artists, in the end they both couldn't do.

A dream deferred: a line that Oliver had once showed him, in a book of poems by Langston Hughes. "Everyone will know," Hector had once told Jed about his own future fame. But *what happens to a dream deferred?* Hughes asked. It might *dry up like a raisin in the sun*, as it had for Jed and Reg. Or maybe, Langston Hughes wrote, *it just sags*, *like a heavy load. Or does it explode?*

At last Jed would see. Jed hadn't set eyes on Hector in years, but in the weeks *after*, Jed would see the kid's face every day on the local news, in the hospital waiting room. And that was when Jed would know that he could have stopped it, years before. He could have done *something*. He could have brought that boy's artwork to the attention of the school counselor or Officer Filipovic, the cop who patrolled the school halls from time to time. He could have sent Hector and Henry to Principal Dixon's office that day; he could have spoken with the principal about the immensity of Hector's rage, very unlike the little shoving contests that had broken out in his classroom over the years. But his old worries about Hector Espina would not be the worst fact Jed would never speak aloud.

November fifteenth. Oliver wanted to stay home. Oliver *would* have stayed home, if not for Jed. And yet, just outside the gymnasium doors, Jed phoned Zion's Pastures that night. "Now you want me to show up alone," Oliver resisted, but still Jed managed to talk him into it. "Rebekkah was asking me about you," Jed even lied to his son, to convince him to come that night. It was just a playful little conversation with Oliver at the time. Later, it would become the sickness Jed would swallow down, unable to admit it to his wife or to Charlie. Jed would have to grow a second organ in his gut to hold it all in. But deep in his black stomach, the unspoken words would only fester, a sickness that would seed his body with infectious growths. *It was my fault Oliver was there. Mine. Me.*

CHAPTER THIRTY-ONE

Years later, so many of those nights with Mr. Avalon would remain unplaceable. His eyes, rampant and dark. Cicadas droning, a deafening static. A gagging in her throat. Somewhere, very distantly, a train bellowing through the desert night. Rebekkah's shame was at its worst when Mr. Avalon kept all the lights burning brightly. What a frail, bruised, freckled girl she must have looked like to Mr. Avalon, what she and Mr. Avalon would have looked like to anyone else. It broke her apart. Rebekkah felt herself shape-shifting then, like a creature in one of the tall tales Oliver had told her. She was becoming a monster, an insect, a toad, and one night, as if it could work like a fairy tale, she found Oliver at the football stadium and let him kiss her once. But it did not work like a fairy tale, at least not for her. Horribly, she could see in his brightened face, it seemed to work that way for Oliver.

It was October now. Everything was building to a climax. At rehearsals Mr. Avalon's Theater Club had nearly perfected their repertoire for the Homecoming Dance. They had ordered their traditional Mexican costumes, which even the white kids paraded around the school hallways, to the befuddlement and mockery of Hispanic and white students alike. No one, not even her fellow performers, spoke much to Rebekkah at all.

Hector had not, as Mr. Avalon had requested, left them alone. A couple more times she had seen Hector, silent in the school parking lot, watching them get into Mr. Avalon's car. One morning just before school, Hector cornered her near the back door.

"Just sing for me. Let me hear what this supposedly amazing voice sounds like," Hector said, his breath flashing on her cheeks. Rebekkah looked at the students filing into the school, saw their eyes watching her.

"Please leave me alone," she said, as Mr. Avalon had instructed her to say. But even if this guy frightened her, Rebekkah felt so alone in her secret that she nearly asked, *What did he do to you?*

What *she* had done with Mr. Avalon on the sofa, the bedroom mattress, the floor of the shed, the backseat of the Cadillac, had made her wiring go wonky. Her body had started to come up with its own odd decisions; sometimes, after she came home from Mr. Avalon's house, her hands reached instinctively for a cheese knife and pressed it into her thigh. Her stomach heaved at unpredictable times, so direly that she worried next time, in the middle of literature class, she wouldn't make it to the bathroom.

Literature class, poor Oliver. She'd still often find him sitting there, pretending not to have waited for her. Sometimes, she'd catch Oliver stealing glimpses of her through the window of the theater room door. She hadn't spoken with the boy in weeks. She wanted only to spare him from more hurt. In truth she thought little of Oliver at all. But then, one day, Oliver did that astonishing thing: he raised his hand in class and read his poem to everyone. That poem Oliver had made of their conversations, of the stars, of her silence toward him. Rebekkah thought it was beautiful, and so it was awful, the distance from the girl he imagined to the person she had become. She wanted only to disappear, to be the object of no one's attention. She stayed at home for three days, wanting it all to stop, until her mother noticed and made her return. She tried to think of a way to tell Oliver to leave her alone. Of course, he didn't understand. She felt she must have worn her secret on her skin, but she perceived anew how alone she was in it.

Or maybe not alone, not completely. Hector came back, just once more. She was at Mr. Avalon's house. They were together on the couch, watching one of the Shirley Temple films he inflicted upon her. No knock at the door this time. Hector let himself in, careened into the living room on unsteady feet.

"What in God's name—" But when Hector collapsed into an armchair, the thing he rested on his lap silenced Mr. Avalon's protest.

"I'm not going to ask you again," Hector said, his tough guy routine slurry and unconvincing, as he ran a quaking finger along the hilt of a sheathed hunting knife. "If you are so special, let's hear you sing." Even in the madness of her fear, some other Rebekkah, the one who had metamorphosed inside her, was relieved that the moment of crisis had at last arrived.

"Hector—" Mr. Avalon said.

"Sing," Hector told Rebekkah. What could she do? She looked to Mr. Avalon, who nodded at her faintly. She put her hands on her knees. She opened her mouth, but no sound would come out.

"You'll be nothing. Nothing. Just like me," Hector said, as if something had been settled. He lifted himself from the chair, knelt clumsily to retrieve the weapon he'd dropped, but Mr. Avalon was faster. The ridiculous way Mr. Avalon waved around that knife, still in its fringed leather casing, was nearly funny. "If I see you again, I'm calling the police."

Edwina snuffled up to this scene. "A dog," Hector said. "Don't tell me you even bought her a dog, too?"

"Her name is Edwina," Rebekkah said.

Rebekkah scooped up Edwina, as if worried that Hector might abduct her. The boy's eyes had gone smoky. He asked Mr. Avalon the question that Rebekkah had never asked. "Just tell me. How many of us have there been?"

"Please," Mr. Avalon said. "Just leave."

Hector turned to Rebekkah then, his eyes emphatic and wide. "The mistake," Hector said, "is to hope. I'm sorry for you. I am."

After that last visit from Hector, Rebekkah and Mr. Avalon tried to continue as before, but the spell was broken, the circuit blown. They hardly touched at all, or at least not in the ways they had. In the days that followed, Hector did not reappear, and Rebekkah just played her music for Mr. Avalon, his favorite songs and a few beloved country hits. "Jolene," "Achy Breaky Heart," "Devil Town," "The Thunder Rolls," "West Texas Waltz."

The only time anyone saw the truth, it was the sad-eyed boy from her English class. It was Oliver's face in the window, as Mr. Avalon hunched over her in a kitchen chair. Oliver was there and then he vanished. Had she just imagined him in the shapes the moonlight etched onto the glass?

And yet. The night of November fifteenth, the Homecoming Dance, and Oliver pulled her aside and told her he would tell someone. She begged him not to say anything; she wanted more than anything for him to say something. A boy from the Theater Club tugged her away, made her follow him to the classroom. Distantly, songs still played: "Baby Got Back," "Push It," "Kiss from a Rose." As the other kids tuned their instruments, studied their lyrics, Rebekkah felt she was watching her bandmates from underwater. She was down there, at the bottom of her own dark sea, when she saw Hector Espina again, framed in the classroom door.

························

CHAPTER THIRTY-TWO

Stashed in the drawer of a desk, Jed kept a certain document, now worn down to the softness of cloth. He'd read it a thousand times. The page was a timeline he'd made, with the assistance of the official police report. The numbers were a torture, but the only containers for the horrors that still flashed through him: the ultrabright gymnasium lights thrown on, a chaos of teenage bodies and squad lights outside, a blind panic hurtling him back down the halls, redness spreading on the shining schoolhouse floors. Arms holding him back, a throat howling. His own.

9:06: Hector Espina enters the school carrying AR-15-style assault rifle.

9:08: Hector Espina enters theater classroom.

9:09: Hector Espina fires first round, striking Brad Rossening in the leg.

9:10–9:11: Twenty-two rounds fired, injuring Jonathan Strom, Brian Hadley, Anna Hoke, Jennifer Schmidt. Fatal shots to Keith Larsen, Vera Grass, Roy Lopez, and Reginald Avalon.

9:13: Hector Espina exits classroom. Hector finds Oliver in the hall. Fires three rounds, two striking the wall, one striking Oliver.

9:16: Ernesto Ruiz tackles Hector in the school atrium, takes Hector's rifle. Hector escapes out the front doors.

9:20: From the atrium, Ernesto Ruiz hears sound of one more shot fired.

9:25: First police car arrives to find Hector's body on the school's front steps, handgun still in his hand.

"Nine thirteen," Jed said aloud, so many times over the years, as if those numbers might bring him back to that instant. The torture, the appalling fact turning a decade old and as unbelievable as ever: that minute had already passed. Nine thirteen: *Oliver,* he could have screamed. *Hector.* He could have tackled the boy. Thrown his body over the weapon. Taken the shot. Killed him. *Oliver!* Too late: 9:13 passed to 9:14, passed to ten years. Jed had done nothing.

CHAPTER THIRTY-THREE

Snap. Snap. Snap. A spot. The bossy girl from Rebekkah's theater class, Vera Grass. A dot on her temple, her face vacant. Stippled, perforated, a seeping punctuation on her arm, her torso. Something was also wrong with the face of Roy Lopez. It took a while for Rebekkah to realize a part of it was missing. There were screams that were not really screams, a combustive silence, blowing out and out. She wanted to say, *You don't have to do this.* As if it weren't already too late. It was already too late. There in front of her. There. No longer quite Mr. Avalon, a mark on his face, an opening in his chest, faintly whistling. His eyes rolled back like those of a man forever appalled. Rebekkah put her hands on Mr. Avalon as if she could piece him back together again. When she looked up, her eyes met Hector's. Hector leaned to her, as if he might explain something. He lifted his weapon and aimed it between her eyes, which Rebekkah closed tightly. But then, without a word, Hector turned and left. He left Rebekkah with the answers she would never speak, and also the questions she could never answer. Why not her, too? Why had he pointed the rifle at her and then just walked away? Was it pity? Was it a kind of punishment for Rebekkah, to make her live with these questions? Or did it have no meaning at all? But Hector left the room, and Rebekkah recoiled at another noise from the hallway. After the sound of footsteps passed, she stepped toward the door, and that was when she saw. *Oliver.*

November fifteenth: the dividing line, the transformational epoch in her own evolutionary process. Mr. Avalon and Hector were gone, and now Rebekkah was a new species. The truth of what had happened was too obvious for her to name. When Rebekkah tried to speak with Manuel Paz, her throat could hardly produce a sound.

Rebekkah showed up just one more time to Mr. Avalon's pueblo. The doors were locked, the windows too. She drifted across the yard, and soon found herself standing in the grayed depravity of the outbuilding.

Rusting nails in mason jars, a few screwdrivers hanging from a pegboard, the smell of skin and sweat and heavy breath beneath the cloying stink of something turned, so powerful that she gagged. She found the single bulb, swinging from a rafter, pulled its chain. Beneath the workbench, a swatch of black fur. Edwina was breathing, barely, surrounded by her excrement.

Rebekkah took Edwina home and she nursed her back to health. She became nothing but a nurse to a dog, it was all she could bear. The extent of her parents' pity for what Rebekkah had survived: they did not make her give the dog away. "I don't know," she said when men came back with more questions. *I don't know.* She would never answer, not in the way they needed. But when Edwina was well enough she brought her to Oliver's hospital room. She did not know until that moment that she had come to give her away. Give to Oliver's family all she had left.

"Her name is Edwina," Rebekkah said.

"Thank you," Oliver's brother replied, but she said nothing else to him. She said to herself every single day that her story was meaningless now, that it was too late to matter. But the truth was that she could have told anyone. The truth was that she could have stopped it.

Time went on. Now she was eighteen, a girl with a GED and a precarious academic standing at a New York community college.

Now she was twenty-three, still without a diploma, aimless and moneyed. Now she was twenty-six when, one night, the past she had tried to give away came back to her. Edwina snuffling at her feet on a Brooklyn sidewalk. "Rebekkah. It's Charlie. Charlie Loving."

In the time before, she had hardly spoken to the kid, but she had seen enough of him to be surprised by the man he'd become. A handsome guy in snap-button flannels, his eyes bright behind fashionable glasses. But she too had changed and then changed again. Her skin had weathered, the freckles expanding to permanent beige spots. The parents who had once wrecked her had dissipated into her grayish atmosphere. She lived alone and jobless, already like some spinster, minus the cats. Charlie was not a boy anymore, and she was not a girl anymore. "What do you want?"

"Just to talk," he said. Charlie's eyes, with their bright gray light, were the eyes of the boy who spoke with her before first period each day, in another life when she still might have become another kind of person. What if she had only kept talking to Oliver? What if she had stopped going to Mr. Avalon's house? The truth was still there, right at Charlie's feet. "Edwina," Rebekkah said.

Just to talk, but how could she? *Mental illness,* people had said on the television, shaking their heads, *violence in the media. Immigration policy. Cartel warfare. Terrorism.* And if it were true that Hector Espina, with his muttering tempers, had been unwell, and if it were also true that Hector had seen the horrific footage of how other boys before him had made a gruesome spectacle of their suffering, Rebekkah knew those factors amounted only to kindling for the fire. It was rage that had set the blaze. It was the outrage of a hopeless, abused, and cast-off child, given false hope.

In a unit on Dante's *Inferno,* one of her college professors described a special torment that Hell reserves for the wrathful. "They are made to spend eternity in the muck of the river Styx," the professor said. "Endlessly lamenting their sins, their words lost in that thick black river. Unbearable, am I right?" But Rebekkah, after years in her own underworld, could put her head into those murky waters, where she could still hear Hector's lament. *I had nothing, nothing, nothing, no one helped me, why did no one help me, why did no one stop him, hope was the worst torture of all, why did no one help me?*

And now Rebekkah was twenty-seven, standing outside her family's empty house. The cottonwoods that lined the man-made gully in the backyard had nearly doubled in height. Edwina hopped through the dense, bunched grasses that carpeted the ground below. The pug gamboled about, diligent and delighted, more youthful than her years, as if searching for a shotgunned mallard. "Edwina!" Rebekkah shouted, and the dog ran to her heel. Rebekkah was seventeen years old, giving Edwina to Charlie. She was twenty-seven years old, crouching over the same animal, who was going gray at the snout now. Edwina licked at her face. This poor pug, bound to her own sad history, twice nursed to health from death's brink. "I'm sorry," Rebekkah told the dog as she gathered her up and turned for the car.

CHAPTER THIRTY-FOUR

Tonight, almost ten years *after,* Jed was in the cab of his Nissan pickup. Seven thirty in the desert and the sun was a low, unblinking orb. When he reached the road to his wife's house, it took all the strength he had to turn.

Maybe Jed's greatest crime was self-pity. After all, his whole past wasn't just the tragedy he'd often narrated to himself. There had been actual miracles. His sons. Their skin and muscle and bone and bright eyes flung wide on just another ordinary Sunday morning as they flew through the air, arcing to him from the rope swing over Loving Creek. *Cannonball!* Maybe the happiest hours of his life, if only he'd known it then. But each day he had failed to be the father he had imagined; he loved his boys so fiercely, he knew he'd make the same mess of it that he made of all things he loved.

History doesn't repeat, but it often rhymes: a quote that Mrs. Henderson had tacked up in her American history classroom. It was true, and not only in the ways his life echoed his own father's. As his truck thundered down the county road, Jed found himself thinking of that man he hadn't thought of in years. He was thinking of Reginald Avalon. Reginald and Jed, Hector and Oliver: two couplets in rhyming verse, four young men with dreams of art that would never come to be. History rhymes, but there is something not quite graspable in the symmetries. The truck seemed to know its own way. He was at that strange and new cracked house of Eve's now, no home. He was at her door, knocking.

"Jed," Eve said.

"Hi." He spoke to his hands, his old man's hands. "Is Charlie here, too?"

"Charlie? You came here to speak with Charlie?"

Jed shrugged down at a brown doormat that said WELCOME.

"Well, he isn't here," Eve said. "I honestly have no idea where he might have gone."

"Oh," Jed said.

"So, what? What is it?" she asked, and Jed looked up.

Eve. Once Jed had painted better universes for his family, but the only better universe he had really tried to believe in was the one she had offered. Belief, silence to the facts. Their perfect son, withering, sightless, untested for years, too horrible to see. The true story of Jed's life? His silence was the jail keeper. He had never told Eve, *This is wrong, you have to let Oliver go. You have to let Charlie live his own life.* He had never told his family, *It was I who made him come that night.* He had never told anyone, *That boy Hector needs some help.*

But now Jed spoke. He opened his mouth and all the contents of the black stomach at last came spilling out. He only had to let go, and the words came and came. Eve said nothing for a long while after he had finished.

"I don't understand," she told him at last.

"I know."

"It was because of you? That he came that night?"

"Yes."

"And Hector—"

"Yes."

"Why? Why are you telling me these things? Why, Jed? Why now?"

"I couldn't not tell you. Anymore."

"About ten years too late."

"You are right. Of course you are right."

Eve turned, stepped into her broken living room. Standing there for a long while, they made no sound but their own breathing. When he tried to reach for Eve, she shuddered away. "Please," Jed said, and she shook her head. Jed had an image of himself bursting apart, his flesh splattering the walls. Somehow he managed to remain upright.

"Jed," Eve said at last. She held out a hand, and Jed flinched, anticipating a slap. Instead, she grasped the hair at the back of his head, pressed his forehead hard against her own. Her breath was in his mouth, his tears on her face. "I'm very, very sorry for you," she said, renewing her hold on his head. "But it is too late for you to come tell me these things now and think you can just be forgiven. Too late to think that everything will somehow change."

Jed pulled gently away, held her hands between his own. "There's still so much we've never told each other," he said.

"Meaning what?"

"We have to stop," Jed said. "We have to stop going on like this. You have to stop."

"I have to stop what?"

"Eve—"

"Fuck you. I mean it, Jed. Fuck you. I don't have to listen to another word from you."

"But you never did, did you? You only hear what you want to hear."

"Easy for you to say."

"Nothing is easy for me to say."

"Leave. Just go. It's what you deserve."

"But what about what Oliver deserves?"

"Go." Eve pointed at the door.

"Listen to me," Jed said.

"I can't," she said. "I won't."

"Listen to me," Jed said again, and his hand found the corner of a television. For three decades of marriage, Jed had found ways to make no sound. He was always careful on the floorboards, nodded through dinners, at last retreated into his father's silence in the settler's cabin. Tonight he grasped the TV and slammed it into the wall. Jed was a different man now, and Eve gaped at the person he had become. Or not become. Revealed. "Okay," she said. "So I'm listening."

And they were still speaking there in Eve's kitchen, at six the next morning, when her phone rang.

CHAPTER THIRTY-FIVE

Midland. Rebekkah soothed herself with the thought of the concrete low-rise hotels she'd seen from the tarmac. She would drive back now, spend the night in an anonymous pod of the Hilton, and in the morning she'd fly away. With a snap of her foot, she fed the engine.

And yet, as if it had some last vindictive point to make before it let her go free, her rental car's GPS system guided Rebekkah past the pueblo that would always stand at the black center of her memory. Its stucco walls now badly chipped, its yard littered with detritus. That same old Cadillac on cinder blocks, a tattered blue tarp, a child's rusting tricycle. Rebekkah told herself that she would pass quickly, yet her Fiesta slowed nearly to a stop. And there her memories still lumbered, walking from shed to house. Mr. Avalon's familiar hunch, something disjointed in his knees, his arms with their simian swing, a parade of children—*How many?* He'd never answered Hector's question—trailing behind him. "No," Rebekkah said to the driver's-side window. The memory vanished, leaving a field of dead weeds in the deepening twilight.

Once upon a time, Oliver was just the lanky love poem writer in her English class; how could she have known then that he would become the only person who had ever seen, the only one who might have had words for it all? Oliver. He still came to her in strange places. He was in the cozy smell of aging paper at the Brooklyn Public Library, the ended possibility of those thousands of pages he would never write. The quiet between notes she still plucked on her guitar. Oliver was his brother following her through the streets of Brooklyn. His eyes were Charlie's eyes. Gray, brownish around the pupil. "It isn't right," Charlie said over the phone. "We never thought about what he might need." In one of the two trees that stood in the front yard of Mr. Avalon's house, a shredded kite rustled in the branches.

Rebekkah turned the wheel. Could she really do it? She imagined the scene that might await her at the hospital. A bedside lamp clicking on, her face coming into focus.

Once, Oliver had looked at Rebekkah like an angel descended. How, she wondered, would she look to him after all those years? Rebekkah knew: in the end, she had become a different sort of angel, the one who brought death.

Oliver

....

CHAPTER THIRTY-SIX

"The whole cosmos," your father once told his Young Astronomers Club, "will end just as it began, collapsed back to a single spot of brightness. The Big Crunch, they call it, which in turn becomes the next Big Bang, the universe reborn." Maybe your father's arty astrophysical stories had always been more metaphor than science, and yet, once more, it was just as your father had described it. At last, after years of spreading darkness, a sudden contraction; the immeasurable weight of past and present rejoining to a single point of light. A brightness that woke you.

It was the bulb at the end of the flexible stick of your bedside lamp, and you could make out just the shape of a wrist as your eyes ached to adjust. Whose wrist? The wrist became a hand, which reached to direct the light upward. You blinked, and you blinked, and the image shook slowly into focus.

Suddenly, I turned around and she was standing there: that was a line from your favorite song in the last of your walking years. Bob Dylan's "Shelter from the Storm." In the few months you'd known her, Rebekkah had never exactly been the shelter, she had at least as often been the storm. But *in another lifetime,* maybe?

Well, here you both were now, *in another lifetime* indeed. You might not have been able to turn around, but it was just as Bob Dylan had promised. Suddenly, she was standing there. But not with *silver bracelets on her wrists and flowers in her hair.* Those famous amber ringlets of hers were drawn back in a neat ponytail, and she wore a half-unzipped hoodie over a purplish blouse.

The hands that were Rebekkah's hands reached to hold your face steady so that you could not look away. You wanted very much to look away. *Enough,* you told yourself. You knew your brain had at last torn down the final boundaries and conjured her back for you, but you found that you didn't have the courage to look upon this pleading hallucination. Rebekkah as you remembered her was one thing, a marvelous flightless bird petrified in iridescent rock. But this dream of her now, looking down at you after all those years? Her parted lips, her widened eyes registering the kind of heartbreak that is lodged between shock and disgust? It was too much, too close. Oh, even her vanilla smell was so achingly convincing. You willed her to vanish. Yet this dream Rebekkah persisted there, and she cleared her throat.

"Oliver," she said.

And still the illusion remained, in such remarkable detail. Even the light throatiness of her breathing, which you had forgotten, was back in your ears. You cheered with the thought that this, at last, was just the true, merciful form your own angel of death had taken.

"I'll bet you are surprised," Rebekkah told you, and that was when you began to believe. Rebekkah, the living, the actual.

But you were not surprised, not exactly. You were—what's the word for when your most persistent daydreams take tangible, breathing, ginger-hued life in front of you? Just one word for it, of course. *Rebekkah.* You could not rise to take in the changes with your arms, and so you did your best to take her in with your eyes, which vibrated across her at a high frequency.

"Oliver?" Rebekkah's tone was distant, a voice on a bad telephone connection. As if testing something, she pressed her mouth to your forehead and retreated. "How is this you?"

In the harsh black and bright white of the bedside lamp, she looked like she had passed through more than a decade. Gray strands wound through those amber ringlets now. As with your mother, her face was a furrowed cartography of the many bad years. And her voice, which you had so often conjured in your memory, was a whole octave lower than you would have expected. She had changed. It was nature's way, and you accepted it. It was in that acceptance that you found yourself appalled.

"I can't, I couldn't. I'm sorry," Rebekkah said. "I should have come to see you. Years ago. I just couldn't."

"It's okay," you couldn't say.

"It's not okay," she said.

What appalled you was the way that, even still, a crazy, vanilla-drunk feeling once more staggered its way upright inside you. Even still, at the mere sight of this half stranger, you felt the old urgency. Everything you still needed to tell her.

Of course you knew that to the woman presently bent over your bed, you were now Oliver the Martyr, Oliver the Buried Truth, Oliver the Secret Shame, but you had never been Oliver the Lost Love. You were, in fact, just one boy she had kissed; there were many before you, and very many had followed. The tragedy of love, you had learned from ten years spent looking up at your mother, is that it is only possible to love perfectly a person who is lost to you; only a lost person, lodged in a place before the narrow, clumsy gates of language, could ever understand you perfectly. And so maybe the great love of your life was only a crush, blown up to operatic proportions by impassable distance, only a name for your vanished future. But when you had spoken those mornings before school in Mrs. Schumacher's literature classroom, Rebekkah had seemed to offer the possibility of a new kind of fluency, and maybe it was that better, impossible language you needed even more than you needed her. That better language, more expansive and full of strange beauty, which you needed to tell everything that had happened and not happened, the ways you had survived because you had no choice but to survive.

Rebekkah clenched her face, released it, clenched again. When your gastrointestinal machine made a little gurgle, Rebekkah startled, and her words came out of her like something she'd spilled, sloppy and wet. "And I know it's way, way too late. To say I'm sorry? But I am. I am so, so sorry. I'm sorry that I never came. That I never told anyone what was happening before it was too late. That I still haven't told. For years. Years, like this. Oliver. I'm sorry, I'm sorry. I'll say it, I think I'll really keep saying it to myself like a little prayer forever. *Sorry*. But what does that word even mean?"

You might have made Rebekkah into the Penelope at the end of your own bed-bound *Odyssey*, but even if you could have spoken to her now, you would have had no idea what to say. Rebekkah blinked very rapidly, as if she weren't seeing straight. "I want to show you something." She relinquished your face and leaned to one side to extract a paper from her bag. Your eyes, of course, could never focus on the text, but you recognized the shapes of your lines as you would have recognized a photograph of your old school. It was, in fact, the poem about your school, "Children of the Borderlands," the last poem you'd written for her. In another lifetime. The page was torn from a magazine, worn nearly to a pulp, the words smeared and creased like old money.

"Recognize it, Oliver? I still read it, all the time. I've memorized all the words, but to see them there, on that page? It is like you are still out there somewhere. I read this thing you wrote, and I still feel—I don't know, Oliver. So glad. That I got to know you."

"Me, too," you could not say. Maybe your hands would never again rise to meet hers. All the promise of your mornings in Mrs. Schumacher's literature classroom would never be yours. But at least you had this, and maybe it was the best anyone could ever hope for: a roomy idea in which you were not alone. Long seconds passed.

"Good Lord!" Another voice—the familiar West Texan twang of the current Crockett State receptionist and former Bliss Pies N' Stuff waitress—filled the room. "Is that Rebekkah Sterling?"

"Excuse me?"

"It's Peggy. Peggy! From the old diner!"

"Oh, right. Hi there," Rebekkah said, her voice fumbling. "I was just visiting Oliver, but now I need to go."

"What are you even doing here? I heard you were living in New York."

"I am. Just passing through and thought I'd make a little visit, but I really have to run."

"Not so fast! Don't you want a picture with the boy? I bet he'd want it. His folks, too."

Please, you thought. Better for there to be no picture. Better for this memory to remain where it had taken place, behind your changed and strange skins. But of course you could not protest when Peggy produced a camera and gestured for Rebekkah to come huddle near your bed. As if this visit were just some excellent excursion you were all taking together, Peggy fixed her face into a wide grin, and she extended her arm for a group self-portrait. Rebekkah strained to brush the wetness from her face.

And then whatever relief this visit might have brought sucked out into the Chihuahuan night. Peggy held her camera at arm's length, snapping photo after photo. It was not the photos that you begged to end. It was the horrible thing that this camera of Peggy's showed you. The screen lit with a bright image: an electronic mirror, the three of your faces pressed together.

Your eyes, unfocused and scuttling, took a long while to find yourself and see. You only held the gaze for a second at a time, before your vision scared off in some other direction. But you did see, over and over and over. It was your face in the screen. And also, terribly, not. Your jaw had grown thick from the labor of its constant tremble. Your hair, as if from shame for the face beneath it, had begun to fall away. Your eyes looked at your eyes, like a senile man groping out of sleep for a clue as to where he'd woken. And you felt now that all the stories you had told yourself weren't really true. Your buttons weren't magical wormholes, just very lucid memories. In truth, you were just trapped in a hospital bed, not a passage between dimensions. You weren't really a ghost inhabiting some other slain boy's body. And yet, the only bit of yourself you could find in this vegetable staring back at you looked just like a ghost of you trapped in something else. A monster.

After Rebekkah left that night, your only hope was that maybe, at last, you really could will your brain to pull its own plug. Yet that was just a fantasy, too.

In the morning, Margot Strout arrived once more. "Here I am!" she said, that tragic woman come back to happily write her fictitious Oliver while the actual Oliver had only his silence. You tried to go slack, to will yourself to fall into that other place, where voices could once more become as meaningless as storm clouds over your roof. But the explosion of the floral hand grenade that was Margot Strout's perfume was enough to rouse the dead.

"A? B? C? D?" Margot asked. At last the computer replied, "Missed you."

That morning, for perhaps the blackest minute of your Crockett State years, there was nothing beneath your graying skin but rage. And it was not the usual anger at the young man who had put you into that bed, nor was it at the pungent woman writing her stories with your thumb. The fury, just then, was at another woman, the one who had spent all those years hunched over your transformation into this hideous creature. How many times, in your screaming silence, had you begged her to let you go? But Ma only carried on, as if her daily devotion to you were an act of selfless love, when it had always, or so it seemed to you now, been the opposite. Your mother, whose unspoken and darkest dream was always plainly visible to your brother and you: that you remain the perfect recompense for her sad, wandering childhood, that you and Charlie never grow away from her, your needs giving shape to the life of a woman who had never quite been able to make any other shape of herself. "I always believed," she'd told you. But her belief was the cocoon in which you'd metamorphosed in reverse, turning into a grublike, wingless insect.

And rage, too, at your father. The man who committed his sins with a nod of his head, the man who carried on as if he had no role, as if his family would right itself if only he kept his lips sealed. And Charlie. The boy who had run off into the world, as if your future were still out there somewhere, as if he could free you with a story, as if he could find some better, wholly whole Oliver someplace thousands of miles away.

Over Bed Four, Margot Strout was speaking at you still, something about one of your favorite old books, *Wind, Sand and Stars* by Saint-Exupéry, which apparently Charlie had told her you'd loved. "Once you get past all the racism, he really does have quite a story to tell . . ."

But then, an hour or so into that morning's visit, Margot fell silent at another arrival to the room. Even with Margot's domineering scent clogging your nostrils, the faint smell of vanilla shampoo in the air was unmistakable.

And it wasn't only Rebekkah who came back to your room that morning. "Margot," your mother's voice said. Your eyes jostling over the stippled foam ceiling tiles, you couldn't get a good glimpse of the scene, but you could perceive a contest of silence in the room, the resolution Ma had come to. A body shuffled fuzzily into the wobbling periphery of your vision, but it wasn't your mother's hand that took your own. The crusty, familiar skin on your palm. Your father's fingers.

"Oh," Margot said.

Oh, you thought, as you felt some heft, the weight that kept you pinned in Bed Four, bleed away. You might only have been a paralytic man in a hospital bed, but it didn't seem that way just now. You were a boy who had fallen into a nexus in the universe, a place where any reality might happen, where you really could slip on new skins. And now you put to good use the shape-shifting trick you had learned. You felt the marrow of your bones hollow out. Your vision tightened and telescoped. Your neck skin shriveled, dangled from the question mark of your spine. The hair of your arms rose and blossomed into bright feathers. As wings, you found your arms could move again. You flapped mightily, throwing your visitors into a minor hysteria. Someone had the good sense to open a window, and you cawed as you flew out of Crockett State. There was one Loving missing that morning, and now you rose over your barren, broken country, flapped your way into the distant hills, bound for your dusty state's capital, to call your brother home.

Charlie

· · · · · · · · · · · · · · · · · ·

CHAPTER THIRTY-SEVEN

"You're coming to Austin?" Charlie's friend Christopher, who had quit Brooklyn months before, had seemed less than thrilled when Charlie called him, from a filling station somewhere near Odessa, to announce that he was at last going to take Christopher up on his long-standing, faintly romantic offer to come stay with him and his new friends in their bungalow on Austin's east side.

"You're really coming?" Christopher had asked, again and then once more, the cheer in his question not at all convincing. In the midst of Charlie's erotic spree in Brooklyn, Christopher and he had taken up together for a single exhilarating December week before Christopher left on a long trip to San Diego in his ongoing crusade to help undocumented immigrants. They had not resumed when Christopher had briefly returned to Brooklyn, but in Charlie's long retinue of *Nothing Reallys*, he had often liked to think of Christopher as a *Maybe Something,* and the occasional sight of his name in Charlie's inbox and those protest and beach photos of Christopher in his Facebook feed always sparked something in Charlie's chest.

At the doorstep to Christopher's new house, however, Charlie had seen that the romance should have remained where they had left it, theoretical. "I can't offer you much," Christopher said, sweeping his sandy hair with a nervous hand, "but we do have a little space in the teahouse."

"Sounds like a dream."

Christopher's bungalow turned out to be some sort of dissolute anarchist flophouse, over the transom window of which someone had affixed the stolen nameplate of a grand home called Trevor House, edited away the TREVOR with a blast of red paint, and replaced it with the silver-sprayed prefix ANTI-. The residents of Anti-House were young bearded men and unshaven women who slept like puppies, cuddled together on cushions on the floor. Christopher's own cuddle buddy was a seventeen-looking kid named Tom Zane—most probably, Charlie surmised, someone's runaway son—who clung to Christopher like a baby sloth and who offered, in reply to Charlie's few attempts at conversation, the wild and warning eyes of a boy who had nothing left to lose. By day, the residents of Anti-House dispersed to carry on their missions of organizing labor strikes and establishing communal gardens, and by night they ingested great quantities of hallucinogenics, nattering polemical congratulations to one another for their righteous fury beneath posters that carried such slogans as CAPITALISM IS CANCER, THE REVOLUTION STARTS WITH ONE, and MOTHERFUCK THE MAN. If anyone could have admired the antiestablishment work those unkempt anarchists were up to it should have been Charlie, the son of a borderland that had been caught for a century and a half between two nations, an ethnic tug-of-war that had at last ripped the town of Bliss apart. And yet, arriving to Anti-House from his return to his ruined hometown, all of their activities had seemed worse than futile. It all seemed quaintly deluded, kids playing at anarchists they'd seen in movies.

A grim few days had followed. But Charlie was glad to scowl from the "teahouse" the anarchists had granted him, a glass box that heated to approximately four thousand degrees under the Austin sun. Charlie had told himself, on the long and windburned journey, that he only needed to get his head straight. Much like his decamping from Zion's Pastures more than five years earlier, he had decided—no, not decided, he had known it just as physically as thirst or hunger—that he could not perform the necessary cranial recalibrations when still in such close proximity to Ma and Pa. *Let me know when you are ready to tell me the truth,* he'd told his mother, and yet his phone never rang. Once, Charlie even called Crockett State to ask Peggy, "Is my ma around?" "Charlie!" she said. "Where did you go? Yes, she is, she's just down the hall, with Margot and your brother." "With Margot," Charlie said. "That's right. Should I get her?" "I think," he said, "I'll just try her again later at home." Before Peggy could protest, he'd hung up.

However (and this would be a late-blooming *however,* visible to Charlie only later, in retrospect) it was also possible that Charlie had not been willing to accept a truth himself. After all, the date of Oliver's next test in El Paso, with that cognition expert and all her sophisticated neuroimaging, the exam that would finally and decisively determine what was left of his brother's mind, had only been a few days off, and perhaps Charlie had not so much been fleeing his mother's illusions as coddling another one of his own, preemptively absenting himself from whatever those results might show. Amid the copious marijuana and poppy plants the anarchists were growing in the teahouse, Charlie had tried halfheartedly to plot his own next chapter.

No more schemes, he'd actually written in his Moleskine after hanging up with Christopher at the filling station. No great ambitions. A nice quiet life. Over the arduous, arm-numbing motorbike trek, Charlie had searched his mind for his archetype of such a life and decided, by the time the city's lights began pinkishly to smear the eastern night sky, that he might never return to the Big Bend or New York, that he might just apply for a job at an Austin library. And if a future as a librarian seemed constitutionally impossible, Charlie resolved to keep his brother's old journal close, hoping an occasional perusal would remind him how thoroughly he had failed.

But this surreal anarchist existence in the Austin suburbs had turned out to be something else entirely, not a great failure's aftermath but a strange new thing, and Charlie's forays into his revised future had been as forbidding as his attempts to engage with the trippy milieu of Anti-House. Charlie spent most of his time in the teahouse, sweating to the verge of unconsciousness as he paged through the few novels the anarchists kept, the predictable collection of Bukowski, Miller, Kerouac, Vonnegut. At night, from the living room of Anti-House, it sounded as if a large family of stringed instruments were being slowly tortured to death. Charlie listened enviously to the anarchists' heedless good cheer, wondering how those people believed in that sort of camaraderie, wondering what the hell was wrong with him, how he could have made his life into something as small and illusory as a series of abandoned word processor documents and a rumpled, coffee-stained, unfulfillable contract.

Charlie had been staying there, among the blooming psychedelics, for three days when Christopher one night managed to grope his way clear of Tom Zane to come alone to the teahouse. Christopher attempted a sort of reenactment of the time they met, in a backroom dance party beneath the Williamsburg Bridge, kissing before they exchanged a word. Christopher came in someone's second- or third-hand robe and a snug pair of boxer briefs, his face a little silly in its lascivious intent. He lowered himself over Charlie, pressing their mouths together.

When Charlie slipped his hands against the young man's sternum, and he felt the unusual convex shape he remembered, as if Christopher carried a doubled heart beneath his ribs, Charlie's face went hot with tears. Christopher, at first mistaking the sound for encouragement, increased the friction on his cock, until at last Charlie pulled the hand away.

"What happened to you?" Christopher asked.

"I don't know."

"If this is about Tom—"

Charlie grinned. "It's nice, how you're helping that boy."

"Is it? Sometimes I think it might be better for him if I just made him go home."

"Well, I guess we can't know."

After Christopher had left that night, Charlie lay on the crummy futon, listening to the deep bass thump of the nightly revelry inside the anarchist bungalow. Some shadow appeared in the back door and fired a Roman candle into the night, white contrails arcing over the glass roof. Like someone's grumpy neighbor, Charlie worried about the fire hazard. He was thinking, *What do you have to celebrate?* Yet he knew they had everything to celebrate. It was just being young and everything being in the future. They were at the beginning of their story, and Charlie felt at the end of his own. Charlie was only twenty-three, but he felt his bones aging beneath his skin, and as for what was beneath Oliver's skin? Charlie felt that all of his journal obsessing, writing, and street stalking had been for naught, that all he had were his wrong stories.

However. Here was the strange paradox: liberated at last from any possibility of knowing, of any hope that he might at last find his way to one of their old mythic passageways, Charlie felt freed to fail. He felt freed to indulge the nostalgia that pained him that night, free to set aside his doomed journalistic ambitions, free to imagine his own imagined, incomplete Oliver back into existence, if only on the pages of his own Moleskine. Just Charlie's idea of Oliver, which had always seemed much clearer to Charlie than his idea of himself. *Your name is Oliver Loving,* Charlie wrote.

When Christopher had come back that night with a hamburger in a Styrofoam clamshell he'd smuggled past his vegan cohort, he asked if Charlie might want to "take a stab at this Twitter account we've been talking about starting. Tweets from people who could never have access to a computer. Who often can't read or write. Nigerian sex slaves, Vietnamese factory workers, the imperiled indigenous people of Brazil. That sort of thing. We'll call it 'Tweets from Hell.' But the thing is that we'll need a really good writer, and I was thinking that's maybe where you come in."

"Who knows," Charlie said. "Maybe that's a job for me."

But, in the meantime, Charlie continued to fill pages. He purloined a stack of anti-McDonald's flyers from the anarchists, the backs of which he filled with more words.

Charlie knew his mother would call it *textbook Charles Good-night Loving*. Charlie was still inhabiting a dream version of his brother, which he could describe with all the empathy in the world, as he meanwhile shut the actual Oliver away, just as he had turned away the daylight hours, turned off his cell phone and not turned it back on. Charlie had become a nocturnal animal, too busy in his moonlit foragings through the past to think much about the present-day Oliver, the ongoing drama at Bed Four, the next exam in El Paso. The guilt pangs only made Charlie write more quickly.

But now, a week after his arrival, Charlie woke in the midst of one of his daylong naps to find that for once his skin was not crisping in the heat. He went outside, and he took a deep breath of coolish September. Even the mockingbirds sounded less ornery that late morning, as chirpy as orioles. Charlie tried to write in the daytime, but he felt blank, sun dulled. He thought a little ride around town might sharpen his mind, but he couldn't get his bike to start. His loyal Suzuki apparently had been a desert creature; in the verdant, humid Austin streets, it had finally expired.

It was that evening, as Charlie was pissing against a backyard live oak, shaking out the last droplets, that something furry brushed his ankle. He swung around wildly, clumsily stuffing himself back into his jeans, to find a black pug weepily clawing at his legs. The dog's cockeyed face, features all cinched into an expression of lovable peevishness, was as unmistakable as it was impossible. Charlie stooped to pick up the pug, her overlong tongue working his forehead as he investigated the collar, where he found a pink rhinestone band, bearing a tag in the shape of a dog biscuit on which was printed the name EDWINA and Charlie's own phone number.

"Edwina," he said, and the animal wept afresh. "How?"

"Reunited and it feels so good."

Charlie pivoted, Edwina's legs cycling in the air. A figure was standing on the slab of pavement just outside the back door.

She was a vision from a film noir, her hips swaying gently to one side.

"Rebekkah?"

"Surprised, I'll bet," she said. "But the truth is that I didn't have much choice. Edwina here wouldn't stop talking about you."

"Funny," Charlie said. "It was you that she used to go on and on about."

Rebekkah shrugged. "I guess times change."

"You found him," Christopher said, joining them a minute later.

"I'm getting the feeling I had a spy in the house."

"I'm sorry for that. It seemed wrong not to tell your mother you were okay. I found her number in your phone. Remember this thing?" Christopher gave the device a few wags, tossed it at Charlie.

"And she sent *you*?" Charlie asked Rebekkah. "What are you even doing in Texas?"

"I volunteered, actually, said it was about time I talked to you anyway."

"No way," Charlie told the impossible fact of her face in front of him. "I don't believe this. Why would *you* come find *me*? And why now?"

Rebekkah grimaced, nodded for a few seconds. "It's a good thing we've got a long drive ahead of us. It's going to take a while, what I have to tell you."

"A long drive?"

"They need you. There's this big test . . ." Charlie nodded, held up a palm to suggest she didn't need to say anything more. She didn't; the shame of his disappearance was argument enough, but the much more prominent sensation—the trembling in his ears, the cool blue behind his eyes—was relief. Charlie gathered his pages from the teahouse, stuffed them into his bag, and checked out of Anti-House by giving Christopher a firm squeeze. But Christopher? He pressed his mouth against Charlie's again, the friction of their stubble generating static electricity.

CHAPTER THIRTY-EIGHT

In the rental car, Charlie rode with Rebekkah through the chaos of stars, the humped black Hill Country. Under the bright beams of the Ford Fiesta, the asphalt was a wire, threading them home.

The first hour or two passed in near silence, as if the gas stations and subdivisions and hill towns were too distracting, as if to tell what Rebekkah needed to tell she had to be in a nullity, a perfect void. As the world was reduced to the occasional streetlamp, burning dimly over the western plains, it felt as if they were the last people alive. "It was a hard year for me," Rebekkah began. "It seemed like nobody saw me until Mr. Avalon . . ." But as Rebekkah pressed on into her whole horrible story, Charlie did not exactly listen to her words. Her words transmuted him; Charlie became thirteen years old again, on that first day in the hospital conference room. But the room was different now, the name *Mr. Avalon* a noxious gas, thick and gray, filling the memory, choking out the air.

Later, after stopping for a bathroom break in Ozona, Charlie took the wheel to let Rebekkah rest. As soon as he turned back on to Interstate 10, Rebekkah fell quickly asleep, Edwina dozing on her lap, her snores mercifully cured of that terrible watery sound.

Mr. Avalon. Their vanished town's faded deity, their failed musician, their imagined martyr. *Why?* Even after Rebekkah had at last fallen silent, and the shock of it had passed, Charlie knew that not even this story could ever truly answer the question that had become the organizing principle of his life. Rebekkah's story might help explain, but there could be no full answer for Hector and the decision he'd made, Charlie saw that now. And, out the windshield, Charlie also saw this: they were already on the border of the desert that had seen five hardscrabble generations of Lovings.

That blue country looked like no place for humans. Charlie was thinking that maybe the wrongness, "the vexation," as Granny Nunu had always claimed, was in the land itself. The evil, the sickness that had led to his brother's confinement, his father's withering, the wasted years, the slain schoolchildren, the silenced abuse of Rebekkah, Hector Espina, and who knows how many others. All of it, taken together, was like some legend Charlie and his brother might once have whispered about in their bunks. A family curse, begun generations before they arrived on that grim stage. *However:* it was not only Charlie's life that bent around that damning conjunction. *However* was his region's ancestral affliction, the whole story of that Texan borderland, a lifeless country where utopian visions had come to die for more than a century. The last hope of an Apache homeland, the entrepreneurial ambitions of the white settlers with their cattle and mineral enterprises, the parched aspirations of hundreds of thousands of immigrants: to all of those dreams the desert had intoned its ancient reply. *However.* And, on the night of November fifteenth, his country's ancient green-grass delusion and the violence it stoked had transformed but was as present as ever, the bloody sequel to the faded tall tales still spinning out in his digitized century, in a country psychotically armed for end times. *However* was the story of Hector Espina's West Texan existence, too, a young man who every day must have carried in his pockets the crumpled dream of his own fame. And yet, as a navy selvage of dawn rimmed the eastern horizon, exposing hills that looked like ancient sea creatures, fossilized in the moment of breaching the surface of the long-drained ocean, the sight entered Charlie's eyes like a key clicking into all its tumblers, unlatching a sensation that even still Charlie could only call *home*.

Rebekkah woke as Charlie pulled the Fiesta over at a filling station–cum–diner outside Fort Stockton. She narrowed her eyes at the sun pouring back into the desert morning. "And now for the next bit of news," she said.

"The next?"

Rebekkah shrugged. "Ha. You know what? I think I'll leave it as a surprise for you."

Charlie was still too adrift in the floodwater of all these new facts to muster anything beyond a survival instinct, throwing his arms over his head.

"But Rebekkah? Have you told my parents? Do they know what you told me?"

"I told them everything. The day after I came back, I told them." She set her jaw, glanced at Charlie, nodded at his next question, which he didn't even need to ask.

"It was just seeing Oliver there, I guess. I saw Oliver, and I thought, Charlie is right. I had been so worried for myself, so sorry for myself really, but I thought, Charlie is right, what does Oliver need? And of course I knew what Oliver needed. Had always known. Just the truth."

"The truth," Charlie said. "And did my parents tell all this to Manuel Paz?"

"I told him myself. I don't even know what he could do about it now. What any of us can do now. But I told your mom that if she needed someone to come get you in Austin, that was a thing I could do."

Rebekkah and Charlie watched a wren pick at an empty box of fries, give up and flutter away. "Hey," Rebekkah said. "Go grab us some coffee, and then I'm taking the wheel."

An hour later, Rebekkah turned off Route 385 five miles before it came to Crockett State. Oddly, no words passed between them as the destination became more evident, the crumbling gravel and frowzy buildings of Route 90 dusting themselves off, buttoning up for the one spot of sophistication in the whole of the Big Bend.

"Uh-oh," Charlie said.

Rebekkah didn't reply as she worked the car through the grid of downtown Marfa. At last she put the Fiesta in park before the vine-choked little ranch house, which now sat far on the feral side of bohemian. "Your father's place," she said.

"I see that. What are we doing *here*?"

"He told your mom that she shouldn't have to be alone, with everything that's been happening." Rebekkah said. "She's been here for almost a week now."

"Seriously? I—" Charlie was silenced by the unlikely sight of his bedraggled mother—her curls akimbo, her gaunt frame in a bathrobe of unspeakable pinkness—emerging from the battered front door. Charlie turned back to Rebekkah, his mouth still gaping, to find the girl waving faintly in the direction of his mother.

"Looks like someone wants to say hi to you," Rebekkah said.

"Looks that way, doesn't it?" Charlie turned away, watched a turkey vulture make its slow clock-like rotation in the sky.

"She's been kind to me," Rebekkah said. "Though I must admit she isn't always the easiest person to talk to."

"Come in with me?"

Rebekkah shook her head. "I have the feeling my work here is pretty much done."

"Done?"

"I told your mom that I wanted to stay, at least until that test, but she made me promise that I'd get myself away from all this. I don't know if that is her being kind or just wishing me gone."

"Welcome to the Loving family."

"Hm," Rebekkah said, looking at the distance down Paisano Lane.

"So," Charlie addressed her profile. "Where *are* you going, then?"

"Who knows," she said. "Back to New York, I guess? Though I'm thinking that it's maybe time for someplace new."

Edwina was panting in Charlie's lap, and he felt for her ears, pinched them away from her head in that way that made her look like a jumbo-sized bat.

"Edwina—" Charlie said.

"We're not even going to discuss it," Rebekkah said. "She belongs to you. Or maybe you belong to her? Ha ha. You and Edwina belong together, anyway."

Rebekkah, even after her long conversation with Charlie, still could not quite bring herself to meet his sightline, and so Charlie cupped the girl's cheek in his hand. To his surprise, she leaned into this touch, pressing her face into his palm. She grinned at him now, a little wistfully. "You know," Charlie said, "I've spent a good part of the last year imagining what I might tell you. 'Thank you' was never very high on my list."

Rebekkah sucked at one of her wounded cuticles, nodded. "No," she said. "Thank *you*." Charlie opened the door and carried Edwina out into the Marfa morning. The engine hummed behind him, and the car disappeared down Paisano Lane.

"Ma," Charlie called across the withered front yard. "What in the hell?"

"Well. Look who's back again."

Charlie paused there, on the broken sidewalk. They were still mother and son; a lifetime of apologies and avowals, attacks and defenses were filing up in their ancient ranks. And yet, after all those years, their locked eyes seemed to carry out the tired warfare and settle the terms of truce in the time it took to cross the lawn and meet for a long, muscular hug.

"Can I just say this right now to get it out of the way?" she said.

"Ma—"

"No. I have to just say this, and you know how it pains me. But you were right. Charlie, I shouldn't have believed. Margot. I should have known better. Did know better."

Charlie bit down on his lip, trying to suppress the urge to nod vigorously. "What finally convinced you?" he asked.

Ma gestured with her chin to where Rebekkah's rental car had just sat. "We brought her to this room, and Margot couldn't even get Oliver to type out her name. Like Rebekkah Sterling was just some stranger. And she was, of course, though only to Margot Strout."

"Ah."

"I was talking to a lie, I think I must have known it all along." Ma put a trembling finger to her mouth. "But it was all I had."

"It wasn't all you had," Charlie said.

"No." Ma showed him her palms. "You are right. I had you."

"Have me. You do."

"I do," she said.

"I'm back," Charlie said. "I shouldn't have gone."

"And Rebekkah told you."

"Everything."

Ma nodded, looking puzzled as to what she might say next. Charlie sucked at the air, particles of dust lodging in his teeth. "But, honestly, maybe you can at least explain *this* to me? What are you doing staying *here*?"

But she only bit her lip, a little guiltily.

Pa's house, on the inside, was not at all the larger, rambling, bottle-and-butt-clogged rendition of his ancient painting cabin that Charlie remembered from his few bad visits, years before. Apparently, as Charlie had been indulging his project at Anti-House, Ma had been heading a little project of her own. Pa's rooms were emptied, the tomb of his solitary years sitting in a Hefty-bag pyramid in the drive. It was an odd, awkward place. What little furniture remained gave them nowhere to hide. But after taking a long, feverish nap, Charlie tried to get into the strange, anarchic spirit of the day. As Pa prepared dinner that evening, a sauce-heavy sheet of enchiladas that

Charlie happily anticipated watching his mother try to choke down, they did their fumbling best to muster a conversation over the heavily dented, corrosion-carpeted stove. "Listen," Charlie said. "About what I said last time, at the hotel?"

"You don't have to explain yourself to me," Pa told him. "If there's anyone to do the explaining, it's me."

"So explain it then," Charlie said. But his old teenage id, that chain breaker with his sardonic quips, was very tired now, nursing a nosebleed in some dim basement of his brain. Charlie looked into Pa's badly worn face, the lines near his mouth a leathery lattice. At that moment, the only question Charlie wanted to ask was whether his father might consider one of those Alcoholics Anonymous meetings they hosted at the Marfa courthouse.

But then Pa really did explain it to Charlie, as best he could. Charlie would later wish that he could remember all the words Pa used, but he would remember only fragments, the sodden debris that splashed around in his father's well-liquored memory: Pa's unspoken worries about his old student Hector, his shame for failing to see the truth about Reginald Avalon, "And your brother, Charlie. Did you know that I was the one who convinced him to come that night? And I've never said that. Ten years, I've never said a thing about it." Charlie turned a burner knob, fiddled with a shirt button as an excuse not to see Pa breathing heavily into his outspread fingers.

Charlie knew that perhaps he should still have been outraged, this one feeble attempt of his father's, a decade too late. But the tragedy of Jed Loving, just then, seemed so much truer than Charlie's own dog-eared indignation. He nodded.

"So, uh, if I recall correctly," Charlie said, "this place only has two bedrooms. If I'm taking the guest room, then . . ."

Pa grinned wearily. "I don't know how to explain it to you. This is all very, very, very strange. I don't know. We're just sorta feeling our way through the dark here."

"Ha! Ha ha!" Charlie bleated, a little theatrically. And certainly it was true that such a revelation—the surprise of his parents' ongoing capacity for romance—would, just a few months earlier, have been shocking to the verge of medical danger. But as Charlie now reconsidered the true substance of Ma's late-night absences from Desert Splendor, the sly grin that would sometimes come into her face, the great shock was that this, after all, made sense. Made sense not only of Ma's behavior but also as the latest, greatest piece of evidence for the revised theory of life Charlie had just cracked in the backyard of Anti-House, that you can never really know the full truth of the stories spinning alongside your own. Maybe, even after a solid year of full-time navel-gazing, you couldn't really even know your own.

"Oh, God," Ma said, appearing in the kitchen doorway, her face blotched with blush. "What now?"

"Nothing," Charlie said with a laugh. "Your boyfriend here was just telling me an interesting story."

Later, after they had polished off the better part of the enchiladas, Ma described a phone call she'd had with a neuroscientist named Marissa Ginsberg, who would administer the most important part of Oliver's examination that Friday in El Paso.

Dr. Ginsberg, Ma explained, working with a machine similar to the one Professor Nickell had driven to Crockett State, had learned of a way she could use the device to remarkable new effect. Apparently, different parts of the brain glowed on the display when people engaged in different mental exercises, and so the clever Dr. Ginsberg had several times used these brain scans as an indirect way of reading a subject's mind, a way for a person to answer yes and no without twitching so much as a thumb. "Think of running when you want to say yes, sing 'Twinkle, Twinkle, Little Star' to yourself when you want to say no," Dr. Ginsberg told her subjects. It was only yeses and nos, nothing more complex she could assess in her machine, and the process, Dr. Ginsberg had admitted, was both laborious and expensive. "It's not like this mind-reading trick of hers is perfect," Ma told Charlie. "Not like it could ever tell us everything Oliver is thinking, but yeses and nos with no Margot Strout in between? It's not nothing."

"You're right," Charlie said. "It's not nothing."

Early the next morning, as the Lovings readied themselves for another day at Bed Four, Charlie heard something disconcerting, a kind of garbled yelp, maybe a squirrel being flattened by a pickup. It turned out to be the sound his father's doorbell made, after he had attempted to repair it. Charlie stood there with Ma, in the empty living room, as his father opened the door to reveal a pear-shaped woman, holding something heavy. "Mrs. Strout," Pa said.

"Margot," Margot said.

"I can't," Ma told Charlie. "I can't talk to that woman."

"Okay," Charlie told his mother, yet he took a few paces in the direction of Margot Strout, whose boots Edwina was already licking. The sight of Charlie, for the first time since that bad morning at Bed Four, made the woman flush deeply. Margot put a hand to her brow as two horseflies orbited her head in wobbly circles, like a cartoon illustration of a slapstick head injury. "I brought you all a casserole," she said in the direction of Ma, proffering the foil-wrapped tray in her hands.

"Charlie," Ma said, employing the old passive-aggressive power move she used to use with Pa, "please tell her she isn't welcome here."

"I just wanted to talk to you," Margot said. "I just wanted to try to explain things. Tell you how very, very, very sorry I am."

"Please tell that woman we're not interested in talking," Ma said.

"Eve," Margot said. "I promise—"

Ma fought back a gasp. "I'm sick of hearing your promises," she told Margot now.

It was a little fuzzy, Charlie's picture of just what had happened that morning at Crockett State when Ma at last dismissed the palm reader from her place by Bed Four. But what was perfectly clear was the familiar way Ma was trying to wield her righteous indignation now, to beat back her own guilt by force of condemnation.

"Listen, Eve, please listen to me." Margot spoke over Charlie's shoulder, addressing Eve in a tremulous, rapid monologue as her makeup began to seep, waxlike, down her cheeks. "I can lose my job. I can stop doing this work altogether, you can hate me, I'd understand it. And I know how this might sound to you, but I'll never stop believing it. I can't. I can't stop myself from knowing that it really was Oliver I felt there. Just like I can still feel Cora is here, listening to every word I say. Listening to these words right now. Even if you think I should know better."

Charlie looked at Margot; he looked at his mother. Maybe Margot deserved Ma's damnation; maybe this woman had come with her Jesus-love and delusions to make of the Lovings a comforting little story for herself. But Charlie was too tired now for this notion to elicit any outrage of his own. Charlie was thinking: Who could understand either of those mothers more than they could understand one another? "Thank you for the casserole," Charlie told her, unburdening her arms. "I'm sure it's delicious. Maybe try coming back later?"

She nodded, and Charlie held Edwina back between his ankles as Margot waddled away. Charlie peeled a corner of the foil, looked at the unappetizing mash-up Margot had made. Walnuts, avocado, potato, and chicken scraps all mashed together into a greenish pap. The Lovings dispersed wordlessly from the room, and Charlie slipped the casserole into the fridge. They didn't speak of Margot that day at Bed Four, nor did they mention her the next day. But that following evening, when Charlie crept out for a late-night snack, he noticed that the casserole tray's foil wrapping had been disturbed, that a little square of it had been cut away and consumed—and Pa, Charlie remembered, hated walnuts.

Charlie had established himself in the house's second bedroom, which, boasting no more than a squeaking queen bed and an antique school desk, qualified as the best room he had inhabited since his childhood. But, for once, he looked at the room's desk without any visions of writing there. Charlie might have had only a few rough pages to show for his sixteen faltering months of writing, but he knew it was time to share what he had with his first reader.

Except, of course, his brother could not read. And so, very late that Thursday evening, Charlie summoned his courage and read for Oliver, out loud from his Moleskine and the reverse pages of his Anti-House flyers, right in front of his parents. Peggy, in a bout of self-aggrandizing defiance, had extended visiting hours to as long as they needed. Over Oliver's ever-searching eyes, Charlie read his attempted sequel to their old fantasy tales, telling his stories to the boy once more in a bed beneath him.

In their bunk-bed sessions, Charlie and his brother had once imagined a great number of battles, piecemeal maps, trickster tests they would first have to pass to be allowed passage from one world to another. But maybe the true answer to the riddle of the gates was this: first you had to fall to your knees, admit that what you would see in the place beyond would only be the hopeful and incomplete images you painted onto the air, and then still forgive yourself enough to stand back up and take a first step over that threshold. *How not to believe, even still, that you were chosen?* Charlie's voice was growing thin as he struggled through his final pages.

His mother put a hand to the back of his neck. "Charlie," Ma said. "I had no idea you had this in you. I had no idea."

"Well, I was the valedictorian of my high school after all," Charlie said. "Though I guess you could also say that I was last in my class."

"Just finish reading," Ma told him.

It was nearly 1 A.M. when Charlie and Edwina at last climbed onto the bed in the back room of Pa's house. Only one night stood between that moment and his brother's final exam. But Charlie wasn't now imagining what might happen tomorrow. He was thinking not of his brother as he had become, but Oliver as he must have once been, that first day Rebekkah sat next to him before literature class. That morning that still existed somewhere, that place where any other future could still happen.

Oliver

·····················

CHAPTER THIRTY-NINE

Forty miles away, you were with your brother in that memory. You knew what was coming—the final test was the next morning—but what could you do to prepare? Even if freedom were in the offing, you were like the hardened prisoner, unwilling to give up your old ways. You picked at the thread of a certain August morning, lobbed into the darkness that lovely button, and quickly found its shape in your hand.

August twenty-ninth, near the start of your last semester at Bliss Township: in the soft morning light of Mrs. Schumacher's literature classroom, a half hour before school began, you were staring into the paper cup of coffee you had bought at Bliss Pies N' Stuff, sweetened with three sugar packets but still hopelessly bitter. You tried to will yourself to gulp down the brown swill, as if it were a slow-acting potion that might straighten the slouch of your spine, ease the awkwardness from your joints, and make you into a man. You took your effortful coffee drinking as seriously as you took the lines of crummy poetry you had crossed out of the open journal on the desk. This was the morning after your father had cajoled Rebekkah into joining your family for the Perseid shower at Zion's Pastures, and you were rehearsing what you might tell her.

"Oliver, hey there."

"Oh, hi! You came early."

"So did you." Rebekkah was nodding. "So here we are. What is that thing you're working on?"

For many days now, you had been watching Rebekkah closely from your spot in the circle of desk chairs. You could have drawn from memory the planes of her face, her Milky Way of ginger freckles. You had studied the amber ringlets of her hair the way Monet studied the haystacks. And now you again beheld, in impossible proximity, the face you had scrutinized from the distant observation point of your desk. You could once more feel the warmth thrown off her, smell the vanilla fragrance of her shampoo. You blinked furiously; your hand flared where it had touched hers the night before.

"Poetry," you told her. You tried to do a gruff James Dean thing with your shoulders.

"Really?" Rebekkah said. "I didn't know you wrote. I love poetry. Walt Whitman. E. E. Cummings. Sylvia Plath. Do you like her?"

You nodded into your coffee. You summoned your courage, drew your breath, and turned to look again at Rebekkah Sterling, who was grinning at you now. A grin to match your own, quivering a little at the edges. This was just your first morning talking together, and in this memory it would always be only your first morning, unbothered by what would follow.

"Hey," she said, "maybe someday you'll write one for me?"

Eve

....

CHAPTER FORTY

There was a blazing, panicked instant the next day in El Paso, when the driver unsealed the rear doors of the ambulance that had conveyed the Lovings from Crockett State, when the noon heat and Eve's dread flashed over her skin as a single incendiary substance. But the orderlies who came from Memorial Hospital were businesslike, unlatching Oliver's cot and lowering it to the pavement, and when they entered the building, they were met by the reassurance of protocol, forms to be signed.

"Marissa Ginsberg," a lab-coated lady named herself just beyond the automatic doors. "So wonderful of you to come all this way."

Dr. Marissa Ginsberg's name, in the fervor of Eve's hope and dread for this day's test, had become shamanistic, but she turned out to be a rather timid woman, with an academic's awkward affability, often pulling at the mop of orange stuff she had for hair. And then, after offering the Lovings a short explanation of the various tests she had scheduled, Dr. Ginsberg performed the one simple, uncommon act that made Eve love her a little. She leaned over the cot, pressed a hand to Oliver's head, and spoke to him in a voice that was mercifully free of condescension. "We're going to give you a little injection now, Oliver. It's a kind of tracer, so we can see your brain working on one of the machines later. We'll give it a half hour to take effect, then we can begin."

The orderlies wheeled the cot into another small room, with glistening medical equipment and a smell of bleach and iodine. A room quite similar to the room at Crockett State, minus the nostalgic Old West bric-a-brac. Waiting for the radioactive isotopes to penetrate Oliver's blood-brain barrier, the Lovings shared a silence as doctors paced the hallway beyond.

"Well, here we are," Charlie said.

"Here we are," Eve replied.

Eve produced a small portable speaker she'd stolen long ago, attached it to her phone. Bob Dylan crooned and moaned his way through the first tracks of *Blonde on Blonde.*

Eve looked down at Oliver's thin and twitching lips, his yellowed eyelids nearly translucent in the sunlight through the window, his thin blue veins like a delicate web that bound him in his skin. She was wondering what Oliver might have made of his first trip away from Crockett State in nearly a decade. The whole ride out to El Paso, Eve's own thoughts had been wheeling, buzzardlike, around an image she'd seen that morning on the cover of *The Big Bend Sentinel,* a picture of the impromptu vigil the old Blissians had held the night before outside Bliss Township School.

With the light-speed conveyance of news in the Big Bend, it shouldn't have been a surprise that the whole wretched tale Rebekkah had brought back with her—about Reginald Avalon, Hector Espina, all those unspeakable things—had spread quickly, but even Eve was surprised by how rapidly those families and Bliss Country faculty had reassembled their old mourning ranks. Donna Grass and Doyle Dixon had both phoned her yesterday afternoon, leaving voice mails inviting the Lovings to the school last night, and the *Sentinel*'s front-page image showed the service she had declined to attend: a couple of dozen bodies, making a constellation with their little votive candles just beyond the school gates. In the picture, Eve had been able to make out the bleary shapes of Mrs. Schumacher, Mrs. Henderson,

Mrs. Wolcott, and Mrs. Dawson. *All those people,* Eve had thought as she looked at that picture, but she had always known that it wasn't her son—or at least it wasn't *only* her son—who had drawn all those visitors to his bed, and it wasn't only her son for whom the town turned out last night. It had been nearly ten years, the memorial candlelight services dimming each November, but the new revelations, the closest to an answer that might ever come, had brought them all out that one last time, the lost town of Bliss temporarily refounded on the old Main Street, to grieve and bury their decade of grieving.

Eve had long ago developed a mental mechanism that converted sorrow into a more useful rage, but this morning, looking at the picture of that sorrowful lot, she hadn't even been able to summon an appropriate fury at Reginald Avalon. It was just a dizzying, despairing sort of confusion she knew when she looked down that hall of mirrors.

"We dug a little deeper into his past, talked to a bunch of his old students," Manuel Paz had told Eve, over the phone. "I'll be honest with you, when I said the man's name to a couple of those kids? They practically came unglued, right in front of me. Weeping, almost sick. Horrible. Horrible, to think how he must have preyed on those children over the years, and no one saw a thing. But we should have. I really was as blind as anyone, just thinking of Reginald Avalon like some saint, and for that I truly don't see how I'll ever find a way to forgive myself."

"No" was Eve's odd reply to Manuel, as if she were also addressing those children now. "*I'm* so sorry. For what I never said."

Hector. Like the rest of her town, Eve had considered the kid human waste, as if his own story could not have been any story at all. But whatever he had done, Hector did have a story, a very grim one. A luckless, powerless boy, with a profoundly poor father and a deported mother, desperate for the attentions of the nice, middle-class teacher who showed him some interest. Confiding in the one man who might have helped him out of his hell, who had ended up doing just the opposite. Still, there was another unfathomable linkage there, between Hector's suffering and what he'd done, and what other word was there for it but *evil*? What else but evil—a bombastic word she'd never truly believed in *before*—could make a boy want to burn down his world?

Of course, it hadn't been the entire population of Bliss on the front page of the *Sentinel,* just a few remaining representatives of its white half. Manuel's decade-old hope for an explanation that might mend his town had been answered too late. The way Hector had died had only deepened the injustice of the way he had lived; now that those Blissians understood the truth about Reginald Avalon and Hector Espina, now that their ten years of xenophobic fantasies had come to an end, they had few Hispanic neighbors left to whom they might make their apologies. *Closure* was just a prayer for an ending that would never come, just a professional-sounding word for another hollow kind of faith. People might have turned Oliver into a myth, a martyr, a metaphor for all that the people of Bliss could never understand, a poignant exemplar of the madness that had seized the world, but Eve knew the truth, had always known. The fantasy that Oliver might wake to offer his town the answers they needed had been only that, a fantasy. There was no real reason why Oliver, why Hector Espina, why it had happened there and not somewhere else, why it had happened when it happened and not at some other time. It was truly only chance that had made her family's quiet little life into a horribly exceptional tale worth telling, just randomness and chaos that had turned the Lovings into a symbol of something unfathomable, that had made her younger son into someone who had no choice but to try to write himself free of the story that would forever be the first thing people thought of when they thought of him. *There is no why,* Eve had always known it. And yet, how was it that even still she could not quite make herself believe it? Eve found herself remembering that long-ago night, beneath the Perseid shower. That evening, lying with her family on the powdery earth of Zion's Pastures, she had looked up into a lucid night sky whose static of stars was indistinguishable from the static generated in the rods and cones of her eyes, and Eve had felt oddly exhilarated to consider it, how little her own eyes could ever hope to glean.

In the little room at El Paso Memorial Hospital, Eve felt the layer of slackness that had gathered over the firm shape of her husband's arm. She found herself wishing, just now, that the room were crowded. That the oxygen were thin, that dense body heat could unsettle any thought. But this room was as inhuman and blank as the worst of her insomnias, as frigid and cramped as the final questions they were still living inside. For a few minutes more. There was nowhere here, among the chrome, plastic, and disinfected surfaces, for wishful thinking to gain traction.

"Oliver," Jed said. He was hunched very close to Oliver now, but still he needed to brace himself to make enough of a noise to be heard. Having suffered hours without a drink, Jed was shaking severely. "I need you to listen."

Eve watched as Oliver's eyes continued, as ever, to speed-read some invisible text. Jed pulled away, and his gaze met Charlie's. Jed nodded, long and slow, as if he had accepted something his son had just told him. He stooped once more to Oliver's ear.

"I want to say that you need to tell the truth. Okay? When you get in there, you have to promise me you'll just tell us what you are thinking. No matter what you are thinking. Do you promise?"

When at last Eve managed to lift her head, she noticed that her fingers had fallen to Oliver's left thumb, which she clutched tightly.

In the end, Eve had learned, she had been right to obsess over that one botched conversation Oliver had tried to have with her just a few days *before*, and she had admitted as much to that task force officer when she'd at last returned his call. "If I had only listened to him then?" Eve had said to the man over the phone, but she had never offered an answer. That question, she understood, would be the unwieldy mass she would have to learn how to carry in the years to come, but for now, at least, she could do what she had failed to do a decade ago. For once, she could listen.

"Oliver," Eve said. "Your father is right. We just need you to be honest now. I know you can hear us. I know you can, and I want you to answer for you. Not for me or for Charlie or for Pa, but just for you. It's okay, that's what I want to tell you. Okay if you are ready. Even if that's what you need to tell us, we will find a way to be strong enough. But if you are ready to go, will you just tell us? Please, just tell us if that is what you need?"

The orderlies returned. The Lovings followed the cot down the bumpered hallways to a set of swinging doors labeled X-RAY AND IMAGING. A half hour later, they were on one side of the glass; Oliver was in the great beige machine on the other. They stood behind Dr. Ginsberg and two technicians who were working the control panel. It was, Eve thought, like a scene on the bridge of a starship from one of her son's beloved old movies. Keyboards clattered, switches turned, and now Oliver's brain glowed, in three separate angles, on the computer monitors. Oliver was a hive of data, arranged on the x and y and z axes.

"Ma." Charlie clapped a hand over his mouth. "I can't."

"It's okay," she said, and she took Charlie's fingers in one hand, took Jed's hand in the other.

"Here we go, Oliver," Dr. Ginsberg was saying into the microphone. "I know you've heard this already, but now it's time to give it a try. First, we need to establish your way of saying *Yes*. So here is what I want you to do. When you want to say *Yes*, I want you to imagine you are running. Imagine your feet lifting off the ground, your legs working hard. Can you do that for me? Imagine you are running?"

Eve's own mind was running now. She was in the air, vaulting a hurdle. She sealed her eyes, and for just a second there, she was at the weightless apex of the leap. One last instant when the only questions that mattered were still just questions.

Despite what her family might think of her now, Eve had never considered herself a very faithful or superstitious woman. Signs and symbols, the densely metaphoric world: that was more the way her sons and her husband saw things. But maybe that was what happened when you grew up in a bounded little land; you ended up fetishizing every inch of it, searching your small world for subtle portents of a better place. You turned a flatulent old steer into a kind of prophet, you assembled Paleolithic monuments out of stone, you chased after a freckle-faced girl as if she were the ticket to paradise. But after her years of confined life at Desert Splendor and Crockett State, after a decade-long conversation with her silent son, Eve better understood her husband and her boys, understood what smallness and silence could make you believe. How you could come to read your life like an invisible text. How you could forever turn one ear to the sound of a lost voice. How that voice, once you began to hear it, would never stop speaking to you in its mysterious ways. For example, in that moment between Dr. Ginsberg's first questions and her son's first response—it was only a single suspended second, really—Eve felt that Oliver had already told her all the answers.

Oliver

....

CHAPTER FORTY-ONE

If pressed to choose among your many Bed Four obsessions, it was perhaps the memory of running that obsessed you most. Your last minutes were horrible ones, but you often found some comfort in the thought that the last time you had been able to use your legs, you used them to their fullest, sprinting along the musty hallways of Bliss Township School at night. Oh, you were never what anyone could call *athletic.* And it's true that at the end of your own walking life, you were already winded, your pulse pounding in your ears. And yet, what obsessed you was a certain moment when you strained at your limits. That speed was like a narcotic your body cooked up for itself, a hormonal oblivion. When you ran then, at least for a few seconds, you were unable to think. You were nothing but thoughtless speed. A blur of sun-bleached lockers and the ancient school trophies in their display cases. Your school might have been a drab place, but to you those were the beautiful sights of your walking life, which you left behind that night.

What was it like, your body forever frozen beneath you, to remember such speed? It was a feeling not unlike thinking of Rebekkah Sterling. That delicious old vitality might have withered to a rind, but the rind remained there, cruelly, under your bedsheets, never letting you forget entirely.

And yet, in certain dreamy hours, as the ticking of the wall clock blurred into a single, timeless groan, it could still seem that you had not yet spent all the momentum of your last great sprint. Just as you could still sometimes hear Rebekkah's voice, speaking to you from the place where you left her, so too could you feel that the memory of such speed was enough to hurtle you back to that final moment. Still, impossibly, you could sometimes feel that you would at last pitch yourself just far enough, that somehow it might not yet be too late to save everyone, that you might even still save yourself.

In the fMRI machine in El Paso's Memorial Hospital, you trembled under the hum of orbiting magnets. Familiar to you now, the fMRI's tube felt almost cozy. It was a liminal place, like a waiting room, a twilight, your creekside cave, a nexus in the universe. A place outside of reality, where reality mattered less.

"Try to put out all other thoughts, think only of running," Dr. Ginsberg told you.

Your legs had not lifted beneath you in years, but you once more motored them along your last memory of running, through the dim halls of Bliss Township School at night. *Yes.*

"Oliver! That's just wonderful," Dr. Ginsberg said. "That's just fantastic! So, okay. How about we try saying no? To say no, will you please sing yourself a song? Your mom said you like Bob Dylan. Me, too. Will you do that now, will you sing yourself a Bob Dylan song?"

And yet, as much as you might have liked to lose yourself in those beloved lyrics, you did not sing, not then. The memory of your legs still powered beneath you.

"Oliver? Will you please try to sing a song now?" When you still refused, Dr. Ginsberg began to sing for you. *"The answer, my friend, is blowing in the wind . . ."*

Over Dr. Ginsberg's singing, the magnets hummed their own penetrating tone. Your twitching eyes turned the neutral arch of the machine above you into a beige smear. It took great focus not to sing along, and yet you kept your attention on your ghost's legs, pumping and pumping.

"Oliver?"

Like your father and your brother, you had always been fascinated by that which cannot be seen: buried worlds and Spooky Action, the mysterious effects of Dark Energy and the mind-bending math of cosmic strings. Those intimations of a secret force behind the forces we can see. And could it have been only a coincidence that a boy like yourself was chosen to bridge the invisible distance between one world and the next? Maybe so. Maybe it was only coincidence. And yet, you had told yourself that you would make a reason out of what had happened, that yours would be a tremendous story of survival, when at last you told it. An interdimensional epic to outdo even the survivalist books you loved most, Apsley Cherry-Garrard's ordeal in the Antarctic, Saint-Exupéry's crash landing in the desert of Libya. But you saw now that no story, if you told it long enough, was ever a story of survival. Survival was not a story you could tell. Survival *was* the telling, and that was the burden and the gift of the living.

"Oliver." Dr. Ginsberg's voice grew weaker in the speakers. "Please. Just please try to sing yourself a song. How about a different one? *Twinkle, twinkle, little star—*"

You knew that you hadn't moved your legs in nine years and 314 days, and also that you would never move them again. You knew, also, that you would never tell your story, just as you knew Rebekkah had never loved you as you had loved her, just as you knew you could never be equal to what Ma's love required of you, just as you understood that all your memories were likely just that: not some lost universe, only days that had passed and would never come back. But you didn't let those facts trip you up now. You let yourself follow your family's example. Your mother, her conversations with an imagined voice. Your brother, reading to you the story he had tried to write on your behalf. Your father, the parallel dimensions of his best hopes. Your town, its last prayer for an answer. That belief, that refusal of the meaninglessness of events, that idea that maybe, after all, your story meant something more than a long series of luckless days, that there really was a reason for it, beyond all logical reason. After all, what was it but those ten years you had endured that had at last delivered your family to the truth and so also delivered you to this day when you could set them all free? As Dr. Ginsberg still tried to cajole you to sing a *no,* you instead imagined that you were back, once more, at Bliss Township School, the bass line beating through the walls. Rebekkah and her fellow performers were still down the hall, buttoning up their costumes. And this time, when Hector Espina arrived, you would run quickly enough to get there first. *Yes.*

After a long while, Ma's voice replaced Dr. Ginsberg's in the speaker.

"Oliver? Please. Just give us a sign? Just tell us what you want?" But, in the examination room, your mother had already asked it. The same question that she had considered every day of the last years. The question that had made her glad, in a way she never let herself consider directly, that you had not been able to answer. *Are you ready?*

And still you were sprinting, faster and faster.

Listen. There will be those who will say that, on that day in El Paso, you did not even say *yes,* that what your family watched on the computer monitors was only a brain's mysterious malfunction. After all, more failed tests followed that first exam in the fMRI. After your family was led out of the room, you were shown patterns, played tones, spoken to, prodded gently, subjected to other brain scans. "The only apparent response, all day long," Dr. Ginsberg told your family in her office that evening, "was just there, in the motor cortex. But we did discover some abnormalities and damaged regions. The frontal lobes, that's where higher-level thought comes from, it's most troubling of all. Twenty percent reduction in mass, almost no activity in those areas. It's incredible that as much of his brain has survived as it did. But I'm very, very sorry to tell you that the Oliver you knew, he just isn't with us anymore. I'm so, so sorry that you'd gotten your hopes up for this."

But your family didn't care what Dr. Ginsberg told them. They knew what they had witnessed there, on the other side of the glass. *Yes,* you had said, and for once in her life, even your mother had silenced her crazed hope, and heard you. *Yes,* your way to ask your family to let you go and also to make the end as painless as possible. *Minimally conscious:* you won that label in a marathon of imagined running, and the rest was a matter of paperwork.

Still, there will be those who say that your replies to Dr. Ginsberg don't mean anything about what you actually wanted. That you have not truly understood a word or spoken for yourself since the night of November fifteenth. That this whole story of you amounts only to imagination, or something worse. A fiction, a hoax, an intrusion, a desecration, guesswork from scant facts, the ideomotor effect spun out over hundreds of pages. That your brother, at last writing this book, telling your family's story as you might tell it now from your place outside of time, has no right to tell it in the way he has. That the voice he still hears is not your voice at all. There will be a great many who do not believe these words, even now. And yet, after so many years spent slipping into the infinite worlds of better memories, you also know that sort of belief is not something you can force anyone into, by argument alone. We all have to decide for ourselves what we believe.

"Okay," your mother told you through the speakers that day in El Paso. "Okay." And still you just kept running, leaping over the land that was cracking open between you.

"Everything in the entire cosmos," your father had once said, "begins where it ends, in a single spot of brightness." And it was then, as you flung yourself from the faltering ground, that the energy Dr. Ginsberg traced on her machines flared explosively inside you. That brightness ripped the lining from your clothes, the substance from your skin, sent all your buttons flying. So terrific was the explosion that this time when your buttons flew they shot in a different direction. After years of backward tossings, for once your precious tabs soared on ahead of you. They whistled through the atmosphere like the opposite of the bullets Hector Espina fired, projectiles that did not end stories but opened them. Your buttons burst forth, into a different kind of universe, one where you would be nowhere but also everywhere. And already you were chasing after them, into the future.

CHILDREN OF THE BORDERLANDS

Quiet children
today's lesson
is on Texas history
that happened
with guns and cows and oil
but also on Texas history
that never happened
because you never said
what was so wrong with us
just speaking
a word
might have changed everything
and yet
today's lesson is on astronomy
that can be seen
on an ordinary night sky
the blackness between stars
is proof that the universe ends
because if it were infinite
the starlight would blind us
and yet
today's lesson
is on cosmology
that might be true
if certain scientists are to be believed
other universes

an infinite number
might somewhere exist
and sometimes
there might be
a crack
in the sky
a darkness or
a brightness or
quiet children
today's lesson is on grammar
when I say nothing at all
when I am very still
and I can hear
my young heart
beating in a someday man
who is old enough to hear
where there should be only silence
there is a something
a sigh
a life
between this pen and this paper
I still can't explain it
but I know that
somewhere
we are still speaking
all the words
we never said.

ACKNOWLEDGMENTS

This novel would never have existed without the enthusiasm, advocacy, and tireless editorial wisdom of my agent, Bill Clegg, and my editor, Colin Dickerman. I'm also deeply fortunate to have found such an excellent publishing team: Marion Duvert, Anna Webber, Chris Clemans, Henry Rabinowitz, Simon Toop, David Kambhu, and the rest of the staff at The Clegg Agency and United Agents; Whitney Frick, James Melia, Amelia Possanza, Marlena Bittner, Greg Villepique, Keith Hayes, Jeff Crepshew, Bob Miller, and everyone else at Flatiron Books; and Will Atkinson and the whole crew at Atlantic Books. I must also give special thanks to the commitment and guidance of all my wonderful publishers abroad.

For their gifts of time, space, and friendship, I will forever be grateful to the foundations that supported the writing of this book and the generous people who make those programs run: Beatrice Monti della Corte von Rezzori, Andrew Sean Greer, Alexander Starritt, Nayla Elamin, Brigida Baccari, and Joao Coles at The Santa Maddalena Foundation; Michael Adams at the Graduate School at The University of Texas at Austin and The Texas Institute of Letters' Dobie Paisano Fellowship program; Pietro and Maddalena Torrigiani Malaspina at Castello di Fosdinovo; and Noreen Tomassi at The Center for Fiction.

For their insights, encouragements, and creative contributions along the way, I'd like to thank Anne Thibault, Steve Toltz, Judith Thurman, Jami Attenberg, David Goodwillie, Teddy Wayne, the Bauman family, Mary Mayer, Peter Mayer, William Paul, and my family: my brother, Aaron Block, and my parents, Andrew Block and Deborah Block. My wife, Liese Mayer, edited this book for the first time when it was nearly a different book altogether, and it was Liese who always showed me the map and compass whenever I lost the trail.

While writing this novel, I relied on the work of a number of nonfiction writers, scholars, and photographers. I'm especially indebted to the following: *Tales of Old-Time Texas, The Longhorns,* and *Coronado's Children* by J. Frank Dobie; *Lone Star: A History of Texas and the Texans* by T. R. Fehrenbach; *Goodbye to a River* by John Graves; *Crazy from the Heat: A Chronicle of Twenty Years in the Big Bend* by James Evans; *The Big Bend: A History of the Last Texas Frontier* by Ron C. Tyler; *Desert Survival Skills* by David Alloway; *Encyclopedia of The Great Plains,* edited by David J. Wishart; *The Elegant Universe* by Brian Greene; *Cosmos* by Carl Sagan; *The Universe in a Nutshell* and *A Brief History of Time* by Stephen Hawking; *Columbine* by Dave Cullen; *The Strange Case of Anna Stubblefield* by Daniel Engber; *Ghost Boy* by Martin Pistorius; and *The Diving Bell and the Butterfly* by Jean-Dominque Bauby.